Dan's War

A Novel

by

Milt Mays

TELEMACHUS
PRESS

Cover Designed by Telemachus Press, LLC

Copyright © iStockPhoto #2796188-delta-twilight; #4737308-pump-jack-in-oil-drop-illustration

Edited by Milt Mays

Published by Telemachus Press, LLC
http://www.telemachuspress.com

Visit the author's website at http://www.miltmays.com

ISBN 978-1-935670-95-7 (eBook)
ISBN 978-1-935670-96-4 (Paperback)

Version 2011.08.16

Printed in The United States of America
10 9 8 7 6 5 4 3 2 1

For Lynn, my love,

My family and friends,

And veterans of War:

Without you, where would I be?

Dan's War

CHAPTER 1

Day 1 0700Z-0800ECT
OPEC Headquarters, Obere Donaustrasse 93, VIENNA, AUSTRIA.

The spiders were ready, but was he? He slowed his breathing and avoided glancing up; security cameras were watching. Hours ago he'd been so sure of himself when he'd placed the writhing ball of arachnids on a ceiling tile and encircled them with a miniscule thread of Semtex. But now?

Impossible. He could not do this. Yet even as his chest pounded, he smiled exactly like the hours of practice in the mirror, and lowered his gaze in deference to the Iraqi delegate who pulled out the Edwardian chair and sat next to him at the linen-draped, mahogany table.

The rapists and plunderers of the earth filled the conference room. Their own Tower of Babel must fall, today. He *must* succeed. The era of oil is over. Besides, how could these idiots stop him? They had been fooled completely by his given name, Abdullah. But a thread of worry tugged at his assuredness: the Saudis had always been suspicious of him, never thought him Muslim enough.

As the din of voices rose, he sat and palmed a ballpoint pen and digital recorder under the table. Practiced fingers unscrewed the oversized ballpoint shaft and coupled it to the digital recorder, a firing mechanism and bullet clip for three .22 bullets he'd pocketed earlier from the laptop hinge. Not for long range, but point blank—deadly.

A slight cough covered the drop of the gun into his coat pocket as he tried not to stare at the visiting guest ambling in—a white beacon in the people of color—Russia. A nice bonus.

He touched the false Mercedes key fob in his pocket and shivered. Such a cold place. Mozart must have felt it too when he died in this frozen hell. The propane fireplace along one wall was for show, like the entire meeting, and contributed nothing to heating. He gazed blankly into the fire, caught in the memory of flames that had licked and clutched Asiyah's charred body at the oil spill. Then relaxation engulfed him and the shivering stopped. Her death would save the world.

The room filled to capacity, and as the most junior delegate he sat at the rear, close to the exit—the only functioning exit.

Perfect.

The daunting task loomed, though every fiber in him ached to feel gulf breezes warm his cheeks at the Boardwalk restaurant in Dubai. But first he must survive.

"Excellencies, distinguished delegates, ladies and gentlemen of the press, I would like to welcome you. The meeting will be called to order," bellowed the Secretary General, Doctor Owoduni Al-Saluz, Minister of State for Petroleum of Nigeria. Streaks of gray in his precise beard highlighted the ebony face, an egg atop his enormous corpulence.

Thoughts of Dubai breezes evaporated and Abdullah wrung his pant leg beneath the table. *Oil was certainly good for you, Owoduni. How about a share of the profits for your starving people? You're nothing but a walrus in a suit, dressed-up but still a fat, blubbering idiot.*

His gaze flashed once at the ceiling and he touched the fob. *Soon, very soon.*

Fluttering of papers and murmurs subsided, and the meeting came to order. The Saudis began and droned on about production, proven reserves, GDP . . .

He crossed his legs and pursed his lips. These endless figures and spreadsheets were for e-mails or secretaries, not for men of power. He wanted to shout at them, make them stand up and be men. *You pitiful weaklings! You let the Saudis bully you.*

The delegate from Venezuela stood and hammered his fist on the table.

Abdullah relaxed his legs and clapped silently under the thick mahogany. How fitting. The beta test in Maracaibo had worked magnificently, destroying Venezuela oil so quickly that today's event would end their world, and begin the new green millennium. Within weeks there would be no more oil.

He leaned forward, thankful for his mastery of language. The translators always missed the flavor, and this would be juicy: precisely the testosterone-filled diversion he needed.

"The chair recognizes the Honorable Romero Sancho." Owoduni's jowls waggled with each syllable.

"Thank you, Mr. Secretary." A sharp mustache creased Sancho's boney face. Coal-black eyes glared and his voice seethed. "I apologize for the interruption of the agenda, but I feel we must spend time on important issues. My country is having a crisis that may soon face *all* of you. These damn bugs, these *bacteria* we thought would help, are not. And they are spreading. First Maracaibo, then the Orinoco wells. How long until they reach the rest of the world? I feel we should *all* share in solving this problem."

He paused and remained standing, glowering at the white-adorned Saudis.

The sheiks gazed back: calm, superior, in control. The pause lengthened. They shifted in their seats and shuffled their papers. Abdullah smiled. The Saudis, those superior, oil-inflated bastards, appeared so much like white lab rats waiting for the next shock. But that shock would be like a slow poison: unrecognized until too late.

Ignoring protocol, a tall Saudi stood and said in curt, British-accented English, "We do share in your concern, but do not see that it is *our* problem to solve."

Sancho erupted, pounded on the table and screamed threats and—

Abdullah puffed through his nose. *Oh, my. Foul oaths about Muslim mothers.*

Pandemonium ensued. Prim, bearded men shot from their chairs, pointed fingers and roared across the table in a babble of native languages.

He could not suppress a smirk. *Speaking in tongues.*

He feigned a coughing fit and, being the polite delegate, not wanting to interrupt these important proceedings, he sidled toward the exit door, placing his hand in his pocket. His finger pushed the small button on the fob and the tiny red light on each security camera blinked off.

The Secretary General pounded his gavel. But it only added to the crescendo of voices, stomping of feet, and screeching microphone feedback.

Now at the door, Abdullah pressed the large button on the fob and breathed, "How about some real bugs, Sancho?"

A puff of white dust, a muffled popping sound, and a large piece of ceiling tile crashed onto the table in front of the Saudi delegates. An inky mound split open and spiders scurried out, dribbling onto the floor as the delegates screamed and backed away. He almost broke out laughing at the predictable reaction. Everyone hates spiders, so they would be stomped and swatted: a perfect mechanism to spread their clinging microscopic oil-eaters.

He gently closed the door behind him and twisted off the key in the lock. A hand clamped his shoulder and his heart sank. It was time.

CHAPTER 2

Day 1 1600Z, 0900MST

The Denver Post headlines glared at Dan Trotter from his pressed-wood cubicle:

VENEZUELA OIL DRYING UP: Chavez Declares Martial Law.

How could he say no? Fred wanted *him* for this mission—to find out why those Venezuela oil wells were drying up. And this might be the one, his break-out mission, the one that set him free. He thought of his dad, an army pilot who died a hero twenty years ago.

So tomorrow it would be sunny Caracas, sweating buckets and swatting sparrow-sized mosquitoes. *Probably end up in a rat-infested military dungeon with that damn dictator-for-life plucking out my toe-nails.* Maybe he should stay here with his computer. He crossed his arms, propped his elbows onto jittering thighs and stared at the keyboard, soothed by repeating each letter to himself, "Q W E R T Y U I O—"

His cell phone rang. He flinched upright and peered at the number. His shoulders slumped and he answered. "Yes, I'm his father . . . I know I should . . . Okay. I will. I promise."

He punched Jeff's number and grabbed a pen. A soothing jazz entre greeted him, and feelings about his son melted him like a Jacuzzi. Then he clamped his jaw. Marci always accused him of being too easy with Jeff. Dan crunched his molars, grinding his cheek, the piercing pain welling up anger he needed. He X-d out *Chavez* on the newspaper with a force that tore the paper.

"Hi, this is Jeff. You know what to do." The beep came.

He flung the pen and raked his thinning pate with his nails so hard it stung, making his voice hard. "Do you *ever* want to drive again? If you don't go to those drunk driving meetings they *will* take your license away. First the Army, now this." Jeff had dropped out of high school, enlisted three months ago in the Army National Guard. Carousing with friends on leave he'd had too many and got caught.

Dan did not hang up, but tongued the salty taste of pennies from the gouge in his cheek, and eyed the photo on his desk—Jeff in mid-laugh, catching a snowflake on his tongue at a Bronco's game. The anger drained. His tone mellowed. "Hey, Jeff. Come on, buddy. Give me a call. Please." He pressed *End.*

The phone rang again. His face smoothed to a beaming smile. Maybe it was Jeff. Finger poised over *Answer,* he froze. The screen blinked *Marci.* He frowned at his wife's name and hit *Ignore.*

He stuck his finger on the laptop fingertip identification pad and smiled. The computer was a gift from the NSA: the newest processor, latest high res screen, largest memory, most powerful wireless—super cool. With it he could modify voice chips, change IDs, hack into security systems, download horrendously huge files, all in complete 256k encrypted security. The screen flashed an Interpol message: *Attack at OPEC headquarters:0800Z.* Eight hours ago. He clicked on a cell phone video clip and shuddered at the spiders, but grinned and tapped his foot as the Saudis shrieked and stomped on the spiders and flung their hands. *A weird hoedown in Mecca. How fun.*

"Shit!" It came out without warning. Ten years of therapy and no cure. Would he ever grow up? He had to admit, though: he loved seeing the Saudis panic.

He peered at the video again and fingered his lips, squinting at the spiders creeping on the table, dropping to the floor like marbles, the delegates smashing them with feet and newspapers.

The video ended and he scrolled to the photo of the suspect, Abdullah El-Hamain, OPEC delegate from the United Arab Emirates.

The gaunt eyes looked like a starving David Berkowitz. *Son of Sam as an OPEC delegate playing with spiders. Great.* His neck hairs prickled.

The other side of his brain barged in and he closed his eyes, seeing a different vision of the man: *Medium build and height—tough to pick out of a crowd. Hair color—some bleach—no, maybe a hat, a blond would stand out there. Weird eyes: add chic, European glasses. Stick on a tidy mustache and pad his coat. From Son of Sam to Monsieur Professor: a few simple changes and El-Hamain would disappear. Probably already in Dubai or Abu Dhabi, sipping a martini.*

He logged off. Tons to do: get supplies, get home, and tell her. He winced. Usually, when he thought about Marci she wore tight pink jeans and a soft green sweater and her eyes caressed him, warmed him all over. People he loved always came to him like prime numbers, floating in his mind in a green as vivid as spring aspen. Lately her eyes were black holes and a snake tongue slithered out between her maroon lips. The doc said his brain's wiring produced strange images, so it might be normal. He thought he was seeing her inner soul, though. Marci had been crabby about his missions, and about Jeff. They hadn't made love for weeks, and she seemed infatuated with the art museum owner downtown. Maybe if he proved he was more than a desk jockey she would come around.

He started counting ceiling tiles. At forty-one he stood abruptly. *Stop that!* The chair scooted out of his cubicle. Why couldn't his brain be more normal? However, he *did* stop at the thirteenth prime. It glowed like a green apple. Weird brain circuitry could be cool.

He hurried out of his cubicle. Agents inside a real office, one with a door, glanced at him, and shut the door. He was sure that was a smirk. Once he'd heard an agent call him an idiot savant. He'd almost blurted, What's 39 squared times 423? Don't know? Who's the idiot? Do you even have a clue as to why prime numbers are so cool?

Entering a white on white, tile hallway, his footsteps echoed: a lone tap dancer in an empty auditorium. Fred stepped out of a side door, blocking the path, jabbing a sheet of paper with his index finger. "Have you seen the latest about Caracas?"

Dan restrained a laugh at Fred's baby face mired in frowning concentration. Disguising him as an aging Venezuelan oil baron was going to be so much fun, he felt like clapping his hands. He couldn't wait. Fred was a superb field agent and Dan's best … maybe only friend. He took a lot of kidding about his name, some calling him Fred Flintstone because he was older, like from the Stone Age.

"Hi Fred. We like danger, right?"

"Quit smiling. You're such a damn kid. This is serious. Lack of gas is turning Caracas to shit. Highways are junk yards; people abandoning cars out of gas; mobs tossing Molotov cocktails; federales killing civilians."

Dan shrugged. He could be as tough as any field agent. "Maybe it'll turn into a real war and we can get rid of the scum down there."

"Are you nuts? We just get in, get the intell, and get out. No friggin' wars."

"Right. Forget wars. Who needs 'em." But Dan thought, At least the Cold War had been global. A skirmish in Venezuela was not what they needed. They needed a real war. Clear the cobwebs. All of them. *He* needed a real war; be a hero, like Dad, and show the rest of those jerks.

Fred's gaze softened. "You're great at what you do. You don't need a war to impress."

"I'm ready for more action."

Fred yanked his polo shirt up, revealing scar dollops on his chest and abdomen. "How about ICU? You need that, too?"

Dan threw his hands up. "Never mind. I'll pick you up tonight at nine. Gotta get home, break the news to Marci."

"You must be joking. You haven't told her?"

Dan stared at the floor and scratched his temple.

"What the hell are you doing? Just tell her." Fred's divorce five years ago had burned him, left a cynical scar. He envied Dan's marriage to Marci and told him so over many a beer. If he only knew about the real Marci, the one who hated Dan's crazy schedule, the one who had recently been seeing a lot of a particular art professor in Denver.

"Look," Fred said, "I asked for you because I need the best down there. This might be—" He shook his head and walked away.

"Might be what?"

Fred kept walking.

"Might be what, Fred? Too dangerous? Is that it? Don't think I can handle it?" Dan's voice had an edge to it.

Fred faced him, hands at his side, palms out. "Forget it. I know you and Marci are . . . Didn't I say you were the best?"

Dan glared at him, then smiled. Fred was green, another prime, a good guy. "Okay. See you tonight."

Fred walked away and Dan studied his wonderful average frame. *I can make that guy melt into any crowd, transform him into anyone, anywhere.*

"Hey," Dan yelled, "don't forget to dye your hair."

Fred waved his hand over his head, but continued walking into the message office, his words floating out. "Have I ever let you down? "I'll do the hair."

I won't let you down either, buddy. Ever.

Dan hurried to the special additions room, tapped in the cipher lock code and entered, waiting for the click of the door behind him. A soothing calm washed over him as he breathed in the peaceful tidiness of the room. The "open-ended" mission time-frame required more than usual. He picked carefully from the neatly organized closets: various silicon facial molds and patches, putty, teeth, flat gel adhesive, skin illustrator coloring, several wigs, hair coloring, bleach, plaster of Paris, foam latex mix. He preferred silicon these days, but the old stuff worked.

From Neanderthal to Mrs. Doubtfire—Fred must be covered.

Well after noon he finished, locked the door and rolled the suitcase back to his cubicle. He unlocked the drawer safe and picked out their new IDs and the Beretta 92FS: standard issue 9mm handgun. The gun felt cold and heavy as he aimed at the dartboard, bin Laden's nose the bull's eye. That bastard was not a real person, but he could shoot him. Right?

He hacked into the Venezuela oil cartel site and came up with something odd. Two names stood out: Octex-Penta Oil, a U.S. oil company based in Texas, and a company named Xoflex.

He froze. *Xoflex out of Louisiana?* He had written a program for them last year—moonlighting money he needed for his family.

He started hacking deeper. After an hour of furious work he got nowhere; their firewalls shut him down at each step. He lost two hours developing a program to better overcome their security system. But he would have to wait until Caracus to use it. It was getting late.

On the drive home he pondered disappearing Venezuela oil, the OPEC incident, Abdullah El-Hamain, and now, Xoflex. The program he'd written for Xoflex had to do with nanobots communicating with bacteria. Xoflex was connected with Octex-Penta Oil. *It was all oil.* Why did El-Hamain release spiders? Scary, true. And yet . . . they weren't even poisonous. So, stomp, stomp, squash, squash, and oh, what a relief. Dead arachnids. Barricading the room for twenty minutes made for pissed-off oil barons, but otherwise, what was the point?

He pulled into the driveway, forgot about El-Hamain, Xoflex and oil, and sighed at the neighborhood: lots of trees, cool neighbors—a great place to raise a family.

Watson gave his best Scottie intruder-go-to-hell barks, until seeing Dan. Then little happy yips accompanied a smiley panting face, and that wonderful wagging tail. Dan scratched the dog's chest and relaxed into his home.

The kitchen table was bare of plates. And the stereo played rap. *Shit.*

Marci stood by the stove, hands on hips, and glared at him.

"The mission came down this morning," he said, "and it's critical. Fred asked for *me*, specifically. He said I was the best."

She stormed by him, opened the door, then slammed it without leaving. Watson skittered out of the room. She whipped around and her eyes bored into him even as tears streamed. "Jeff's talking about going to Afghanistan, serve his country, like *Dad*. Now you're leaving again?"

His cell phone rang. The screen blinked *Fred*. He wanted to talk more about Jeff, about her and the art professor, but Fred never called unless it was important. "I gotta take this."

The door slammed and he jerked his head up so fast he almost dropped the phone. He started after her, but thought about her blaming him for Jeff's patriotism. Was she really going to the art exhibit to be with their daughter, or to see that damn retired professor? Maybe she was having sex with him and that's why she didn't—

To hell with her! He answered the phone. "Hi Fred. What can I do for you?"

"Get moving. We leave in half an hour."

She would come back. Right? And Jeff?

"Dan. You there?"

"Yeah. What's up?"

"Tell you when you get here."

CHAPTER 3

Abdullah had escaped Vienna that morning as planned, but it had not been pleasant. The hand that had clamped his shoulder outside the OPEC conference room now lay lifeless. Abdullah had shot that guard and the other guard, and run. He had exited the back door of OPEC headquarters and jumped into the back seat of an idling night-blue BMW. The stick-thin German woman drove off quickly, though not so fast as to draw attention. Nausea of having killed the two guards disappeared with the exhilaration of success, and one bullet to spare. He had succeeded. The cloak of leadership felt warm. Gunpowder smell hung in his shirt pocket and the ballpoint barrel pressed against his nipple. Nausea bloomed again. He must change clothes, soon.

They passed the Sigmund Freud museum, then the University of Vienna where students in bright parkas milled about, the breath from their erudite discussions steaming above their heads. The car slowed, not to avoid hitting someone, but out of habit. Abdullah knew the driver's son had attended this University before going off to Iraq and not coming back. She crossed herself and sped off. After a circuitous, tail-dodging route, they sped northwest on Federal Road 14 to a private airport. They stopped; Abdullah eyed the rearview and put a hand on her shoulder. "Thank you, Hilda." She put a hand up and waved. In the mirror, tears filled her eyes, her thin lips pressed tight. He squeezed her shoulder, scooted out and boarded a waiting Gulfstream 550. It taxied and took off immediately.

The pilot, Bob, an American, survived a five-year stint he called living on the edge of hell—the Iraq War. He'd lost three buddies, left the Army's First Air Cavalry Brigade, and on return home to Wyoming, discovered the family ranch sold to Octex-Penta. The big oil company leased a part of the land for hydraulic fracturing. That tainted the water, so to keep his father quiet they bought him out. A year later Bob's oldest son died in Iraq. The way he saw it, oil killed his buddies, his hope, and his son. All he had left was payback.

Abdullah's cause attracted thousands like Bob. They didn't think his plan crazy at all. With all those followers, travelling across the globe was easy. He had infected OPEC; now he must infect the non-OPEC oil wells before anyone realized how to stop him.

"Mr. Abdullah, we must change plans." Bob glanced back. "After Volgograd, we'll have to go north, through Russia. Going through Dubai will put us right in the middle of the Interpol radar screen and multiple searches. So that's a no go."

Abdullah smiled out the window, enjoying Interpol's nervousness. "That is okay, Bob. The most important thing is getting to Manila by early morning. Will that be a problem?"

"No problem at all. There will be a new pilot at Irkutsk."

"Another pilot? Do I know him?"

"Ivan Slovatski. I think you met him once."

"Ah, yes. I know Ivan. He was one of the pilots at Usinsk in '94. That will be fine."

"Okay, sit back and relax. We'll be in Volgograd in a few hours, then over Siberia most of the night. With the jet stream we'll make good time."

Abdullah eased back in his chair. Had it not been for spills like Usinsk, the research would never have been done. They would not have the tools. He placed his palm on the briefcase by his side and closed his eyes, trying to visualize the nano-bacteria floating into oil wells. All he saw was the surprise in the OPEC guard's eyes and the blood spurting from his temple.

His eyes snapped open and he shuddered. These were not the thoughts of a leader. He must be stronger. Everyone counted on him.

The scenery below moved from the Carpathian Mountains to the Dnieper River valley to the Central Russian Upland Plateau. Their plane descended into Volgograd, a name he could never get used to. Stalingrad was better. Russians called it the "Hero City" for its role as a turning point in World War II where they defeated the Nazis during six months of war in snow and frozen mud.

He closed his eyes and saw one and a half million bloody corpses on the tundra, their faces contorted in screams: All so Germany could control Russian oil in the Caucasus. Another blink and the OPEC guard stared at him with black holes for eyes.

You must forget the OPEC guards. You will succeed. The reign of oil will end. Now!

Flying into -2°F, he was glad he did not have to leave the plane. They taxied to a private section of the airport. There, a squat man with a Cossack's fur hat rushed aboard, transferred six of the long cylinders from Abdullah's briefcase to his own, and rushed off, with only two words in Russian when he left the plane: "Fuck oil." He would deliver the package to the huge Kashagan field in the Caspian Sea tomorrow.

Minutes later, they flew east over the last town. An icy fog diffused the final rays of sunlight as they entered the Russian Steppe. Darkness deepened, and a frosted-glass etching of snowy grasslands floated below them. Sparse streetlights illuminated a solitary rutted road with rainbow halos of frozen light.

The last streetlight marked the end of electricity and the road seemed to disappear into the void. But it was still there, a winding dark capillary of civilization scarring the vast tundra.

Soon, he would land in Irkutsk: the next step.

CHAPTER 4

Minutes after Dan and Fred rushed aboard, the CIA's Gulfstream 3 jetted away from Denver at 1900MST. Four hours later their plane banked right so quickly that hot coffee spilled on Dan's lap. He sprang forward out of the beginnings of sleep against a seat belt that held him fast. "Shit!"

The pilot apologized, explaining he had to avoid Cuban fighter jets. The water in the bathroom cooled off Dan's loins, but now he was awake. Wide awake. What the hell were Cuban fighter jets doing so far west?

For a few hours he tried to sleep, then gave up, glanced from his watch to the window and back again, drummed his fingers on the Plexiglas and the seat arm, and sniped at Fred, who finally glared at him and moved to another seat. They should have been there by now. He needed time to get Fred ready.

They arrived at 0800 local time, two hours late. The private and deathly quiet airport, Oscar Macha, was a short twelve miles south of Caracas, far enough from the craziness in the city, but close enough to get in and out quickly via the Caracas-Valencia Highway. They jumped into a waiting jeep and headed to their safe house in the hilly jungle. The driver weaved expertly around abandoned cars as their very-official-looking contact assured them they would not be stopped.

That would suit Dan just fine. He yawned and snarled out the window. Screw her. And Jeff. Then he hung his head and counted to eleven. He liked that number—prime, two ones. Great number. It glowed green in his mind. Eleven soothed him, so he could remember how much he loved Jeff and Marci. Two people. Another great prime—the first—two. Then he envisioned her sitting in the lap of that artsy-fartsy guy, grinding her hips, and he wanted to bash the window with his fist.

He thought of Jeff and their last face to face. Last night Jeff came in late from a Nuggets game and bragged about his skills as an infantryman in a Humvee. *He could have been an officer if he would have just waited. And what was he doing driving after that DUI?*

"You *drove* to the game?" Dan said. "Don't you think you should wait until this DUI thing is figured out? I would have taken you. All you had to do was call."

"It's not a DUI. It was a DWAI. And it was bogus. I have my license, so I'll drive when I want. Besides, my phones on the blink."

"Right. Phone's on the blink. I know you're a genius in math, but I'm not stupid. You *are* my only son and I really *do* want to help. You going into law, or just majoring in RPG's?"

Jeff's face had contorted into a snarl. "I'm not a kid anymore. If I want to—"

A loud bang interrupted Dan's thoughts and he ducked and covered his head.

Gunshot?

The driver of the jeep struggled, barely able to hold onto the wheel.

Dan inspected the driver. *No blood.*

Finally, the driver got control and stopped the car.

Dan sighed. A front tire had popped. Spare on the back of the jeep. Simple.

Jumping out, the driver loosened the lugs to the spare, then faltered.

A beat later, a faint but familiar coughing sound spurted from the jungle behind the jeep. Fred immediately grabbed his bag, jumped out, and motioned for them to follow. The very-official-looking contact was out in seconds. No one bothered to help Dan wrestle his kit out.

He crammed in next to Fred at the front bumper in time to see the driver's head bounce once in the dirt, thudding like an unripe cantaloupe, dust frosting his hair. Sightless eyes stared up, accusing, and Dan's stomach felt like a cauldron ready to spew. He wanted to rush out and grab the guy and try CPR. But it was too late. He glanced away. *Sorry, buddy.*

Pings sounded off the metal frame of the jeep and dust spurted inches from Dan's feet, the cough of the silenced gunshot a quick echo.

"Damn!" he croaked. *Great, you idiot. Stand up and wave next time.*

"Sit tight," Fred whispered and then melted into the thick bush.

Dan scooted behind the front wheel. *One guy dead and we're not even to the safe house.* Was the hazardous duty pay worth it?

He took a deep breath and rubbed the scar on his ankle where a sniper in a supposedly safe Iraq hotel had near-missed before Fred dropped him with a great two-hundred yard head shot. Dan had escaped easily, but Fred ... Dan remembered waiting for hours in ICU, studying the bandages around Fred's chest, the oxygen mask on his face, waiting for his eyes to open, and the relief when they did. Dan offered a prayer skyward to a God he'd neglected.

Another shot popped into the ground inches from his foot. Dan's feet took over. He shuffled back and forth, up and down, keeping low, feeling like an Indian rain dancer with serious Tourette's.

The very-official-looking guy squinted at him.

He stared back. *Yeah, so I'm nuts. Big deal. Still have my ankles don't I?*

The rear tire popped, whistling air.

Come on, Fred. Do your hunter-killer thing. My back isn't made for bending over and acting like a chimp on speed.

Two loud shots and Fred strolled out, thumb raised, big shit-eating grin.

Dan nonchalantly stood and stretched his lower back. "About time. I was ready to come to your rescue."

Fred's shit-eater drifted south, faded to a wince, and he grabbed his side. A dark spot spread on his shirt under his hand.

Dan tried to smile. He hurried to his friend and supported his weight on his shoulder. "Great, guess we'll need to lay low. Maybe we can call on the local witch doctor and he'll take out the bullet." The joke didn't feel funny.

"No bullet. Went right through. Big tear. Needs stitches. Bleedin' pretty good. Might need antibiotics." Fred's clipped words and blood-drenched shirt reminded Dan of the ICU. He pressed on the sopping dark spot and shuffled Fred quickly to the jeep, while trying to remember the last time he had stitched anything. Pig's knuckles in the field survival course maybe five or so years ago. "Or so" seemed right. *Hey, like riding a bike, right?* He needed a Harley, though. They were running out of time.

Fred jumped and yelled at Dan's suturing. "Goddamn it! Just poke it through fast and hard. Don't try to be careful or I'll lose a pint of blood."

The yelling he could take, and the uncomfortable position kneeling in the dust suturing while Fred sat in the front seat of the jeep, but then Fred started slapping the side of his head if a stitch hurt too much. On slap number four Dan said, "One more slap and I'll sew your nuts to your navel."

"Sorry. Guess I'm getting too old for this shit."

"Come on. This is only a flesh wound. No hospital needed," he lied and swallowed hard. The exit wound was jagged and Dan wondered if Fred needed more than an amateur. Dan quickly put in ten more stitches and breathed out in relief when the bleeding stopped. Then it hit him: Fred never complained. Something was up.

Fred's phone rang and he held up a hand and answered it. Dan paused, mid stitch, wanting to finish, but curious about the call. Fred's Spanish was too fast.

"What was that all about," he asked when Fred ended the call, but Fred only stared down the road.

Dan raised his voice. "Fred?"

"Oh . . . Uh . . . The meeting's in one hour."

"Okay. So what else is going on?" Dan started stitching again.

"Shit! That hurts like a mother."

Dan finished with a flourish. "Done. Pretty good, huh?"

Fred gave Dan a teenage eye roll, then started to get up, but Dan said, "Wait a minute. Let me dress it."

Fred sat still for all of five seconds before his legs started jittering. Dan dressed the wound and asked, "You didn't answer me. Are you okay, buddy?"

"Fine. Never better."

Dan finished and tried another tack. "Who was that guy, I mean that shot at us . . . that you killed?"

"I dunno. Dressed shabby. No ID. Maybe he wanted the jeep. Probably wanted to get the hell outta this place."

The man's M-4 carbine leaned against the Jeep—a sniper's rifle, with an eight inch cylinder on the front of the barrel. "Why the silencer?"

Fred shrugged. "Hey, there's a war going on here in case you hadn't heard. Probably stole it."

That was a pat answer, like Fred was trying to ease Dan's fear. But Dan pressed him. "You think he was alone?"

"Don't worry. This is the only road in and I called a couple of guys to watch the entrance." Fred's poker face said truth, but he fiddled with his ear lobe, his tell. Fred had just lied.

Dan licked his lips, and twisted his head in a one-eighty search to each side. He clutched his suitcase and scrambled into the rear seat, ready to get moving.

Fred pointed to the tires. One spare tire and two flats. *Son of a ...!* One hour to get everything ready, but first he had to drag his suitcase up the road. If another sniper waited, they would be easy targets.

CHAPTER 5

Dan stuck to Fred's shadow and they force-marched ahead of the now-quite-worried-official-looking guy six hundred yards uphill to an adobe dwelling at the dead end of the well-grated dirt road.

Fred slipped in first. After he cleared all three rooms, Dan sauntered in, trying to appear casual while his stomach flip-flopped. "The last time I sweated this much was in a nice sauna after playing racket ball." *Only then the sweat wasn't mud caked around the edges with fear driving it down my butt crack.*

A rust-encrusted ceiling fan hung motionless. An AC unit of similar vintage perched in a window. He flicked the switch on the wall, feeling like he'd flipped a coin. When the fan actually rotated he exclaimed in his best TV game show host voice, "Hallelujah! Electricity. And, will you look at this, Fred: two nice interior rooms, with a great view of a—you guessed it—your favorite sweaty jungle—a holiday dream come true."

Fred didn't smile. He *always* smiled at Dan's jokes. "The Company *does* have great connections." Fred's words were emotionless. "Probably a vacation home with a foreclosure problem, or political asylum needs, or some other leverage thing going on."

"Right. Vacation home." Still nervous about a sniper, Dan crawled below one window to the one with a window unit and turned it on. Nothing happened. He slapped it on the side. The unit sputtered then smoothed out and soon blew cool air on his face.

"Mother of God! The end of sweat. And, more to the point, the makeup will do best on dry skin, though it should be clean, too." He pointed to the bathroom. "Not that you smell or anything, but a quick shower to get the sweat, dust, and blood off will help my makeup job easier."

Fred grunted.

"Come on, man. Lighten up. You get to be a hero again."

Fred went into the bathroom, and the shower creaked on. Dan thought about yelling through the door, but Fred would tell him what was wrong when he was good and ready. Besides, the rusty pipes screamed too loud to be heard. One good thing he noticed: there were nearly new cable modem hook-ups for his computer. He took out the Berretta and stared at the door, occasionally glancing at the official-looking-guy, who had brushed off his dusty pants and sat on the couch, mute and looking nervous, but official.

After his own abbreviated cold shower, Dan started to work on Fred who would be impersonating an oil man come to Caracas to ferret out the problems with sagging production of the oil wells. Finally doing his job was Xanax for Dan's nerves.

First, he combed and further straightened Fred's still curly, but brunette hair, and added streaks of gray. More streaks of gray. The disguise called for an *experienced* oil man. All the real old guys were on other missions. Those guys would need less makeup, but they weren't Fred. Not at all.

He added a neat Boston Blackie mustache and chuckled.

"What?" Fred said.

"You ever listen to Jimmy Buffet?"

"Sure."

"I was just thinking Jimmy would love to have this mustache."

"Right. That mustache song."

"Yeah. He'd like it right up until the time you impersonate a slick Caracas businessman in front of ten of their oil Mafioso."

"That's funny?"

"Forget it." Maybe Dan would just concentrate on his job.

Less was better on the face, and with this heat, probably no brush-on at all. He stuffed one cotton ball into each of Fred's cheeks to give him the bulldog look, like Brando in *The Godfather.* He stepped back and surveyed his work.

"Gonna be hard," Fred paused, adjusting the cotton in his cheeks, "talking like this." His voice sounded chocked full of hot potatoes, or in this case wet cotton.

A cell phone buzzed in Fred's shirt pocket, and he held out a hand like a stop sign. He took out the cotton and discussed disposal of the driver's and sniper's bodies, and a new vehicle.

When he hung up, Dan stuffed the cotton back in his cheeks. "Leave it in and you'll get used to it. Also, this will help." He glued and disguised the micron-thin voice-changing chip just above Fred's Adam's apple. It was programmed to lower the frequency of his exceedingly boyish voice, communicating with the micro-surgically implanted modulator near Fred's vocal cords.

"Here." He gave Fred what appeared to be a butane cigarette lighter. It housed the power pack and wireless communicator for the voice chip.

"Something new?" Fred sounded bored, not the usual interest in gadgets. What was wrong with him?

"Yeah, and better. These batteries will last for eight hours continuous use. Range is only twenty feet, so if it's on you or close you're good." Sometimes they had to empty pockets for metal detectors.

He tried to perk Fred up with the coolness of the gadget. "Just flick this hidden switch here, and it's on. Don't forget to slide the cover back or you may accidentally turn it off. It's also a functional butane lighter that can be used as a weapon." He thumbed on the lighter and a half-inch flame popped up. Then he pointed it at wooden cabinet two feet away and thumbed the dial over. A flame bored into the cabinet. That should get Fred happy. The official-looking-guy decided to walk to the next room.

Dan thumbed off the lighter and handed it over. Fred pointed it at the adjoining cabinet, burned a neat, one centimeter diameter hole into it and grunted. No smile. He turned the voice switch on, closed the cover and stuffed it in his pocket. "How far does the flame go?"

"Twenty nine inches. Close range only. By the way, the voice sounds good."

Fred cranked down a doubtful eyebrow.

"Okay, still a tad gauzy and not quite slick, but passable."

Fred closed his eyes and sighed out his nose.

"What?" Dan said.

"Just finish this."

Dan nodded. Fred had saved his life less than an hour ago, so a little latitude was in order.

After twenty more minutes of body latex and clothes padding, Fred stood transformed from a muscular, round-faced, blond-haired American to a slightly plump, baritone, *Godfather* image.

Dan beamed. Fred ignored him and strode outside.

Dan's shoulders slumped as he eyed his friend's back. He gritted his teeth and followed, leaning on the front door frame. Fred usually wasn't rude.

The new vehicle arrived, a Mercedes. Dan whistled and tried to be perky. "Gotta' act the part, right?"

Fred gave a weak smile, his voice a flat monotone. "This is it for me, Dan. I'm done after this mission."

Dan's legs got weak. There it was.

Fred yanked out the cotton, tossed them at Dan and strode to the Mercedes. "This is not working. I'm sorry. I lied. There are no other guys watching the road. Be careful."

The car drove off with Fred invisible in the backseat while the very-official-looking dude gave a movie star smile out the front passenger window.

Dan picked a wet cotton ball off his shirt, flung it at the car, sneered at the grinning ignoramus, and plopped onto the floor, sitting cross-legged, all his energy gone. Fred was quitting and Dan was alone. What else could happen?

CHAPTER 6

Dan hung his head. A drop of sweat fell from his forehead onto the crystal of his watch and he realized he hadn't slept for thirty hours. Maybe he'd heard Fred wrong, or jumped to conclusions.

He quickly set up the portable motion detectors, alarmed each entrance, then placed his gun beside the laptop on the coffee table, and got plugged in. The computer always cheered him. He tried the new program on the oil cartel site. A name came up: John Sinclair, son of the ruthless oil tycoon from Octex-Penta Oil—something about him taking over the Texas branch and partnering with Xoflex. When Dan saw the name Xoflex he started breathing fast. Maybe he still had that nanobot program on his computer.

After searching all his files, his eyes got blurry. There wasn't much chance, anyhow. He remembered Xoflex had strict security; they made him destroy all the files and program codes. He tried to download the rest of the Sinclair file, but a brand new security program bumped him out. The cheeriness of the computer gave way to glances at the bed.

He turned off the laptop, grabbed the Beretta and lay down on one of the two twin beds. A framed print hung on the wall: red roses on a trellis attached to a crumbling brick wall, somewhere in Europe, France maybe. It reminded him of a moment, eighteen years ago—a single perfect red rose, the first bloom that spring of the American Beauty he'd planted the previous fall when Jeff was born, their first child. Beads of dew had danced on the petals in the morning sun that played through the waving aspen in the front yard. He had wet the tip of his nose on the crimson petals, and breathed in the aroma, a sweetness that could change your whole day. He could use that rose now.

He rolled onto his back and placed the gun on the night stand. Fred would return in a few hours, and explain everything. With any luck they'd be home tomorrow and Dan could speak to Jeff.

He counted revolutions, of the ceiling fan, round and round and . . . the last number he remembered was one hundred and thirty one.

He dreamed of being eighteen with Marci at a drive-in on the bench seat of Dad's old '76 Duster three on the floor. The windows had fogged and were beginning to frost on a cold fall night. "Billy Jack" blared and crackled through the window speaker. Marci moaned louder with each stroke in time to Billy's calm, cool voice, "I try, I really try. But sometimes I just go berserk!" His dad and mom cheered from the back seat.

Not now! Someone was knocking on the window. He was so close to climax. Though he'd never been to a drive-in with Marci. And why were his parents in the back seat?

The knocking confused him even more. *Just a few more strokes.* The pounding wouldn't stop.

He woke up sweating and dazed, his loins aching.

The sound whopped in the distance. No police baton on the window. He blinked hard and tried to shake his head fully awake. But he kept rerunning Marci's groans and his eyes drifted closed.

The sound pounded louder.

The secure satellite phone bleated.

Waking up was like running uphill in mud.

He keyed the talk button on the phone.

"Yeah."

"Get out of there. Now! It's the Nano guys. My cover is blown, and—"

A gunshot cut off Fred's last words.

Dan jerked awake. The whop-whop was a helicopter. He shoved his equipment out the door and into the bush, then heaved it onto his shoulder and ran.

After minutes of stumbling through the thick bush, sweat pouring off him, a loud detonation sounded behind him.

The sound of the blast tripped him onto his suitcase. He twisted around to see what had happened. Smoke rose above the ragged remains of the house. The smell of burning wood and plastic wafted in. The jungle holiday home was gone. He already missed the rusty window AC unit. His heart seemed to join with his stomach and lungs, all three trying to jump out and run. He would have to watch them run away because his legs were paralyzed.

What just happened? Who did that? The Nano guys? That was Xoflex. Shit! What should he do? First, find Fred and help him. Really? His brain seemed a black hole and had obviously joined his legs. No way could he find Fred.

He felt like weeping, screaming, and wanted just one prime number to come in his head. Confusion crammed every thought hole. The shrink said it was okay to cry. But real men didn't do that, right Dad? Dad would know what to do. But he was dead. Maybe Dan could call Fred on the radio? Maybe not.

He slapped his neck and wiped the maroon glob from his palm onto his pants. *Damn mosquitoes ARE the size of sparrows.* He doused his face and arms with repellent, then forced his legs to move away from the blast, heaving the suitcase forward several feet until he tripped and landed on it again. He slathered on more repellent. Would he have enough to ward off a trillion mosquitoes? Maybe he would O.D. on DEET. *Who gives a shit? Fred's probably dead.* He was losing it. *Concentrate!* He flung the bottle away.

The helicopter pounded closer. He pushed the suitcase under the brush and lay supine, banana leaves swaying between him and the passing helicopter. He muttered in a disgusted tone, "You were right, Einstein. This *is* the mission you get to be a field agent."

Yeah, well, screw it. I can do this. Though his chest constricted at the thought of leaving Fred, his organs seemed to have rejoined him and were under reasonable control. He must go by protocol. He changed the frequency on the radio and keyed 666 three times, then turned it off. Meet at rendezvous site beta.

CHAPTER 7

Remmy St. James stepped out into the afternoon of honking horns and humidity in northwest Caracas. He felt right at home, including the wet trickle between his shoulder blades. He wiped his forehead with a handkerchief. The heat wouldn't be so bad if it was the *only* nuisance. Bad attitudes and incompetence had been eating away at his patience. Now this.

Time to end this shit and git.

Venezuela Oil had tried to lull him last month with air-conditioned luxury at Hotel El Paseo in Maracaibo. *A damn Best Western no less. Who woulda guessed?* Great sunsets over Lake Maracaibo, too. But two days ago the oil platforms pocking the surface of the lake sprouted black smoke from riots in Maracaibo, so he was forced to fly to La Guaira, a quaint village north of Caracas. His hillside bungalow overlooked the Caribbean, and was minutes from the plane, which he would probably need. Soon.

The next hour would be grim, so he walked outside for one last survey of the historic Hotel Avila. Nelson Rockefeller built it in the '40s on George Washington Avenue. The morning sun glinted off beautiful old lines, reminding him of the Garden District in New Orleans, though with no AC and two steps from the slums, this place was more like Bourbon Street, including the tree frogs. The barrios ran rampant up the hillsides a few steps from the hotel front gate. The hotelier had warned him to stay away. "They are dangerous, señor."

Right. Try the Ninth Ward after midnight.

He strolled back inside the hotel and meandered toward the meeting room, still unsure how to handle the situation. As head of the nanobiotechnology division of Xoflex he'd climbed his share of hardship stairs, but this threatened to ruin his kingdom, which now encompassed a 200,000 square foot building southwest of New Orleans, near Houma. No one else wanted the land after Katrina, but the swamps had been his home as a kid; floods and snakes didn't faze him. Besides, he'd be long gone before the next hundred-year hurricane. So he might as well dip into the pot of gold now, while he could still enjoy it.

But now he worried he'd dipped into something different than gold. Not even the black gold he'd been sent to check on could protect him from death.

He rubbed gris-gris bag in his pocket, a constant talisman companion, concocted for him by his Great Aunt Verene. Made of red flannel, exactly two inches by three inches, it contained cayenne, a gator tooth, a mustard seed, his eye tooth lost at age eight, and rose petals, all soaked in the olive oil from an ancient tree that grew next to his great grandfather's cabin. He needed some luck today. Then he adjusted the tea rose on his silk lapel, sniffed it, and knocked on the door. A thin Creole man opened the door, greeted him quickly and closed the door behind him.

Remmy padded into the boardroom, glaring at the other Venezuelan "businessmen" crowded around the table. They kept their eyes down, except for the guilty glances at the corpse laid out on the elegant teak table, now ruined from the puddle of blood under his head.

Goddamn grease balls. Quicker with guns than the Mexicans after Katrina. Dumber, too.

The rain-gray eyes of the stiff they had shot an hour ago reminded him of bayous in the winter. They stared at Remmy, daring him to figure out their secret. Someone had torn off half of the stiff's fake mustache—a cheap ruse. Remmy bent to inspect the man's neck. He peeled off a silicone disguised voice chip—far from cheap. That and the thick, muscled body spoke of . . . danger. *Must have been into weights with those arms. Waste of time.*

At five eight and barely one-fifty, Remmy had a wiry strength that bested most weight lifters, especially ones who teased him about his size, or being gay.

If only he could extract pieces of memory from the brains that splattered the table.

"Get fingerprints, a shot of his face, and fax it to this number." He spoke tersely, wrote down a number, and flung it on the table.

One picked the paper up and whispered to another. The others looked at each other quizzically.

"Now!" Not loud, but he said it like the master, the captain, almost a growl.

It wasn't the words or the tone that got them moving, though. It was his dark eyes. He'd cultivated that look. Dead fucking serious.

They scurried around. Phones popped out, and they babbled gibberish into them. One of the men stepped forward, squinted and smiled. "Mr. St. Jaim. We know not how do this."

The man paused, then smiled and tilted his head. "I call Santiago. He come. He know how."

"Gracias." Remmy gave the man a thumbs up.

Damn spics. It'll probably take three times forever.

"You know where to reach me. We must figure this out before tomorrow. Understand, before mañana. So get the lead out. Vamanos. Rapido." He pocketed the corpse's cell phone and waved a hand over his head as he walked out the door.

He could feel their collective sigh as he left. Tension was his middle name, and down here he needed to use it. Daily.

Once outside the hotel, he crossed the busy street and eyed the bric-a-brac shanties on the hillside. Odors assaulted him—rotting vegetables, fruit, and definitely excrement, likely human. He pulled out a mint and popped it in his mouth. *If this is a progressive South American city, hate to smell the others.*

The Avila perched on the edge of the upper crust of Caracas, the last area of high rises and luxurious gated communities before the barrios, where the only sewage system was outside and gravity made the lowest shacks smell very far indeed from the penthouse shanty one mile uphill.

He dodged cars crossing the street and caught the limo back to the jungle bungalow, pocketed in the hillside jungle overlooking the beach. The limo left and he tapped a number on his own cell. A man with a thick Cajun accent answered and Remmy said, "It's getting too crazy here. Might want to get things ready."

Once inside the bungalow, he picked out the rose and placed it and his cell phone on the nightstand. He threw off the leisure coat, unbuttoned his shirt and flopped on the bed. With his head propped forward on a pillow he examined the stiff's cell phone over his flat, bare abdomen.

Nothing in the memory or in the outgoing or incoming calls.

He hit *Redial* anyhow.

Fine print, but the numbers and letters were crisp with good resolution. *Not allowed. Good Bye. Code 911.*

The screen went blank.

He hit *Redial* again.

Nothing.

Again.

Nothing.

He tried to punch in his home number. The screen remained blank.

Must be a low battery.

He opened the back.

"Jesus!" He yelled and flung the phone away as it hissed and smoked and dripped a liquid that burned like a lit cigarette. He jumped off the bed, brushing off his abs.

He tore off his shirt and ran to the sink, throwing cold water on the burn. Blackened spots like hot grease marks speckled his abdomen. That was going to scar. He hated scars after his teenage acne years. But Tony would be okay with it. He might even kiss it.

After dousing it for several minutes, the water did its job and the sting began to subside.

What the hell...Who WAS that guy?

He'd seen industrial espionage before. Usually they would pay off a key worker to take pictures, and the dolt would put the money in a traceable bank accounts. But voice chips and a self-destruct cell phone?

What have I got myself into?

Two months ago he'd been sent down to get the Venezuelan wells back on track. Their oil production had peaked and now decreased every year. That's where Xoflex came in. His division had developed Makers—nano-bacteria that could refresh old oil wells, raising production to new highs for many more years. In the past those bacteria had been used to clean up oil spills, and took months to work. But Remmy's extra punch—self-replicating nanoparticles sped the process and made the bacteria hold onto the oil, and bring it to the surface for harvest. The number of bacteria doubled so quickly that oil levels would jump in weeks. Just toss some of the Makers into the well—they go get the oil that couldn't be got before and come back to the surface with oil, oil, oil.

But that's not what happened.

Two weeks ago he'd traveled here to figure out why the wells produced *less* instead of *more*. Not a little less, *much less*. They were drying up. He wondered about the computer program that linked the bacteria and nanobots. Had it gone bad? Had someone modified it? He had no time to figure it out. That G-man probably had back-up.

Get the hell out.

He donned another shirt, threw his stuff in the suitcase, and put the rose in his pocket. He grabbed his phone from the nightstand and hit *Redial*.

A knock on the door raised the hair on his neck. He ended the call and erased the memory. He pulled his pant leg up and touched the Rorbaugh R9.

CHAPTER 8

A familiar male voice accompanied the knock at the door, "Remmy? Dat you? Okay, you?"

Remmy relaxed and pulled his pant leg down. The size of a cigarette pack, the Rorbaugh R9 could put six 9mm bullets into a forehead at seven yards. He opened the door. "Uncle Joe, you scared me shitless. How did you get here so fast? Thought you were at the plane."

Joe Doucet was a sable-haired, wiry Cajun, barely five and a half feet, who could out-work, out-wrestle, out-drink, and out-fox almost any man alive. Remmy already owed Uncle Joe for saving his life once. Today was looking like number two.

"Oh, Lola got de plane. You sounded kinda nervy on the phone, so thought I'd stop by early. You okay, boy?"

"Yes sir. So far. Except for a Mission Impossible self-destruct phone from a G-man."

"G-man? How you know dat?"

"Who else would wear a thousand dollar disguise, and have a phone that burns itself up?"

Joe cocked his angled face. "Where dat guy at?"

"He's dead. But his friends might be close." He grabbed his suitcase.

Joe did a one-eighty and led them out of the room. "No grass grow here, no."

A dilapidated Range Rover waited outside. Torn seat covers, dents and cracked paint disguised the machine beneath. A hint was the new off-road tires. When Joe turned the key, a low rumble smoothed to a purr.

In minutes, they cruised onto a rutted and pot-holed side road behind the bungalow. Remmy didn't care; he was glad to be getting—

The windshield fissured with a loud crack and something whistled by his head.

They both ducked low and Joe pressed the accelerator to the floor. The ride got very bumpy very fast. Remmy cinched the seat belt, gripped the grab bar on the dash, and peered up at the spider web of broken glass spreading out from a neat bullet hole.

How did they know we were going this way?

Twenty yards ahead an Army jeep was parked sideways on the road, blocking their path.

"Fuck!" he shouted.

"Not quite dat bad." Joe's voice remained calm and he smiled at Remmy, the sun reflecting a twinkle in his blue eyes and a glint off a gold incisor.

Joe wrenched the wheel to the right and the Rover plunged into the bush down a steep hill. After two bucking bounces, screeching metal on rock, and grinding gears, Joe popped his head up and floored it.

Remmy craned a peek behind them. Only banana leaves and vines. It seemed they knew their every move, though. He yelled, "They'll be waiting at the plane, Joe."

Joe cackled, his gold tooth sparking like steel on flint, his hands working the steering wheel around trees onto a rougher road: a madman driving a carnival ride.

"We gone plan 'B' already."

Remmy threw his head back and laughed too, cutting it short to avoid whiplash and broken molars. "Uncle Joe, you de man!" he screamed.

" 'Course. Just for you, though." Joe's features softened in affection at Remmy.

A minute later the Rover bucked onto a paved road, twisted and screeched and blew by three Army jeeps by the road. Remmy peered out the rear window. They were not following them. Why not?

In minutes the Rover plowed to a stop next to a dock in a protected industrial cove, a completely different location from their landing of two days previous. Uncle Joe knew how to escape the authorities, and he had proven himself once again, him and his Venezuelan baseball card-trading pals.

A modified Grumman Albatross waited with engine idling. Uncle Joe had found the sea plane in an auction, replaced the old turboprops and added three extra gas tanks.

They hopped out and ran to the plane, casting off the mooring lines and jumping in. Lola, Joe's carrot-topped wife of thirty years, sat in the cockpit and revved the engines once they climbed aboard. Beads of sweat studded her freckled forehead, and when she leaned forward her white cotton blouse was striped wet down the center of her back. She tipped a can of Dixie beer while chewing on a smoldering Tiparillo.

"You boys strap in. Got a little chop, but wind should help with lift. We gone."

Her voice lilted, the accent more genteel than Joe's. But her wiry muscular arms spoke of work, not pianos.

Remmy buckled in as the plane nosed into the cove and started out into the Caribbean where heavy waves splashed as high as the windows.

A little chop. Right, Auntie.

He cinched down the safety belt as they accelerated into a spine-jolting take off.

Lola's hands gripped the wheel like eagle claws on a flopping fish. The plane rose, the flopping ceased, and the ride smoothed as the vintage but well-tuned motors proved their worth.

Her gray-green eyes peered at him as she smiled and reached for the beer.

"Boy, what you got into down there?"

The wind whistled through cracks in the closed doors, the sun glinted off the windshield, and the seat tilted under him as she banked north, towards home.

"Don't quite know yet, Auntie. But I'm gonna find out soon as we get home."

Joe cracked a cold Dixie and handed the foam-topped can to Remmy from behind. He popped another for himself, took a long swig and back-handed the foam off his lips with a loud smack, "Ahh boy. Dats good."

Remmy was enjoying the first swallow of beer when he felt Joe's vice grip grab the nape of his neck and firmly twist his head around to face him. "You better find out. We got plans next month for you trent-trois. And ain't no G-man invited." He let go of Remmy's neck and play-fully slapped him on the back of the head.

Lola's eyes got wide. "G-man! Oh Lord. You're thirty-third birth-day comin' up and there's a G-man chasin' you? We need to go into the bayou, cher?"

Remmy studied the wispy clouds covering the lush green moun-tain top of El Avila as Lola banked left to follow the beach west. "Maybe so. If it is a G-man, his friends know where I live."

The plane leveled off and the engine whine decreased to a cruising hum. The weight of the extra fuel tanks kept the ride smooth.

Lola drained the beer and tossed the can in the bag at Joe's feet. "Gimme dat thermos of coffee. Need to be sharp going into de bayou at night."

Soon they were over Lake Maracaibo and Remmy could see the hundreds of oil platforms dotting the surface, and the swirls of green duckweed that had infested it. He stretched his neck to scope out the entire lake. Something bothered him.

Was it the paucity of birds on the vast lake? Or the distinct feeling he was not being chased, but herded?

CHAPTER 9

Dan lay on his back under brown and green banana leaves, waiting for that persistent, searching chopper to leave. Please. Sweat dribbled into his ear. Fred's last words and the gunshot replayed. What had happened?

The chopper moved off, he let out a held breath and stood. He slapped off the detritus and trounced through the bush, holding the suitcase on one shoulder. The chopper rotors sounded close again, and he flopped, belly first, onto the wet humus, under plants he prayed had no relation to poison ivy. He turned over and peered through thick leaves at the helicopter cruising by. Ants crawled on his chest. A large centipede meandered across his abdomen. He shuddered and stifled an urge to stand up and brush them off. He hated bugs. Finally, the helicopter retreated, and he jumped up, swatting and beating his body, contorting like a crazy African dancer.

He picked off every square millimeter of his torso, and pushed on, occasionally checking the GPS. After two hours and changing direction several times, he studied the GPS and dropped the suitcase. This was the designated spot; had to be. GPS didn't lie. It was electronic. He and electronics were buddies.

Twilight settled in and he hunkered down. A huge yellow spider weaved a web between two trees.

What had Fred said? "The Nano guys." Fred loved only the best. "The Dolphins" would only refer to the undefeated Miami Dolphin team under Shula, and "The Mustang" equaled the '68 Shelby GT500KR.

So, "The Nano guys?" No mystery there. *Xoflex.* Oh, yeah. Dan knew about them.

Xoflex started as a tool company in the '60s, their motto: *We have a tool for every business need.* In the '80s they delved into nanotechnology. Xoflex's CEO, Jack Scorlotta, was a genius. He realized genetics needed nanotechnology, so he bought Genetrax, one of the biggest genetic companies in the world. Last year patents on about two hundred bio-nano tools were issued, a hundred and eighty of them to Xoflex. Now, it seemed, they were involved in oil, with Octex-Penta and John Sinclair. Maybe Octex-Penta didn't want us to rescue Venezuela? And how were they using Dan's program. Could Dan be responsible for the oil drying up?

Stars crowded the night sky. The black silhouette of the spider poised in the center of the web, a specter between Dan and the Milky Way. The web shuddered and the leaves shuffled in a breeze from the hills. Dan twitched at scurrying noises. A big swig from his canteen sounded like a monstrous frog gulping on a loudspeaker. The adrenaline rush petered out and his concentration melted into the night.

He started counting the rungs of the spider web and when he got to twenty-three, he stopped. That number usually glowed blue, not green, but still another great prime number. Tonight it was red and stopped him. He focused on one thing: once he got out of this bug-infested slime pit, he was going straight to Louisiana where Xoflex had built a brand new nanobiotechnology center. Maybe he could find some answers there. Fred's last mission would not be in vain. Dan would avenge his ... *Jesus!* His vision blurred but he clenched his jaw and forced himself to think of Fred in the *present* tense. Fred would show up soon.

He slapped and flinched for a few more minutes and twenty-four hours without sleep caught up. He nodded off; woke once in panic feeling the heat and noise of an explosion at his back. Then realizing it was a nightmare, he thought of Fred's baby face laughing at him from a time of happiness, and fell back asleep.

He awoke, groggy. Darkness surrounded him. His sleep-hung eyes wouldn't focus and he felt eerily detached, as if in a dream. The moonlit shadow of a Huey hovered nearby while a faint swoop-swoop of the rotors waved banana plant leaves in what seemed to be a black and white, slow-motion, silent movie.

Something stung his cheek, and he slapped it. Everything changed, every motion became real time, the sound of the rotors deafening. This was no dream. The chopper had a U.S. flag decal. He grappled with the suitcase, dragging it to the rescue ship, and hoisted it into the cabin, his shoulders aching, and rotor wind on his face.

A raven-haired beauty in camouflage grabbed his hand and heaved him inside, her strong arms engulfing him next to soft breasts. He reveled in not retaining his boyhood revulsion at being touched. Sometimes psychiatrists can help.

If this is no dream then I must have lost it. What the hell is a girl like this doing here, rescuing a geek like me?

He squeezed his eyes shut, then opened them to blue eyes of a depth he had never known.

Definitely Looney Tunes.

He glanced around the plane. "Where's Fred?"

She shook her head. He hung his. She raised his chin with her hand and looked in his eyes. "It's okay, cher. We find him. You cheer up, you. Okay? I'm Sergeant Lisette Boudreaux."

He found out she was a Marine assigned to the Company sent to rescue him, and raised in the Louisiana delta. That got his attention. She might come in handy going to Xoflex. Could someone leading this show actually be thinking ahead?

Hours later they boarded a C-130 cargo plane in Grenada, headed for Pensacola and debriefing. He yawned for the eleventh time. *So tired Visine will never get the red out.* But he couldn't sleep. Hell no. Not with her sitting next to him. Not to mention the heat slathering his back in sweat in the non-air-conditioned plane while the never-ending turbulence bounced his head off the aluminum frame of the cargo webbing.

She shed her outer fatigue shirt. "That's better. Feels like a dry bayou in August in here."

Dan studied her camouflage tee-shirt. It had a very intricate pattern.

Her soft accent mesmerized him for hours. He felt drunk with fatigue but focused hard so as not miss a detail about bayous, couche-couche, and sucking the heads of mud bugs. She also shared her iPod loaded with Zydeco and country music.

One of his favorites by Garth Brooks played, and he unconsciously sang along. He really loved that song, though singing along reminded him of Fred—he had hated country music.

When he turned around and wiped his eyes, he caught her look, a kind of you're-an-okay-guy look.

Finally they flew over Pensacola Beach. Each wave of the turquoise Gulf of Mexico crested foam and blended into the sugar white sand. He was supposed to be skiing champagne powder at Breckenridge with Marci today. But she didn't like his job and was probably screwing the art professor. He felt as unfettered as a teen swinging on a rope over the river, about to let go into cool depths and currents of wonder.

The cool turquoise water moved below in hypnotizing waves: irre-sistible. He subconsciously let go of the rope and felt his conscience click off. All those years of being straight, following the rules, it all fell off as easy as a coat that was too big. Maybe it had been fading all year. Marci seemed a distant empty-eyed cheater, Jeff an ungrateful son, and Fred—he was gone.

He needed to feel good, feel wanted. This sexy Cajun beauty seemed to like him, and after being with her only hours, coupled with the sights, the songs—he felt free and bold, like he'd lost twenty years.

So much Freudian Id stimulated I'd probably make love to a butt-ugly barmaid at the Florabama Lounge.

But that's not who was next to him. He glanced over at her.

Not even close.

At 1400 Pensacola time, they landed at Sherman Field, Naval Air Station. A skinny airman, who looked all of sixteen with braces and acne, gave Dan a sealed written message: *Proceed with Sergeant Boudreaux. Debrief in a.m..* He could do that. No problem.

They rode in an open Jeep to a quaint motel on Pensacola Beach. The road was pot-holed, construction-ridden, and the Jeep had no shocks, but he thought it the smoothest ride of his life.

The scenery was pure Deep South: live oak trees draped with

Spanish moss, numerous railroad crossings, seagulls squawking, and two long bridges so close to the water you could toss a rock and feel the splash. He saw it, but concentrated on yellow and red: Lisette's yellow short shorts and the red tank top she'd changed into at the base. All he heard was her voice, lilting like that of a Bonnie Prince Charlie in a Parisian court, telling of the Civil War and cannon shots fired back and forth between the Rebs at Fort Barrancas and the Yanks at Fort Pickens.

"You know, cher, the cannons, they did'na have the 'umf to put one across the bay, so neither fort ever landed a shot."

Yeah, he knew. But he only nodded and raised his eyebrows, aching to hear more words from her lips.

She continued in the lullaby that kept him wide awake all the way to the motel. She spoke of the great Apache chief, Geronimo, imprisoned at Fort Pickens, and the more recent Hurricane Ivan that almost completely demolished the Fort, and all its history.

"That terrible Russian did what our brave Confederate troops could not: cut off any travel except by boat."

History stuff. Yeah. That's what I'll tell Marci. I learned a lot of history stuff. Not really. What did she care? He'd never known another woman. Maybe that was his problem. Lisette could be the cure for his social inadequacies.

They arrived at a motel by the beach and she grinned. "Here we are. Are you up for a margarita?"

CHAPTER 10

After escaping Caracas, Remmy's Aunt Lola flew the Albatross for hours before entering the Gulf of Mexico. Remmy peered out the west window and saw the boot of Mexico punching into the blue water, remembering great Cancun trips in highs school when he first realized he was gay. His wan smile disappeared instantly when the plane banked left and began descending. A fighter jet roared overhead.

"Looks like the Cubans are out." Lola said. "We might have to park this thing overnight and have some tequila."

Remmy frowned. He had to get back, find out what the hell was going on with his nano-bacteria, not to mention escape the trigger happy shooters in Venezuela. Then he wondered if that's what they wanted: to scare him right into a trap at Xoflex.

More jets roared by, a noise so loud it had to be three. "Guess you're right, Auntie." Remmy said. "This oil problem in Caracas has got everyone touchy."

"We got other problems, too." Lola pointed out the front window. Large thunderheads bloomed ahead, glowing pink and orange with the setting sun.

As she splashed down in a small cove south of Cancun, the rain began, and didn't quit all night.

Remmy spent a soggy night on board. Though the plane had plenty of room for all three of them to stretch out, a few leaks plinked at random like Chinese water torture. Remmy finally got up and put a shirt under the drip and fell asleep.

The next day, he realized he had to go back. Xoflex held all the answers—why his nano-bacteria were taking, not making. The rain and clouds finally cleared off enough for them to depart at eleven.

The plane droned on over the Gulf, now mostly clear of clouds and jets. After two hours he dozed, and the next thing he knew the plane bumped down at a private airstrip in Mobile, Alabama.

Remmy peered through sleepy eyes at Lola's favorite customs agent, a red-cheeked rotund man named Calhoun, waving and smiling at her from the tarmac beside the gate. New Orleans had too many Yankee agents. Here Calhoun cleared her quickly. Maybe it was because she had dated him once, or he'd been a tight end for LSU, her alma mater. Lola *was* like most Southern women: they ruled, whether you knew it or not. Of course, Calhoun had suffered from that Russian bitch-storm, Hurricane Katrina, and her preceding bastard cousin Ivan, not to mention the oil spill that had nearly wiped out the region's economy. Bonds of disaster were stronger than superglue.

Calhoun walked up the boarding stairs, peered in and waved his hand at Lola and Remmy, winked at Joe, signed the form and left. They refueled, and sliced the air again.

They followed the coast and finally descended, the landing a soft shudder in the Louisiana bayou. The seaplane's radial engine purred and flung burnt JP5 into the surrounding musty sulfur odor of the swamp. The sun's orange crescent flirted with the Gulf's horizon. Remmy watch it and waited. There. The spark of green after the orange winked out—a rare phenomenon of winter Gulf sunsets, shared only with sailors far out at sea. Mist crept onto the water surrounding the building, reminding Remmy of a haunted house, though it also warmed him with memories of summers as a child. They motored forward, and Lola killed the power. The plane touched the dock.

Quiet.

A few thumb-sized frogs started: *nee-deep, nee-deep.* Within minutes thousands joined in. Several bass players throbbed along with percussive squawks of nearby water fowl.

The Swamp Things chorus.

The plane's occupants listened and nodded. Stress lines relaxed and eyes closed.

Remmy sighed. "Good to be back, y'all." But the relaxation at the familiarity of his teenage vacation home soon faded. Work awaited. He wondered how long before his pursuers found him.

"You right, you." Uncle Joe eased out onto the floating dock.

Lola threw a rope to Joe and jumped onto the dock. She sighed and stretched arms high at the zenith of wispy purple clouds catching the sun's last rays. "I could do with a snort of lightnin' and handful of bugs. 'Bout you, Remmy? We got a mess of 'em."

"Throw in some gumbo and I might make it through the night." Remmy grabbed his bag and followed them into the shadows, not seeing, but feeling his way. Helen Keller feet. He'd been there, done that, blind drunk. He peered into the distant marsh, a ghostly place even in broad daylight, but now the mist thickened, an opaque blanket on the water that could hide even real demons.

The siding of the shack resembled a patchwork quilt, not cloth but different ages and types of wood that, in the waning light, returned an optical illusion of a modern multicolored brick home. But brick was not useful here. Wood ruled: easier to get, cheaper, and quicker to rebuild after hurricanes and floods. A way of life. And death.

Remmy's Cajun ancestors had been exiled from Nova Scotia to this harsh ground in the 1760s, and the land had been in the family ever since, not for its real estate value, but for its roots and an escape from the revenuers during Prohibition. An old still continued to operate in a distant wood using new parts that Remmy had scrounged for his uncle. The resulting product, white lightning, was pure, clean, and high octane. Sips taken with clenched teeth added to the flavor of any mudbug feast and helped loosen newcomers into "sucking heads."

Joe poured a shot glass of the clear liquid for each of them while Lola put on a big pot of water and Old Bay seasoning. From the freezer, she pulled out a bag of gumbo, and dropped the contents into another heating pot.

Remmy offered a toast, "May the winds be gentle, the rains not too much, and fishing great."

"Dat too," Joe said.

They all downed the liquid simultaneously, and slammed the glasses on the table.

"Laissez les bon temps rouler!" Lola and Joe sung the words together at top volume.

Remmy put his open palms out. "Sorry, y'all. That's it for me. I gotta' keep my brain straight for thinking tonight. Tomorrow I need to be fresh."

Lola pinched him on the cheek. "Eat up, Remmy. Need strength for them G-men."

The meal went down easy with a glass of lemonade, and finished off with rich pecan pie.

After supper, the other two cleaned up while Remmy sauntered onto the covered porch. The swamp yielded few sights from the moonless night. The lilt of his aunt's and uncle's Cajun melded with the clink of dishes. Remmy breathed in this home and heard his cousins screeching in his memories of them jumping off the dock into the cool water. He wished he could call Tony.

But he would only call him to warn him, and that call might be a hangman's noose.

After they finished the dishes, Remmy cocked an ear to the swamp.

No frogs. No chorus. Water lapped the dock.

Too quiet.

CHAPTER 11

Remmy stepped into the house, flicked off lights and whispered, "Uncle Joe, someone's coming."

The remaining kitchen light outlined two huge aardvarks riding on the mist. No. They were men wearing night vision goggles. The single lens stuck out like a long snout. One sat in the front while the other stood on the rear of the low-slung pirogue, poling silently through the dark water, weaving through the cypress trees like a snake.

To the side of the pirogue two water born orbs reflected the kitchen light. The curious gator's eyes sank. Remmy hoped the gator would upend the pirogue, thinking it a new flavor of nutria.

The aardvark snouts pointed directly at Remmy and he turned off the remaining light.

Lola let out a squeak when the lights went out. She touched his shoulder and handed him a shotgun. "Where they at?"

"A few yards from the plane."

Joe had disappeared, and Remmy wondered if he was already dead. "How did they find me?" he muttered.

He squinted into the darkness, halfway wishing he would have left the light on. A scant wind cooled the back of his neck. Movement caused an immediate twitch of his eyes. Spanish moss fluttered in the trees like hanging ghosts.

He spotted them, still hovering in the water, several yards out from the plane. What were they waiting for?

The man in the rear pushed on the pole and the pirogue glided forward.

The breeze brought in the musty fish smell of mating sea trout, and Remmy longed to be on a quiet boat, fishing in another bayou, with different company.

Another push on the pole. Twenty feet closer. Both night vision snouts peered side to side, inspecting each cubby hole.

A skittering splash came from the other bank and the snouts turned to it. Remmy figured Joe would make a bigger splash. Probably a nutria or deer. He raised the shotgun and pointed it at the men's backs.

The rear snout faced forward and poled the pirogue until it bumped the dock. Remmy relaxed his trigger finger. Perhaps he should only wound them. He needed answers.

Before he could aim again the man in front grabbed the dock and leveraged the pirogue around. Usually, a pirogue tipped easily side to side, better exited with stabilizing earth and swamp on either side. But these were no amateurs. In a silent blink they flipped onto the dock and disappeared.

"Where the hell is Joe?" said Remmy.

"He gone to cover the still. Should have been back by now."

He motioned her to go to the rear door, hoping she could escape. He would not. *Should have shot them when I had the chance.* He'd seen men like this before. Hunters: Silent, swift killers. And now they wanted him.

His heart skipped and he licked dry lips. The pitch black offered no solutions to his searching eyes. Maybe if he flicked on the outside flood lights it would blind them in their night goggles long enough to give him an advantage. The switch was across the room. He took a deep breath and ran for the switch.

Flinging open the front door he gawked at where they should have been.

Someone wrenched the rifle from his hands and thick arms snaked around his body, quickly crunching him in a full Nelson. Remmy hoped Lola made it out the back door.

CHAPTER 12

The next morning Dan sauntered onto the cramped, but private, patio outside his room at the beach motel, feeling like a prince. Aquamarine waves crested, phosphorescent in the morning sun, brushing the sugar white sand paper smooth. He sipped a Corona, smiled into the sun just winking over the peninsula of Pensacola Beach, and savored warm feelings in all the right places.

Lisette surfed on a long board, bouncing up and down on the waves in a bathing suit that weighed less than an ounce. No wet suit and that water had to be cold, though it fit with what she told him last night. She had barely survived Hurricane Katrina, and seeing it destroy so many people's lives she had decided to enjoy every minute of life and help everyone else do the same. She said it freed her, completely, like a free spirit from the '60s. No drugs, but sex ...

She waved. Her wet breasts strained at the tight bikini. *Freedom rules.*

Last night still percolated in his amygdala, a part of the primitive brain he remembered from college psychology. Take the amygdala, add endorphins, and humans did things without thinking—some good, some bad, but they always *felt* good, at the time. Last night's massive endorphin release into his amygdala pleasure center still simmered enough that Lisette's bouncy-bouncy juiced him up to medium heat.

That's when the frontal cortex crept in. He spit out the beer, stood and shook his head.

What the hell are you thinking?

After a good night's sleep, doubts about Marci seemed a flimsy veil of smoke, and he ached to hug Jeff, tell him it was okay. But most of all he had to get to Xoflex and find out if his program had anything to do with disappearing oil in Venezuela. He also wanted payback for whoever killed Fred. The company would go along with that, surely.

He walked inside and made a call to the office, using his encrypted cell-phone. Listening to it ring, he studied the wall. The plain beige wall. *That's it. No more great views of . . . of anything. Put last night out of your head. Stick to business.*

The office told him a guy named Sam Houston would debrief him. They said he had contacts down here with Xoflex. They patched him directly through.

Sam answered, "Yeah." He sounded hung over.

"Is this Sam?"

"Yeah."

"Well, uh, Sam, you want a debriefing now?"

"Who's this?"

"Oh, I thought they told you. I'm Dan Trotter and my good friend, Fred Pollak, was . . . uh . . ." He pushed thumb and index finger into closed eyes, then opened his eyes and squeezed the bridge of his nose. The thought of Fred actually dead left his head devoid of colors, only black. He had to force himself to finish. "I think he was murdered yesterday while we were on a mission. Maybe you heard about it?"

"Tough break. Fred was a good man. So, what else?"

Jesus. Hung over AND stupid.

"Is this a bad time for you, Sam? Maybe I should get someone else."

"No, I'm fine." A whooshing noise hazed the words, like he was driving a car with the window open.

"The Company told me you had connections with Xoflex Corporation in Louisiana."

"Xoflex, huh? They're into pretty crazy shit. Sure you want to ride those waves?"

"What?"

'Ride their waves?' If he says 'dude' I'm hanging up.

"Listen, Fred and I were—Never mind."

"Dan, why don't you go back outside and enjoy the view of Lisette? I'll be there in five."

He frowned at the disconnected phone, then at the window, and snatched the binoculars and peered out through one tilted slat of the Venetian blinds.

A black guy with flopping dreadlocks flew over the waves on a Jet Ski about a mile south.

Can't be on a Jet Ski. Didn't sound that loud. Where the hell is he?

He glassed up and down the beach. Finally he gave up, took a deep breath, ambled outside and sprawled on the chase lounge. High in the sky a bright yellow advertisement trailed behind a plane. It said *Bubba's—A Gentleman's Club.*

Not even eight and already advertising for a strip club. Then the sign collapsed, the plane banked back toward the mainland, and another yellow object floated towards Lisette, a parachute with a guy pulling strings.

Mine and his.

The guy waved at him.

Dan saluted him with his middle finger.

Sam Houston laughed and used the morning land breeze to float in about ten feet off the waves, hitting the beach at a gentle run, his feet slapping on the wet sand.

Dan shook his head. The Company was smooth. But this guy was oiled butter.

Sam rolled up his chute, and Lisette strolled over to him, took his cell phone and gave him a hug and a ... long kiss.

Goddamn. She knew this guy was coming all along. Throw out the Coronas. No more Tequila.

Sam trotted towards him, sinewy legs and tanned muscular body rippling with each step. He was shorter than Fred, with a buzz cut, and peered at Dan with dark opals that glinted in the sun.

They shook hands.

Grip like iron. Of course.

"Hello, Dan. I'm—"

"Sam Houston." Dan said. "Nice name. You must be of a Southern bent. Having an enjoyable morning? I see you and Lisette know each other."

Sam squinted one eye. "Didn't mean to piss you off, but I was in Ft. Lauderdale last night, needed to get here fast, and decided to scope out the place. No better vantage point. Sorry about Fred."

Fred's name ebbed Dan's anger. "Oh yeah, thanks."

Dan glanced at Lisette and his voice sharpened. "You could have told me about him last night."

Another captivating Cajun smile. "Could I? Are you sure you would have heard me?" Her soft lilt melted his anger despite the sarcasm.

He shifted his gaze to the sand. *Need to rearrange my thinking about this girl.*

"Am I interrupting something?" Sam said. Then he chuckled, which made Dan clench his fist. The Jet Ski cruised towards them.

What is this, a convention?

The man skidded the machine to a stop on the sand right next to them, jumped off and grinned at Sam before shaking his wet dreadlocks like a dog.

"That's Ron. He'll be helping me and Lisette. You got your stuff here, Dan?"

He was accustomed to working fast, but this was . . . light speed. *C=299,792,458 meters per second.* They could be to the sun and back in about sixteen and a half minutes. He shook his head and refocused.

"Okay. Sure, I'm ready to go. Could you brief me on exactly what we are going to do? It might help my brain reorganize and avoid mistakes. Besides, we can't all fit into that Jeep out front."

Sam strode inside, Dan following on his heels, wanting answers. Sam grabbed clothes hanging in the closet and went into the bathroom, saying over his shoulder: "I'll only be a moment. Lisette, will you go introduce Dan to the new ride."

Poking his head around the door he added, "Yes, I am from Texas, and my mother named me after an honest and determined man. We're going to find out why Xoflex is in Venezuela, see if they killed Fred. That's what you want, isn't it?"

"Yeah. But how are we getting into Xoflex, and what do you want me to do?"

"All in good time."

Sam disappeared behind the bathroom door.

Lisette grabbed Dan's hand and led him. He felt like a first grader being taken out to recess for the first time: No explanation, but everybody else was excited, so he would go along.

The Jeep had been replaced by a tan Ford Club Van with two surfboards on top. The logo on the side read: "Sam's Surf Shop, Custom Boards Since 1982." Below it, a blond, bikini-clad babe surfed a huge turquoise wave on a psychedelic-colored surfboard.

He scrutinized the truck, then Lisette.

"How long have you known Sam?"

"A while."

He wanted to ask her how well she knew him, but that seemed obvious.

"Hey," she said, "Ron's my friend, too. I like Sam and Ron, and I like you."

He felt weird, like when a program solution was just beyond his reach. He changed the subject. "So, what's with the surfing logo?"

"That's what Sam does. He's been surfing and doing boards for a long time."

"Who was the model?" He nodded toward the logo.

She shrugged.

He studied the face on the blond and put dark hair on her. *Right.*

"Where's the Jeep and how—"

"One of Sam's friends delivered the van this morning and took the Jeep."

He blinked. A deer in headlights. *Really bright headlights. I need a double espresso.*

Sam jogged out, dressed in a salmon-colored polo shirt, black shorts and tennis shoes and a beige baseball hat emblazoned in bright red: *Sam's Surfboards.* Dan couldn't help staring at the different colors. Maybe he would like Sam.

He patted Dan on the shoulder. "Are we ready? Where's your stuff?

Lisette motioned with her head, "In the back," and eyed Dan. "I took the liberty while you got your beauty sleep."

"Great! You took the liberty of moving my . . . my *stuff?* Do you have any idea how important that suitcase is?"

He stomped to the rear of the van and jerked on the handle.

Locked.

"Okay, open this thing. And, while you're at it, I want to see IDs for everyone here. I am not some school kid."

Ron ambled around and unlocked the rear door. He opened it with one hand and showed his ID with the other.

The other two joined Ron and flashed IDs.

"Those are driver's licenses."

Sam shrugged. "Wanna show me your ID?"

Good point.

"Okay. Let me look over my stuff. I need to make sure everything is here."

He opened the suitcase, touched each item, felt every pocket, and muttered "okay" after each check. Finally, he picked up the Berretta.

"You won't need that," Sam said over his shoulder. "We're here to take all the risks. And I'm sorry to rush, but if Xoflex and El-Hamain are in bed together, we need get there. Yesterday."

Dan closed the suitcase. *Okay, I'm the heel here. Should have known.*

"I get a bit edgy when someone else touches my equipment."

Sam offered his hand. Dan shook it.

They piled into the van and Dan said, "I know about Octex-Penta and Xoflex, but what about El-Hamain and Xoflex?"

"I thought you would have put that together by now." Sam glanced sideways at Lisette and raised his eyebrows. "Maybe you've been busy with other things. Think about this for a minute. Why do you think Venezuela oil disappeared about the same time OPEC was attacked?"

Dan frowned at the back of Lisette's head as she drove them away and muttered, "I wouldn't call it an attack. I mean spiders? Come on. They weren't even poisonous."

"Maybe so, but I don't believe in coincidences. OPEC oil is drying up, just like Venezuela."

Dan blinked. Outside, seagulls dove at a splashing school of fish in the Gulf and a young couple dragged a cooler across the fine, white sand. A tow-headed toddler ran behind. Everything was happening so fast. All he wanted to do was go to the beach and build a sandcastle with that little boy. The biggest oil spill in history seemed distant history. And more oil wells loomed only miles away in the Gulf, waiting. He thought about Jeff, Marci, Fred, and last night, and oil.

Twenty four hours. Everything had changed. Was it for better or worse?

He needed Maalox for the burning bitter reminders of last night's Corona seeping up his throat. Cool sweat beaded his temples and his heart danced liked he'd run a mile. If someone was suspicious, they might say he looked guilty.

After Venezuela his body didn't trust his mind to keep it safe. But with Lisette driving, things couldn't be all bad. She liked him. That was okay.

"Let me catch you up on things," Sam said. The van accelerated.

CHAPTER 13

Thirty six hours earlier, Abdullah arrived in Manila. He rubbed his red eyes. Flying east through seven time zones and fifteen hours, he'd only managed fitful naps. Despite the glare of morning sun, his body rebelled against awakening.

Last week's super typhoon had smashed Manila, with uprooted trees and helter-skelter boards piled high against the foliage, and leaning buildings at the edge of the beaches. That and landing at a private airport should make security even less than the usual Philippine laziness.

At customs a Cockney-accented Englishman in a ponytail, flowered shirt, white Bermuda shorts, and yellow flip-flops greeted him. *Probably some aging hippy who came here to live cheaply,* thought Abdullah.

The man sized up Abdullah with smiling eyes. "Anything to declare, governor?"

He shook his head and handed the man his fake passport for a Mr. James Sabbat.

"What a bloody shame, Mister . . .uh, Sabbat. We was hoping you might have pharmaceuticals or maybe a bit of cash for the hurricane relief effort." He raised his eyebrows and flashed crooked, yellow teeth.

Abdullah pondered the floor and scratched the back of his hand. The man was right. He should do something. He pointed to his throat and whispered, "Laryngitis. Can't talk. Sorry, I didn't bring—" He winced and grabbed his throat.

The man frowned, pulled a handkerchief out of his shorts pocket and placed it over his nose and mouth. "Bloody hell. Could have told me sooner. Don't need no Asian flu, now do I? Sit over there, mate, while your fancy jet gets petrol. The pilot will arrive shortly."

He stamped the passport rapidly and waved Abdullah through.

Abdullah sat and closed his eyes and let his head fall on his chest, easing breaths in and out, concentrating on the task ahead. He should be in Cepu by eleven. Indonesia was not a major producer, but it all had to go. No exceptions. He would simply deposit several grams of his modified nano-bacteria outside the gates of the Cepu oil compound and, similar to the HeLa cells disaster of the '60s, they would spread like black magic. Air, water, people, animals, insects, and whatever else managed to wander close to the wells would transport the nano-bacteria. They would self-assemble and multiply to a kilogram of nano-bacteria overnight—a sure end to billions of gallons of crude in weeks.

After Vienna, he probably could have relied on them infecting the wells here within a month. But speed was imperative. It must be over before anyone released the Regulators—that could stop everything.

Soon he would be home, feeling the sea breezes in Dubai.

He glanced around the waiting room, recognized the courier, and strode into the bathroom behind the short oriental man. Akio was Japanese, and once again proved efficient. He transferred two tubes from Abdullah's briefcase in the time it took for Abdullah to thank him with a smile and a pat on the back. Akio left without a word. The Chinese oil wells would be taken care of.

A blond man watched Abdullah as he strolled out of the bathroom, reminding Abdullah of the Russian at the OPEC meeting. He chuckled through his nose. He didn't have to use a courier to spread the nano-bacteria to Russia. They had spared him the trouble.

How ironic. Usinsk—where everything began. 1994: 100,000 tons leaked out of the pipeline break onto the Arctic tundra. Oil companies promised a cleanup. Photos of the site weren't taken for years, and only released then with oil company comments such as, "As you can see, everyone overreacted to the spill. Due to our clean-up efforts the area is even more beautiful."

Greenpeace finally got a formal written plan answering their demands for remediation in 2001. Seven years. The profits of the major oil companies never waned. Fix the pipeline and continue. To hell with the environment, and anyone who got in their way. The Americans got a taste of that with the Deepwater Horizon spill.

The blond man stood and walked to the window. *Too fat to be of danger.*

Outside, Akio strode across the tarmac towards an awaiting Gulfstream III, an older jet, but nondescript, with no corporate name. Abdullah's environmental splinter group worked hard to avoid publicity. Unfortunately, early on they had also focused their attention in the wrong direction, not realizing the solution existed right under their noses the whole time. Common bacteria did precisely what was needed: eating oil spilled from accidents—only too slow. The bacteria names— *Pseudomonas aeruginosa, Bacillus subtilus, Acinetobacter baumannii, Alcanivorax*—were common to bacteriologists, soon to the world. Now, thanks to Xoflex and a slight modification, those previously slow bacteria were lightning fast and already on their way to Russia. Payback was hell.

The fat blond man shuffled away from Abdullah, but kept eyeing his jet.

Another plane arrived outside, a red cross painted on its side. The door opened on the Red Cross plane and a slim, chestnut-haired young woman carried out a huge box that should have sent her toppling. She reminded him of Tamara: only a wisp, but stronger than most men, with a beauty that started at the skin and penetrated every ounce. He popped rose hips from Tamara's organic garden into his mouth. *Helped keep the immune system strong. Might need that.*

He crunched the rose hips and tented his fingers, thinking on a different tack. He turned on his cellphone and made a call, noting the exact second on his cell-phone.

Tamara's normal loving tone was absent when she answered, and she proceeded to berate him for risking a call. He interrupted her. "I know. But I must do this. Please listen."

After instructing her for exactly twenty-eight seconds, he turned off the phone and scrutinized the area. The fat man was gone.

Tamara listened to his instructions and hung up, still peeved that he called, but understanding why. She snuggled into the covers and fell asleep in minutes.

The next morning she fingered the curtains apart and glanced outside her flat in London: no signs of surveillance. One van parked across the street—Mr. Green's, the florist. All the other cars—empty. A good day to leave.

While she showered and rubbed dried rose petals over her shoulders, she remembered 1996 and her first meeting with Abdullah. She was working for Greenpeace. She still couldn't believe it, a damn oil baron and she fell for him. *Dear Abby, I hope you know I love you as much as your dead Asiyah.*

She'd worked oil remediation after the Gulf War and traveled to many of the OPEC countries trying to convince them of the importance of cleaning up their act, and how easy it would be with the new bacterial techniques.

Who knew he would join our side, and lead us to something so important?

But he had. And in the process she'd come to love an incredible man. Wanting to help out with the Manila hurricane relief fit her Abby perfectly.

If only he could have waited another couple of days.

He'd told her he wanted to live each day as if it were his last, make each one count.

She toweled off and muttered, "I hope your charity didn't make this your last day."

Once dressed, she combed her long auburn hair in the mirror, and made a decision. Searching for scissors she gave herself a quick, monstrous haircut and inspected her reflection. Uneven, but modern.

In another fifteen minutes she walked out the door, past the red brick Richard Hoggart Building of Goldsmiths College. The vibrant autumn scarlet of the ivy-covered walls had faded to winter brown. She carried everything she needed: two changes of clothes and two IDs: one hers and one Priscilla's.

Two should be enough.

To hide in London she should only need her tinted glasses and hood. It depended on how much they knew, and who was after her. If they only scanned crowds she could change her hair to blond and eyes to blue in seconds. However, if they pulled the hair on thin women to check for wigs, she would need a sink and privacy. And changing her five-foot, hundred-pound frame to a large woman like Priscilla would take even more unobserved time.

That was why she chose the Tube. From New Cross Station she would get on the East London line to East Canada, the Jubilee line to Greenpark. There she could decide on a train out of town, or to Heathrow. Greenpark had a lot of people, and several big loos. She could spend time there changing if she needed to.

"East Canada, White Chapel." The announcement came over the speakers as the train pulled in.

She casually glanced around the station.

No bobbies. Only an Asian man talking on a cell phone.

Tinted glasses were the rage. And the hood over her head? It was winter. But of course it could have been August in England and still have been winter. As someone once said, "English summer: beginneth June 30, endeth July 1."

She strode to the queue at the ticket counter, and opened the paper to wait like a good Englishwoman.

CHAPTER 14

Abdullah had spent an entire day frustrated before Tamara awoke to leave her flat. Due to the recent cyclone, all flights to Cepu airport on Java Island had been cancelled. He finagled a flight through Da Nang, and arrived on Java late, too late for any action. At least, while in Manila, he had delivered nano-bacteria to another Japanese courier, this one headed for Australia. In a sleazy Java motel he managed a few miserably short hours of sleep. Then, by the first rays of morning, he spread his destructive beauties around the gates of the Cepu oil compound, and caught a taxi to the airport.

He paced and surveyed the almost empty Cepu airport several times, waiting for his private charter to refuel. The fat blond man from Manila had not reappeared, but Abdullah wondered about the lovely Asian woman who'd come out of the restroom and flashed him a smile. He smiled politely at the woman and sat in a chair close to his gate, keeping her in view.

Tamara should be out of the U.K. by now, having spread the nano-bacteria and on her way to meet him for some fun in Dubai. He ached for her and his home. He stifled a yawn. He'd pushed himself to the limit for thirty-six hours and felt it. A few more details and he could rest. Once he arrived in his warm and beautiful Dubai tonight, he would enjoy Tamara's company. Tomorrow she would pick up more of the nano beauties and fly across the big pond to Texas and the Gulf of Mexico. Other couriers would go to Canada and Alaska. Then he could sleep.

He rolled his head around to keep his eyelids from closing and out of the corner of his eye noted the TV news. A middle-aged, well-tanned man with manicured hair said in a smooth baritone, "CNN reporter Julie Craven reports from Caracas. Julie, how are things down south?" That woke him up.

Julie told of the escalating civil war in Caracas. Then her face faded out of focus as the camera jerkily focused on the distant scene unfolding. An angry mob of mostly college-aged men and women marched toward the capital building. Five Humvees, manned machine gunners on top, surrounded the crowd. A warning blared out through a megaphone in Spanish that Julie quickly translated: "Stop or be shot."

The crowd waved their hands, guns, knives, pitch forks and cricket bats in the air and jeered at the soldiers in the vehicles.

The Humvee gunners fired warning shots above the crowd. But this only enraged the crowd. They swarmed forward.

All five machine guns fired into the crowd.

A female hand covered the lens of the camera, and Julie said reflexively, "My God. It's horrible. This is not anything like Egypt. We don't need—"

"Julie?" John started, but the T.V. screen flickered and returned to the CNN newsroom where John shuffled papers. He glanced up, momentarily confused. "We seem to have lost our up-link to Julie. We'll get back to her momentarily."

John flashed his perfect white teeth to the other reporter at the desk. "Brittany, I know many Americans are glad to see Venezuela lose their prominence in the oil cartel, but I see nothing good coming of this."

Brittany, a stunning brunette with a flawless complexion, dazzled the camera with her smile and uttered what would probably be her last words as a newswoman, "Except maybe less pollution in Caracas."

John's eyes widened in alarm. Abdullah laughed at the stupidity of the man and the brazenness of the beauty. He placed his palms together in mock prayer, pointed his fingers at her and said, "Exactly." Perhaps he could hire her.

The beautiful Asian woman smiled again when he stood to board his private plane. This time he did not smile. The plane taxied for take-off while he buckled in and mused on Tamara. What would she wear for him tonight?

CHAPTER 15

At the Green Park station in London, Tamara got that inkling—someone was watching her. She'd spent the morning on the Tube, and finally made her way here, pretending to window shop, but carefully observing for any signs of a tail. That's when she spotted him in the reflection of a window. A plain-clothes bobby? Maybe. Or maybe someone worse.

She ducked into the nearby loo, slipped into a stall, and took off her glasses. Holding her oversized compact in one hand she rapidly applied make up around her left eye: brown and green. That would have to do. She put her dark glasses on and went to the mirror, waiting. Luckily she didn't have to wait long.

A woman with the same physique as Tamara traipsed into the loo. Though shabbily dressed, she had jeans nearly exactly like Tamara's. When the woman finished and came to the sink, Tamara caught her eyes in the mirror and said, "I'm sorry to bother you ma'am, but could you help me?" She held out a twenty pound note. "Would you wear my dark glasses and hooded jacket out of the loo?"

The woman cocked her head back, like a snake ready to strike, and frowned, but never took her eyes off the twenty.

In hushed tones, Tamara explained while toilets flushed in the background. "My bloody husband beats me when he drinks. I ran in here to get away from him. He's out there looking for me. All he wants is to pinch more money and bruise me ribs. Bloody lunatic. If you could mislead him for about fifteen minutes, I'll make it to the train to me auntie's."

She took off her shades and pointed at the shiner under her left eye.

The woman clapped a hand to her mouth. Another woman primping in the mirror behind them overheard the comment and glanced at the shiner in the mirror, snapped her compact closed, and rushed out.

Tamara fit her shades on and dropped her head as if embarrassed.

The look-a-like removed her hand from her mouth, and squinted angry eyes. "Glory be! Bloke needs a lesson. Happy to help you, poor lass. And I'll have me Jim take care of him right proper. He's up the road beggin'."

Tamara puckered her lower lip and nodded.

"Okay. Give me at least fifteen minutes after you leave the loo."

She added a bit of reverse psychology, hoping to punish whoever followed her. "But please, don't let him catch you or Jim. You see what he did to me. He might hurt you."

She gave a description of her "no good husband:" the man in the shopping window that had been following her.

A lull in the loo's business prompted Tamara to hurry. She peeled off her coat, and gave the woman her shades. Quickly donning her new duds, the woman pocketed the money, put the shades on and turned to walk out.

Tamara put a hand on the woman's shoulder. "You don't know how much this helps. I hope he doesn't hurt you."

The woman patted Tamara's hand. "Now, now. Don't you worry, Dearie. You get to your auntie's. I'll take care of this bloke. Just let him touch me and Jim will make him eat fish 'n chips through a straw the rest of his bloody life."

After the woman left, Tamara glanced around and, seeing no one, ducked into the stall. In less than two minutes she'd cleaned off her left eye, inflated a tummy shaped donut around her midriff, stuffed extra padding in her bra, and wriggled into a plain, buff-colored moo-moo.

She heard the door to the loo open and someone entered the next stall. A fart echoed out of the toilet bowl, a lighter clicked, and the smell of burning wet hemp filtered from the stall.

Tamara smiled and popped in blue-tinted contacts, rouged her cheeks, and pulled on a neatly-combed, straw-blond wig. She finished with BCG's, black-framed glasses that Abby had termed birth control glasses.

The smell of marijuana filled the loo.

She pulled on white jogging shoes and made a final check with her compact. Unfolding a flowery canvas tote, she shoved anything left inside, opened the stall door, and walked to the sink.

A policewoman entered the loo and glanced at Tamara, now the maidenly prim and proper "Priscilla," washing her hands at the sink. The female bobby wrinkled her nose at the odor.

Tamara raised her eyebrows at the bobby's accusing stare, then lifted pinched thumb and forefinger holding an imaginary joint to pursed lips and pointed to the stall where tan smoke curled over the top of the door.

A grunt and another fart from the stall.

Tamara brushed on more rouge and applied ruby red lipstick while the policewoman walked over and knocked on the gaseous stall.

An annoyed gravelly voice answered the knock with, "Can't a girl have a piss? Bugger off!"

Tamara smile grew as she exited the loo with Priscilla's walk, face, body, and new flowery bag.

Timing and luck. Sometimes you had 'em, other times . . .

The rest of the trip proved easy. She took her time getting to the airport so as not to arrive too early and appear to be a loitering terrorist. As a shy, overweight spinster she kept to her knitting and reading, and boarded the plane from Heathrow to Dubai at the scheduled departure time of ten p.m.

When she arrived in Dubai the next morning at half past seven, she waited patiently in line to get through customs, secretly surveying her surroundings every few minutes. Finally, she stepped up to the counter. The customs official smiled broadly at her and asked in a thick British-Arabic accent, "What is the nature of your visit to Dubai?"

"I'm going to study some of your rare arachnids."

The agent raised his eyebrows. "What?"

She smiled and showed him a magnified picture of a large red-backed spider: inky bulbous body with a bright red stripe down the back: Dubai's own black widow, not native to Dubai, but an arachnid hitchhiker from Australia and twice as deadly as the North American variety.

"You know, spiders." Her voice was almost a whisper.

He shuddered, stamped her passport quickly, and waved her off.

At the Burj Al Arab hotel, she checked in as Priscilla, but once in the room she shed wig and clothes in seconds and padded naked over the plush carpet through the large suite to the oversized bathroom. A hot shower, a bit of sun on the balcony and a gin and tonic were all she could think of. That and Abby.

In the shower, the gentle, warm water jet on her nipples was not what she wanted. She adjusted the spray until it stung. Better. She pinched one nipple, closed her eyes and took down the removable shower head, aiming it at her mons. Leaning against the marble wall she wallowed in the trichotomous feelings: the cool hardness on her back, the hot spray titillating her loins, and the stinging pinch of finger-nails on her nipple.

Abby's face and manhood filled her mind. Her eyelids quivered, her groans echoed off the marble walls, her hips tilted against the spray, and one nipple tented at her pull.

She held her breath in longer . . . longer.

"Mmmmhh."

But before climax she stopped.

Save it.

Abby would be there soon. She was tweaked. She loved to dance and show off her body for him at the Planetarium. Now it was time to enjoy the warm sun.

She toweled her hair and ran her fingers through it, approving in the mirror. Her face and physique fit the mussed look perfectly. Water dripped from her body and left a trail on the carpet while she mixed a gin and tonic and licked her fingers of the squeezed lime. She eyed the Chinese finger traps hanging from the headboard. Abby did love his toys. In the meantime the private balcony beckoned, and she strutted out, feeling freer than she had in weeks. Au naturel—the only way to sunbathe at eighty degrees.

She lay supine on the chase lounge and her quivering thighs

relaxed. The hot sun heated every inch, a feeling she had missed in London.

Sweat puddled in her navel and between firm breasts that now rose and fell with each gentle deep breath. The days of worry and tension drained, smoothing her face as she slept, the heat a welcome lullaby from the British winter she'd left behind.

On the table beside her the half empty glass of gin and tonic beaded dew that gradually trailed down the sides. The melting ice gently settled with dull tinkles.

The sea breeze swayed the curtains and a man slipped in the front door.

CHAPTER 16

Dan awoke with a start at Sam staring at him. "Sorry." He wiped the drool from the corner of his mouth. "Didn't get much sleep last couple nights."

The van droned west across I-25, and Dan had fallen asleep listening to Sam's briefing about Abdullah El-Hamain. That had been maybe an hour after leaving Pensacola.

Sam smiled. "Yeah. I heard."

Lisette reached out and slapped Sam's knee. He grinned at her.

Lisette eyed Dan from the rearview. He sat straighter, rubbed his neck, and yawned. "You got any coffee?"

A cold mini-can tapped him on the thigh with Ron's hand wrapped around it. "Try this." Ron said.

He took the can, popped the top, but his arm froze, the can inches from his lips. He did not recognize the label. "Nothing illegal in here, right?"

Ron shrugged.

Dan started to put the can down and Ron grinned at him. "No way. Drugs aren't my style. It's just an energy drink."

Yeah right. Dan eyed the open can, then drained it and asked. "What's with the surfer logo? You guys don't actually surf do you?"

"What? You don't think we're capable?" Ron chuckled.

Dan gave Ron the once over: shoulder length dreadlocks, a white tank top over a muscular torso, and dancing café au lait eyes on a handsome black face. A good cover. Smart, too.

"Sorry about the drug thing. I never thought anyone that worked for The Company had surfing as a business."

Sam twisted around, one side of his mouth dimpled up. "Beach bums don't usually enter your head when you think about hard work and espionage. Is that what you're trying to say?"

His pupils seemed to consume his eyes, black holes under the brim of the cap. Probably late forties, but appeared ten years younger. Deceptive in a subtle way. He'd long since graduated from the old days of shirt-and-tie men in an overseas embassy.

"Okay. Right. You're one of those guys." Sam had to be a NOC-list agent: Not Official Cover. When caught they disavowed working for the government and the government forgot them. Like lone wolves, they lived on the edge or died falling over it. As an international surfer who designed surfboards, who would ever think the guy was CIA?

Sam's grin widened, crinkling the corners of his eyes.

"You're sharper than you look, Danny boy."

Dan pursed his lips. Though Sam had a soft red aura to him, he seemed closer to the assholes in the office than Fred. He decided to talk more, instead of keeping his feelings in. "You like to poke at geeks?"

"Well, you are pretty white. And what's with the dress shirt and designer slacks?"

Lisette squinted at Dan through the rearview. "Come on, you guys. He's no field agent. Give him a break."

Dan grinned. *Guess I DID make an impression last night.*

"Thanks, Lisette. I appreciate the effort. If it weren't for us desk jockeys and hackers, those glory guys wouldn't stand a chance."

Sam touched the brim of his hat, tipping his head. "You got that right, Danny Boy."

Ron gave Dan's shoulder a gentle squeeze.

"Man, we was only joshing with you."

Dan felt warmth in Sam's nod of respect and Ron's affirmation. Joking was cool. That's what Fred said people did who liked you, joked with you. Maybe these guys were okay.

"My dad served in the Navy," Sam said, "so I always lived close to water. I learned to surf at seven and since then it's been a way of life. And I never forgot the need to do something for my country. The Navy wouldn't take me; said I was too small. So, I tried a different route. And, you might not believe it, but my international business has done so well I rub shoulders with a lot of important people across the globe. A multi-million dollar corporation makes being a NOC-list agent easy."

"And he makes great boards, man," said Ron, as he reached over Dan's shoulder with all fingers flexed except his thumb and little finger sticking out like horns.

Dan smiled. "Hook 'em horns. I like Aggies football too."

Lisette's suppressed laugh sounded like a muffled snort. "First of all, it's the Longhorns and that's the pinky and index. Second, that's surfer lingo for *hang ten,* and it means *everything's cool.*"

Need to get out more.

"Maybe I'll shut up."

"Nope," Sam said. "Now it's your turn. How did you get into this shit?"

"I went to college, got a degree in computer science and after working for IBM decided to do something different and joined the CIA."

Sam took his hat off, rubbed his forehead with the heel of his hand and glanced up.

"We got that from your file. I want to know *why?*"

Dan gazed out the window. Only Fred and Marci knew him down deep, and that had taken years. *Don't have that luxury now.* Sam needed to trust him, and he needed to trust Sam. Fred was gone.

He swallowed and studied the southern winter passing by: dormant browns with only the hint of green life beneath—his life twenty years ago. His father, an Army pilot was killed in an air accident, just before the Gulf War. Dan missed the funeral to study for finals. Dad wanted him to finish college, so he did, a major in computer science and minor in theater. Alcohol got Mom. Driving drunk, she took his brother. Marci asked him once if he ever cried about it. Back then he hadn't learned to cry. For a long time he didn't like … no he hated the Army for taking his family.

A studio apartment became his shell, nights programming and hacking, day job at IBM a joke. People were absent from the equation. Something his father said kept nudging him, though: Freedom will die unless you fight for it. A CIA recruiter came to the office and when he took Dan to dinner, said, "You're quite the hacker, Dan. We could really use someone like you." They wanted his makeup skills, too. He met Marci and Fred and they nursed him back into the world of people.

He glanced at Lisette, then Sam, and dropped his head and studied his shoes. "Guess I'm like you, Sam. My dad was Army, so I believe in fighting for freedom, and will support you guys or die trying. I wish I could have saved Fred, but . . . Anyway, that's about all I got." He wanted to tell Sam more, but he wasn't ready. And besides, Sam was no Fred. He peeked at Sam, almost afraid to say it, but decided he had to. "If that's not enough, maybe you should turn the van around, or drop me off, and I'll find somebody else."

For a long minute the whirr-thump, whirr-thump of the highway sections reverberated under the speeding van.

Lisette broke the silence. "Great."

Her eyes flashed angry at Sam who fiddled with his hat and studied the floor.

Ron touched Dan's shoulder. "Sorry, man. Sam was only ..."

"Hey, no problem. I'm okay with it if you are. Maybe we should talk about how best to get into the Xoflex security system."

Sam tugged on his hat and looked Dan straight in the eye.

"Sorry if I hit a nerve. I agree. Let's move on."

Dan nodded and glanced at Lisette. *That's twice she rescued me.*

She stared at him in the rearview, her eyes wet.

He blinked. *Shit. I'm in trouble. First my dick, now my heart.*

He leaned over and made a pretense of retying his shoelace. This time he pulled the laces way too tight. *Damn. That hurt.* He needed to blot out Lisette. No way she could like him more than Sam.

He sat up, and cleared his throat. "So, what do you think Xoflex has to do with Venezuela oil drying up?"

"Not sure yet." Sam said. "Xoflex has been up to their neck in oil companies for a few years, and they were there when Fred was killed. Something about nanobiotechnology. Any ideas?"

"Maybe." He knew about Xoflex, maybe too well, and had formed a theory since Fred had uttered, "It's the Nano guys."

Sam turned around and peered over his sunglasses at him, grinning and raising an eyebrow. "Okay, I said I was sorry. Care to share?"

He scratched his chest, glanced at both rearview mirrors, out the window, and then at Sam. He had to make sure he didn't say too much—nothing about his programming.

"Yeah. I think I have time." It felt good making a field agent sweat, especially Sam. He also noticed two things: She was smiling at him and a blue truck was tailing them.

CHAPTER 17

Dan pushed back into his train of thought, despite worrying about the truck that followed them, and his tight shoelaces that began to ache. "Okay, Xoflex's technology melds nanobots with bacteria and genetics to help end peak oil."

"Yeah, but that's only the end of new reserves. Not like in Venezuela when it started disappearing," Ron said.

"Right. The peak of production was reached and there should have been a gradual decrease. In the U.S. that happened in the '70s. Venezuela, in the last five years. Saudi Arabia, with the largest reserves in the world, is peaking now, and they are the last. Every oil-producing country would jump at ways to increase production, especially now that there's a lot more buyers."

"Like China," Sam said.

"And India." He wanted to finish this and ask about the truck. "Now, enter Xoflex. Years ago we used bacteria that ate oil to clean up oil spills. Xoflex's patent utilizes those bacteria, and they're getting filthy rich because they tapped the estimated fifty percent of reserves that used to be non-extractable. *And* I think Xoflex went one step further." Not only did he think it, but he knew it. They had used his program.

He leaned down and loosened his shoe. It was okay if he enjoyed Lisette's smile and glances without pain. Besides, he enjoyed having Sam wait for the answer.

Sam took off his hat and slapped him on the back of the head. "You know I have been schooled in torture, the kind that really hurts."

Dan raised his hands. "Okay, okay. Just getting comfortable."

He smoothed out his hair and glimpsed the truck again. "Anyway, in the past the bacteria that cleaned up oil spills ran out of energy, so it took months to clean up a ten-thousand barrel spill. I think Xoflex found a way for nanobots to supply endless energy, and communicate with the bacteria, so they can eat billions of barrels in weeks, and somehow bring all that previously unavailable oil to the surface."

The rearview reflected Lisette's confused eyes. "But that should have made the Venezuela wells make *more* oil, not *less*."

"Yeah, something must have gone haywire. Maybe his program malfunctioned. Marrying nanotechnology with genetically engineered molecules and bacteria is very new."

"And scary," Ron added.

"You mean the gray goo scare."

"Exactly."

"That's pretty much been eliminated."

Sam held his palms out. "What the hell is gray goo?"

"The original theory," Dan said, "held that because nanobots could self-assemble, one would become two; two four; four eight; etcetera, and on and on, until you had so many that you had gray goo."

Sam shook his head. "But who cares if you have a puddle of gray goo. I mean even if you had a million of those molecules you wouldn't have much mass."

"The problem *is*—" Ron began.

"The problem is that there is a blue truck following us." Dan blurted and glanced to their rear.

"Yeah, we know." Ron said.

"You *know?*"

"He's a friend." Lisette said.

"I was about to say—" Ron tried again.

Dan held his hand above his head like a stop sign. "Let's get this over with. The gray goo theory stated that nanobots with endless energy would assemble so fast that in hours there'd be seventy billion, in a day they'd weigh a ton, and by three days they'd weigh more than the sun and all the planets in our solar system, and the human race would be plutoed." He loved that new word—plutoed—obsolete, caput, no longer a planet. It was so galactic.

Lisette's eyes smiled at him and he wet his lips. Marci used to like his silly little words, too. But now she had that artist, the funky brush slapper. He smiled back at Lisette, deciding to enjoy the moment.

"But," he raised an index finger, "there are regulators, nanomolecules preprogrammed to interrupt replication, say every millionth replication, or stop several different steps. Policing organizations for the FDA and the EPA oversee all nanoscience projects to prevent gray goo or any other runaway assembly nanobots."

Sam frowned. "There's a problem with police."

"Yeah?"

"Crooked cops."

"But these police are mostly scientists with several levels of review."

"Are these scientists getting paid?"

"A little."

"Big money in nanotechnology?"

"A trillion dollars in the next ten years." *And I got how much for that program? Man!*

Sam shook his head. "So hear me out. The scientists, who we all know don't get paid shit, are keeping others from making a lot of money illegally. Oh yeah, I forgot the most important part. The scientists are human beings."

"Sounds like New Orleans cops policing narcotic dealers to me," Lisette said.

Sam smiled at her. "Except for us. You know, the *good* guys. We make sure the police are honest, and the bad guys go to jail, because we *always* do the right thing."

Dan's stomach knotted. He thought they always *did* do the right thing. Sam made it sound like doing the right thing was a joke, or that he operated under different rules. *I need to watch Sam.* He thought about the program he had sent Xoflex. *Or maybe he needs to watch me.*

Sam stared through the windshield like he was studying the most interesting road in North America.

Dan closed his eyes and sighed. "You're more right than you know. The nanotechnology policing organizations have no teeth. The field is too new. Most of the nanotechnology companies do whatever they want, whenever they want." *With my stupid program, no less.*

He opened his eyes. "Now who the hell is in the blue truck?"

CHAPTER 18

The previous night, Remmy struggled to breathe. Strong arms controlled him easily in a full Nelson, a wrestling hold he knew to be potentially dangerous. If this guy knew what he was doing he could... snap Remmy's neck. The hairy arm gripped so tight Remmy could not speak, barely eke in a breath. The smell of sweat would soon be replaced by something worse if he didn't get away. He kept thinking about a broken neck and puttering about in a motorized wheel chair, and he relaxed and put his hands up, hoping the man would ease up.

The man whispered in his ear. "Dat's better, Remmy."

The grip loosened and Lola tittered in the dark. The lights came on, and she broke into a laugh.

He barely squeaked out, "What the—?"

The arms let go, and he squinted through the sudden brightness. Lola flanked Joe and held a bottle of moonshine. Beside them stood a rangy man in hunter's camouflage, his tooth-gapped grin familiar. Twisting around, Remmy saw another familiar camouflaged man, taller and wider, but with a similar piano-key smile.

"Shit!"

The room erupted in hee-haws and cackles.

"Good thing Bear got you or Dad would be feedin' bugs," Lola choked between giggles.

The rangy man held out his hand. "Kinda jumpy aincha, Remmy?"

The big man slapped him on the back. "Kinda slow, too."

Remmy shook their hands and said to the big man, "Just out of practice. Give me a couple days, Bear."

Bear was not named for his huge size, but for his prowess as the best bear bow hunter in the South, his first kill at age eight. After the Special Forces, he worked the offshore oil rigs. And Dad? Not a father. The nickname referred to Crawdad. After the Forces he made a name for himself running shrimp boats and finding those tasty mudbugs when others came home empty, almost like he was part mudbug himself. Calling him Dad got confusing at times, but what was Louisiana if not confusing. And oh, how interesting.

Dad said, "We was checking out these new night vision specs. Man, 'dey good. Come in handy tomorrow."

"You two could have warned me." Remmy eyed Lola and Joe.

"We was just goofin' with you, boy." Joe smiled and held out the bottle. "Sides, we need all de hep we can git."

"Probably right." Remmy sighed and the tension drained. He would get some sleep tonight, not having to worry about getting his throat slit.

Everyone settled down, sipping moonshine and talking about old times, including close calls with revenuers. Bear and Dad stood guard. Night hunting flowed in their blood, so staying awake presented no problem. That was one of the reasons they did well in their brief stint with the Special Forces. It also helped in detecting night raids from many a revenuer. They respected their government, even taught the Special Forces a thing or two, but they liked their own freedoms, including moonshine. They didn't last long in the service.

Remmy slept like a dead man. He woke once, but the normal creaks of the swamp and the cool musty air lulled him back to sleep until dawn. He made coffee and was frowning out at the swamp when Joe walked in.

"You still mad at us?" Joe asked as he poured a cup.

"No, just thinking about what I'm going to do today."

"You mean what *we* gonna do?"

"I think I'll go into the office by myself this morning. I need to do some research."

Joe peered over his coffee mug at Remmy. "We be there, just de same. You and dat oil are our life here, so we be there for both of you"

"But—"

"Don't worry. Nobody see us. Bear and Dad be—he waved his hand—invisible." He put a hand on Remmy's shoulder and looked him square in the face. "Dat's just de way it is."

After the trip across the bayou, Remmy cruised his Porsche Boxster over roads lined with Spanish moss-laden live oak trees. Joe and Lola followed in an old Buick sedan with Bear and Dad hunched in the rear seat.

When Remmy arrived at the Xoflex gate, he entered his code, and glanced into the rear view mirror. No Buick. Already invisible.

CHAPTER 19

Thirty-nine miles away, if a brown pelican flew straight, Dan stared at the blue truck in the rearview mirror. What was Sam trying to pull, now? The van suddenly jarred sideways and he snapped his head to the left, craning to see out the window.

"What the hell was that? You run over something?"

Lisette answered flatly, "Yeah, the Louisiana state line. Welcome to the worst roads in the U.S. of A."

"Don't they ever repair them?"

"Oh yes, cher. Just never before you get there." He loved that word, cher, and the way she said it.

The van lurched to the side and a resounding *bang* jolted and tilted everyone to the right, then the left.

"Nice recovery, Lisette," Ron picked his can of pop off the floor and wiped up the spill. He frowned at Dan. "What's wrong, man? You okay?"

Dan crouched low, eyes wide, fingers gripping the seat.

His voice seemed to run away from him on legs without direction in a high staccato. "Yeah, no one tells me anything: Whose in the blue truck?—that bang reminded me of Fred getting—probably good for me, back in the saddle and all, that's what the shrinks say, right? Of course they also said I was a difficult case—emotional lability, social naïveté, coupled with extreme mathematical genius."

He relaxed his grip and a sheepish smile cracked his bloodless face.

Sam twisted around and said gently, "The guy in the blue truck is one of Lisette's buddies helping us. You want a real drink?" He offered him a flask. "J.D., Black Label?"

Dan's head twitched toward the flask, then away, then back again. He grabbed it and drained down two gulps. The burn felt good, like squeezing a boil. His voice croaked, "Thanks."

Ron's gentle hand squeezed his shoulder and his old revulsion at being touched surfaced. "No gun's yet man. Surveillance first. You can help with that."

Lisette cracked her window. Odors of dead crawfish, beer, and swamp mud floated in. "How about some air? You need me to stop?"

He shrugged off Ron's grip, and held up his hand, nauseated at the smell. "AC's fine. You can roll up the window. The whiskey hit the spot."

She rolled up the window and minutes passed. The wheels hummed over the rhythmic bumps of the road.

"How long did you know Fred?" Sam said.

Dan took a deep breath and gathered himself. He studied the upcoming bridge, a beam bridge, with concrete pier supports crumbling a bit, but probably safe. Colors and numbers flashed in his mind. "Sixteen, maybe seventeen years."

He hung his head. "Good friend. Great guy. Saved my life, again." Gritted teeth. Clenched fists. "Fuckers."

Whump, whump, whump. The concrete highway sections slapped as regular as a metronome, and he could not help counting them. It calmed him.

"Agreed." Sam's voice thudded cold, hard, determined.

Lisette cleared her throat. "Here we are."

They exited the highway before he could get to thirty-seven. She unrolled her window all the way. "Can't stand AC. Live with it all year. Shouldn't have to in December."

Traffic noise faded. Two '70's vintage pickups were parked abreast and faced away from them on the frontage road, one the rusty, sky-blue Ford that had been following them, the other a faded white Chevy. A .30-06 Springfield rifle hung inside both rear windows, easily visible despite the translucent mural painting of the rebel flag. A boy's caricature pissed a white stream on one corner of the white truck's rear window. The blue truck had a pointy-breasted woman's silhouette as a rear bumper sticker.

Dan rubbed his forehead and slapped a mosquito buzz off his ear. *White Pee Pee and Blue Titty. Redneck City. Jesus.*

Lisette studied him in the rearview mirror. "Yep, and those guys are between us and Fred's killers. Good thing, huh?"

She turned onto a dirt road: fields of green on one side, brambles and swamps on the other.

Reading my mind. That can't be bad.

"Guess you're right. We could use a few good old boys right about now."

To the right, a large gator slithered off a sun-cracked mud bank, leaving only a dark line of green floating scum in the caramel water. He made a mental note: No swimming. A hee-haw startled him, and he twisted his head to the left where white cattle egrets pecked at the feet of two piebald long-horned steers grazing on tall grass beside the dirty white donkey. Straight ahead the dusty hot road disappeared into the cool twilight of cypress trees, palmettos, and water.

Dan swallowed. *Where's the weird guy with the banjo?*

The road maintained itself above sea level and meandered for another twenty minutes through a black and white kaleidoscope of shadows, cypress trees, palmettos, vines, and swamp grass. Intermittently, fingers of dark water touched the berm of the road. At the end, a cabin materialized.

Jesus. How the hell did they get that built here?

A redwood and cedar house stood high on sturdy pilings, and appeared as natural as another cypress tree. It occupied a quarter acre island surrounded by swamp, the only access a wooden bridge that rattled and creaked as the van rolled over it.

Barking and crooning of dogs began at the first creak of the bridge. A man with a ZZ Top beard and a double-barreled shotgun walked out of the house and down the long stairs accompanied by the barking dogs: a giant, auburn pit bull and two lean, black and white-spotted hounds.

The man recognized Lisette and stomped his foot, hissing at the dogs, "Shhhtt!" The dogs immediately sat and noise ceased, though they watched the van, ears forward and muscles tense.

"Dat you, little girl?" His voice was gravel mixed with song.

"Yes, Daddy." She jumped out of the van, strode over and gave the man a hug and tugged on his beard. "That thing gets any longer and you gone trip over it."

His grin sported three gapped teeth. He twisted his head, deftly squirted brown liquid out of the side of his mouth into the swamp and backhanded his lips and beard. "Ain't gone get me shave, no."

He addressed the hounds, "What you say to Lizzy? Give her some love, you?"

The dogs immediately stood, whining and licking her hands.

She squatted and grabbed the monstrous pit bull's face in both hands and kissed his soft nose and lips. His large pink tongue slurped her cheeks and she said, "Yeah, I love your mush too, Bruiser."

The other two bowled her over backwards and licked her face. She talked softly, ruffled their ears, and scratched their chests before standing.

"Daddy, meet my friends: Sam, Ron, and the man we're to help, Dan."

He shook their hands. "Name's Lester. This here's Bruiser. The other two are Salt and Pepper."

Dan squatted and smiled at Bruiser, who meandered over to him wagging his tail.

Lester cocked his head and shook it, the beard tip tracing a figure of eight. "Will you look at dat. Bruiser got his self a new friend."

Lester turned and winked at Lisette. "Et vous, cher?"

She smiled.

Dan stood and pointed at the black and white dogs. "So, Salt is the one with the white ears and Pepper with the black?" It seemed right, though the white eared hound did have a mostly black body.

Lester tilted his head to the sky and cackled long and hard; a laugh that made everyone smile and want in on the joke. After wiping his eyes he said, "You got it right, you. Most go for de body. You good. How 'bout lunch?"

Lester grabbed Dan's arm and led him into the cabin.

Sam and Ron stared with wide puzzlement and Lisette grinned, rubbing her chin. "Daddy just loves a dog man."

CHAPTER 20

A day earlier, Abdullah awoke, feeling much more rested after sleeping most of the all day flight from Cepu to Dubai. The pilot announced their approach to Dubai's private airport while Abdullah finished toweling off his torso. The thought of Tamara dancing quickened his breath. His manhood throbbed as he donned his favorite black silk shirt and white linen pants.

Once the exit door opened, distant salt spray sweetened the air and golden pink clouds glowed in the sunset over the Persian Gulf.

Ahhh. Home.

Dubai was *his* city, from the Burj Khalifa needling the sky, to the white sand beaches and raucous night life. Even the Saudis let down their turbans here because, of course, Allah could not see beyond their border. His Christian-American expatriate mother had entertained many of them.

He threw off the oppressive thoughts of the OPEC Islamic fundamentalists. His pulse raced. Tamara's body would soon be his.

A white limousine waited on the tarmac. Sliding into the rear seat, he breathed in the leather like a good cigar, pulled out the Old Raj Dry Gin and tonic water from the liquor closet and said to the driver, "The Planetarium." They had agreed to meet at her favorite nightclub.

The driver nodded and the car eased forward, accelerating so smoothly Abdullah knew no Old Raj would be spilled tonight.

Cutting and squeezing a lime into the mixture, he licked his fingers and took a sip, rolling the taste of juniper, lime and tonic around his mouth, and finally swallowing. *A gentleman's drink. Civilized. Something good from the Brits.*

When he arrived at The Planetarium, one of Dubai's premier dance clubs, he discreetly entered through a side entrance. Chords of music pulsed on the lower level. He caught himself scrutinizing every person, not to find her, but to discern anyone dangerous. Why be careful? They would never look here, thinking him too religious. Fools. His bodyguard preceded him and they eased around tables, shouldered through the throng of thrusting, jumping dancers. Women laughed, their slender necks swaying to the rhythm of the bone-vibrating bass. He eyed each of them.

She's not here.

Upstairs: the same.

She should be here.

He sat at a corner table with a good view of the main floor. His bodyguard cruised, invisible.

René had easily been the best choice for bodyguard, not due to his substantial skills, or because of his Arabic features, but because he dedicated himself fully to the cause. He hated big oil because they had murdered his family. They started with his father because he had designed an automobile engine that ran off household garbage. They fire-bombed his family in their home on the Nigerian delta. Big oil did not like witnesses. René survived only because he had been visiting an uncle in London, an uncle with ties to Abdullah.

Abdullah saw the fat blond man from Manila. At the same time René appeared out of the shadows. "Sir, we are being watched. I recommend—"

A tiny, bloody sausage landed with a slap on the table and rolled in front of Abdullah. René started moving around the table when the fat blond man grabbed him and pinned his arms behind his back. For a fat man he was quick.

An Arabic man with a full black beard, luminous eyes, and a white taqiyah hat pulled up a chair and sat down across from Abdullah. He nodded toward the sausage and his voice oozed silken evil. "You wanted her. Granted, it is not all of her."

Abdullah scrutinized the sausage through slitted eyes. His nostrils dilated and his jaw clamped so tight it hurt. Though hard to discern in the club's mood lighting, he made out the knuckles and fingertip—Tamara's finger inside one of the Chinese finger traps he so enjoyed being placed in while she teased him.

He grabbed it and put it in his coat pocket. He closed his eyes and eased breaths through flared nostrils, and spoke in a steady monotone. "What do you want?" Octex-Penta could not be behind this. They hated OPEC. The man had to be from OPEC.

"It is very simple. We want you to stop. And we want your plan. If not," he paused and smiled. "More pieces."

Abdullah flipped the table forward, smashing the Arabic man's face. The fat man's head flew backward, smacking the floor; René's foot thudded on top to ensure unconsciousness. Abdullah held a knife to the Arab's throat and whispered in his ear, "The only other piece will be your head if you don't tell me where she is right now."

"You'll never find her." A coarse whisper, but his eyes betrayed him—a glance, yet sufficient.

Abdullah motioned with his eyes to the men's restroom, and René vanished into the restroom.

Several dancers in the crowd started staring at the prone fat man and the upset table.

Abdullah inserted the razor sharp stiletto an inch into the Arab's right armpit.

The man whimpered.

"If I push the knife deeper you will lose the use of your arm and, after a bit, bleed to death. Now move."

He held the man by his upper arm, one hand clamped on top while the other pressed the knife tip into his armpit. They waited, pressed against the wall.

René popped his head out and nodded. "She's here. Let's go."

Abdullah mouth curved up but his eyes remained flat. "Take her to the car. I'll be there in a moment." Then he spoke to his prisoner. "You were a fool to bring her here."

The man whimpered, "I wanted her near so when you gave us the plan you could have her and we would be finished."

A young woman, fresh from the dance floor, walked around the corner toward the restroom while talking into her cell phone. Abdullah glared at her. White fear circled her irises and she ran the other way.

René bumped through the door and whisked by, Tamara wrapped in a blanket and limp in his arms.

Abdullah gripped his captive so close they could be mistaken for entwined dancers. They pushed through the bathroom door.

A man lay supine with sightless eyes staring from a head twisted too far behind his shoulder. Another kneeled in a permanent prone crouch, head in the toilet. Otherwise the bathroom was empty.

Abdullah pushed his captive to his knees, and twisted the blade, deep. The man cried out, and started to fade from the pain.

Abdullah grabbed his face and squeezed it to wide-eyed alertness. "I have spared your life because you brought her, and to allow you to tell them: The days of oil are over."

He stuffed the man's taqiyah into his mouth and left.

CHAPTER 21

Abdullah held her bandaged hand with one hand, while the other touched the severed finger in his pocket. *Tamara. My sweet Tamara. How will you play Brahms now?*

Her sobs of pain had ended about ten minutes ago after the morphine injection had taken hold. René was good, always prepared for violence, usually to repair damage inflicted on his own body. Yes, he was good, but not good enough to fix this one.

They had severed her left small finger at the base. It had been a crude device, crushing before it pinched off the finger. Undoubtedly she would need surgery to clean up the splintered bones and keep infection from setting in on the mangled flesh. But there would be no replacing the finger. Abdullah's entire body tensed to prevent his weeping and screaming in rage. *Barbarians!*

She moaned and he cradled her head as she rocked like a wounded animal. For this they would pay even more. They would lose not only their precious oil, but their lives. But first they would see their profits die.

He clenched his teeth and a low growl escaped from deep inside as his rage churned. He thought of Flex Fuel, and big oil's deceitful advertising: they were doing their part to decrease pollution and save the economy by lowering the price of gas while helping farmers whose crops made ethanol. But the coal plants they used to manufacture the ethanol polluted more. The price was falsely driven down by government subsidies. The stupid Americans paid more through taxes, higher prices of food, diverting more water to the thirsty corn, and the need for more antipollution devices.

The old sores festered and bled through his mind. *They were in it to their necks with the big auto industries. How else could all those GM cars have already been 'Flex fuel ready' two years before the stuff even hit the pumps? At least the Japanese pushed hybrids. But profit was profit no matter what color your skin or which way your eyes slanted. Why get one-hundred miles per gallon like the first prototype GM electric cars, when you could get forty? Even with peak oil, years remained, more like decades that produced enough profit to retire several oil and auto CEO's on Caribbean islands.*

The limo slowed, and the privacy window rolled down. René kept driving but spoke over his shoulder. "Sir, we are at the hospital. I suggest you stay in the car. I'll get her taken care of."

They came to a stop. René opened the rear door, and gently lifted the now semi-conscious Tamara and carried her in.

In minutes he returned to the driver's seat and spoke over his shoulder while he started the car. "It will take about two hours. Stan is with her and will wait. We need to get you out of here."

Abdullah nodded. "Stanley is good. I trust him. But I want you with her as soon as possible. I will have to go to the States instead of Tamara. After she is stable meet me in Dallas. I'll need you there."

"Don't worry, sir. I'll be there within twenty-four hours."

"Thanks René, for everything." He added, "I need some time to myself," and rolled up the privacy window.

Contaminating the U.S. oil wells solved the most difficult part of the puzzle. That's why Tamara had been chosen. She was the best. There were others he trusted enough for this job, but he needed them on the other side of the globe. Not only that. Now it was twice as personal.

He'd lost Asiyah years ago, and it had taken years to recover. Tamara had filled that void. She knew him, and despite that, still loved him. At one time she had played violin for the Vienna Philharmonic. Never again.

There never was a doubt. He had to go. He knew the instant he recognized her finger on the table that he would be going to Texas.

Time to cowboy up.

CHAPTER 22

Dan jumped at sounds of gunshots and sat up from a sound sleep. He rubbed his eyes, found the loaded Berretta, cocked it and thumbed off the safety. Creeping toward the door he felt giddy from waking so quickly. Who was shooting? A sliver of sunlight creased the wall. His watch read 1300 and he remembered falling asleep after lunch in Lisette's bedroom. Only an hour gone and now gunshots.

He cracked the door of Lisette's comfortable bedroom. It *was* comfortable, too—surprising in this swamp-cabin. AC worked great, hot water, firm mattress. Only bad thing: too close to the living room.

And the TV.

The news captured riots in Caracas with angry mobs shooting at militia who returned fire.

Gunshots on TV. Get a grip.

He thumbed the safety down while easing the hammer home to prevent a loud click. Before the door shut he did a double take on the next scene that flipped up on the TV. He held the door open.

Tanks rumbled on the streets of Houston, the squared-off city hall building in the background. The newsman said, "The National Guard has been called out in many major U.S. cities due to last night's riots in LA and Miami. When the price of gas jumped to ten dollars a gallon overnight many people just snapped."

The team had gathered around the TV in various states of dress. Sam wore jeans and a T-shirt with an airbrushed surfer being chased by a great white shark. The caption read: *The Only Boards Faster than Jaws.* Ron sported orange and black swim trunks and munched on a piece of pecan pie. Lisette brushed her teeth in a half T-shirt and skin-tight short shorts. Real short. Now that was an ass.

Thank God everyone was facing the TV. He maneuvered his lust back inside the slit of his boxers.Embarrassed, he glanced around for Lisette's dad, but remembered Lisette had sent him to her Aunt Delilah's after lunch. The thought of more pecan pie called to him, but he pulled the door back and watched the remainder of the news, imagining himself as a sideways Kilroy-was-here graffiti from WWII along the edge of the door. Only one hand remained visible, though. The other pushed the cold flat of the gun against his groin. *Keep your eyes on the TV and your dick in your shorts, shitbird.* The thought of the gun being loaded also helped. He pointed the gun at the floor.

Apparently the President had called out the Guard after declaring a "national" state of emergency. Miami and LA had the only riots so far. The governor of Texas had assigned extra guards and barricaded the roads near the refineries and wells. Dan recalled Texas had most of the major lower forty-eight refineries. But no one messed with Texas.

Alaska presented another problem—wilderness on one side and mostly water on the others. The Canadian Mounties helped guard the wilderness side. But the U.S. Navy was already overcommitted with the Middle East, Korea, Japan, and China. The President parleyed with the Russian president late into the night, asking for help with the Bering Sea.

That's a switch. First Russia decides it's time to point their missiles at Europe again, now we are going to ask them to provide defense for us, their enemy of five decades.

The TV picture became a shower of salt and pepper.

Sam stood and pointed the remote control at the TV trying to squeeze life into it. All they had here was satellite TV. Lots of reasons for that to go down, but if they were in a national emergency...?

Dan eased the door closed after one last peek at the curve of her leg up into—.

Better take a shower now. Might be the last of the hot water.

He was stepping into the shower when there was a knock on the door. Lisette's voice sang, "Oh Danny boy. Hurry up. We've got work to do."

"Be there in a jiff."

He turned off the hot. *Goddamn that's cold. But good. Think about something else, like, how the hell are we going to get into the Xoflex building?*

He turned off the water and shivered. *What an idiot. Last chance for a HOT shower.*

He wondered if Ron had left any pie. Then an idea came to him. He threw his clothes on and burst into the living room to tell Sam his perfect plan. No one was there, but the TV blared again, with a rerun of Gilligan's Island. The Professor and Gilligan argued about how to get off the island. The Professor explained detailed plans for a raft. Gilligan wanted to wait for a good ship to rescue them.

For a moment the TV mesmerized him. *Oh, to be Gilligan.*

Sam walked in, dressed in a salmon polo shirt, light khaki pants, and black athletic shoes.

Dan blurted, "Hey Sam, I got a great plan for how to get into the Xoflex plant."

"Okay."

"I thought I could disguise you as the janitorial help. You'd be able to wander about anywhere in the Xoflex building. They probably don't keep track of all the janitors, so security checks would be minimal."

Sam folded his arms.

"You don't like it?"

"We don't even know if they have janitors. We don't have keys, not a clue about their security systems. Today recon. Tonight we hit them. Okay?

Dan pursed his lips tight and crossed his arms.

Sam patted him on the shoulder. "You know computers, right?"

It didn't feel bad having Sam touch him. Of course he *knew* computers, 0=off, 1=on. Neither one or zero were prime numbers. Interesting. He gave Sam his best Jackie Gleason eye roll. "Yes."

"Can you hack the Xoflex security programs?"

"You must be kidding." He didn't tell Sam he'd already been in several times trying to find out how they were using his program.

Ron and Lisette walked in. Both wore Sam's color scheme—Ron a salmon tank top, tan swim shorts, and black sandals; Lisette a midriff-revealing tube top, short shorts (*uh-huh*), and lace-up, black sandals with heels.

Dan found the pie tin, and poured a cup of coffee. He munched and sipped, knowing he needed caffeine and sugar. Then he looked down at his bland clothes. "Got a cool pink and beige outfit for me?"

"You're dressed fine. You'll be in the van, doing your computer thing."

Dan raised an eyebrow and said between bites, "You think they will have Wi-Fi way out in the boondocks where the Xoflex plant is?"

"How about positive waves?" Sam pointed to the door. "Shall we?"

Dan washed down another bite with several gulps of coffee and got his laptop. They all loaded into the surfer van. It had been transformed inside. Beige curtains covered the sides and rear windows and a floor-to-ceiling curtain dividing the front seats from the rear. Dan and Sam sat at the rear on either side of a two-by-two table centered between previously hidden side walls that bristled with electronic plugs and connectors. Dust and the sulfur smell of the swamp drifted in before they closed the doors.

Lisette drove and Ron navigated. The two trucks, White Pee Pee and Blue Titty, followed behind.

With Sam's help Dan got plugged in, gleefully rubbing his hands. "Damn, this is a great connection. How did you ...? Never mind."

After typing the Xoflex website in, the screen went blank, then multicolored tools floated across the screen: wrenches, drills, microscopes and more. Dan smiled. He liked the colors. The screen faded to a new background of miniature animated robots holding tools, scurrying about, quickly building a beautiful house, with a caption over the top: "Tools from Yesterday Made Better for Tomorrow."

His grin broadened. Even though he'd seen it before, it was still cool. He began navigating through the site, testing for weaknesses. He paused and frowned.

Sam squinted and tweaked his mouth to one side. "Tough huh?"

He chewed his lip and Sam patted him on the shoulder. "But you're good, remember?"

Dan's knees jiggled and his fingers flew. Symmetric primes assaulted him: 107,701;113,311;337,733. He raised his right index finger and dramatically hit the *Enter* key.

He sat straighter and pushed his clasped hands away, popping all the knuckles. "Yes! I'm in."

Three more keystrokes and he found the security program for the entire plant.

"Pretty simple for nanotech wizards." *Too simple. Something wasn't quite*—"Shit!"

"What?" Sam asked.

"I'm out."

Outside the scenery had changed to an antebellum street, lined with live oaks. It dead-ended in a wrought iron gate. On the other side of the gate a manicured, green lawn gently sloped up to a large, very new, beige building. *XOFLEX* was printed in a salmon-colored papyrus font, outlined in black. An entrance door beckoned. Dan turned his attention back to the computer.

The van stopped in front of the security camera, Lisette lowered her window, and the humid warmth trickled in.

Sam moved to the front of the van. "How long until you're in again?"

Dan continued typing and staring at the screen while he mumbled under his breath, "Not sure... kinda weird stuff... haven't..." This wasn't the same security setup he'd seen before. Maybe he could try the back door.

"Dan!" Sam's shout made Dan jump.

"Okay, already. It's complicated. Might take a while."

The security camera interrupted a smooth side-to-side scan and telescoped out to focus on Lisette's face. Sam's held out an ID

The gate clicked and eased open.

"You've got ten minutes," Sam said.

Dan didn't blink and muttered, " 'nkay."

Ron shook his head. "We might need a plan B."

Sam sat next to Dan and put a hand on his shoulder. "Not with Danny Boy the Mad Hacker."

Ron cocked his .45 and put it under the seat. "Just in case."

The cocking sound jerked Dan's head up. The gunshot that killed Fred racked his memory. He glanced up, blinked hard and let out a long breath. "How the hell did you get us in here?"

Lisette laughed. "Had an appointment."

Dan frowned.

Sam ran his hands down his body like a sexy model. "Xoflex makes great swim and beach wear that protects you from the sun and keeps you cool. Nice colors, too. Nanotechnology really is great stuff. So, my company bought quite a bit, in their standard colors, and Xoflex offered to give us a tour if we were ever in the area."

"So you don't need me. You have an invitation. Hell, you can go in and find out all you need. I'll—"

Sam held up a hand. "We *do* need you. Right now we do a product tour. We'll have micro-cameras taking video clips inside the building. You stay here and crack the security for our raid tonight. We'll leave the van on with the AC going and the curtains drawn. I'll tell them you were sick and needed to stay in the van. Act innocent if someone knocks."

Sam waved goodbye and the three departed.

Dan drew the curtain. His fingers danced, eyelids half-closed, and he hummed the *Flight of the Bumblebee*. He felt at one with the violet hue of the computer while a vivid rainbow of colored numbers and codes flashed through his mind.

CHAPTER 23

That morning, Remmy tapped in his code and the Xoflex gate whirred open. He drove around back to his private entrance. The rearview held nothing but trees. Bear and Joe were out there somewhere. He parked the car and took the elevator to his office on the top floor, overlooking the swamp. A piece of home.

The smell of coffee greeted him as did Jean, his secretary. She was a wisp of a woman with the determination of a pit bull and a face to match. She handed him a cup of her chicory coffee. "Mr. St. James? What a surprise. Thought you were still enjoying the Caribbean." Her voice was part of the reason he had hired her—soft, kind, and Southern around the edges.

"Plans got rearranged. Oh, can you get me the Maracaibo file, please?"

"Mr. Phipps has it. He took it a couple of days ago."

"What about the disc? And I also need the Texas and Alaska file."

"I think he left the disc. And the other files are here. I'll get them. Is this about security?"

"Something like that."

Before he closed the door, he heard her murmur, "The National Guard should be enough."

Out of habit, he turned on the wide-screen TV in his office to listen to the news. The top story was about the National Guard on the streets of all the major cities.

Jean brought in the files and the disc.

"Hey Jean, what's this about the National Guard?"

"You haven't heard? The price of gas topped ten bucks a gallon yesterday and there have been riots. The President called out the Guard for security in the cities, including New Orleans, and no one is being allowed into Texas or Alaska. That's why I thought you wanted the files."

"Oh yeah, that. I thought maybe they were coming here. Thanks."

He dismissed her, closed the door and whispered, "Jesus. Leave for a few days and everything goes to hell."

He popped the disc into his computer and scanned the technical files. Spreading out the paper files on his desk, he glanced between the computer screen and the paper. There had to be a something missing from Maracaibo that Texas and Alaska had or ... didn't have. They'd used the process in those two states first, and their wells had increased in production, not died.

What was different about Maracaibo?

He studied the files and computer for hours, then took a break and peered out the front window. A van was parked in the visitor's parking lot. The surfing logo on the side touched a memory: *Sam's Surfboards.* Oh yes. They had a big account of swim and surf wear. He glanced at the computer screen and papers covering his desk. If they were here on a tour, this was not the time—

The intercom buzzed and Jean said, "Sir, the people from Sam's Surf Shop are here. Do you have a spare moment?"

They did have a very big account. He pushed the intercom. "Sure, I'll be right with them."

He began to gather the paper files together. The door burst open. A short, dark-haired man strode in, with Jean bustling behind, her eyes wide, lips thin. The man raised his hands like he was about to hug Remmy. "Mr. St. James!" It sounded like a cheer. "I am so glad you are here. I wanted to thank you personally for the wonderful product. Our customers all love the shirts, suits and hats."

Remmy moved his body between the man and the files on his desk. "Jean, it's okay. I'll see him now." She held her hands out as if to say she tried.

He faced the man, who was surveying the room.

"Are you Sam Houston?"

"Yes, how did you guess?"

"Saw your van outside and I think we have a picture of you. That's probably how you were able to get a tour."

Ron and Lisette walked in, and Sam did the introductions.

Sam glanced at the files on the desk and the computer screen. "I can see you're busy. But I had to let you know how great your product is. We even wore them out here to see how they did in your Louisiana heat. And they performed miraculously. Anyway, we'll leave you alone. We'll send you another order soon. Keep up the good work.".

"I was only doing a bit of file maintenance. Why don't you stay a minute? Would you like coffee or iced tea?"

Sam studied his watch. "Actually, we are on a tight schedule. I appreciate it, but we should get going. Besides, with this gasoline crisis, you guys probably have a lot of work to do."

"Maybe another time then?"

Sam wrung Remmy's hand. "Your business is at the top of our To-See-Again list."

After they left, Remmy closed the door. His armpits dripped and he turned the dead bolt. *No more surprises.* He walked to his desk, then turned quickly around and squinted at the door. *Had Sam looked a bit too long at the papers and computer screen?*

He shook his head. *Why would a dumb surfer care about this stuff?* He shuffled through the papers and began reading the files.

After an hour of careful study he stopped and gazed out the window, tapping a pencil on the desk. He stared at one of the paper files, then the computer screen. He turned on the scanner, stuck a flash drive into the USB port, and scanned and saved several pages of the paper file into it. After a few more typed commands he hit *Enter*, then placed the files and the disc in his safe and dropped the flash drive in his shirt pocket.

He ran a shredder program to erase any evidence of the files, then punched the intercom.

"Jean, can you come in here a minute, please."

He unbolted the door, let her in and walked to his desk. "Close the door, please."

She frowned, easing the door shut. "I'm sorry, Mr. St. James. He just barged in."

"That's okay. Don't worry about that. This is about something else."

He peered at her. "I have a very important question I want only you to hear. Think very carefully. Is there any other record of these files you gave me on any computers, e-mails, copied files?" He leaned forward. "Anything?"

She scratched her lower lip with her upper incisors and scrunched her nose. "No sir. Mr. Phipps got all the paper copies. And he hates computers and e-mail. You remember his memo."

"So if he asks, tell him there are no computer copies, exactly like he wanted in his memo. And right now, go out and erase any e-mails about Maracaibo, Alaska, or Texas. Use that shredder program I gave you."

He leaned forward. "You have any discs copies of the files?"

"Well, yes, I keep one."

"Destroy it."

"Destroy it?"

"Yes. Run the shredder first and go home. If anyone asks, tell them you got sick. Take the disc with you and destroy it there. Break it into pieces. Better yet, melt it in your incinerator. Whatever you do, get rid of the disc as soon as you can."

"What's wrong, sir?"

"It's better if you don't know. Just make sure you get rid of any trace of those files. You're sure Phipps got all the paper files?"

"Yes."

"Okay, double check and shred any paper evidence, too. Then go."

She frowned.

"Don't worry. It's only a tiny glitch. I'll see you tomorrow. Enjoy the day off. Now get out of here." He shooed her out the door with his hands.

She put a hand on the closing door and murmured, "Sir, does this have anything to do with the meeting Mr. Phipps is having with Mr. Croner this afternoon?"

"Croner's here?"

"I think Mr. Phipps is giving him a tour in about a half hour."

"Thanks. I'll have to go say hi. No, nothing to do with him."

He closed the door and leaned his back against it. The acrid smell of his sweat reeked. *Shit!*

He'd wanted to run the shredder program for a few hours to ensure complete erasure of all files. No time now. Croner *was* Penta Oil in Louisiana *and* Texas. That meant they would be coming to his office.

He gathered the sampling rod and other necessary items, revised the security camera program, then paced for precisely three minutes, the exact time needed for the cameras to start turning off. He left his office. Jean was gone. He must get samples and get out before Croner and Phipps arrived. And he must accomplish this feat without anyone else seeing him.

CHAPTER 24

During Sam's "tour" of Xoflex, Dan's fingers flew. He was hip deep in the main security program of Xoflex, his mind totally focused on avoiding complex security traps. A high pitched chime startled him. *A security alarm?*

He shook his head. Not the computer. *Gotta change that ring-tone.*

He wrangled his cell phone out of his pants pocket and studied caller ID. *She knows not to call, unless—*

"Marci. What's wrong?"

"Dan, thank God I got you. I called this morning and only got your voice mail."

Crap, forgot to check the messages. Too busy watching Lisette's ass.

"Sorry babe. Been busy. I'm kinda rushed now, too. What's up?"

A pause. "It's Jeff. The night you left he was in an accident."

Dan mind stopped; the numbers, programs, colors evaporated into a void that left him as empty and cold as deep space. He couldn't breathe.

"He's okay, a few scratches that's all. And he was not driving."

He managed a quivering breath and his face flushed. Thoughts clicked again. His son was alive.

"His unit deployed the next day to east Texas."

"East Texas! What ...?" He felt better. East Texas wasn't like Iraq. Maybe Marci was overreacting.

"With the jump in oil prices, people are starting to go crazy. Haven't you seen the news?"

"A little bit, about the National Guard in Houston. I've been real busy."

"Well, I guess there have been attacks on the east Texas oil wells, so they sent the Guard there. Things are escalating fast."

He glanced out the window. Sam and the others walked out of the Xoflex building.

"Honey, I gotta go. I'll call you tonight. Maybe I can fly home soon." Silence.

The screen said, *Call ended*. Damn. Maybe he should call her back.

Sam opened the door. "How we doing, Danny Boy?"

The humid air wrapped him like cellophane. He stared at the laptop, his face hot, and his chest still tight, wondering about east Texas. He tapped several keys and folded the laptop. *Focus on the job. Be tough.*

"Why the glum face?" Ron asked.

"I got a call from my wife about my son, Jeff."

He glanced at Lisette but could only see her forehead in the rearview. She kept her eyes low. Why was she avoiding him? Then he realized: she didn't know about Jeff.

The doors slammed shut and Sam nodded. "Family problems. They do put a different perspective on things. Do you need to go home to help with . . . What did you say his name was, Jeff?"

Dan gripped the laptop as Lisette accelerated around the corner and out of the gate. Her eyes remained hidden, only her forehead visible in the rearview.

What could Dan do about Jeff, after all? Jeff was in the Army, and still in the states. He'd made it clear he didn't need Dan's help. It wasn't like Jeff was going to war.

"Yeah, it's Jeff. And he's okay. Only a small blip on the radar screen of life."

Sam twisted around and peered at Dan over his sunglasses.

"Really. It's okay," Dan said. He could not show weakness. That's not what a field agent did.

Lisette's glance in the rearview said, *Liar.*

"Okay then." Sam said. "Let's get at it. We need to research Remmy St. James. He's their program manager for the nanobiotechnology branch here in Louisiana. I glimpsed files on his desk and on his computer."

"Let me guess," Dan said, pushing out Jeff and remembering the Xoflex files he'd seen, "all about Maracaibo."

Sam nodded. "That and Texas and Alaska."

"Right up our alley," Ron said.

Sam pointed an index finger at Dan. "Oh yeah. Can you see what his computer file says on Maracaibo?"

Dan opened the laptop. The Wi-Fi icon blinked *NO SIGNAL.* "Didn't have time to save anything. We need to get close to another Wi-Fi transmitter first."

"I could use a cappuccino, so let's head into town. There's bound to be a Wi-Fi transmitters along the way."

A couple of minutes later the computer screen changed to two-and-a-half bars. Dan shouted, "Stop! The reception is great here."

Lisette pulled into a grove of trees next to an eight-foot tall, wire-mesh fence that surrounded a trailer park. Dan noticed several trailers had satellite dishes, and about three hundred yards behind them the two sentry trucks, Blue Titty and White Pee Pee, motored into a side road.

She turned off the key. "I need some fresh air." Her voice carried no soft lilt, but flat-edged with either bitterness or sorrow—he couldn't place it. He tried to catch her eyes as she got out. She walked to the fence and leaned against it with her hands clasping the mesh, like she wanted to crawl over the top. She stood back, pulled out her cell phone, and made a call. The odor of burning charcoal wafted in the open door. Someone was barbecuing in the trailer park.

Sam tapped Dan's shoulder. "Come on, Dan. Get busy. We need this file."

His fingers flicked over the keyboard. He stopped and frowned at the screen. Then he glanced at Sam. "I'm pretty sure I saw a file about Maracaibo, and you saw it on his computer screen, right?"

"Absolutely."

Dan thought of something else and played the keyboard again. "Sorry, there's no evidence anywhere of a Maracaibo, Texas, or Alaska file. I even checked his secretary's e-mail account." He scratched his head. "I could have sworn his secretary had a lot of e-mail stuff. I started to enter that file when you guys returned. But it's all gone now. There's only one e-mail, and it went out about ten minutes ago to her husband, saying she was sick and going home."

Lisette jumped into the van. "We got company."

She started the engine and tried to pull out, but a Humvee blocked her. A man stepped out of the passenger side. His camouflage clothing matched the Humvee's color to a tee. He walked to the van and with hand signals asked Lisette to roll down her window.

A convoy of military vehicles rolled behind them. Dust from their passage filtered in the window when Lisette lowered it. Dan folded the laptop and put it under his shirt to protect it.

"We'll only be a moment, ma'am," he said. "I need you to wait here while we get the trucks by."

"What's going on? Is there a problem?" Lisette asked.

There's no problem. We're goin' up the road a piece to help with security. You know, with the oil situation folks are a little jumpy. So we're helping out."

The last Humvee stopped. The man waved at Lisette, got in, and the vehicle joined the tail of the caravan.

Lisette put the van in gear, but Sam put a hand on her shoulder. "Wait a sec. I want to see where they're going."

He looked in the side rearview mirror. In a minute he grunted.

"Xoflex?" asked Dan.

"Yep."

"Now why would Xoflex need military security?" Ron asked.

Sam smiled. "Looks like we're on the right track."

"And we made it out of there just in time," Lisette said.

Sam took his hand off her shoulder and pointed forward. "Forget about the coffee. Get us back to the house, if you can."

CHAPTER 25

The overnight flight to Houston left Abdullah tired but successful. Money bought lots of things in Texas, and private airports were commodities the wealthy enjoyed most, especially Scottish oil tycoons. He would have been suspect had he come directly from Dubai, but not from Aberdeen's offshore rigs. There'd been one stop, change of plane, slight disguise, and now he enjoyed the royal treatment. Customs proved just as easy too, managed by his Scottish flight attendant and security guard, Ethan. The pilot, Craig, had logged many hours here, and had connections in the highest Texas oil society. Both men had reasons to help Abdullah: Ethan had lost his wife; Craig lost his best friend in the Iraq war. Abdullah had wanted to keep René with him, but left him with Tamara until she stabilized.

"Sir, your car has arrived," Craig said.

The noon sun beat down on Abdullah as he walked down the stairs from the corporate jet. He stopped and turned around and saluted Craig. "You know you might not be flying much longer."

"Okay by me, if things get better."

"Don't worry about that. It will get much better."

Abdullah gave him a thumbs-up gesture and walked down the stairs to the waiting car chauffeured by Ethan. The smell of diesel fuel and humid air accompanied him into the back seat where a large metal briefcase sat—delivered as planned. The contents beckoned him, but first he called René, and got only voice mail. He left a message to call him about Tamara.

He checked their route, reviewing a paper map of Texas while simultaneously checking Google Map on his cell phone. They would be heading to northeast Texas, the location of the East Texas Oil Field, the largest oil field in the lower forty eight, and centrally located in the Midcontinent oil region that encompassed Texas, Louisiana, Arkansas, Kansas, New Mexico and Oklahoma. Until the discovery of the Middle East oil, this had been the largest known oil reserve in the world.

The AC filtered out the diesel odor as Ethan drove off. Abdullah flipped open one of the clasps to the briefcase. But no sooner did the car move forward than it eased to a stop. Ethan said, "Sir, we may have a problem."

Two dark sedans and an open jeep with two uniformed guards waited at the side gate.

"Show them the ID. Don't get excited," Abdullah said. "We are covered."

Ethan lowered the window and one of the guards said, "I am sorry, sir, but there is a slight detour. You'll have to go the Toll road. Fifty Nine is closed."

"What about I-45?"

"That's clear all the way to Dallas."

"Thanks, Sarge. Can we go now?" Ethan held out the ID. The sergeant peered at it and motioned him through.

Abdullah studied the map. "Turn north on highway seventy-nine when we get to Buffalo."

He touched the smart phone screen and double checked the map. "How ironic. Palestine, Texas."

He unclasped the briefcase to reveal two rows of cylinders cradled in a form-fitted cardboard divider. His heart pounded and hand shook as he lifted the top row of ivory cylinders, and counted the row of gray cylinders, beneath. All there, ten each. He closed and refastened the case, leaned his head against the headrest and exhaled. His heart rate slowed. "Let me know when we get to Buffalo."

Ethan nodded, and Abdullah closed his eyes, forcing even, slow breaths. Soon he slept.

The recurrent dream was more vivid this time. His wife, Asiyah, had just rescued another Canadian goose out of the oily sea. Her name fit: *The one who tends to the weak and heals.* She lost her footing with the goose still in her hands. She went under. But she had dressed well for the Arctic spill. She bobbed up, covered in oil, and smiled—spitting image of a black mammy from silent pictures.

Out of the corner of his eye he saw it: the spark. One of the newbies had been smoking and a cinder from his cigarette blew into the oil covered sea. Oil in tanker spills was not usually flammable; it should not have happened. But neither should the tanker have hit an old submerged German U-boat. Maybe volatile liquid in the hull of the old sub had been dislodged by the tanker collision and floated to the surface. Maybe the oil tanker spewed out flammable petrol. The reason was moot; it responded to the cinder like an ignition switch.

The sea erupted in flames. Asiyah submerged herself, but not in time. The flammable liquid had coated her down parka, so water did not extinguish her fire. She resurfaced, thrashing, and screaming, all in the slow-motion torture of dreamland. The smell of her fried flesh made him nauseous. She pleaded, "Abby, ABBY, HELP ME!" He reached for her, but could not move. Tears welled and bled from his heart. His stomach churned. He could not take his eyes off her.

Thankfully his legs caught fire; he would suffer and die with her. Then someone behind him wrapped his legs in a wet towel they had been using to clean off the birds.

"NOOOO!" he cried and struggled to free himself from the man who was extinguishing his legs. He flung himself backwards, hoping to drown. But he landed in only inches of water, flat on his back, and the cold water seeped into his parka. A shroud veiled the white arctic sun, a shroud of smoke from his burning wife. They helped him stand. Her charred lump smoldered and floated in the finger paint of the oily, opalescent sea. Two men flung a net and dragged her blackened remains to shore.

He awoke sobbing, tears streaming down his cheeks. Ethan, who knew of the dreams and the tragedy, had pulled over and was shaking Abdullah's shoulder. "Wake up, sir. Please wake up."

"It's okay, Ethan. I am awake. Thank you. Please drive."

Ethan pulled onto the road. Abdullah rubbed the scars on his lower leg and wiped his cheeks.

"No more fires," he whispered. "Oil is finished."

In two hours they made the turn north at Buffalo, Texas onto U.S. Highway 79. Within a half hour they arrived: Palestine, Texas. He hadn't planned it like this. But how fitting. Palestine in the Middle East meant religious conflict, hatred, and wars between Muslims, Christians, and Jews. His plan would end the fueling of the U.S. war machine. It would end the reign of President Streeter and his oil cronies. They could not fuel the Israeli efforts. The destruction of OPEC oil would take the money out of Muslim fighting. Maybe his act would spell peace for Palestine.

He shook his head. You can't end a thousand years of hate.

They stopped outside the wildlife sanctuary. He grabbed the brief-case, got out of the car and walked to the edge of an embankment over-looking a bog. The squawks, croaks, tweets and melodious songs of birds filled the air—a pit stop for birds on their way to points west or east.

He sat the briefcase down on the ground, opened it and selected two of the white tubes. He loosened the screw tops and threw them deep into the bogs. He grabbed two more white tubes and walked down the edge of the embankment, loosening the tops as he walked. This time he tossed one into the prairie and the other into the dormant dogwood forest. Birds scattered.

Gray-brown dogwoods reached long fingers into the blue sky and balanced the brown grass of the prairies and the mossy bogs—stark winter beauty. He breathed in the freshness and felt content. This was his destiny: to save nature from man. Lost in a reverie, he walked back and gazed upwards, blue heavens filling him up.

A shot rang out and he twisted around, eyes wide. In the distance he saw the man with the shotgun—a hunter. Alarm at being discovered and anger welled up. He turned and ran, but his feet tangled under him and, in anger, he kicked the obstruction, realizing too late it was the open briefcase. The briefcase slid on its smooth metal side like a hockey puck on ice, carrying the rest of the contents over the side into the bog. As the briefcase gradually sank, the last row of white tubes stared at him before easing under the muck.

His legs buckled and he hit the ground on his hands and knees, eyes fixed on the spot where the tubes had disappeared.

Ethan jumped out of the car. "What happened?"

"It's okay. We can get more." Quiet, calm words. In a way, he felt relieved.

He lay supine on the carpet of prairie grass, hands clasped behind his head, eyes lifted to the sky. "It's so peaceful here. Don't you think?"

Ethan stared at Abdullah, frowning in puzzlement.

Abdullah hummed and noted Ethan's look. "*Beethoven's Sixth: The Pastorale*. It's all about birds. Tamara played the parts so well."

He stood and carefully brushed off his pants. "We replace the microbes. Louisiana is not far."

Ethan drove the car out of the natural area, quieting the birds momentarily. A flock of egrets flew off to the west, and pintails flapped quickly to the east. Winter migration was not finished, and its purpose had just been expanded.

CHAPTER 26

Remmy crept down a hallway inside Xoflex and stopped outside a door labeled *Makers*. His watch second hand ticked around—one more minute. Most of the plant was automated, so he didn't have to worry about live people, only security cameras. Before he left his office, he'd arranged for timed shutdowns of key cameras, two minutes each. That gave him thirty seconds of extra time, just in case.

He held a large briefcase in one hand, the sampling rod in the other. This was the room that held the *Makers*—nano-assemblers already coupled with the bacteria—the entire component helped *make* more oil. The security camera panned towards him. The red light winked out and the camera halted.

The sound of a door shutting and footsteps echoed in the hallway. Damn! Were they coming to get him? He couldn't tell with the echo which way their steps moved. The seconds ticked by, fifteen, sixteen— the footsteps receded and he slipped into the room.

Temperature-regulating motors hummed and the room smelled of ozone and disinfectant. He stuck the needle of the sampling rod into the side port of a silvery, two-foot diameter, one-foot high cylinder. The cylinder maintained an anaerobic environment, no oxygen, using cheap liquid nitrogen that also maintained the temperature around -200° F. Keeping the nano-assemblers cold avoided self-assembly, or multiplication, and no oxygen was what the bacteria preferred. So everything lived, but did not grow. After he took the Makers out, they would survive a maximum of ten days in well-insulated, leak-proof tubes, which he had designed. To obtain a good sample of the Makers he ticked off twenty seconds on his watch, then pulled out the needle and stuck it into the top port of each white tube in the briefcase: five total. Each needle stick and withdrawal elicited a spurt and hiss of steam from the super-cooled contents. Finally, he stuck the needle in the magnetic pulse and UV sterilizer for ten seconds, sheathed the needle, snapped the briefcase closed, and left. Ten seconds later, the security camera's red light blinked on, the motor clicked and whirred and resumed scanning.

Outside successive hallways he paused for camera shutoffs. Once in the Regulator room, he repeated the sampling and transfer into the five gray cylindrical tubes.

White for the good guys, gray for the bad guys.

He had picked the colors for their symbolism. The Makers were the best thing that could happen to the world: make something useful out of mere molecules. Good guys wore white hats. But things could get out of control, so they invented nano-regulators and labeled them gray. Not black. That was too strong. They weren't bad guys, merely the end of the Makers, temporarily, until reactivation.

He colored them gray for another reason: *To remind us of what might happen if we don't use them: gray goo.*

After he finished, he let out a deep breath and walked to the stairwell. Murmurs and shuffling of feet sounded around the corner. Phipps giving Croner the tour. He ran, easing the stairwell door shut behind him. If someone opened the door, he was toast. His heart thudded as he vacillated on holding the door closed or running. He sprinted down the stairs and glanced up before bursting out the door to his private parking lot. The security camera in the stairwell—he'd forgotten that one.

He prayed the security guard continued reading his usual Louis L'Amour novel instead of watching the screens. Deciding to make a non-hurried show for the outside cameras, he drove at a leisurely pace. He rapidly punched in the security code to open the gate while his heart pounded. On the other side Bear waved from behind a tree, directing him left, instead of the usual right. The reason appeared down the road to his right—a caravan of military vehicles were headed this way.

The gate did not move.

His finger quivered as he entered the code again, this time more slowly.

The gate opened.

Bear got in and they sped away from the caravan, Bear directing, until they came to a dead end at a rickety dock beside a bayou. Joe's Buick sat under a live oak tree. A twenty-foot, aluminum bass boat was tied to the dock, with Dad at the rear, his hand on the throttle of an idling, one hundred horsepower Mercury outboard. The motor purred and sputtered water and silvery smoke. Lola stood at the bow and waved for him to get in.

Remmy grabbed the briefcase and got out of the car. Then another thought struck him, and he rifled under the car seat. Teasing out a black plastic garbage bag, he popped the bag open with a quick pull and stuffed the briefcase inside.

"Whatcha got there, son?" Joe stepped from behind the live oak tree and zipped his pants.

"Wondered where you were. Prostate acting up?"

"Sheeatt! Can't a man take a piss without someone reminding him of his age?"

"Quit the lollygagging and get in da boat," said Lola. "We gots to get outta here. Vite, vite!"

They jumped in, Lola threw off the ropes, and they puttered through the shallows. Once in deeper water, Dad twisted the throttle and they rocketed through the winding bayou. Remmy gripped the side with one hand and clutched the briefcase to his body with the other, the trash bag flapping and snapping in wind.

"You never answer me 'bout dat!" Joe yelled over the engine noise and pointed at the trash bag package.

"Research!"

Brackish spray peppered them but offered minimal respite from the baking sun in the open bayou. The boat slowed and entered the cool haven of a cypress marsh. Dad killed the Merc and tilted the blades out of the water. The boat glided and Dad squinted into the shade, his face pinched in concentration.

A distant helicopter vibrated. Dad pulled them close to a cypress laden with Spanish moss, and peered up. The sound dissipated and he pull-started the Stump-Jumper. They motored gently over cypress knobs and logs into a world of fluttering shadows, through an eerie twilight that flickered like an eight millimeter film. Only Dad's memory could navigate this maze of channels.

Remmy pointed at Lola. "How'd she get here?"

Joe pulled a handheld CB radio out of his pocket and smiled, his gold tooth winking. "Dis *is* de twenty-first century, ya know."

Remmy gave him a wry smile and mumbled, "Maybe not for long."

Several minutes later they bumped into the dock and tied up between the pirogue and the seaplane. Once inside, Remmy excused himself to the bedroom where he turned on his laptop and assembled the portable testing machine, a two-inch square by one-inch thick gray box he'd brought from Maracaibo. He set one of the white tubes on the table, and plugged the box into his laptop, and a wire from the other end into the port of the tube.

He entered the data into the laptop, the numbers loading up the screen.

A roaring sound and a loud thump shook the room. He jumped from his chair and held onto the white tube to keep it from clattering to the floor.

He leaned over to get a better view out the window. *What the hell is a supersonic jet doing way out here?*

A knock on his door. "Remmy," Lola said, "you need to watch dis stuff on da TV. Things are gettin' crazier'n a coon dog chasin' a skunk."

He frowned at the laptop and moved closer to the screen.

"Remmy! You hear me, boy?" Lola's voice vibrated an unusual chord for her. *Panic.*

"Yeah, I'm coming."

He closed the laptop and entered a room that reminded him of a funeral: standing statues gazed solemnly at the TV. No pleasant smell of lilacs or roses here. Only the smell of the swamp mixed with an acrid odor of sweat.

A young black newsman faced the camera, voice calm, but his eyes shifted and he fidgeted at gunfire and explosions in the background. "The GM plants in the heart of the Midwest have been attacked by a number of individuals with military-like rapidity and planning. The SUV assembly plant in Janesville, Wisconsin has been demolished by explosives. About twelve of the executives and scientists have been taken hostage. We have yet to hear from the group responsible, but—" He pushed his fingers on the ear piece. "Here's Kathleen with breaking news."

The screen flipped to a quaffed brunette newswoman, whose frail physique and business suite contrasted to the military men surrounding her on the assembly-line floor of an automobile plant. Camouflage extended from uniforms to their face and scalps. Four cradled rifles, one a rocket launcher. The man standing by her wore a hip-holstered .45 handgun.

The newswoman tried to appear calm, but seemed flustered and inexperienced to Remmy."Tom, I'm here interviewing the leader of the attack on the GM plant, former Army Colonel Frank Lodster." She faced the holster man. "Colonel Lodster, can you tell us what happened today, and why you are doing this?"

Lodster was lean with pale, serious eyes. "What happened here was a lesson. The reason should be obvious. We will no longer tolerate gas guzzlers made by money hungry auto industries that are in cahoots with big oil."

"But why have you taken the scientists and executives hostage?"

His lizard eyes blinked at her like she'd just added two plus two and got eighty-nine.

"They know where they are, and how to get things started again. That's why we left the other plants operational. We can start producing them right away."

"Colonel, I'm sorry, but you have me stumped. What are they going to produce?"

"Jesus Christ, you're as stupid as the rest of them. The electric cars! The hydrogen cars! They've had them for decades and kept them out of the market because they wanted to make all the money on the gas guzzlers."

She widened her eyes, her inexperience showing, apparently thinking only the camera could see her.

He caught her gesture and the reptile eyes became slits. "Bitch!"

He pulled the gun and shot her in the head.

He extended the gun at the camera, and the screen went dark.

"Mon dieu," Joe whispered.

"Holy shit." Bear said.

Remmy returned to his room and closed the door.

Lola opened the door, marched over and got so close he smelled coffee on her breath. "Remmy, what's da matter wit you? Dis country fallin' apart and you just turn yo back and go to yo room. Dat's not like you."

He sighed. "Auntie, I might be able to fix it all if I can figure this out. But I need some time. And it seems I haven't got much of that left."

He opened the laptop. "Please, Aunt Lola."

"Okay, you. We be waitin'." She closed the door softly behind her.

He started typing in commands and another sonic boom rattled the room. He held onto the white tube with one hand, kept typing with the other hand, and stared at the screen.

CHAPTER 27

Dan jostled in the back of the van on the road back to Lisette's house and stared at his laptop. "The world has gone mad over oil." He was watching video clips of the latest news he had downloaded before they left the Wi-Fi hot spot. He had decided to concentrate on work, and leave Marci and Jeff for later.

"So what's new, the world has always been nuts about oil?" Ron said.

"Yeah, but now they're not just crazy, they're angry as hell."

"What do you mean?" Sam asked.

"Watch this." Dan rotated the laptop around and played the video of the colonel in Michigan shooting the newswoman. Next he ran a clip of SUV's and pickups carrying gun-wielding men and women over the rolling hills of Texas and Oklahoma towards oil refineries. Suddenly, an explosion of dust and smoke replaced the vehicles. The newsman explained U.S. Air Force laser-guided bombs were meant to hit the ground in front of the caravan, but hit the trucks. The next shot showed large holes in the ground draped with the gruesome remains of bodies.

"Jesus," Sam said.

"There's more." Dan played the last two clips.

Alaskans, according to the narrator, had decided they would stop the oil from leaving Alaska. A bush pilot contingency flew Pipers, DeHavillands, and Cessnas into Prudhoe Bay to try and take over the pump station. Fishing boats gathered to jam up the ports outside the Kenai and Valdez refineries. The Marines and the Army were waiting with anti-aircraft missiles and guns. Several Pipers were hit and crashed, the fiery wreckage and smoke bleak and foreboding against the backdrop of snowy tundra and herds of caribou near the Prudhoe oil fields.

In London, Tokyo, Peking, and Moscow, similar civil wars had broken out; a clip showed widespread violence. A Russian peasant appeared, his head bandaged, his interview translated: "The big oil companies raise our price too much. We have had enough. All they want is more money. We must stop them."

The last clip enumerated the price of a gallon of gas around the world: Miami-$11.00, London-$20.00, Moscow-$16.00, Tokyo-$35.00

Dan wanted the numbers to be more accurate and more fun, like $11.17, or $35.27. He flipped the screen around. "That's about it."

"That's enough," Ron said.

Sam frowned. "Why is the price of gas so high?"

"Oh, yeah. I forgot the first bit of news." Dan started searching the clips.

"Just tell us," Sam said.

Dan folded his arms and sighed. "Okay." He knew he sounded like Eeyore, but he loved to show things on the computer. "The gist of it is that oil production at all the OPEC countries has taken a nose dive. During the last twenty-four hours every producing well has lost ten percent. Even the Saudi's cannot make up for it, because their wells are down even more—fifteen percent."

"What about the SPR?" Sam said.

"SPR?" Dan felt his face twist into a little boy's puzzlement.

"We have billions of gallons of oil stockpiled in case of emergencies to stabilize prices. It's called the Strategic Petroleum Reserve. Why aren't they using those until they get it figured out?"

"Maybe they are." Lisette pointed at the convoy of military vehicles passing them. The din outside made it hard to be heard in the van, especially when the helicopters and jets flew over.

"Why would so many Army vehicles be out here in the middle of nowhere?" Ron said.

"Those aren't all Army," Sam said. "There's Marine amphibs on those trailers."

"Couldn't be just for Xoflex," Lisette said.

"What about the Gulf oil wells?" Dan said.

"That's it!" Lisette said. "I think there's a military port about five miles down the road."

She turned onto a narrow dirt road that led to their hideaway. Dan repressed the urge to wave at Blue Titty as the pickup drove by. His head swiveled to find the other, but White Pee Pee had vanished.

On their walk into the cabin, his phone chimed. He stayed outside and answered Marci's call.

"There's something I didn't tell you about Jeff." She blurted it out.

"What?"

"We had a fight the morning he left. I thought he should stay home, get the drunk driving stuff figured out. He said you told him he was old enough to make decisions for himself. Since his country needed him, he was going where they needed him."

Dan paced. She'd told him to be firm with Jeff, to let him act like a grown up. Isn't that what he did? A breeze rustled the fallen leaves of live oaks.

"Anyway," she continued, "he said they needed him for the new Oil War. That's what they're calling it. You've seen the news?"

"Yeah."

Dan closed his eyes. Sun warmed his face. No colors came to mind.

"You didn't cause this," he said. "Jeff is a big boy, now. He made that clear to me."

Sobbing filled his ear. "How could you?" She said. "The kid is head-strong anyhow, then you tell him he can start making decisions for himself. What were you thinking? Why did I have to yell at him? I—" She broke off, the sobs louder.

"You said he's almost a man, remember?" He mimicked her voice, "He's eighteen, Dan. We need to treat him more like an adult. That's what you said. Besides, I told him school is more important than joining the Army over and over. That never sank in."

He hung his head. *That was a stupid thing to say.*

"Oh Dan. What am I going to do now?"

He looked at the cabin and at his feet, shook his head. "I wish I could be there, but things are a bit crazy right now."

"Of course they are." Not a simple affirmation, but an icy rerun of prior arguments when his job had taken priority over family.

"Look, I gotta go. I'll call soon. Don't worry. He'll be alright."

"He better be. If something happens to that boy . . ."

"I know."

He hung up and blew out a deep breath. Jeff's last conversation with him drifted back: "I'm not a kid anymore. If I want to drive you can't stop me. I know what I'm doing. You couldn't stop me from joining the Army, could you?" Then he walked out. And Dan had let him go. He should have followed him, talked to him, tried harder to convince him. If he would have done that, or called in and told Fred he couldn't go, maybe none of this would have happened. Maybe Fred would still be alive. He kicked at the ground; dust billowed and dirt splattered the water.

Frogs nee-deeped in the swamp and something splashed. A cool breeze riffled the water and he stared at the shimmering wavelets. Then he peered up. No sign of flying frogs. Trees still swayed, moss still fluttered, and the sun still shown. Moving forward was his only choice.

When he walked in, Lisette sat at the kitchen table eating an apple. Her nose seemed bigger, and her lips thin. Her eyes found his, but he averted his gaze to Sam who talked on his cell phone.

Sam ended his call. "Everything okay?"

Dan shifted his eyes. "Yeah, sure." He eyed Sam. "What about you? Who was on the phone?"

"Doesn't look like we'll be going anywhere anytime soon. One of our good-old-boy truck drivers just told me the Army's barricaded all the major roads."

CHAPTER 28

The barricaded highway outside Dallas prevented Abdullah from retrieving René from the airport, a minor problem. But when he called and had to leave another voice mail for René, alarm flags waved in his head. The voicemail beeped and Abdullah said, "We are going to—" But he stopped. René would find them. If he lived.

They traveled east on I-20, but outside Shreveport police cars with lights flashing blocked the way. Darkness fell. The last motels had been in Terrel, Texas, so they flipped around and drove into the downpour. By the time they saw lights, the wipers skittered across a film of ice on the windshield and Ethan had to slow considerably to keep from sliding off the road. They were in an ice storm.

"We better stop at the first motel or we may be stranded out here for days," Ethan said.

The first and only motel at the Terrel intersection blazed three neon red X's in the window of the attached adult book store.

Abdullah shook his head. *The land of Bible-beating Baptists and I must stay in a whore house.*

They got out of the car at once. Ethan slipped on the glare ice, grabbed the car door and caught himself.

Abdullah's reflexes were not as quick. He saw a blur of red neon X's and—

Blackness.

After an eternity of strange dreams, Abdullah awoke to the smell of bleach. Remembering the three red X's, he guessed the sheets had been bleached many times. Neatly pressed green drapes hung over a large picture window that overlooked scenic I-20: gray highway and pine trees. How lovely. The room vibrated with a passing semi. René sat beside the bed, smiling. A splitting headache, dry mouth, and the thought of being trapped in this motel beside the pornographic book store tainted Abdullah's return smile.

"You gave us quite a scare, sir. That damn ice storm nearly killed you. Ethan tells me your head sounded like a coconut cracking. I was in baggage claims when he called, so it didn't take me long. That was forty-eight hours ago. Ethan wanted a doctor, but—"

"You knew I wouldn't want that. Thank you, René."

"I have to say, if you hadn't awakened I was ready to call a doctor."

Abdullah sat up, winced and lay down.

"Might take that a bit slower, sir." René placed another pillow under his head.

He squeezed his eyes tightly shut and opened them. "When can we leave for Xoflex?"

René turned up the volume on the TV and motioned at it with his head.

"That should answer your questions."

Two news personnel, a man and a woman, gazed out with sunken eyes, rumpled clothes, and not a speck of makeup covering their blemishes.

"Jill," the man said, "it looks like the worst could be over, but now we are probably in for the long haul."

"To recap, our world as we knew it only days ago is now in the throes of a disaster worse than any World War III we could have imagined. The oil supply has been—"

The screen went chartreuse green and the emergency signal screeched three times. A monotone male voice said, "This is not a test. This is the emergency broadcast network. Please standby."

Then, electronic snow.

Abdullah sighed. "Perhaps you could fill me in."

"Yes sir. Over the last two days there have been worldwide riots and civil war due to the oil supply dropping precipitously from all OPEC countries, Russia, Europe, South America and the Far East. Since the U.S. and Canada's production has not been affected, Russia is accusing them of collaborating in a plot to monopolize all oil production."

Abdullah cackled briefly, stopping to hold his head in his hands. Then he continued laughing, unabated. He couldn't help it. He laughed, and laughed, not caring about the pain.

René's smile faded to parted lips and widening eyes. "Perhaps I should call the doctor." He reached for the phone.

Abdullah stopped laughing. "Soon the shoe will be on the other foot! Don't you see?"

René's hand froze mid-reach, and he shook his head.

"Didn't Ethan tell you? The Regulators. They're gone. We were on our way to obtain more when the ice storm hit."

"You mean you released the Makers, but no Regulators?" René's hand fell, and he breathed out like he'd been punched.

Abdullah waved his hand as if this could calm the storm blowing through René's mind.

"There's still Alaska oil. I know we wanted to save some of the oil for us here, but we'll be fine. We have people in place up there to take over the wells. There will be enough oil for us to use until the biofuels arrive. Maybe a month at most. It's more fitting that Texas oil is gone. Don't you see?"

René dropped his head and closed his eyes. "Sir, Boris Yanikovich arrived in Alaska yesterday as an envoy from Russia."

Two semis rushed by outside, rattling the framed print of *Whistler's Mother* on the wall.

Abdullah's face drained of the returning color. "Boris was in Vienna."

CHAPTER 29

Remmy had a revelation in darkness. It had taken much longer than he wanted to figure things out, but after two days and only four hours of sleep he ran the test two more times. All three results were identical.

He burst out of the room to tell someone. The night filled the house. Bear and Dad traded snores on the fold-out couch. A breeze from the swamp ruffled the drapes and delivered the sweet-sour smell of sea trout milt and dead crayfish.

"Fuck!" he shouted a whisper at the half moon.

"Notchyet. Maybe later, after you're asleep," came the soft answer from the screened porch outside. Aunt Lola's pipe added a pleasant sweetness to the air.

He sighed and tried to calm himself. He walked to the porch, eased the screen door shut and sat on the cypress bench beside her. "I figured it out."

"'Bout time. You been workin' on dat shit for two days now." She blew gray smoke over the water. An alligator splashed its tail in the distance and a bat fluttered over their heads.

"Why do you smoke that thing?"

"Better'n chewin' an' spittin' like Ma, don'tcha think?"

"I guess."

"Sides, I only do one bowl at night. Heps me unwind and put everything in its place 'fore I hit da hay."

He did enjoy the sweet smell of pipe tobacco. Slate clouds floated over the crescent moon. The stars shown brighter.

"You gone tell me or just sit there?"

"It's bad, Aunt Lola. Someone put a different bacterial strain in the Makers vat. So instead of Makers, we have been delivering a destroyer, or we'll call them Takers."

"How 'bout you translate dat for your poor dumb Aunt?"

"Auntie you're not du—"

"Yeah, yeah, just tell it to me simple like."

The moon came out of the clouds and deepened the shadows of her frown.

"Okay, it's like this: the amount of oil in the world . . . the world oil supply . . ."

He stopped, closed his eyes and sighed again. "Simply, there is no more oil in the world to discover, and existing oil wells are producing less and less each year. My company patented a way to wring more oil out of existing wells using what I call Makers, nano-bacteria we spread into the oil wells. They work so fast, the oil well is back in high production almost immediately. Someone switched the bacteria, though. So instead of Makers, we've been delivering Takers—the nano-bacteria wolf down the oil, and in two weeks, or maybe less, all of the oil in that well is gone."

"Butchyou just delivered it to Maracaibo, nowhere else, right?"

He found Orion's belt in the stars and scratched the two-day stubble on his jaw. "Yeah. But I think I know how it got everywhere else."

"How dat?"

"Do you remember about the OPEC meeting and the spiders that fell from the ceiling?"

She chuckled. "Sure. I seen it on de TV. Them scairdy cats all ran from them spiders like they was rattlers or something."

The door creaked open from the dining room. Uncle Joe stepped out. "Whatchoo doin' out here, lady? Tot you was comin' to bed."

He paused when he saw Remmy. "Oh, did'na see you Remmy. What'ch y'all talkin' bout?"

"Hi, Uncle Joe. I was telling Auntie about what caused this problem with the oil."

Lola pointed the stem of her pipe at Joe. "And he was gittin' to de good part, so shut it and sit."

Joe put his hands up. "Okay, okay. I'm all ears. Go ahead, boy. Spill it."

A breeze from the bayou whispered through the trees and caused the pirogue to rattle on the pier. A gray wisp of cloud knifed the moon.

Remmy sighed with the bayou and began again. "Those spiders at the OPEC meeting had the Takers on them. When they came out of the ceiling the spiders helped spread the microscopic demons into the air and onto the clothes and shoes of every person there. Once the OPEC members returned to their countries, the Takers would have quadrupled in number. With the help of the HeLa effect, the Takers then spread to the oil wells. After a week, production slowed. Another week and . . . Well, you saw it on the TV."

Lola puffed out silvery smoke. "How da hell can those tings spread from the bottom of someone's foot to oil wells miles away? You need to talk sense, Remmy."

"Auntie, like I said, it's the HeLa effect."

"Who dat?" Joe said.

"In the early fifties someone discovered a cell line taken from a black lady named Henrietta Lacks, who had cervical cancer. These cells, abbreviated HeLa for her first and last name, had a property that allowed them to live forever if given food. They were so persistent that they got into everything, contaminating labs all over the world, even twenty years later. No one ever solved the mystery as to how the cells got everywhere. That's the way these Takers act. They're so small they get into everything, and the very air currents take them to where they want to be."

Lola had been concentrating so hard her pipe bowl went out. She tamped and relit it, puffed a few times and blew out a snake of blue smoke. "Dat sounds like voodoo to me." She gazed at the smoke floating over the bayou. "What now?"

"The infected oil wells will be big holes in the ground. No more oil."

"Good ting we got dat thousand gallon tank over yonder topped off 'fore we left," Joe said.

Lola pointed at Remmy with her pipe stem. "And you think you can fix it, you?"

The frogs *nee-deeped* in high pitched harmony across the edge of the bayou while the Spanish moss waved rhythmically in the breeze: conductors of the frog symphony.

Remmy rubbed his stubble. "If I can get to the wells that are still producing maybe I can at least save those. The others . . . I don't know."

A thrashing sound came from the other side of the bayou. The squeal of a deer ended abruptly with a big splash.

Silence.

A shallow wave moved across the water and lifted the pirogue and the floating dock, bouncing them together like two hollow trees hitting in the wind.

CHAPTER 30

The next morning Dan awoke early and peered through slits of sleep-encrusted eyes. After spending most of the last two days barricaded from driving, he and Sam had tried to figure out what Xoflex was up to, but Dan was severely hampered with no cable and no land line. Right after they saw the army caravan, cell phones had gone on the blink with very spotty coverage. Sam thought the military had destroyed cell towers to impair civilian coordination of attacks. They tried the satellite phone, but their code didn't work. After two nights of fitful sleep Dan had finally crashed last night and slept like a stone.

Lisette sat on the edge of his bed, staring out the window. He tried to avoid any action that signaled his awakening. He glanced at the bayou and wondered if they would still be here to see the beauty of spring. His eyes fell on Lisette again. He noticed that her lips were not voluptuous, but thin, and her nose almost bulbous. Otherwise . . . Shit! What was he going to do about her?

He closed his eyes and concentrated. The number two vibrated spruce green. Two—him and Marci, or him and Lisette? Three was next to two, undulating blue: him and Jeff and Marci, for sure. He tried to transport good thoughts to Marci and Jeff, tried to blot out Lisette, and make this war disappear.

What he really needed was a land line, and he could get back to work. He'd tried his best to ignore Lisette the last few days. Once he'd gone off on her about the land line. "Why would you have a TV here but no phone?"

She'd pondered him for a minute before a gentle answer: "We did before Katrina and Rita."

"But wouldn't you want to get that repaired fairly quickly afterwards. I mean communication with the outside world, relatives, friends . . ."

"What?" Her voice grated now. "You think after Katrina those telephone repairmen were like grapes on a bush? Just go out and pick one and they'd be real sweet and do the job right now?"

"Okay. Sorry. I thought that a new house like this came with a phone?"

"Cousins built this place. They didn't know how to do phones. And besides, there were no phone lines to be had."

She had Dan cornered this morning. He hated confrontation. Maybe he could talk about something else. He fluttered his eyes open and stared at her beautiful blue twinklers. Unfortunately, she frowned.

"We got to talk," she said.

He rubbed his eyes, tried to disguise combing his wisps as scratching his head, and sat up. "I told Sam, without a land line or Wi-Fi I can't do anything. Maybe we could drive back to that—"

"Not that shit. I mean about you and me."

He closed his eyes. *Damn!*

"What?" she asked.

"Lisette, I—You know I was kinda screwed up that night."

"Yeah, we both were. But so what?"

What the hell was happening here, he thought. He loved Marci and Jeff and Katie and Watson—his family. How could he love her? How could she have feelings for him? This is not the way field agents did it. They had overnight flings and never looked back. She was just a crazy-assed Marine, a free spirit, should move on, forget that night—great while it lasted, enjoy the moment. She was crazy and beautiful, and always stuck up for him and gave him space when he needed it, and . . . He'd never had any woman but Marci. He wanted to call Fred and ask him what to do. He eyed the laptop on the desk. Maybe just ignore her and get back into the programs and numbers—the violet hue of calmness.

She stared at him.

"I'm old enough to be your father. I'm not good with people. Look at me. Almost bald, baggy eyes in the morning, can't even make good decisions after no sleep and a few beers. You wouldn't want me."

A breeze blew through the screened window beside the bed and flipped her hair over her eyes.

She studied the ground. "I know that. But I like you. You remind me of a friend I lost once. I don't want to lose you." She closed her eyes and a tear dribbled down one cheek, tracing over her beautiful lips. Her tongue licked it away. He sighed.

God! I'm stupid. Just because she's a Marine.

He folded his arms around her. She hugged him and sobbed.

Sam peeked from behind the door, raised an eyebrow, then eased the door shut.

She cried on Dan's shoulder and he kept quiet, afraid that if he opened his mouth something stupid would come out.

Then, as though resolved, her arms tightened and her sobs lessened.

She pushed away from him. His gaze faltered at her pouting lips and sad eyes.

"Okay Lisette. I'm stupid. Dumb. Insensitive."

The sides of her mouth started to turn up.

"Aaannnd married," he finished.

Her lips parted and disbelief crossed her face. She shook her head and turned to leave.

"Wait. Let's talk this through. I can't leave it like this," he said.

The door opened and Sam stuck his head in. "You both need to come in here and see this."

She slid by Sam and Dan followed, shaking his head. "Don't even ask."

"Yeah, well, we have more important things to worry about right now." Sam motioned toward the TV.

On the screen, a newswoman stood before white and gray camouflaged American tanks. Soldiers milled about on snowy ground.

The woman wore a parka and spoke slowly and distinctly to be heard over wind gusts, "Here in the Alaskan tundra the US Army has deployed over five thousand troops in the last five days."

A huge black helicopter flew over her. She shouted and pointed up. "That is not an American helicopter. It's a Russian Werewolf, also known as the Black Shark. Every minute or so one will make a pass-over."

The Werewolf moved away. The camera zoomed in on her intense gaze. Her voice became low and calm. "I don't think this close-in surveillance, or show of force, or whatever they think it is will last another day. There will be shooting before morning."

The screen switched to the news studio where a sallow, unshaven anchorman shook his head. "That was Ann Kaslowski in Prudhoe Bay, Alaska. It's looking like Texas did four days ago. Now we take you to those precious oil wells in east Texas, with John Stevenson. John?"

Dan peered at the screen. *What's with their makeup guy? The anchorman looks like shit.* Then he slapped himself mentally. *I may have started this. My program.* He *must* get back on the internet, and into Xoflex. Maybe he could stop this escalation.

The camera panned from left to right over rolling hills peppered with mesquite bushes and oil wells, and settled on a disheveled man wearing stained jeans, western shirt, and a military vest. Behind him tanks, Humvees, military jeeps, and desert-camouflaged armed soldiers stretched in either direction. They faced fifty feet of razor wire coils behind a freshly dug twenty foot ditch. An open field stretched out to the right where ragged smoking craters defiled the smooth hills of Texas. Orange flames licked from burning wrecks of Tahoes, Explorers and civilian trucks. Hundreds of bodies littered the grass like a monstrous truckload of zombie ragdolls had spilled.

"Yes, Phil," the newsman said, "Eastern Texas is under control, at least military control. We didn't have the Russians to contend with here, but it was still no picnic. As you can see in the background, there were a lot of civilian casualties, and—"

The camera view jerked around, viewed the ground. The newsman yelled, "You can't do that. This is a free country. We have the right to be here!"

The screen jumped with wavy lines, then flashed to the studio with the anchorman, Phil.

"Apparently we are having minor technical difficulties," Phil said. His eyes jerked sideways and got wide. "We'll be taking a short break."

The TV beamed multi-colored waves and emitted white noise.

Dan remembered the sour stench of dead bodies in an Afghanistan mass grave presumed to be suffocated Taliban prisoners of war. He felt nauseous.

Sam turned down the white noise but left the TV on.

A gentle flap of wind blew the curtains. Ron's rocking chair creaked. Lisette sniffled once.

Dan felt numb. East Texas. His son could be one of those corpses.

CHAPTER 31

Dan stumbled towards the door; had to get outside, get some fresh air. "I'm going to try Marci, again. Maybe I can get better reception outside."

Sam nodded. Ron gave him a weak smile. Lisette tilted her head and scrunched her face like she was going to cry again.

He walked outside and shouted "Damn!" at the exact moment he slammed the door, wanting the noise to disguise his anger. *Don't need them to think I'm weak. I can take the pressure.*

His phone revealed a half a bar. He tried to dial: *No Signal.*

He walked to the edge of the bayou. Half a bar, still. He couldn't walk further, not adept at walking on water. He hit speed dial #1. *Number one. That was Marci. Always had been. Always would—*

"Dan is that you?" The reception crackled in and out.

"Yeah. How you doin', Babe?" If he pressed her too fast she might hang up.

"Good."

Nothing else.

"Good?"

A slight whimper. A sniff. "No. Not good. Not really."

A mullet jumped twice out of the water like a stone skipping. The morning sun beat down and sweat ran off his forehead. *Gonna be a hot one.*

"Sorry I'm not there. Have you heard from Jeff?"

A cough. More sniffs. Her voice became a controlled tremble. "I got an encrypted email yesterday."

"Is he okay? What happened?"

Her words came in a torrential high-octave quaver. "He's okay, or at least he was yesterday. He's in eastern Texas defending the oil wells and had to kill people. People! Humans! Americans! Civilians! It's not—" She choked off, sobbing.

Yesterday he was okay. They said all that happened yesterday, and most of the casualties were civilian.

He forced his words into calm, slow sentences. "I know, Babe. It's not right, not supposed to happen this way, not good, not . . . right."

Sunlight skipped off the water in pieces of brightness against the side of the cabin. A blue heron jabbed its knife-like head into the shallows, retrieving a silvery, flopping breakfast.

His stomach growled, yet he felt queasy, though better, now that he knew Jeff was okay. One hundred and one—101—flashed green and red like a mixed-up traffic light in his mind—yes, no, yes. One of the few computer-literate primes.

"I thought," he said, "he would just set up some barbed wire fences, stand watch, maybe fire the machine gun at bushes or something. Being a corporal, and with all his math and language skills, he should be isolated from any fighting."

"That didn't happen, did it? He's only a kid, Dan." She ended again with sobs.

She quieted and Dan asked, "Did he say anything else?"

"Yeah." She cleared her throat. "He said the guys are great, several from around here. Good company commander, gave them all a pep talk before the . . . shooting began and . . ."

The reception kept crackling in and out.

Marci's voice returned, "Members of his platoon from Texas recognized dead friends on the other side after the battle. Jeff said they were having a bad time afterwards."

He waved off a cloud of midges and the rotten egg smell of low tide.

"They're killing more kids over oil. Why can't they do something else? Why didn't they see this coming? Is this the end of the United States?"

Dan sighed, "I think it's the end of what we've known. But we have to protect the oil. Our whole economy runs off it. Without it we'll be paralyzed." He suddenly wondered if that was true.

The reception faded and buzzed. She did not answer.

"Marci, if you're there I'm going to try to do something about all this."

The screen blinked *No Signal*.

He peered north, beyond the cypress trees and fingers of Spanish moss waving in the breeze. Somewhere out there his son risked his life, creating future nightmares. Brothers fought brothers. Could Dan's program have done all this? It was a small thing, a way for nanobots to communicate with bacteria. Xoflex was supposed to be the good guys in all this, making more oil, not less. Yet Octex-Penta and Abdullah El-Hamain had been in that Venezuelan file with Xoflex. The principle of simplicity told him all of them were responsible for the oil shortage.

He breathed faster and felt his whole body tense. He must do something. Xoflex wasn't far. He had to find out what they'd done, and then maybe Sam and Ron and Lisette could . . .

The closed door to the cabin beckoned and glowed in an orange hue. *Lisette.*

His gaze shifted from cabin to bayou, cabin to bayou. But he didn't move. Sweat rolled off his nose and the shirt stuck to his lower back. His palms felt slick as oil as he gripped his hands over and over.

He relaxed his hands. Warmth and Lisette's orange glow flooded over him like high tide in the swamp. For an instant he felt the freedom of that first day with her when they flew over the Gulf of Mexico.

He blinked hard. He was in way over his head with Lisette and Sam and this save-the-world bit. All he really wanted was to get his family back.

CHAPTER 32

Abdullah paced and muttered and harangued René about the need to move, take action. Abdullah had taken a few days to regain his strength after his concussion, but now, this afternoon, he must act.

René argued, "You're still fuzzy, sir. Besides, the highways remain barricaded."

"My mind is crystal clear," Abdullah said. "Damn the barricades. Call in reinforcements."

"The cell phones are not working, sir."

He flopped onto the moldy couch and turned on the TV. At least it still worked, though only two stations were broadcasting. This afternoon's news about the Texas civil war started him to chuckle. He thought of fellow Texans killing one of President Streeter's cousins over oil, and laughed. When he remembered they fought over something that would be nonexistent in a week, he roared.

His laughter ceased. President Streeter stood framed in the foreground of Prudhoe Bay and a Russian helicopter strafing American tanks.

It's what you always wanted Mr. President, to have all the oil. Now you've got it. How's it feel asshole?

The President's erect stance matched his firm gaze and voice. "We have the situation under control in Texas, and Alaska will follow suit in the next day. We will overcome this, just as we did the 9/11 attacks.

Terrorism will not prevail. The Ring of Jackals will meet their end soon and justice will win out. God bless America."

Abdullah hit the power button and stared at the blank screen. Streeter loved his new term for terrorists. But he will have more than a gang of dogs on his heels very soon.

"Perhaps God will bless something, Mr. President. But I don't think it will be America, or American oil. In another week there will be no oil, and where will that leave you, you moron?"

René squinted at his boss from the corner of the room.

Abdullah presented an open hand, as if inviting René into his mind. "It's what we all wanted. No oil. They have to wake up. The earth can't take it any longer. She's getting hot, angry, spewing out more hurricanes, drying up crops, starving out these . . . these human ants that have been choking her breath, clogging her arteries. We're helping her, you and I: equalizing the playing field so she can recover. Just because the human ants are all fighting it's not the end of the world. It's the beginning of a new one. Those remaining will keep the agreement with her, fill her lungs with clean air, use her resources in renewable ways to keep her mountains green, oceans blue, and all her guests, animals and humans alike, living in harmony. After these skirmishes they will be forced to find other ways of traveling. That's when we will help the most."

Suddenly he felt utterly exhausted. "Tomorrow we will go and fulfill the final plan. It is time."

He lay on the bed and closed his eyes.

René watched his boss go to sleep, then gazed out the open window at the late afternoon. Sparse brown leaves hung motionless from the trees. Torrid waves welled from the asphalt and cement that surrounded the pathologic motel. No tractor trailer trucks rattled the windows. The highway had been deserted for days. Two distant military jeeps blocked the way. The sky held scattered puffy clouds. A raven soared overhead, searching for the usual road kill that would never come again. Deer slept in the cool grass under pine trees beside the highway. He breathed in clean air. Not a hint of diesel. An armadillo sidled across the exit ramp, not even bothering to look both ways. Some things never changed.

A world without cars.

Abdullah breathed even and regular; the unfettered sleep of the blessed innocent, René thought. Or perhaps the uncaring damned?

Outside, the black limousine gleamed, the clouds moved lazily, and the armadillo eased into the tall grass by the exit ramp. René sighed and twisted his torso to dislodge the gun holster pinching his chest. He closed his eyes and soon he breathed regularly.

One hundred miles south, larger birds circled: turkey buzzards. The air contained no freshness. Oppressive heat netted the odors of thick diesel fumes, freshly dug earth, burning rubber, and another acrid smell. Hunters knew it. Men of war hated it. The smell of dead meat brought the buzzards, and coyotes. Before the dawn of white men and roads, the bears and wolves that had roamed these hills would have scared the coyotes off and taken over the carcasses, fed until full, and moved on.

Jeff peered at the coyotes from behind a tank. He fidgeted, wanting to bury the dead, but knowing if he ventured into the fields he would be killed by the snipers beyond the tree line across the field. As a new corporal he would not be assigned the burial detail. All those language classes and math had earned him a higher rank right out of boot camp. Prior practice on the weekends firing all the Army's gun's also allowed him real action. They needed soldiers not interpreters.

The field was pockmarked by mortars, and littered with smoking vehicles and dead bodies. It reminded him of pictures of the Civil War. But unlike the Civil War, those men behind the trees on the other side of the field had good weapons, M-60s, AK-47s, grenade launchers, long range sniper rifles: all aimed at any soldier not shielded.

Two days ago they had lured the tanks down the road five miles and managed to cripple two before the platoon made it back to the compound. Those two tanks still smoldered. The episode had cost their unit valuable fuel.

How the hell did they get grenade launchers? His new buddies filled him in: Ever hear of the black market? Drug dealers? Where you been kid?

Not in their world.

Yesterday at dawn a surprise rush of those men had succeeded in breaching the tank line. Grenades had destroyed two water buffalo, their fuel dump, and killed ten soldiers, one of them Jeff's friend Jason. Jason had been returning from the latrine, hunched over, running behind one of the tanks when Jeff heard a metal clank. A grenade bounced down off the end of the tank like a flat tennis ball and burrowed into the freshly dug dirt in front of Jason.

Jeff stared at the spot now, a crater in the ground, the dirt stained dark at one edge. He closed his eyes. But it didn't help. It replayed over and over. Jason skidded to a stop, pushed his hands and rifle forward and lurched to one side. The explosion blinded, percussed Jeff's chest, blasted his ears. Then, smoke, dust and quiet, a quiet dullness from ear drums being rattled.

A breeze scattered the smoke, and at the edge of the crater stood Jason's left boot and his lower leg. It ended at the ragged knee. How had the leg stayed upright? No one could explain it.

They had collected the rest of Jason, bits plastered on the tank and pieces flung in the dust—like mud clods Jeff had thrown as a kid, only these had Jason's blood, flesh, and bone inside. They'd dropped everything they found, including his leg, into a bag smaller than Jeff's backpack. They put it in the makeshift morgue, and would fly the remains out tomorrow. Or whenever.

More like, whenever.

That had been twenty-four hours ago. The attack had been repelled, the tank line reformed, the rest of the day without event. Empty.

When the sun went down everyone relaxed. Snipers popped ten relaxed soldiers.

Someone said it must be Nam or Iraq veterans with night-scoped rifles, or maybe local hunters, good old boys that could shoot.

They guessed at that, but he didn't have to guess at what they wanted. The oil.

He couldn't understand why Central Command didn't order an air strike and bomb the shit out of the tree line and beyond. He found out this morning. His CO reported everything that flew, except the turkey buzzards, operated in Alaska, or perhaps in Afghanistan. So, no air support. More exciting news—the last fuel truck arrived empty two days ago. If they didn't get more fuel soon, the tanks would be no more than a stepping stone the enemy could use to get over the razor wire.

How could they run out of fuel with a refinery and oil wells in their lap?

The coyotes tugged at something with their teeth and growled at each other over the meal. He leaned against the tank. Bile played tag with his tonsils. After Jason's gruesome death he'd begged the medic for a transfer, leave, get the hell out. But the medic said he wasn't hurt and the best thing was to go right back out there. It would prevent long lasting psychological problems.

He closed his eyes and tried to think of his life four months ago; tried to visualize the basketball court, hitting a three pointer at the buzzer and his dad cheering in the crowd. He tried to visualize Krista smiling, the day she gave him the news.

All he saw was Jason's leg.

CHAPTER 33

Dan strode inside, his talk with Marci a cattle prod for action. Now!

Sam met him at the door with the other two. "We need your help. There are four different routes we need to observe, so I need every available pair of eyes. I've got some lunch and water."

Dan wanted to punch Sam. Surveillance? More waiting? But he had no choice. They spent that day and the next watching for a possible way out. The good thing: Dan had respite from Lisette. He paced more than he watched, frustrated at the inability to connect to Xoflex and call his wife.

On the second afternoon he'd had enough; he started walking to find Sam. Sam grabbed him, slapped a hand over his mouth, and pulled him behind a tree. Someone had spotted Dan and had been following him. They waited.

The sentry peered into the bush, M-4 carbine gripped at ready, barrel nosing through leaves. Sam readied his Sig226, his trigger finger outside the guard. Something snapped under the sentry's boot. His radio crackled a call; he mumbled a few words into it and left.

Dan breathed again. "Sorry Sam." Sam grunted and they left for the cabin.

That night Dan tried to reach Marci without success. The next morning, after little sleep, he tromped out of the room to demand more action. They must do something besides watch.

Sam and Ron walked out of their bedrooms, backpacks already on, Ron's chest holster bulging with a .45 pistol. Three M-16s rattled over Lisette's shoulder.

"Okay, keemosabi," Sam said. "We're ready. Grab your shit."

Dan blinked and shook his head. Maybe he *could* transport his thoughts and they actually listened to him. Then again. "Where are we going? What did I miss? How should I dress? When?"

Lisette winked and gave him a half smile.

Ron said, "Outta here. A lot. Something cool, with hiking shoes. And I'm guessing at your last question with, NOW!"

"Okay, I'll be right out. Finally we're doing something!"

He rushed into his room and changed into his Venezuela outfit: synthetic khaki pants, a beige long-sleeved shirt, a baseball-style fishing cap with a neck flap, and waterproof hiking boots. He grabbed his pack, slipped in the laptop, his handgun, a bottle of water, and walked out. He thought of the right-truncatable prime 73939133: take away a number from the right side and get another prime. If he took away each addendum he carried would it make him just as interesting? No; merely more vulnerable. People weren't like numbers—they did not have eight interesting layers.

"Looks like you're ready for safari," Sam said.

"Just because I'm a computer geek doesn't mean I haven't been in the bush."

Sam gripped his shoulder. "You're dressed perfect. Get in."

Sam drove, Ron sat in front, Lisette beside Dan. White egrets picked at the feet of grazing cows on the way out of the marsh. Through the open van window, warm humid marsh air mixed with cow dung and a whiff of the van's exhaust.

"Are you going to tell me or do I have to guess?" Dan said.

Ron and Sam traded looks, smiled, and simultaneously said, "Guess!"

Lisette chuckled. "This I gotta hear."

Dan scratched his head, peered outside and cleared his throat. "The war's over and all the oil is back, right?"

"Right." Ron stuck his tongue out the corner of his mouth.

"Just kidding. Though, I was hoping. How about, your boss called and is flying us to Alaska to save the day?"

The van stopped at the highway. Dan scanned the area. Blue Titty and White Pee Pee appeared behind them. Watchers and guardians.

Sam pulled out onto the highway. "We did manage a brief call to the boss. They're too busy to help, what with Alaska and Texas and all. We're on our own. Ron found a possible way in, so we decided to make a stop at Xoflex and retrieve a few things."

"Xoflex? Last time we were there, half the Louisiana army reserve units were taking over security. How are you planning on getting in?"

Ron faced Dan. "You can get us into their security system. Right?"

"Of course. But I need an internet connection."

"Leave that to us," Sam said over his shoulder. "You sound pretty sure about getting through their computer security system?"

"I did it before. What makes you think I can't do it again?"

"Like you said, there have been a few changes at Xoflex."

Sam pulled the van behind a patch of trees, still a good distance away from the Xoflex perimeter fence. He handed Dan the binoculars.

"Take a look."

Bullet holes pockmarked the Xoflex sign and building, and the perimeter fence had huge gaps torn out. A Humvee patrolled the perimeter with one man and a large machine gun swiveling on top. Sand bags and cement highway barriers stood in front of the entrance door. Helmeted heads and machine guns sniffed over the top.

Dan quickly lowered the binoculars. "Can they see us?

"Doubtful. But you raise a good point." Sam put the van in gear and they moved off.

"Turn right at the break in the fence," Lisette said. "Then it's about another mile."

"It? What is it?" Dan said.

"You'll see," she said and rested her hand on his shoulder. No sign of previous tears, and her voice sounded cheery. He wondered why.

CHAPTER 34

After Remmy's revelation, one question remained for him: Who switched the bacteria? They started out early for Xoflex the next morning to find out. A boat ran along the bayou less than a mile away, forcing them back. All that day, the sound of the patrolling boat got closer. Joe thought them military boats, protecting the Gulf oil wells. At dusk Bear ventured out for reconnaissance, and returned with the report: "It ain't no military guys. They got beards and no uniforms."

That night Remmy woke with a nightmare of someone garroting his neck. The next morning, while he sipped chicory coffee and rubbed his neck, Bear took care of the boat and the men in it. Their IDs read: "Octex-Penta."

They'd hounded Remmy since Venezuela; probably suspected *he* switched the bacteria. If he didn't find the real culprit, he'd be gator food in the Octex-Penta aquarium in New Orleans.

He decided to revise his plans for return to Xoflex. He took all day carefully mapping out his visit to Xoflex the next day: where and how to enter, rooms to explore, how to avoid the military, his boss, the cameras, and how to get out. Then he planned his trip to Texas, and on to Alaska. He must reverse the destruction of oil before the too-late clock ran out of time. He felt his chances as good as a trapped crayfish escaping Aunt Lola's pot of boiling water. But the plan helped him sleep.

An hour after he awoke the next morning, dawn sifted through the cracked door in his room. Over the *duddle-duddle* of the Stump-Jumper outboard Joe yelled, "Come on, Remmy. Les go."

He grabbed the oversized briefcase, placed it in a large dry bag, and closed the door behind him.

Joe stood high in the front of the boat. "Thought you was in a hurry?"

The fresh morning air mixed with the smell of gas. Remmy eyed Bear in the stern holding onto the till of the Stump-Jumper. "You gonna drive this thing?"

"Okeedokee," said Bear. "Untie dem ropes and let's git."

He threw the ropes off and jumped in. The pirogue was gone. Dad must have already slunk away.

Bear steered them through the swamp using a new route. Habitual routes could get you found. The Stump-Jumper blades slurped in and out of the water as they slid over roots. They maintained a steady, though rumpled ten knots, squeezing through cypress knees into a narrow channel in the grass that widened to the main bayou. Bear cocked the Stump-Jumper out, tilted the Merc in, and soon they rocketed through the bayou at thirty-five knots.

A misty vapor coated the milk-chocolate water; the cotton shroud seemed untouched by the boat, the only trace of pushed water a distant slosh on the bank. Voodoo ghosts and Cajun stories reared in Remmy's mind. Would he be John Lafitte and conquer all? He needed a voodoo doll with Phipps's suit coat and Army camouflaged pants. A pin here and a pin there and his pursuers would crumple while he got the magic treasure.

He tapped Joe on the shoulder. "Does Aunt Lola still throw the bones?"

Joe yelled over his shoulder. "Dat you can be sure of, you. Last night dey say you gone have some kind a day today."

"What kind, good or bad?"

Joe shrugged, "Da bones not say. Maybe dats up to you." He laughed a high pitched cackle and ducks took flight.

Remmy rubbed the gris-gris bag in his pocket, once again feeling the need for good luck. The red flannel felt smooth and the contents of the gator tooth and his baby eyetooth chattered together. Taking his fingers out he smelled the rose petals, mustard and cayenne, with a hint of olive oil, all mixing together to ease his anxiety. A thought struck him odd, though. Gris-gris meant gray-gray in French, and he was attempting to balance the black magic of the Makers and Takers to prevent gray goo.

The mist cleared, a dock materialized, and the boat glided in, the motor killed to a rebound of silence. They emptied out and walked toward a dented, olive-green Ford Fairlane station wagon. The trees sprouted soldiers, and Remmy's hope of a good day from da bones ended.

CHAPTER 35

Dan noted the familiar Wi-Fi trailer park as Sam drove around the next bend. But Sam didn't park outside. He drove through the fence gates of the trailer park and stopped about halfway down the main drag in front of a beige fifth-wheel trailer. Colorful Chinese lanterns, Christmas lights, and several Disney characters hung from the front awning. Green AstroTurf covered the ground beneath the awning with a picnic table parked in the middle, giving the feel of springtime. Six place settings with Wookiee faces festooned a Star Wars motif tablecloth. A blond woman bent over the barbeque and tended the spicy smoking contents. The smell made Dan's mouth water.

The woman faced them at the sound of the closing van doors. "Wondered when ya'll were coming. Didn't want the sausage to burn." Her voice crooned honey and cream southern aristocracy, and her face, though wrinkled and tanned, still gave Dan pause: A previous belle of the ball.

"Aunt Bernadette," Lisette said, "meet my friends, Sam, Ron, and Dan."

She held out her hand to each, and said, "Enchanté," and bowed her head with a slight knee bend that would have been a curtsy had she worn a dress.

Greeting Dan last, she winked. "I have heard about you, cher."

"Oh," he said, wondering what else Lisette had told her.

"Auntie, you promised," blurted Lisette.

"I promised I wouldn't embarrass *you*." She flourished the tongs at

Lisette, as if to parry any response, and faced the men. "Hope y'all are hungry. There's black-eyed peas, rice, okra and turnip greens, andouille sausage and spicy shrimp. Sweet tea's in the pitcher, Dixie beer and wine in the cooler under the table. It's such a nice day I thought we could sit outside. Don't get many young men come to see me nowadays."

"Yeah," Lisette said, "she likes to see 'em sweat!"

"Child! What's got into you?"

The two women traded squinty-eyed frowns.

Sausages sizzled. Paper Chinese lanterns bumped against Goofy and Mickey.

Sam cleared his throat and Ron shifted his feet.

Both women smiled and broke out laughing.

Bernadette plucked the sausages off the grill and while she cut them into bite-sized pieces Lisette hugged her waist from behind and kissed the side of her head. "How you been Auntie? I sure have missed you."

Sam and Ron gazed at the sky and shook their head before they sat down at the picnic table.

"Can I help with something?" Dan asked.

"Oh, a gentleman. I do approve, Lisette." She handed him the bowl of cut sausages and another piled high with pink shrimp. "Thank you, Daniel. Please take these to the table and sit down. We can handle the rest."

Dan liked Bernadette already. His mom had called him Daniel, said she named him after the biblical Daniel. He hadn't read the bible in ages. He did remember Daniel survived the lions. Did Wookies and beautiful Marines count?

Bernadette nodded at Lisette, "If it's too hot out here we can go inside with the air conditioning. What do you think, dear?"

"It's okay. I like to see 'em sweat, too."

"We can eat out here," Sam said, "but we should probably go inside for the main event."

Lisette and Bernadette brought the rest of the food and sat down. The air dripped with odors of grilled meat, butter, fresh vegetables, and a touch of Bernadette's perfume, similar to one of the girls at Dan's Denver office.

Bernadette raised her hands out like a conductor of an orchestra. "Don't just sit there. Dig in. We don't stand on ceremony. And about the main event, they don't bother us trailer trash over here, so you can speak freely, outside."

Lisette pulled a couple of Dixie beers out and gave one to Dan. He caught her eye and passed the bottle over to Sam. "Think I'll have iced tea, thanks. Need to stay fresh for the afternoon."

Sam and Ron nodded in agreement. Bernadette grabbed the bottle and popped the top. "A cold Dixie never clouded the mind." She chugged a third of the bottle before setting it down with a big, "Ahh."

"So," Dan said, "you're a Walt Disney fan, a Wookiee nut, a great cook, a computer whiz, and what else?" He paused. "Oh yeah. A spook for the Army."

Bernadette sipped the beer, swirled it in her mouth and swallowed. "Lisette has looser lips than I thought."

Lisette shook her head, her mouth open, palms up, like a child accused of stealing cookies.

"Okay, sorry, my dear. But to set things right, it's a Navy spook." She frowned at Dan, and added, "Retired."

"You had to have computer expertise, or why would we be here. I figured a connection with the service so we could get through their local jammers, and you had to be in the clandestine service to be close to these guys." He waved at Sam and Ron. "And, this close to a bunch of Army guys ... Two out of three's not bad."

"To be fair we work a lot with all the services, so you might even say two and a half right." She smiled at him, more a wan grin of temporary conciliation.

Something else. What's she hiding? Maybe he stood closer to lions than he thought. He decided to test her. "Eighteen thousand, one hundred and eighty-one."

"Dihedral prime." She smiled at him. He smiled back. A dihedral prime number looked the same in the mirror, upside down, or upside down in a mirror: 18181. Working with Bernadette was going to be fun.

"Danny boy, you are the right man for the mission. I'm impressed," said Sam through bites of food.

Sam's compliment sounded flat.

Lisette's eyes twinkled and she half chuckled, "I told you he was good. But you guys had to keep picking at him."

Dan tracked from Sam to Lisette to Bernadette. *Okay, what's the big secret?*

Bernadette grinned slyly. "Alright, Daniel. Finish up, and let's get inside. Your little toy will work much better out of the heat. Or, you might want to play with something a bit more ... powerful."

Washing down a particularly hot sausage and shrimp combo, he shook his head.

Retired, my ass. She still likes to keep secrets.

CHAPTER 36

"It's all right, Bear," Remmy said when the soldiers surrounded them. Bear could easily take out several of the soldiers, but Remmy didn't want him killed in the process.

Joe glanced at the bayou and whispered to Remmy, "Don't worry, you. Dad got gone."

A tall, lean soldier with serious, gray eyes and silver leaves on his shirt lapels said, "Mr. St. James, I'm Lieutenant Colonel Hargrove. We don't want to harm any of you. Please, get rid of your weapons."

Remmy nodded for them to obey. Three handguns, a shotgun, and several knives splattered down in the mud, the last Bear's pearl-handled, ten-inch Bowie knife.

Hargrove raised an eyebrow at the haul, but studied Remmy's briefcase. "Anything else?"

Remmy tapped the briefcase. "Nothing in here but the end of the world. But you've been to Xoflex, so you already know that."

"Why don't you let me hold onto that? We'll keep it in a safe place until we can x-ray it. Let's go."

The Colonel held the briefcase at arm's length and motioned with his handgun toward the rear entrance of the Xoflex building. A short walk inside and they stared at four soldiers and a haggard Phipps who said, "Hi, Remmy. Glad you could make the party."

"I'm a bit more than fashionably late, but it is the South."

The Colonel separated Remmy from Lola, Joe and Bear, and walked him down the corridor with the pear-shaped Phipps at his side. The others were herded in the opposite direction.

Remmy called out, "I'll be back, Auntie. Don't you worry."

"You better, you. Or we come git you."

Remmy said to the Colonel, "If you hurt them—"

Hargrove cut him off. "They're going to get a good hot meal and a nice soft mattress tonight. Nothing more."

"The Army is here to help us, Remmy," Phipps mumbled. "They only need some answers. That's all."

The Colonel gently laid the briefcase onto a conveyor belt. He pressed a button, the motor groaned and the briefcase moved into an enclosed housing. He peered at the x-ray image. "What's in the tubes?"

"Plastique of course."

Phipps shook his head and rubbed his forehead. "Remmy, please."

Remmy eyed Phipps but spoke to the colonel, "Something's not right in lower Louisiana, is it, Colonel? The rest of the world is fucked, too. Maybe it all started right here, perhaps with me. Is that what you think?"

The colonel motioned him to enter the boardroom.

A cadre of soldiers and business-suited men sat around several computers and TVs. The humming and clattering office noises continued, but murmuring and hand gestures ended when Remmy and Phipps entered. Someone turned the TV's down.

An overly tall, thin man stood and approached Remmy. His sallow, acne-pocked face seemed to fit with the rock-sharp cheekbones and jaw. He wore a lavender suit and dark purple tie. "Welcome, Mr. St. James. We weren't expecting you quite so soon. But we are glad to have you." His precise words exuded confidence, touched with a scant Texas accent.

When they shook hands, strong boney fingers completely enveloped Remmy's hand like a huge eagle's talons.

Where had Remmy seen him before?

"I'm John Sinclair."

Remmy nodded and closed his eyes in memory. "Right. Of course. You're the Texas center whose knee got blown out in the NCAA championship with LSU."

The man smiled, lips only, eyes cold steel, voice flat. "That was a long time ago."

Remmy felt the need to have this man like him. "Yeah, but you were a hell of a roundballer. What happened after that?"

The man waved his hand, and the grin disappeared. "Another time, Mr. St. James."

"Remmy. Call me Remmy."

"Remmy, then. Right now we have more pressing issues."

He held his hand out for the briefcase, and the colonel handed to him.

"So what's in here?"

"I'm sure you already know." Remmy glanced around at the various monitors showing the outside perimeter, oil wells in Alaska, the Regulator and Makers rooms, and one with a red and blue Chevron on the left side of the screen, Octex-Penta's logo.

CHAPTER 37

"If I knew I would not have asked." Sinclair's smile was definitely gone, and Remmy remembered the name: The son of the oil mogul that founded Octex-Penta.

The side of Remmy's mouth ticked. *So much for getting him to like me.* Still, he wanted to see how much Sinclair knew. So he waited.

Sinclair's eyes glanced at one of the computer screens, the x-ray of the briefcase. "I'd say they are sampling tubes, likely of the Makers and Regulators. Only they're not Makers now, are they? They destroy oil. Perhaps you were cooking up a new batch to take to your Arab friend?" He glanced at Remmy who frowned but remained silent.

"It looks pretty bad for you right now Mr. St. James. And if you don't start talking—"

"Come on, Remmy," Phipps blurted. "They already know the Pseudomonas is contaminated. They think we're trying to control the world oil market, in cahoots with the Chinese or the Russians or other nonsense. Please, tell them what you know. They want to prevent more destruction. Haven't you seen the news lately? My God! Anarchy is not the word."

Remmy surveyed Phipps's worried face and decided.

"First, I'm not in cahoots with any Arab. I know *I'm* trying to help, but I'm not quite sure about Mr. Sinclair. I need his assurance that my friends and family will be released. They were only giving me a ride and protecting me. They have no idea what is truly going on."

Sinclair's eyes remained cold. "Okay . . . Remmy. First, you give *us* something. Please have a seat."

Remmy sat. Sinclair's long arms guided Remmy's chair around in front of a monitor. The screen filled with a face.

"Do you recognize this man?"

"Of course. Abdullah El-Hamain. He's the one that screwed with OPEC."

Sinclair clicked the keypad with a long index finger. The screen showed a color photograph with Remmy shaking Abdullah's hands in front of the Xoflex logo on one of the Maker's vats. Abdullah carried a briefcase identical to the one Remmy had given Sinclair.

"Oh come now . . . Remmy. It's quite apparent you and Abdullah are old friends. He even buys his briefcases at the same place. So you see, I don't know whose side *you* are on."

Sinclair spun Remmy's chair around to face him.

Remmy tried to make his gaze confident. But it was difficult looking into the predatory eyes of this huge man waiting to sink his talons into the soft underbelly of his prey.

How the hell did he get that photo? I destroyed the files two weeks ago.

"Yeah. I knew him. But he's no long lost friend like you seem to think. He needed our product to help with U.A.E.'s flagging oil wells. We did business. He left. End of story."

Sinclair's mouth twisted and he glared. Ugly, but confident.

Remmy's thoughts raced: *What kind of game's he playing? Octex-Penta wanted me to help Abdullah. Is it for Phipps's benefit?*

Remmy glanced at Phipps, who averted his gaze.

Must be for Phipps. Play along.

"Okay. He contacted me a month ago and said he wanted more product and would be visiting the first of this month."

Sinclair's lips flexed slightly, a hawk's smile.

"Look," continued Remmy. "I think this guy contaminated our cultures. That's why I came here today: to prove it."

Phipps studied the floor, shook his head, and sidled away from Remmy.

Sinclair clasped his talons in front of his face and squinted over them. "Come now, Remmy. Abdullah's a businessman, an oil man. He would need someone who knew about nanobots and DNA modification of bacteria to do the things he's done. He would need someone . . . someone exactly like you."

"Right. I'd partner with this guy to destroy the oil wells of customers that paid me to help them out. Really? I want to continue doing business with these guys for a long time. I want success, not failure. I like my job and," he waved his hands around, "all the perks. Why would I destroy this great lifestyle and the oil that made me rich?"

"Power can be more of an enticement than money. Though, Abdullah could easily triple what you have here. He has done well in Dubai."

"You're talking to *me* about power! I would never leave Louisiana. My family has been here for generations. Speaking of my family, I told you what I know. Now why don't you let them go?"

Sinclair pondered Remmy. "Okay, Remmy. We will let your family return to their . . . swamp." He spat the word "swamp" like a curse word. "I'm not sure I believe you. But we can easily pick up your family again, should we need them."

He pointed a finger and one of his men walked out of the room. Remmy's chair spun around and he faced the monitor again. Lola, Joe and Bear were being escorted out of the building into a waiting van.

After the van drove off, the view switched to a video of Remmy weeks ago in his clandestine sampling of Regulators and Makers.

How did they get that video? He'd shut down all the cameras.

Sinclair's hands gripped the tops of Remmy's shoulders from behind, and his alien countenance reflected in the screen. "Guess you missed that other video system we advised Mr. Phipps to add. As you can see, Mr. St. James, we have a lot of incriminating evidence that you are involved in bioterrorism."

Remmy tried to stand but the man held him fast. "Hey, you know why I got those samples. I had to figure out what happened."

"So you say. Perhaps our Homeland Security representatives can find out for sure."

Hands pried open Remmy's eyes and sprayed a stinging liquid into them.

He tasted sweet honey, the room blurred, and darkness extinguished the sparks of fear.

CHAPTER 38

Dan sighed and gawked, feeling like a kid with a new toy. *So this was their secret.* Sam and Lisette grinned at each other.

Bernadette's state-of-the-art, multi-screened array computer stared him in the face, and before long he flexed the new found power, his laptop a distant memory, closed on the couch. Once into Xoflex's security system, he found a new batch of electronic hounds sniffing his fingerprints. Bernadette sat beside him, typing on a separate keyboard, keeping the dogs at bay while he tried to unravel the puzzle that had stumped him for weeks.

He knew Remmy St. James had files on Maracaibo, Texas, and Alaska. Where had they gone? Using one of Bernadette's special programs she named Snoop Doggy (for an elderly lady she did have unusual taste in music), he had uncovered parts of erased files from the hard drive. He found nibblets left by a shredder program, like names of bacteria: "E. Coli" or "Pseudomonas." Sometimes he found sentences, such as "East Texas test site was successful." But mostly he found gibberish.

Three codes kept recurring, imbedded in several files: 'S_Am1,' 'US1,' and 'N3.'

Bernadette groaned. "If you got what you want we better get outta here or—" She squinted at the screen.

"Little Pac-Man is right on my ass." She hit a key and the entire array went dark.

"Sorry, Daniel. Had to skedaddle. Get what you needed?"

"Kind of."

"That doesn't sound too promising."

"Someone, I'd say St. James, ran a shredder after he deleted the files."

"Yeah, but Snoop Doggy should have found something."

"Mostly ghosts and shells. A few coded initials keep recurring, but I didn't have time to get anything else."

"What's a shell?" Sam asked.

Dan's head twitched to the side. He'd forgotten about Sam. "It's a piece of a file that the erasure program missed. But they're very fragmented. St. James ran an excellent shredder. The ones I found had only initials and letters and a few partial sentences."

"Anything on Maracaibo, Texas, or Alaska oil wells?" Lisette said.

"Maybe."

He sat for a minute, frowning.

"You wanna share?" Sam said

"Yeah. Okay. It's kinda weird, so bear with me. I found three recurrent codes: 'S_Am1' , 'US1', and 'N3.' 'S_Am' might be short for South America, and the '1' . . . could be for the first trial there. Maybe Maracaibo?"

"So 'US1' is Texas?" Lisette said.

He nodded.

"And 'N3' ?" Sam asked.

He sat back and observed the ceiling. "The 'S' in 'S_Am' was South, so maybe 'N' is North. Alaska maybe?"

He pondered Sam and Lisette. "Weak huh?"

"I don't know." Sam said. "It *does* match the files he had on his desk: Maracaibo, Texas and Alaska. Though, following your previous logic, if 'N3' is Alaska that would imply that there were three northern wells. So what were the other two?"

"I think the only way we're going to find out is to ask Remmy St. James."

Sam nodded and stood. "We received good intell on his possible location a couple of days ago. I've been wanting to check it out. Guess it's time. Ron and I will go. Lisette, you stay here and keep an eye out while they try to get something else. If you get something let me know."

Dan shifted in his chair, thinking of being with Lisette and her matchmaker aunt. "I can take care of myself. If you need Lisette, she doesn't need to stay here to watch after me."

Sam had a foot out the door when he swung his head back. "Who says she's watching out for you? Bernadette is one of our most valuable assets."

The door closed.

The van drove away, gravel crunching and engine groan fading. The blank array of plasma screens beckoned Dan to crawl inside and escape.

He flinched when the array lit up and computer keys clicked next to him. Bernadette was typing furiously, her eyes locked on the screen. "You heard the man. Let's get to work."

Lisette's warm hands massaged the tight bands on the back of his neck. The faint odor of Bernadette's perfume seemed distant to Lisette's musky smell and hint of gun oil. He resisted at first. She persisted and her capable kneading relaxed the tension from his neck to his brain. The number three kept floating into his mind, changing from green to red.

Marci jumped into his head. *Jesus!* He pushed her out. Jeff replaced her. They were playing one-on-one in the driveway when Jeff was twelve, and Jeff sunk an impossible long shot, beaming at Dan afterward. That moment had been a milestone. Soon after, Jeff became more of his own person, less a child. And now, Dan felt he had no control over Jeff's decisions.

He took a deep breath and concentrated on the screen. He had to end the fighting.

His fingers became a direct extension of his thoughts and moved over the keyboard like a fast-forward video of a spider spinning its web. A partial name in a file pushed him faster: ". . . Hamain . . ."

CHAPTER 39

A day earlier, René bumped the car onto the median around another fake roadblock—nothing but empty highway patrol cars and cement construction dividers. Abdullah had nearly cheered hours before when René told him they could move to their headquarters. The ride smoothed again and the trees flipped by, the morning sun fluttering into the car like a strobe light.

The television message from President Streeter had prodded something deep in Abdullah. Not a gentle prod; more like a jolt of electricity that had kept him awake most of the night and still coursed through him as the trees oscillated by. Finally he traveled to his destiny, to raise a pulpit for his message. The masses needed a real leader, not the bumbling Streeter. After Streeter's idiocy, they would bow down to Abdullah, once they heard his revelation. He would show them the real reason why their world had been turned inside out, why no more gas existed for their cars, no oil to heat their homes. The military probably had a hint—not the lowly fighting men placed in the fields as fodder. They didn't have a "need to know." Rumors would spread from on high, though: "The wells finally dried up." or "The Saudis have been lying all along about the reserves." or "They are trying to up the price of oil again." Moving to the top of the information ladder, the so-called "higher authority" would not want those below to know the truth.

Abdullah had experience with these "special" people, many of them the very wealthiest people in the world—his father's cronies whose monetary sleight of hand ruled the rulers. They made sure even the President remained uninformed so he had "plausible deniability," and could stay in power so the "special" people could continue to pull his strings.

Streeter was not a real leader. A real leader took responsibility for anything in his command. Anything.

The car slowed and turned onto a dirt road. Abdullah lowered the window and spat outside, disgusted at the last twenty years of American presidential rhetoric. A cloak of humid hot air enveloped him. Dust silted the window edge. He raised the window. A glint of metal in the distance caught his eye, but did not register right away; his mind unable to climb off the treadmill of racing thoughts.

The ache in his head from the concussion unveiled everything to him, with thoughts so clear and quick he felt like a god on a higher plain of understanding. Everything made sense: how the politicians sidestepped the truth and used alarmist tactics to shift blame. In the Cold War they'd blamed "the communists" or "the Russians." "For God's sake, man, don't you know the Communists are trying to bring down the American way." Now it was "the Terrorists," "the Iraqis," or "the Ring of Jackals." And they targeted more than just Americans. So the politicians coined the term a Global War on Terror. Keep the focus on "them," the bad guys, the conspiracy against "us" the good guys. But somewhere between "them" and "us," the truth got lost.

The truth was politicians wanted power. Needed it. Power needed money. And money needed oil.

He would stop them dead in their tracks: the politicians, the terrorists, the power mongers. He would show the masses that the only conspiracy was parked in their garages.

They would worship him as their savior, the one who had shown them *real* truth: that he, Abdullah El-Hamain had spoiled the Profit Party that big oil and big auto enjoyed for the last century. He alone had brought them to their knees *and* their global political machine fueled by petroleum and automobiles. He would take away their puppet and the strings that made him dance. No oil, no power. No power, no strings.

The rolling hills out the window stretched for miles without any sign. They were surely using all their resources, confident they could find him and that their vast technological resources could reverse any damage, believing they would soon ride high in the money saddle.

Where were they? In days their war machines would halt without fuel. But his machines would not.

Black smoke roiled into the air a few miles ahead, smacked him back to reality. This might spell trouble.

"René?"

"I believe that is our people."

The previous glint of metal now registered. Could René be wrong?

The car slowed and came to a barrier of pine trees across the road. Three men in green fatigues materialized from the woods, moved towards them, and pointed AK-47's at the limousine.

"I'm sorry, sir. They should be expecting us."

René's window descended and he dangled out an ID card. The closest man inspected them and lowered his gun and said in an east Texas twang, "We were expecting y'all a few days ago. 'Bout time."

They pulled the fallen trees back with ropes. René drove through.

Abdullah eyed one of the soldiers. "Are you sure about these people?"

"I believe they are good people, sir, though I have not met them all."

Abdullah sat in silence trying to regain his thoughts. But the previous clarity eluded him. He would have preferred Tamara to do this. She could spot an imposter instantly. He should be in Dubai, enjoying the warm salt water on his toes and having a gin and tonic.

He glared at this land of dead trees and Texans that spoke like Streeter. "Are they ready?"

He had instructed René to prepare a television announcement. They would tap into the local news media camped out at an east Texas oil refinery and use their broadcasting equipment. The world would get news, and so much more.

"We will be ready in another hour, sir. We need a bit more power for the feed override. Several generators and a tanker will arrive shortly from Gulfport, Mississippi. They had to corral them from the Katrina relief, but sacrifices have to be made."

Abdullah winced at the word Katrina, but nodded. "We will make it up to them in the coming months. They will be the first to get power in the New Age."

The car stopped and they stepped out into a scene reminiscent of a secret military command center Abdullah had visited in Iraq, only without the uniforms. A large metal Quonset hut stood before them, radar-reflective camouflage netting draped over the top to fool any snoops in the sky. Inside buzzed a multitude of people and two large computers. TVs and radios blared. Papers fluttered from a constant breeze of fans and air conditioners. An underlying deep thrum vibrated his chest, a hint of the powerful biodiesel generators that ran day and night. Tentacles of power cords ran along the floor, temporarily covered by mats while technicians worked furiously to organize the wires into more neatly bunched conduits. Canvas and plastic floorcovering crackled underfoot.

It had taken months of skulking and secrecy to gather here, hidden in the backwoods, but still close to the oil fields. Not perfect, but they had all worked in even more stoic conditions, having chased corporate greed and pollution around the world. This time was different: they ran the show, the end game.

Abdullah felt tentative at first, suspicious of all the strangers, and worried they would not see him as the ruthless leader Tamara would surely have been. But many smiled at him, a few even saluted. His heart leapt at recognizing old friends: Johann Jorgensen, a huge Swede who'd been part of the crew that confronted whaling in Japan; Rema Katau, an eloquent Indonesian woman who battled pollution of the Ganges River; Jenna Hoffman, who'd lost an arm when netters rammed her dolphin-protecting boat and she fell overboard. Many had lost friends and family to cancer from pollution, or suicide or homicide from loss of jobs due to the price of oil. Some needed payback. Others liked the adrenaline surge of a war between good and evil, knowing they supported the good. There were so many—so, so many. It touched him to lead this group who cared so much.

So many months ago he had wondered how the world would view his destruction of their way of life: the end of oil and all its ramifications on human existence. Now, he did not care.

I will force the world into a new era: green power, not black. I will show them their ignorance, and make the world better in a decade, not a century. Sacrifices will be made, yes, but in the end, the earth will be a better place. Human beings will live in harmony with the rest of the planet, not decimate it like a plague of oversized alien locusts.

He sequestered himself in a small cubicle and read over his speech for the last time. Soon he would go on the air to millions. *They will understand. I will make them.*

Minutes before their broadcast, two biodiesel generators quit. No power, no broadcast. They finally fixed them in the afternoon, and the black clouds that had threatened all day let loose a lightning display like he'd never seen. One bolt destroyed a generator, fried a minicomputer, and downed a tree that ripped through the camouflage covering. Several of the technicians had hearing problems after the deafening clap of thunder.

What would he do now?

CHAPTER 40

Jeff squinted into the morning sun and wondered how the U.S. Army got into this predicament in eastern Texas. Yesterday things had quieted down, so Jeff's company commander had sent out burial details to collect their fallen comrades. Sniper shots sprinkled in, but then nothing. The dozers and front-end loaders rolled in to move the rest of the unidentifiable bodies into three mass graves.

There were problems, aside from the nauseating smell. The initial operators couldn't stomach the sight of the dead bodies flopping into the loader at odd angles and various states of decomposition and dismemberment. The first operator jumped out of the cab while the loader remained in forward gear. After the ten-foot jump he threw up, and then stumbled fifty yards back to the gate on what later turned out to be two broken ankles. Jeff had opened the front gate to the stumbling man whose wide-eyed derangement reminded him of his own inner turmoil.

The loader he'd jumped from remained in forward gear and rolled into the pit with the other bodies. It took an hour to get it out. First, two "volunteers" had to unload the bodies out of the big front-end shovel by hand, literally piece by piece. Those two had been butchers before the war, though they preferred the term "meat organizers." They said it was just another slab of meat to them. But when they returned, Jeff had caught their eyes: lost.

They had plenty of MREs; he heard they tasted ten times better than the old C-rats. How nice. Another grenade attack had taken out two water buffaloes and half their fuel depot. The choppers would not return—no air support or reconnaissance. Bottom line—they'd be well fed when they died. Or starve if they tired of MREs.

The CO ordered a ground unit for recon, water and fuel.

Jeff raised his hand first to volunteer for the recon detail. No burying for him. His platoon commander asked for Unmanned Aerial Vehicles to fly over and video the area. All UAVs were en route from Iraq. Make do with what you have. Move out.

The five tanks had too little fuel left for a reconnaissance mission. That meant Humvees. Jeff asked for the turret position.

He'd studied the M998 High Mobility Multipurpose Wheeled Vehicle, HMMWV, or Humvee, the most commonly deployed tactical vehicle used by the U.S. armed forces. It had originally been designed for the changing nature of war—urban and guerilla conflicts required speed, compactness, and agility.

The urban guerillas developed a weapon that often defeated hundred thousand dollar vehicles and a squad of the best trained soldiers armed to the teeth—the IED. It cost less than a GI's CD.

To avoid being soldier coffins, the soft sides and underbelly of the Humvees were reinforced with lightweight armor or FRAG protection kits, adding a mere seven-hundred fifty pounds and another fifty grand. Special Forces and Marines opted for these vehicles to maintain light weight and maneuverability. The Army opted for a heavier beast, the Up-Armored Humvee, UAH, fully armored from the factory, weighing about two-thousand pounds more than the original. The next generation, the MRAP, Mine Resistant Ambush Protected vehicle, was a magnitude better, what every soldier wanted, but a cheap one went for a mil, and hen's teeth were more common.

To one-up the million dollar Humvee improvements, the guerillas built a better IED, up to a whopping twenty bucks. They used a kid to detonate it—no charge.

The CO traveled in the one MRAP. Jeff's platoon consisted of five Humvees, the point vehicle an UAH: Jeff's assignment. Thank God. Maybe the combination of Jeff volunteering and grieving over his friend's death had colored the platoon commander's choice. Jeff didn't care.

He rode in the best seat of the house—unobstructed vision and fresh air, if he held his sleeve over his nose when passing the putrid mass graves. Also, if an IED exploded under his Humvee, he could jump out and run, though he must jump fast to avoid being crushed if the vehicle flipped. Despite having the M240B, 7.62mm machine gun in the turret, or "two-forty Bravo," he also carried backup: a Beretta handgun and his M-16. He felt naked without the rifle, but there was no room in the turret.

Jeff's turret position was critical. He had to be vigilant, constantly searching with and without binoculars. IEDs could hide anywhere out here—fresh piles of dirt from exploded ordinance, abandoned vehicles, dead animals and garbage, not to mention the trees and bushes. He also searched for any signs of an operator, a person watching the road and ready to detonate the IED with radio frequencies from a cell phone, walkie-talkie, or a MacGyver-rigged doorbell. He saw no one. The final possibility remained—a monofilament line stretched from detonator to a tree. How the hell could he see that?

Something glinted in the trees ahead. He whispered into the mike, "Something in the tree. Two-hundred yards at two o'clock. Kick in the jammer."

The jammer blocked the most common IED radio frequencies, but occasionally screwed with the communication between Humvees.

"Ten four. Can you eliminate operator?"

He hammered the tree with the 240 Bravo. Chunks of bark and leaves spewed out, and a man with a gray tee shirt and jeans fell. The man hit the ground and a deer carcass fifty feet from Jeff's Humvee exploded. The explosion toppled pine trees and rocked the vehicle. If they'd gone another thirty feet: Wheels up. End of mission.

Despite the helmet and ear phones, his ears rang. He felt something wet on his cheek. Had he been hit? He picked off a chunk of deer fur complete with hide and blood-stained yellow fat.

"Shit." He threw it away and wiped his hand on his shirt.

He adjusted his body armor and something pricked him. A shard of deer antler stuck into his left deltoid. He plucked it out and winced. It reminded him of a toothpick, only with a handle of mottled brown deer antler. Pulling his shirt revealed a tiny nick in the skin, an inch outside the protection of the armor. He dropped the splinter into his shirt pocket. Future war stories.

"Hey, Jeff. You alright?" The voice in the headphones sounded far away and had cotton in his mouth.

"Yeah. Got fragged by a deer antler, but no real damage. You need to turn up the volume. Hardly hear you."

"Got it up all the way, buddy. The blast must have affected your hearing. Sure you're okay?"

"Yeah, I'm fine. You sound closer already." He wondered how long his hearing deficit would have lasted without the earphones.

He peered down into the vehicle. "How about you guys? Everyone okay?"

"Yeah, Lonnie got a nick in his ear. Only had one window cracked for air. Frag must have come through that millimeter. Won't do that again. See anything else?"

Jeff scanned the forward perimeter. "Nah. But they probably know we're coming now."

The intercom got quiet. Jeff adjusted the shoulder holster again, took a sip of water and a bite of a food bar. The quiet headset continued. Someone pondered options.

Jeff thought, too, about the three Humvees all stopped and idled, Jeff's in the middle. Sitting ducks.

"We should move," he said into the mike. "We're easy targets out here."

As if the other Humvees had heard his intercom, their engines roared. One drove off to the right, the other to the left.

Spread out. Good move. Though, exploding IEDs would shred the sides of those other Humvees. He glassed the area. He had to protect his buddies as well as his own skin.

A flare and smoke trail headed straight to the Humvee on the right flank. A faint whoosh sounded seconds before the vehicle disappeared into the yellow and white light of an RPG explosion. He raised his arm as a shield. Heat and vibration rippled over him.

He lowered his arm. In the burning Humvee's turret, scarecrow arms feathered and flapped with flames. He hadn't known JJ very well. A good poker player, straight-faced and lucky. Until now.

A strangled scream, flailing fire, and finally a quiet burning hulk. Pitch-black smoke streamed from orange flames licking out of the turret and windows. The smell of burning flesh caused a sour eructation of bacon and egg MRE.

Their vehicle surged forward, fast and erratic, like Ricky Bobby had taken over the wheel, determined to get to the tree line before a rocket of death found one of their windows.

He thought of JJ and fired the machine gun, straight ahead, right, left, up, down. He mowed down saplings, cut off tree branches, whatever it took to clear everything in his path. His eyes widened and jerked to each target like following pinballs. "Take that, you fuckers! Eat my lead! Die! Die! D—"

A hard yank on his pant leg. "Jeff, cool it! We need the ammo."

But he couldn't stop. His finger gripped the trigger as if the harder he squeezed the more likely he'd kill. Kill them all!

A fist pounded into his thigh.

"Shit!" The pain in his leg broke the trance and he released the trigger. He reached for his hand gun, retaliation a necessity for such pain, but caught himself.

"Goddamn it!" He pounded his fist against the side of the turret. "They burned up JJ. All of them. Dead. Burned alive."

He shook his head, closed his eyes and tears streamed down his cheeks. His words came out soft and unbelieving. "Burned alive. Fucking burned alive."

In his headset he heard a firm baritone, "Corporal, we gotta keep going. If you can't handle it, let me know. I can send someone else up."

He gritted his teeth, backhanded the tears off his cheeks and shook his head. "I'm okay, sir. Let's get going. Get 'er done."

Peering into the dust made by his 240 bravo he saw the mesquite and pine trees thin out into an open space with no vehicles. Nothing moved. Maybe that was it. Yet, something told him as soon as they moved forward another surprise waited.

CHAPTER 41

After waiting patiently for ten minutes, the driver gunned the engine. The UAH crashed into the first line of young pine trees and they broke through onto the rolling hills of mesquite and tall grass.

Immediately, Jeff's head snapped right from a Pac-Man ninety-degree left turn. They traveled twenty yards and whipped around to the right.

Pwang. Jeff's helmeted head banged onto the turret shield with the sharp turn and he almost lost the binoculars.

"What are you guys doing?" he yelled into the microphone. "Just do a little jag here and there. You're going to tip us over if you make one of those crazy-assed turns at a ditch."

Ditches and dips abounded, so even though the severity of the turns lessened, they traveled so fast it felt like a roller coaster ride. Good luck avoiding any IED's at this speed.

Another two miles and they came to a clearing and stopped before they punched out into the open. Jeff's headset crackled, "Corporal, which way?"

He scanned the field: a low flat valley of light green grass with winter killed platinum tips, a grizzled mother earth. In the middle sat a burned-out shell of an olive Chevy Avalanche, its charred remains alongside freshly formed ruts through the grass. The grass grew so tall that it hid the lower half of the truck. The grass moved. Was it the wind?

"Stay left behind the trees. In fact, backup about twenty yards so we can't be s— Wait!"

The movement in the grass proved to be nothing. Movement on the other side of the valley looked more suspicious. Could be a bayou. The green grass indicated low lying land, and beyond that probably water. But the line of the valley rose to dry land, and shadows moved on the other side. He focused in with the binoculars and saw a large Quonset hut covered in camouflage netting. Men walked in and out.

"Lieutenant, you better get up here and take a look."

Second Lieutenant Robison, known to the men as "LT," stood up in the turret after Jeff wriggled down. LT scanned with the binoculars. "Huh." The statement implied they had found something useful and not altogether unexpected.

LT's silhouette, frozen in the hole of the turret against the blue sky, appeared picturesque to Jeff, peering up from the dark interior. LT ticked his fingernails on the stock of the 240 bravo, mirroring Jeff's thoughts: What the hell were they going to do now?

LT wriggled down into the Humvee, indicating with his hand for Jeff to go up. "Corporal, keep an eye out. We're going to back off into the shadows. Let us know if we go too far."

They parked about fifteen yards in the shadows of the trees, still with a nice window to observe. Jeff heard the radio conversation below. Low murmurs suddenly flared louder. "But sir, we need more backup." Then a resigned, "Yes sir. Aye, aye sir."

The pit of his stomach twisted. *They want us to stay here. Probably no backup. Great.*

The intercom crackled, "Listen up. We need three men from each squad to hop out with me and move forward for recon."

Jeff felt the need to move, leave this big target and stretch his legs. Cover abounded in the bush. If necessary he could hide—a much smaller target than the Humvee.

"I'll go." He slipped off the headset helmet and jumped down, out of the turret.

The other two Humvees motored about thirty yards on either side of them, one down in a depression and the other in a cluster of pine trees. The side doors opened and men stepped out and walked toward Jeff's UAH.

LT got out, gave Jeff his other helmet and the M-16, and they formed up.

"We'll have backup in about two hours," said LT. "In the meantime we need to gather as much information on that camp across the valley as possible. Sergeant Rector will take you four around to the left. I'll take the other five right. Use only the walkie-talkies for comm. No radio. Switch to alpha two-one before we leave. That's alpha two-one. After fifteen minutes—up five, the next fifteen go down seven. Keep repeating. Got it, Sergeant?"

Rector nodded, "Yes sir. Alpha two-one. Up five in fifteen, down seven in fifteen."

"Okay. On my mark synchronize watches at twenty after. Ready. Five, four, three, two, one, mark. Everyone got it?"

They all nodded.

"Keep your heads down, eyes open. Anything new let me know, otherwise check in every hour. Move out."

Jeff thanked God he was with Rector. LT had never seen combat. Rector had been in Afghanistan for six months, and before that Iraq and the Gulf War. He would get Jeff back to Krista and hopefully a new family.

As they slunk through the brush, Jeff thought about Iraq. Operation Enduring Iraqi Freedom, OEIF, a nice name they gave the Iraq War. Sounded like they would free the Iraqis. He wondered about the acronym for this war. Operation Enduring American Freedom? Or perhaps more truth, like the Oil Civil War, or The War Between the States II. Whatever they called it, he hoped it would end soon.

He glanced at Sergeant Juan Rector. Word had it that before he had joined the Army, Rector nearly died in a gang war in Albuquerque. His salvation had been the U.S. Army. He'd done well, carrying the gang mentality of protecting his own at all costs. He was loyal to the Army and expected the same of those under him. His juniors knew they could follow him to hell and still return in one piece. Some said he'd fought in one too many battle, and once lost several men. Perhaps that's why he got flaky at times, especially after Afghanistan: Something about spooks, CIA types.

A hand signal from Rector caught his attention. Everyone hit the dirt. The moist ground smelled of fresh grass and pine. He couldn't believe so many pine trees grew here.

Lying supine with his head held low he heard a faint panting, irregular trudging steps, and intermittent whines. He peeked through the grass and around a pine tree. Pit bulls and German Shepherds pulled on leashes held by men dressed in military fatigues, not the newer, patterned cammies but solid green, or "greenies," a much less expensive variety. Whoever they were, they probably couldn't afford newer cammies.

Over his shoulder, the Humvee was barely visible. Maybe he should have stayed there. The sun squeezed sweat down his flanks and over one eye. He shut his eyes. Maybe if he kept them closed long enough this would all go away.

A seasoned veteran had told him that fear never left you in combat. You slept with nerves on idle, took a shit too fast, and ate while scanning, pausing every other bite to listen. The medics called it "hyper-vigilant." Some people handled it better than others. Those whose pulse never went above eighty were either born leaders, or loved killing so much that you had to watch your back.

Jeff felt his chest hammer so fast it surely vibrated the ground. The dogs wouldn't need to smell his fear; they'd find him by feel.

When he opened his eyes, Jeff saw Rector positioning his gun, ready to shoot. As if Rector's action had scared them, the dogs and their masters turned around and moved toward their camp. Jeff's head fell forward onto the cool earth and grass and he let out a breath. That had been too close.

After a minute Rector tapped him on the leg and whispered, "Let's go."

They stood to a crouch and crept forward toward the camp, spreading out to get different vantage points. Jeff's mouth felt so dry his tongue stuck to his teeth. Yet, his rifle felt slippery in his damp palms. He took a deep breath of air filled with humus and pine smell. This was it. The real deal. He was being all that he could be.

He smiled. Really? He hadn't even killed anybody face to face.

Rector had told him the real test—the one that separated the makers from the breakers—when you met someone face to face, mano a mano, hand to hand combat, and then killed them.

Would he make it, or would he break?

Krista's smile and Jason's bodiless leg flashed in his mind.

He forced his tongue under his upper lip, loosened the dry suction against his teeth, and walked forward, hoping hand to hand combat did not lie ahead.

CHAPTER 42

Remmy awakened and shivered at the damp air blowing over his naked body. *So this was a Homeland Security interview.* He opened his eyes wide, attempting to see ... anything. Nothing but darkness. He wondered if he was still in the same dark room they had kept him in yesterday while they bombarded him with questions over a loud speaker. Then he groaned at the knifelike jabs in his aching shoulders when he struggled. This new position was a step in the wrong direction. Any movement exacerbated the pain because his arms were pulled as tight as bowstrings behind, and his wrists chafed at handcuffs. He felt like he sat slightly tilted back in a straight-backed chair, his legs jutting out from his waist at ninety degrees, spread wide and strapped in a rough, canvas-like support, like a birthing chair he'd seen from the '50s. A wide band strapped his chest and hips, pinning his back against a cold flatness. Air cooled him from above. His head and manhood remained free, the latter feeling extremely exposed, right next to his puckered anus.

He tried to relax. But the tightly stretched shoulder muscles involuntarily contracted, causing painful spasms that soon became constant searing fire.

He breathed in and out slowly, trying to put the pain aside.

Something like paper rustled to his right.

Thankful for the mobility of his head, he twisted to the far right, touching his cheek to a cool headrest. A slice of light penetrated under a door about ten feet away.

A cramp in his neck forced him to relax. If he could just—

A blinding light sprayed the entire room. Footsteps approached.

Blinking through the light, he peered at a bald, sallow-faced, gangly man followed by two, thick-armed men in camouflage fatigues. The tall man walked like a praying mantis.

Remmy forced a grin. "Ya'll could have at least brought some hot women with whips. Reminds me of Mardi Gras last year. I like kinky shit."

The stick man pulled a chair over and sat. He leaned close to Remmy's head and smiled, but only with his lips. His eyes seemed to observe the head rest, not a human being.

"Now why would we bring women when you prefer men?" The man barely moved his lips, his voice matter of fact, with no intonations, less emotion than a computerized greeting. His breath proved without a doubt that he did not believe in oral hygiene.

Remmy glanced at the two muscled attendees. "They are such handsome boys, but not my type. Too much brawn, if you know what I mean."

The man's lips momentarily ticked up at the corners. He directed each attendant with a sideways movement of his eyes and head. He nodded at Remmy, and backed away.

Cold water hit Remmy's chest and abdomen forcing him to suck in a deep breath. One of the attendants held a hose. Not a garden hose, either. A fire hose.

Remmy glanced over at the camouflaged hulk. "Hey, it's nothing against you, but—"

The full force of the water hit him in the face, cutting him off.

The water stopped, footsteps receded, and the lights went out. The breeze got stronger and much colder. Involuntary shivers waved through him and soon became constant.

Remmy took in a deep shaky breath and shouted into the dark, "I told you everything I know. This is illegal. I know my rights. I want a lawyer."

Nothing.

Through chattering teeth he swore. "Motherfuckers. I hope Dad—" But he stopped short, not wanting to implicate another friend.

After five more minutes of shivering and wiggling to try and relieve the shoulder pain, the lights came on again. More footsteps. The boys were back.

The praying mantis sat again and studied Remmy, like a science project. "Tell me about Abdullah El-Hamain. What exactly have you two done to the oil wells and where is he?"

Remmy's teeth chattered through his words. "Gimme a blanket and a hot toddy and I'll tell you all you want to know."

The face disappeared and frigid water slammed Remmy's testicles like an ice hammer.

"Goddammit! That hurts!"

The glacial water pummeled his crotch. The deep ache soon changed to a searing claw that penetrated his core and extinguished other thoughts.

The blast stopped and the sallow face leaned over again, filling his field of vision.

"It will only get worse, Mr. St. James. I suggest you tell us what we want to know soon, or you will no longer be of any use to your boyfriend."

The attendant to his left chuckled and uttered a disgusted whisper, "Fucking fag."

Remmy shouted, "You think I give a shit about your homophobia? And I already told you, El-Hamain was a customer only. If you let me out of here I will show you what he's done."

A strong pair of hands grabbed his head and strapped it to the metal head rest.

The hollow-cheeked face came into view.

"I'm not convinced. I think you are a terrorist like El-Hamain. And because you are a terrorist we can do about anything we want to in order to find out what you plan on doing."

The face disappeared and the arctic blast hit his groin again, but then moved to his abdomen and chest. The face of one of the pit bull attendants smiled. "Open wide."

The full force of the water hit him in the mouth. He closed it, but the water went into his nose. He opened his mouth to take a breath and the water crashed into his tonsils.

His entire body tensed as he coughed and spit.

The water kept coming.

He closed his mouth, held his breath, and relaxed. But within seconds another cough racked him, and the water pushed into his mouth and nose.

He'd read about this, near drowning victims pulled out of a pool after having sucked fresh water into their lungs. They usually occupied ICU for days, hooked to IV's, oxygen, or maybe a ventilator if they'd been under for a long time. It took only six minutes of no oxygen to the brain to get brain damage. The more brain damage, the longer it took to come off the ventilator. Too long and a ventilator wouldn't help.

He grayed out, hoping they kept him under for . . . way too long.

Instantly the water stopped and someone slapped the side of his face.

He coughed, and coughed, waking gradually from somewhere he preferred to stay.

He opened his eyes and the ice water smashed his groin. The claw returned.

The water stopped and the thin man's ghoulish visage appeared.

"You see. We can do this for an hour, leave and go have coffee, then return for more. As strong as you are, this could go on for the rest of the day if you don't give us what we want. So, what will it be?"

Remmy's wheezy voice sounded like it came from someone else, yet he could feel the sting of his vocal cords pushing out the words. "Okay. I know how Abdullah modified the bacterium to destroy oil and I think I can reverse it. And I know where you can find Abdullah."

He heard murmuring. Spray stung his eyes. He couldn't see and breathed faster. A hand held something over his mouth and he tasted a fruity sweetness.

Wonderful, dark unconsciousness washed over him, but it didn't last long enough.

CHAPTER 43

The computer flashed a file name at Dan. It disappeared before he could register all of it.

The screen died.

Sam had left hours ago with Ron, leaving Dan with Lisette and Bernadette. Bernadette sipped iced tea and leaned back in her chair, not seeming to care that all the screens remained dark. "Automatically shuts down when the sniffer gets too close."

He threw up his hands. "I had something. Motherf—"

"Relax, honey pot. We'll take five and go back at it."

She studied him. "What did you have?"

He sat back and rubbed his eyes. After ninety minutes of searching, he'd seen the first inkling of anything useful since "Hamain." He shook his head trying to remember.

"I only caught a glimpse—a file name with a few left-over characters."

"Where were you searching?"

Closing his eyes, he clasped his hands on top of his head and spoke haltingly, seeing it in his mind. "I went through his travel itineraries. Nada. Then his schedule for the last month and then one file on special visitors: 'VIP'. I opened it and there were a few initials. I think."

The mind-film went blank. *I never have problems with remembering files. What's wrong?*

Lisette lay supine on the couch across the room, her breasts rising and falling in a peaceful slumber, the warm afternoon sun highlighting every curve.

He slammed his feet on the ground, stood up, and paced, keeping an eye on her. She had confused him. He had to concentrate, but how could he with her just—laying there like that.

She rolled over and faced him, cracked one eye, a glitter between long lashes. Her cheeks glowed pink from the heat.

"Are you done Danny boy?" Her voice caught him by surprise, low, husky. So sexy.

Jesus. Don't know if I can stay here all night with her. He wanted to talk to her, tell her he could not give up his family, but that meant another confrontation.

It wasn't bad, this thing she had for him. A lot of men his age would have given in a long time ago. Let it fly. It wasn't like the world was getting any better. Maybe he should enjoy the moment.

He ran his hand over his head, hoping maybe more hair had grown out in the last hour, though it didn't seem to matter to her. She liked him for what he was: an older geeky guy, going bald, who still had enough in him to have a blast with her one night. Two weeks ago. More like a lifetime. How could she like him, or from the other day's conversation, even love him?

Maybe he'd misunderstood. Perhaps she'd only wanted to comfort a guy rescued from the jaws of death, company agent, out in the field, exciting, action packed guy who traveled all over the world, could mold computers to his own mind waves, could—

She sat and ran her hands through her black hair, yawned then stretched both arms over her head, revealing her taut abdomen and smooth white skin.

This is war, right? Take it while you can. Might not be alive tomorrow.

The conversation with his wife a few days ago about Jeff surfaced. His eyes shifted from Lisette's navel to the window and he turned around.

"Not yet," he said. "I'm trying to remember something I saw on the screen before it shut down."

He moved to refill his tea and felt like the Tin Man needing oil when he poured the last half glass from the pitcher. Everything felt jumbled, and when he couldn't think, he moved very slowly.

"Shut down? Did we lose power?" She jumped up and banged her rifle on the wall when she snatched it from the floor.

"No. We're okay. The computers shut down when the hacker-tracker programs got too close. We'll be online again soon."

She laid her rifle on the couch.

He sipped iced tea and sat down. Bernadette's chair swiveled, empty. The trailer door squeaked open and banged shut and the balance of the trailer shifted. *Must have stepped out to get some fresh air.*

The blank screens stared at him. A jumble of pastel colors and numbers seemed to float across the screen. One kept repeating: three. *You're going to have to turn around and look at her again.*

He twitched when her hands kneaded the back of his neck. Then he closed his eyes and dropped his head forward.

She kissed one ear. "Kind of jumpy aren't you?" Her breasts pressed against his shoulder. He turned to meet her lips and he forgot everything: computers, trailer, war, son, wife. He was connected to a beautiful woman whose lips were soft, hands magic, and heart his. Her nose bumped against his cheek and then her lips felt tight, not so soft.

The trailer door creaked open and Bernadette sang out, "Is it back up again, Daniel?"

Lisette broke the kiss. "Not yet, Auntie. Could you bring us more tea, please?"

He dropped his hands from around her waist, came out of his trance, and stared into her moist baby blues, avoiding looking at her nose or lips. She winked and spun him around, started massaging his neck again, and murmured, "Don't worry. We got all night."

He reflexively placed his hands on the keyboard and the screen lit up: *Booting System.*

That's what he needed: a swift kick.

He called out to Bernadette, "We're in business again."

Bernadette brought fresh tea in, poured it into the half-full glasses, added a few cubes of ice and sat down next to him. She hummed a tune he thought he knew, but couldn't place.

"Auntie," Lisette said. "I think Dan has figured out what he couldn't remember."

Shit! How did she know that?

"As a matter of fact I did. Guess I needed to clear my head."

Bernadette gave Lisette a sideways glance, "Lisette has a way of doing that."

"Yeah." He murmured. But he thought, *Are you kidding? Every time I look at her, I lose my brain.*

He typed and stared intently at the screen.

"So are you going to tell me, honey, or just sit there and type while I hum *Black Water*?"

"Oh, yeah. Doobie Brothers. Nice."

She smiled and tilted her head expectantly.

"Sorry. I think the letters in the file were *UAE*, followed by *bac-ass diff.*"

"Did you say back ass diff?" Bernadette asked.

Lisette gave a one grunt chuckle. "Huh. Back ass difficult. A riddle. Maybe it's the opposite of what it should be and not easy?"

Bernadette cackled. "Like what we've been doing for the last two hours, right, Daniel?"

He sighed and smiled at Bernadette's twinkling eyes. "Not exactly. There's a slash after the ass. I think it means something else." He wrote it on a yellow tablet and twisted it around on the side table so Bernadette could see it.

Lisette stopped massaging and moved so she could peer at the paper over Bernadette's shoulder. Branches of a tree blew against the trailer outside—fingernails on a chalkboard.

Bernadette sat up. "What do you think, Daniel?"

He sipped more tea and sat back in the chair. "I think UAE is United Arab Emirates."

Lisette nodded. "Do you think it's related to that guy . . . What's his name? Abdul Hamain?"

"Yeah. Absolutely. Only his name is Abdullah El-Hamain. I thought he was a nutcase trying to scare OPEC with those spiders in Vienna last month, but it appears Sam was right: There are no coincidences . . ." His voice trailed off as he put more of the puzzle together.

"So how does he relate to Xoflex," Bernadette said, "and what does bac-ass diff mean?"

He squinted at her and tilted his head.

"Daniel!"

He blinked. "Right. Sorry. It's all coming together. See if this makes sense. I think the UAE is like every other OPEC country. Their oil wells have peaked out and they can't let the gravy train stop. Xoflex has a nifty product that allows dying wells to squeeze out more oil. Maybe UAE sent Abdullah here to get that product."

Bernadette rubbed her nose with an index finger. "But if this Abdullah guy bought Xoflex's product, why did all the OPEC wells start going to hell after he disappeared? Xoflex's product should have *increased* production, not decreased it."

"Yeah, that is where the next letters come into play I think. Hear me out on this. It kind of popped into my head, green and pink, like when I read computer codes."

The both squinted at him.

"Colors are how I see numbers and codes sometimes. The best ones are usually green."

He crossed his legs and rubbed his thighs. "Okay, well, bacteria are used in Xoflex's product right? So I think 'bac' refers to bacteria."

He kept thinking and Bernadette said, "You wanna put this on fast forward?"

"Right. The 'ass' might be short for assemblers—the nanobots that facilitate the bacteria. The 'diff' could mean a strain of bacteria, like *Clostridium difficile*. Though I've always seen that abbreviated *C. diff.* And it's been *Pseudomonas* bacteria that they have used in the past."

The two women stared again.

He threw up his hands and sighed. "It seemed perfectly logical a minute ago. Now, I'm not so sure."

"So," Lisette said, "the 'bac-ass' could be short for bacterial-assembler?"

"Maybe. The more I think about it the more confusing it gets. I think we need more information."

Bernadette started typing on her keypad. "I think you're right."

After another hour of work, they had nothing else. Dan's mind filtered and sifted in other directions. That corner of his brain tugged his inner sight to the edge of a cliff. He had to get on the computer without Bernadette watching his every move.

CHAPTER 44

When Aunt Lola, Joe, and Bear were escorted by armed guards out of Xoflex without Remmy, Lola figured they'd have one chance to get away. She suspected their release was being used to coerce Remmy and she vowed to get reinforcements and rescue him. As soon as they walked out of sight of the cameras she felt sure the guards would shoot them or haul them to another prison for future leverage against Remmy. So she gave Joe and Bear a sign when they stepped into the woods.

It was all over in an instant. The soldier who was prodding Bear with his rifle woke up an hour later, spitting broken teeth, a painful lump on his forehead, and no rifle. The other guards who lasted longer would later fill him in on what happened. But first they had to get untied from around the cypress trees, find their pants, and explain to their sergeant how five armed men had been overcome by three hillbillies.

Lola got the spare keys from under the seat and had the boat cruising through the swamp in no time. Bear stowed the guards' M-16s and radios, except one radio they monitored on the return trip to the house. Joe laughed at the sergeant cursing when no one answered after hailing his men for five minutes. "Dey gone get KP duty for sure tonight."

"Probably worse. Lot worse," said Lola.

"They deserve it for takin' Remmy. I don't think they was real Army. Didn't feel right. Anyway, what we gone do?"

"We gotta get some help. Bear, where you tink Dad went?"

Bear scanned ahead of them. "He's probly doin jus dat...gettin' hep.

I'll find him when we get back. Don't worry. And I agrees wit Joe. Those guys weren't real Army. Dat was too easy."

After they docked the boat, Bear slipped away.

Joe and Lola went in and started preparing lunch. Lola put the gumbo on, and Joe started cutting potatoes for frying.

A voice behind them said, "Where's Mr. St. James?"

They both turned around, Lola with the ladle from the gumbo dripping on the floor, and Joe with a chef's knife gripped tightly in his right hand.

Sam aimed a Glock at them. "Whoa there, buddy. Put the knife down. Real slow."

Steam rose from the boiling gumbo and carried spicy smells into the room. Joe held onto the knife, and Lola pointed the dripping ladle at Sam. "Who you? Whatchoo want with Remmy?"

"My name is Sam Houston, and that," he motioned with his head to other side of the kitchen, "is Ron. We need Mr. St. James's help." Ron held a steady stance, also pointing a Glock. Sam motioned with his gun at Joe. "Please, just put down the knife. I don't want to shoot either one of you, but I will."

Joe glanced out the window to the right of Sam, flexed his knees and placed the knife on the floor. Then he winked at Lola.

Suddenly, through the door of the rear bedroom, Bear stepped out with a shotgun. "I don't wanna shoot you either, mister, so why don't you put down da gun."

In the same instant, another huge man materialized behind Ron, held a knife to his throat while his other hand twisted the gun from him.

"Okay," Sam gingerly placed his handgun at his feet. "Like I said, I don't want to hurt anyone. We just need Mr. St. James's help."

Lola turned around, moved the gumbo off the burner, and pulled a sawed off shotgun from under the sink. She pointed it at Sam. "Bout had it wit everyone wantin' Remmy's hep. Put yo hands on top yo head and git with your friend or you won't have no brains to tink wit much longer."

Sam complied and sat next to Ron on the living room couch, both with their hands resting on their heads.

"Now what da hell do you want with my Remmy?" Lola said.

"We think he can help us get this oil war stopped."

"And who exactly is dis 'we' you talkin' bout?"

Sam glanced at Ron, who nodded and said, "Might as well tell them. We need to get moving."

"Okay." Sam said. "We work for the U.S. government."

"Dat don't tell me shit."

"We're CIA."

Joe brandished the knife in front of Sam's face. "You de G-man try to kill Remmy down in South America?"

Sam's eyes became slits and his voice turned flat. "You mean after he killed our man?"

Joe cackled, "You think Remmy kill yo man? Sheeat. Remmy wouldn't hurt a flea. It was those dang grease-balls down there wit da fast guns. They kill your man, we got Remmy outta there, then they found us and got Remmy up at dat Xoflex place."

"Whose got him?" asked Sam.

"Probly your friends in de Army."

"We don't have anybody working with the Army here. We're it. But we think that Octex-Penta is working with the Army to protect the wells. They think, as do we, that Xoflex is responsible for the oil wells drying up all over the world. And since Mr. St. James is the big dog at this plant, and he was in Caracas when all their problems started, it seems logical that he was the one that screwed up their production."

"For the CIA," Lola said, "you pretty stupid, you. Think Remmy is de one? Hell, he barely got away wit his life after somebody killed your G-man down there. And he been tryin' to figure out how to fix it for de last two weeks."

"Yessiree. Dat Remmy so smart he figured it all out, too!" Joe said.

Lola shot him a frowning glance. "Shht!"

"He figured it out?" Sam said, leaning forward.

"Maybe." She glared at Joe. "Big mouth."

Joe looked like a whipped puppy. "I thought they could hep us."

"Maybe we can, sir. You see, we've also been working for the last two weeks trying to figure out what happened. It seems like all our information leads us to Remmy St. James. So we thought if we could find him, we could finally solve the puzzle. If you've seen what's happening in this country right now, you know we definitely need to figure things out quick."

Lola squinted her freckled cheeks and looked sideways at Sam. "How we know you not de same ones tryin' to kill Remmy, or tryin' to take us back to Xoflex."

"I give you my word that we have not been trying to kill him. All we want to do is talk to him. We don't want to take you anywhere. In fact, since he's at the Xoflex plant, we'll just be on our way to get him."

Sam started to lower his hands.

Lola jabbed the shotgun at him. "Where you think you're goin, you? Get yo hands up."

Sam returned his hands on his head. "Maybe we could help you rescue Remmy from the Army, he could help us, we could stop this mess, and everyone would be happy."

Lola thought for a minute. "How you find us, anyhow?"

"I told you. We're CIA. That's what we do."

She shook her head. "Dat's not good enough. Who told you where we was?"

"Come on, Sam," Ron said. "Let's do this and get out of here."

Sam sighed. "Contacts from Lisette Boudreaux told us there had been activity at this cabin recently. So—"

"Lisette Boudreaux?" Lola's eyebrows rose. "I tot she was in de Marines."

"She de purtiest girl of all de Boudreaux," Joe said. "How her daddy doin'? He ain't been gettin' his lightnin' like he used to."

"She *was* in the Marines, but we recruited her about a year ago. We've been staying at her father's cabin about five miles from here. You know each other?"

"A course we do," Lola said. "Anyone that's still movin' in these swamps pretty much knows everyone else."

Ducks flapped and quacked by the open window.

She lowered her gun. "Any friend of Lisette Boudreaux is a friend of ours. Bear, you and Dad let 'em go. Ya'll come on over here and help with supper. Those dumb fake Army guys at Xoflex got de drop on us once, but they got no idea where we is now. And if you help us get Remmy I'm sure he'll help you."

Sam picked his gun off the floor.

CHAPTER 45

Dan squeezed his eyes shut and rubbed them. What the hell had he just seen?

After Sam left, he and Bernadette had spent hours searching computer files. But he couldn't stop thinking about Lisette's kiss an hour ago. Her nose and thin lips really didn't matter. Maybe he could divorce Marci and marry Lisette. Or maybe he could just throw himself off a cliff.

That's when the file had popped up on the screen.

What the hell was *UAEUAE?* Not a symmetric palindrome and only six letters. No symmetric primes had six numbers. He opened his eyes again and the screen appeared blurry. *Staring at the screen too long.*

He blinked a few times and his vision cleared. *UAEAEH_cleanup.vid.*

"Got something." He wrote it down on the tablet and turned it around to Bernadette.

She glanced at it but kept typing. "We've got about ten more seconds, so if you can get anything *else* you better do it now."

He highlighted the file and copied it to the hard drive. The Window's hourglass sifted the electronic sand while the four-runged, green time ladder below indicated progress.

One rung. Two.

Bernadette counted down, "Six, five, four . . ."

Three rungs.

"Two, one. Hasta la vista, baby."

The screen went blank. Had there been a full four rungs?

They must wait fifteen more minutes until they knew—the fourth wait to reboot. The sniffers got faster each time. Soon Dan would have to quit altogether, or attack from another route.

Twilight had eased into the room. Lisette had opened a window before she went for a walk. "Recon," she'd said. Frogs croaked outside, night hawks *pee-yahed*, and the cicadas pulsed like the very heart of the earth.

He stared at the blank screen while shrugging his shoulders and moving his head side to side. *Miss her massage.*

Bernadette rolled her neck around, stood and stretched, arching her back and interlocking her fingers in a reverse knuckle pop.

She saw Dan's worried glance at her hands. "Yeah, my momma told me it would make my knuckles big and give me arthritis. But see." She held out her hands and played the air piano with rapid finger movements. "No big knuckles and no arthritis."

Dan scratched his temple, then blew lint off the keyboard.

"Cat got your tongue, honey pot. Or maybe it's Lisette?"

He sighed and murmured, "It's complicated." Then louder, "Wonder where she went?"

"Yup, life can get complex. But she'll be back soon. Maybe you need time to talk with her alone, cher. She's always been a lover, but after that hurricane hit, she . . . Well, let's just say she loves life and everybody in it. I figure we should give this program a long rest or those security programs are going to figure us out. Besides, I'm too tired to be much help until I get some sleep."

The trailer door creaked open and Lisette's sweet cadence asked, "Are ya'll about done in there?"

"Yes, honey. We're bout done in for the night. At least I am. I need to take a little walk. There's a certain mister I need to check on across the park. It may take a while, maybe even all night. Don't wait up."

She grabbed a sweater, smiled at Dan, and squeezed Lisette's shoulder on the way out.

The door swung shut. An earthy sulfur smell puffed in. The street lights in the trailer-lined road cast a stark cone of light on the parked cars. The fluorescent light had changed a previously blue car to a lavender hue.

The cool green dampness outside contrasted to the cold dry nights of Colorado. The pulse of cicadas vibrated a different chord than the howls of coyotes in the foothills outside his back porch. And the Cajun woman looking into his eyes made him feel different, crazy, and . . . Shit! He was the same guy, right?

Time's beak had pecked away at him piece by piece over the last ten years: the thinning hair, the ache in the knees after a pick-up game of basketball, the bags in the eyes after a night of too much, the bifocals, the weight gain, and last year the white whiskers. He exercised, dieted, and ate right. Yet the hair kept leaving, and each month more white hairs crept into the beard and out of his ears. He thought he had resigned himself to it. Soon the kids would finish college, get married. He would one day maybe be a grandfather. It was okay. It was really okay. Right?

She came along and he was surprised, tempted. Happy? Maybe. Though now he felt more disappointed that she could never be a serious part of his life. He loved his wife. He wanted to spend the rest of his life with Marci, share grandkids, travel to China, finish their garden, and take long hikes through the Rockies in springtime.

He was also disappointed in himself. No, disappointed was too small, too timid for what he felt. He had failed his wife. Guns were made for heads like his.

All this raced through his mind as Lisette's gaze entered his inner sanctum.

Her eyes went flat and she turned away.

The fan on the hard drive hummed, then stopped.

Say something.

The cicadas outside finished the first movement and rested for the next chorus, along with all the birds and frogs. Quiet overwhelmed, no squeaking branches, no creaking doors, as if a giant foam air bag popped and consumed the swamp and deadened every movement.

He couldn't speak. The back of her head, raven hair behind delicate, pink ears, did not move.

Had silence stopped time?

The theory of relativity crammed his head. His thoughts must have moved so fast that the real world seemed to halt. *Could thoughts move faster than the speed of light?*

She moved and his heart restarted.

Gradually she turned and her face came into view again. What he saw dropped his heart. Not crying. He could deal with that. No anger. That would be okay, maybe even good. Not even as bland as disappointment. He'd figured on that, maybe even in a selfish way hoped for it.

No, the eyes, the way she held her mouth, the sag in her shoulders. Remorse. She thought it was *her* fault.

Crap!

"Lisette, it's not your fault. It was me. I had too much to drink that first night. I felt like . . . It was *me*, not you."

It seemed like the blink of her eyes took an hour. She murmured, "I gotta find Sam." The trailer door slammed behind her.

All the noises started again, both outside and inside his head.

CHAPTER 46

Remmy awoke to odors of soap and fresh sheets. He felt swaddled in clouds: everything white, soft, warm, and dreamlike. He wanted to return to sleep, for a long time.

He took a deep breath and heaven disappeared.

His eye sockets ached, and when he opened his eyes bright sunlight filtered in through a narrow shuttered window, blinding his initial attempts at survey. What day was it?

After repeated blinks, he realized he lay in some sort of hospital room, the walls painted off-white, a full-length narrow metal locker on the wall half opened, clothes on a hanger inside.

He moved to get up, but his head swam and tape pulled at his forearm where an IV dripped into his vein. His head steadied, but his throat felt like he'd screamed in a smoky bar all night, and the raw pain brought back memories of coughing water. Cool white sheets slid off his naked body as he sat up and took inventory: sore, stiff shoulders; aching, bruised scrotum; dry eyes and mouth; and his teeth ached.

Not much worse than the morning after Fat Tuesday.

He pulled out the IV and ripped off a piece of tape and slapped it on the leaking needle hole. After standing several seconds to clear the grainy vision, he pulled clothes off the hangers and got dressed. Sitting on the bed, buttoning his shirt, he suddenly recognized his location—the lab tech's room on the ground floor down the hall from the Makers vat. He gazed out the window. Morning, but what day?

The dead bolt lock thwacked open, and he realized he better have a damn good story or he would soon be gargling the fire hose again. Or maybe this time they would shoot him in the head and throw him to the gators. *Wishful thinking.*

Sinclair entered, his lanky tallness contrasting with the tea kettle of a man clothed in all white who followed.

In a voice that made Remmy wonder if the man had ever hosted a TV Halloween movie fest, Sinclair said, "I'm glad you're up early. I understand your interview with Homeland Security last night was a bit fatiguing. Hopefully your rest has not weakened your memory."

Remmy wanted to cheer. He'd only slept for a few hours. If he escaped now he had time to save the oil. He cleared his throat and managed a hoarse whisper, "Of the interview techniques or of why it ended?"

"Mostly the latter, but I wouldn't want you to forget the former either. It is important to remember painful events in our lives and why we got there, don't you think?"

Sinclair's hawkish gaze gave a hint of humor.

Remmy sighed and gazed out the window. "Whatever. Can we get on with this? Coffee and a beignet would be helpful."

Sinclair nodded and swept his talon-like fingers toward the portly man in white pants and lab coat. "Meet Mr. Fielding. He's one of our recovery and maximizing experts. He will help with any technical aspects of your endeavor. We have refreshments down the hall."

Their footfalls echoed as they walked down the hallway toward the Makers room.

They stopped outside the room at a card table with a styrofoam cup and brown paper bag on top. Sinclair gestured for Remmy to sit. "That's for you."

The coffee smelled good, but was lukewarm, and the donut stale.

Sinclair patted him on the shoulder. "I think you'll find we are indeed grateful for your coming to the aid of your country in a time of crisis."

Remmy moved away; Sinclair's hand made his skin crawl and his stomach churn. He put the donut and coffee down. "I'll need the briefcase I brought in yesterday."

Fielding reached under the table and produced the silvery case.

Remmy peered at him. *Such a quiet little gnome.*

"Okay, let's get at it. There's a lab between the Makers and Regulator rooms that we can use. It will be convenient for taking any further samples and has the necessary tools, reagents, and isolation rooms." He opened the door to the Makers room.

Sinclair reached over his head and re-closed the door.

"I need to speak to you for another minute or so." He glanced at Fielding. "Alone."

Fielding sauntered down the hallway about fifty feet and began studying the wonderful Louisiana flora and fauna out the window. *Minds well, too.*

"Remmy, I do apologize for the way you've been treated. When I discovered their barbarism I halted it immediately." Sinclair sounded sincere and his eyes wavered between regret and disgust.

Remmy rolled his eyes. "You actually expect me to believe that?"

Sinclair gently placed his hand on Remmy's shoulder; for the first time his smile seemed warm.

"You and I are a lot alike. We have both been persecuted for a certain . . . way of life. Though, I think it easier being gay in New Orleans than with a Texas football father."

He took his hand away, and the ice returned to his eyes. "Overcoming it was difficult, but with enough money and power—which brings me to the point. The United Arab Emirates have been buying up companies and land in this country over the last decade for a reason. And now we can see that reason. Can you?"

Remmy wished he had a quart of water. The coffee smelled good, but . . . He took a deep breath, and sighed. "Who is this *we* you keep referring to?"

Sinclair's eyes darkened. "Why, the U.S. Government. Who else?"

"So you're saying that the UAE is trying to overtake the United States by buying up land and companies?"

"That, and now making sure that UAE has a monopoly on oil production."

"By destroying your company, Octex-Penta Oil?"

Sinclair stood straighter, squared his shoulders and motioned for Fielding to return. "Mr. St. James, please give me the location of El-Hamain."

Remmy had to tense every muscle to keep from laughing. *Hit a nerve, huh?*

"Okay. Every time he came, Abdullah would stay near Dallas at a private B&B called the Eye of the Camel. It caters to Persian tastes, and especially oily ones, if you get my drift."

An Army soldier came out of the stairwell entrance carrying an M-4 carbine. Sinclair motioned him over and said to Remmy, "This soldier will accompany you wherever you go, even into isolation and sterile rooms. He has familiarity with isolation techniques, but most of all he will make sure you are not tempted to elope."

"Where the hell would I go? The place is crawling with Army and God knows who else. Besides, I'm not up for another party like last night."

"Nevertheless, he will be your shadow."

Remmy shrugged. "So let's do this. Or, do I need more babysitters?"

Sinclair stepped to the side to let them pass. "Thank you, Mr. St. James. When this is all over, perhaps you will be able to understand and forgive us for our methods. We will have a place for you in our organization."

Remmy avoided Sinclair's eyes and entered the next room, followed closely by the white fire plug and camouflaged assassin. *Yeah right. I'll be dead meat the minute you get what you want.* The soldier's eyes had the calculating look of a careful killer. He wouldn't miss. And Fielding, the smart little gnome in white—Remmy would have to make things appear genuine, at least for a few minutes. Once he got into the lab, he had a surprise. He only hoped no one had emptied out the freezer.

All three geared up into isolation suits: typical beige disposable paper pants and gown, hair and shoe covers, and a surgical mask. Typical, except this suit felt stiffer. Still smelled like paper, though. Xoflex had necessarily invented a special weave of paper and carbon polymer that repelled nanobots. They didn't want to take any of the critters home with them. They also had a five by nine foot decontamination room where they shed all the paper, and a miniature Electromagnetic Pulse, or EMP, transmitted to completely deactivate any nanoparticles still clinging to skin, or exposed respiratory or gastrointestinal mucosa. But Remmy would never get to the decon room.

Once they entered the lab, Remmy started his spiel, "The key to our process is that the Makers have an extra oomph in their design. They are able to create ATP, and thereby give the Pseudomonas an endless supply of energy to keep going and replicating. This allows us to extract oil out of spaces that were once like the end of a toothpaste tube—acceptable waste. But in an oil well, that could be twenty percent or more of the total reserve. And twenty percent of billions of barrels is a lot of profit."

Fielding interrupted, "I thought Pseudomonas was only used for oil spill cleanups, not extracting."

"That's another bit that our company has tinkered with and modified. The Pseudomonas species that we developed still has an affinity for oil. But instead of the bacteria digesting oil, we modified them to store it, though only in an anaerobic environment, like deep inside the oil well. After they have all that oil stored, they seek out an aerobic environment, i.e. the hole in the well, where they regurgitate it and we recover it. In the process they refine the crude oil a bit, getting energy out of it. So, it's a win, win situation. They get food, we get slightly more refined oil, and production of the well increases."

"Until the well runs dry," Fielding said.

"Right. But that will be in another fifteen to twenty years. And by then, the oil companies will have figured another way to make money. Right now oil is a major cash cow that keeps them flying high and selling cars. But I don't have to tell you that, Mr. Fielding. You're in the belly of the beast."

Fielding blushed. "I'm j-just in r-research and development. They don't pay me t-t-too much. Anyway, go on. What destroyed all the oil?"

Remmy hoped that the low-end security cameras and sound system they had installed in the lab had missed the chink in Octex-Penta's armor that Fielding had just volunteered. Maybe he could use that.

"It was amazingly simple. Someone, not me, but someone else, outside of Xoflex, planted a colony of the oil-eating Pseudomonas into the vat of Makers—you probably know them as nano-assemblers. At the temperature we keep the vat, the extraction and improvement Pseudomonas species, our Makers, stay relatively dormant. But the bad boys grow quickly at that temperature and overrun the good guys. I found this out by sampling the vats two weeks ago. The Makers vat no longer has any good guys, only bad boys. Let me show you."

He opened his briefcase and took out one cylinder of Regulators and one of Makers and placed them inside an airtight hood. He poured crude oil into a graduated test tube and stuck a rubber stopper in the top. The stopper had a sealed port that he accessed with a syringe he filled from the Makers cylinder. He hit the large timing clock. The big red second hand began its course.

"Watch the markings on the test tube," he said. "In three minutes there will be one millimeter less. In four minutes three less. By ten minutes, voila! No more oil and the bacteria die."

While Fielding and the assassin scrutinized the tube in the hood, Remmy put on protective eye goggles.

After a few minutes Fielding said, "But if the oil disappears, how can you get it back?"

Remmy kept facing away from them and opened the freezer door, blocking their view of the contents with his body. "That's where our new prototype comes in."

Inside stood a bottle of yellow fluid labeled: WEAR EYE PROTECTION. He surreptitiously peeled off the label, pulled the cork out enough to allow the contents to leak out, and placed it on the table, saying. "Gotta let this warm up a bit, then I'll show you. I need to get the Regulator tube from my briefcase."

Still with his back to them, he stepped away from the table and opened his briefcase, carefully moving his body in front of the camera, obscuring his actions. He quickly upended the Regulator tube enough to get a spot of the broth on his left index finger. Tube in hand, he faced them and shook his head. "That stuff they put in my eyes earlier still stings." He rubbed the edges of the goggles with the wet finger, as if rubbing stinging eyes. Next, he scratched his surgical mask absent-mindedly. The Regulators now coated the sides of his eyes and the surgical mask to protect him.

Within twenty seconds Fielding and the soldier shook their heads and coughed violently. They pawed at their eyes. Remmy had secretly released nano-assemblers that attacked mucous membranes.

"Shit!" Remmy yelled. "Goddamn Abdullah must have done something else to the Makers. I'll have to lower the temperature in here to prevent further growth." He grabbed a fire extinguisher and sprayed it at the two men, making sure he hit the surveillance camera, too.

When the fog of the fire extinguisher cleared, Remmy St. James had vanished.

CHAPTER 47

Abdullah did not sleep well two nights ago because of the fiasco the day before: the computer breakdown and the lightning strikes. He began to think all his plans would fall apart.

Yesterday, in the early morning light, he surveyed the damage to the computers and became more optimistic. The grinding whine of chain saws had ceased an hour ago. The men had worked all night and removed the tree that had fallen onto the building from the lightning, repaired the camouflage netting, and brought in another generator. He unfolded the paper he'd found outside his door. It was a note from the head computer technician assuring him that they had plenty of computing power to give him what he wanted.

He smiled. If this had been any type of operation in Saudi Arabia, the workers would have left, sure that the natural disaster had been a sign from Allah to cease work. *Allah. Who was Allah but a figment of Muhammad's imagination? And Muhammad was just a man who conquered and plundered and wanted control of everyone's thoughts and beliefs. I'm better than that.*

He laughed, startling one of the passing guards.

I will be the new Muhammad for mother earth. Earth! Real, tangible, something worth believing in and saving.

He walked inside to add that line to his speech. Things were looking up after all.

Not two-hundred yards away, Jeff woke up. Having to stay prone on the ground all night, the rain had seeped into almost everything, despite a rain poncho. If they had been allowed to fall back, they could have set up a tent and kept dry. But orders were orders. Stay on station.

He chewed on the protein bar and sipped water from his third and last canteen. His second canteen had a bit of rain water collected from yesterday, but by evening he would need more.

Fitful sleep had snuck between trickles of water meandering into warm spots and intermittent chainsaws from the camp across the way as they dismantled the fallen tree. Not wanting to even crouch for fear of discovery, he'd finally taken a piss on his side after feeling like he would burst.

What he would do for a couple of swallows of hot Starbuck's, sitting in the coffee shop with Krista, talking about their future. His tongue explored his mouth trying to extract the taste from memory. Only remnants of the protein and granola bar.

He took another swig of stale water, grimaced and forced it down. How long does water have to sit for it to taste like it had been filtered through dust? A leaf fluttered into a puddle of muddy water under the tree. Soon he might have to taste *that*.

He put the canteen away. Conserve.

He shifted his head, trying not to move his eyes out of cover of the poncho but still locate Sergeant Rector. Rector lay prone about twenty yards to his right, binoculars trained on the camp.

Rector let the binoculars hang from their tether around his neck, and brought up the walkie-talkie. He spoke into the radio, listened and frowned. Then his lips moved so forcefully and rapidly spittle flew out. Jeff could not hear the last whispered expletive, though he easily lip-read: *Motherfucker.*

Who would Rector say that to? Who *could* he? LT? Probably not. Rector wouldn't do that. Rank and order were too important to him. Another sergeant? Maybe. More importantly, why was Rector so upset?

He tried to make eye contact with Rector, needed to. But Rector never stopped glassing the Quonset hut. After two more minutes, Jeff inched to a better vantage point and did the same.

Whatever happened next couldn't be much worse than yesterday.

Yesterday had been that flash of terror they talked about: that part of war that punctuated long bouts of boredom. Maybe that was it. All of it. *Please.*

That must be why Rector was pissed, staying here another day, bored, in the swamp, wet but thirsty.

The image of JJ burning alive flashed in his head.

Boredom is not so bad. Not bad at all.

Abdullah finished his revision and decided to make a walk through the compound to get a firsthand view of where they stood. Halfway to the generators, René called from behind him.

"Sir, I'm glad you're up. I think you need to see the latest news clip."

René had dark circles under his eyes, a two-day beard stubble, and coffee stains on his normally impeccable white shirt.

"You should be sleeping," Abdullah said. "Let someone else worry about that."

"I prefer to do the worrying when it comes to you, sir. Please, follow me."

They entered the eight by ten, soundproof communication room. The room smelled of cigarette smoke. René closed the door behind them, lowered the shades. "This came in early this morning." He clicked on the mouse and the video played.

A familiar talking head, Jonathan Creuter from CNN, also sported stubble, only his seemed at least a week older than René's. Abdullah thought he should look tired, but his eyes shone like he'd discovered King Solomon's mine.

"Jane Roberts in Tokyo has this latest development."

René fast-forwarded through the thin blond's intro right to the meat. The camera panned streets and alleys of downtown Tokyo and the major highway. Abandoned cars, trucks, buses, and taxis littered the roads. Close-ups showed dealer stickers on a few of the cars. Others appeared gutted; doors open with dangling tentacles of wire reaching out from the dashboard.

The video switched to the port of Tokyo. Piles of the abandoned cars and trucks had been bulldozed to form a wall. A woman's voice said, "They call this 'The Great Wall of Nissan.' It barricades the oil tankers from the city's angry citizens."

The camera zoomed in on military trucks and tanks on the water side of the Great Wall. Cement partitions and rolls of barbed wire stood between the wall and the military vehicles. On the city side of the Great Wall seethed a mass of civilians, shouting, throwing anything handy including the occasional Molotov cocktail. These invariably fell short of the barbed wire, but burst into flames nonetheless. Intermittently, the flames erupted higher and a bulldozed car exploded, presumably from bits of gasoline left in the tank. Staccato pops of automatic gunfire preceded several civilians falling to the ground. The civilian side launched an RPG that exploded one of the military jeeps.

Similarly, scene after scene across the world played out, including Afghanistan where, the reporter said, all of the U.S. and allied military support had been pulled out.

The next view of the frozen Alaskan tundra contrasted with the handful of Army trucks two weeks previously. Now, a city of Quonset huts, tents, tanks and bulldozers crawled with soldiers. A flock of helicopters cruised overhead. Offshore, Navy destroyers, battleships, and a distant aircraft carrier plowed the seas. On the ice-hazed horizon, black smoke billowed in three different areas.

The scraggly face of Jonathan Creuter filled the screen, his face and mouth a dead calm. He continued describing the atrocities. But no matter how far he lowered his voice or how tightly he pursed his lips he could not disguise the elation in his twinkling eyes.

Abdullah puzzled at this newsman's enjoyment of worldwide disaster, but only for a moment. The corners of his lips rose ever so slightly. Of course, he was a news-hound, an action junky, and getting his drug mainlined twenty-four seven. Abdullah recalled the man as a fixture during the beginnings of Afghanistan, the Gulf War, and Iraq.

Always in the beginning, but never later.

He smiled broadly and spoke to the man as if he could hear him. "Get it while you can, Jonathan. This might be your last hit for a long time."

The President of the United States came on the TV, his eyes and face more synchronous in their grave message. "I know that many of you are wondering why all this has happened. Why is the world in a crisis that matches the Plague of the Dark Ages? It is all because of this man."

The OPEC picture of Abdullah filled the screen. Abdullah glared at it.

The voice of the President continued, "This man is Abdullah El-Hamain. He is a Muslim extremist who is trying to take over the world by destroying all the oil while keeping his own supply in China. He even sold out his own country in the United Arab Emirates. He contaminated all the members of OPEC with a type of oil-eating bacteria that's infected and destroyed all OPEC oil wells. We believe we can restore these wells, given time. Luckily for us, he was unable to get to the United States oil wells, and our military will keep them safe. However, he is still at large and may be in Texas. If anyone has seen this man, please call the FBI at the following number, or contact your local law enforcement agency."

The President's sincere face replaced Abdullah's. "I am in Air Force One overseeing and coordinating the defense of our country. I want you to know that we have the situation under control and will keep you informed of the progress. I know that there have been skirmishes throughout our fair country. Please, do not take matters into your own hands. Let the military and the Red Cross and local disaster agencies do their job."

Scenes flashed of Navy ships launching jets, and Army tanks destroying two enemy tanks.

"I repeat, do not take things into your own hands. That's why we have a government, to come to the aid of the people in times of crisis. As your President, I promise you that we will overcome this and move on to a brighter future."

The American flag flapped on the screen and faded to a bald eagle flying through a backdrop of snow-covered peaks and a crystalline Alpine lake. The *Star Spangled Banner* played in the background.

The newsman's beard-scruffy face, sparkling eyes, and stifled smirk returned to the screen. He coughed and said, "There it is, America. China and the U.S. are the only world powers with oil, and we are currently trying to avoid World War III. Stay tuned."

Abdullah punched the mouse and abruptly ended the clip. He grabbed a handful of papers on a desk and twisted them in his hands, then thrust them at the sound proof window. The papers flittered all around them. René did not move.

"They think I'm a Muslim extremist? A terrorist? That inadequate leader has the gall to accuse me of crimes?"

A thought stopped his rant: Perhaps he could turn the public's head in the right direction. He still had a few tricks up his sleeve. *China? You must be kidding.*

"How soon will we be up?"

René eyed the floor. "Probably not until noon."

"Is your intell on the Texas wells correct?"

"Yes sir, I believe so. They have sent all their air power to Alaska. They have stopped running their generators during the day, and only one at night to conserve oil. However, we will only know for sure that their wells are dry when we get inside."

"Very well. Could we make the same transmission and overload their circuits from inside the Texas oil wells?"

René squinted one eye and cocked his head. "Yes. We would have to overcome their paltry forces and move all the machines and computers. It might take a day."

"Okay, I will wait until tomorrow. Let's start the move now. I need to have proof for the American people that their President is a liar. We will show them that Texas oil is nonexistent, and I will tell them the real reason. I am no terrorist. I am their savior."

He walked out of the room feeling like a great weight had been lifted.

CHAPTER 48

Jeff forced his sleep-deprived eyes open. For the last half hour he'd observed the same three men repair the camouflage netting torn by the fallen tree. Twice he reached for his canteen and changed his mind. Rector had a water filter and Jeff had used one many times in the wilderness streams of Colorado, but pushing that muddy brackish water through that filter? Nope. He would have to make the canteen last another hour or two. He eyed the brackish mud. Maybe even a day.

He peered up through the canopy of trees at the cloudless dawn sky. The front that brought the thunderstorms yesterday also brought cold air. Not twenty-degree snow-skiing weather, but still he shivered. Probably above freezing, but the combination of the damp clothes and inactivity felt like the time he got hypothermia after a thunderstorm caught him above timberline without a raincoat. Luckily Krista had hugged him, kept him warm.

The roar of an engine startled him and he glassed the Quonset hut. Two deuce-and-a-halfs flanked the building, the distinct growl of their engines accompanying the blue-gray smoke billowing out of the stacks. Men carried equipment out the large side door of the Quonset hut and loaded the trucks.

In another instant several Humvees appeared off to their right across the waterlogged field.

Rector signaled to fall back.

Jeff slithered on elbows and knees backwards, keeping low, his joints so stiff he swore they squeaked. When he got close, Rector said, "They're moving out. Let's get back to the truck."

Within minutes, they all piled into the Humvees, except Rector and LT who remained outside. Jeff stood in the turret and kept his intercom helmet cocked up to hear their conversation.

"Sergeant, if they are making another assault on our command center, our orders are to slow them down."

"With those deuce-and-a-halfs, they'll need to travel on that dirt road. I'll rig a few surprises. There's a—"

The LT raised his hand. "We need to do some damage sooner than that."

Rector's face clouded. "Sir, we only have four RPG rounds. Once they're gone we'll be sitting ducks. What about that air strike we asked for?"

"Same answer as yesterday, Sergeant. No air support. Use those RPG rounds now, and don't just sit there after you're done. Get the hell out."

A flock of grackles flew and squeaked overhead, spooked by the oncoming enemy entourage that had grown louder.

LT went to another vehicle. Rector jumped into the UAH and crammed up into the turret, his face inches from Jeff's. "Corporal, lock and load. We're gonna slip in, deliver, and slip out. Once you fire, hold on because we'll be moving fast. Got it?"

"Yes, Sergeant."

Rector slid down into his seat. Jeff snugged his helmet, pulled up the RPG, and braced himself.

The UAH moved forward with a jerk. Enemy Humvees came in sight.

"Fire!" The Sergeant's orders crackled loud and clear over the headphones.

Jeff aimed through the sights, pulled the trigger, and a millisecond later a trail of smoke plotted the course of the grenade.

A second before the explosion, the UAH reversed and jarred left. Jeff braced with one arm while reaching down for the next RPG round.

Stop again, aim, fire, hold on for dear life, grab the next round.

Twice more and the Humvee accelerated out of there. Jeff tensed every muscle in his body as they bumped up, down, around, and through spindly willows, gulleys, and cattail marshes—evasive as a scared jackrabbit.

A pine tree shredded to their left. An instant later, he heard the distant report of a machine gun, behind them. Jeff's Humvee broke through the tree line into the clearing, almost to the dirt road, and jerked to a halt.

Rector erupted through the passenger door and ran with a light duffel bag over his shoulder. He placed two claymores with trip wires across the road, and ran back.

Before Rector made it to the UAH, an artillery shell whistled. Jeff yelled, "Incoming!" and instinctively ducked inside the UAH. The driver panicked and the vehicle charged forward before Rector reached the door. The shell burst twenty yards to their right and the UAH halted.

Rector jumped in. "What the fuck? You gonna leave me out there?"

"Sorry, Sarge. Foot slipped," said the driver.

"Probably from that shit coming outta your pants when that shell hit, huh, private? Never mind. Just get us the hell outta here, and stay off the road."

The Humvee's jackrabbit run across the fields soon had them in site of camp.

The first explosions tore through the computers. Abdullah ducked under a table. After no others came, he stood.

René sprayed a fire extinguisher, then spotted him, handed the extinguisher to someone else, and ran to him. "Are you all right, sir?"

"Yes I'm fine. How much will this delay us?"

"Not a bit. We already have backups for everything."

"What about the attack?" Abdullah held out his hands and gripped his fists in frustration.

"Don't worry, sir. We have a regiment of men and fighting machines already arriving. The surprise will be all theirs."

Jeff traded helmets and pulled up his M-16. When they reached camp, he jumped out of the Humvee and ran for cover behind a tank. The RPG's he'd fired did nothing more than piss off a beehive. Bullets ricocheted off anything metal and flicked mud and dust all around him. The fire-power seemed endless, making the diesel engines of the newly cranked tanks seem pitiful. Still, it reassured him when the big diesels roared, smoke billowed, and turrets swiveled, ready to deliver a considerable retort.

He peeked through binoculars from behind a muddy tank tread. All reassurance left.

What the hell? Where did they get all the Humvees and armored vehicles?

Someone made a big mistake. We are the Army. THE U.S. ARMY! Bigger, badder, more powerful than any other force in the world. Right?

The riot of vehicles surged forward. *Not really.*

They were completely outgunned. How could a civilian force do that? Not only Humvees, but a shitload of civilian SUV's and souped-up monster trucks bristled with camouflaged men firing automatic weapons, flanked by Land Rovers, Mercedes, and what seemed like hundreds of black Suburbans.

Shit! This was more than black market and drug dealers. Someone had been planning this one for a while, and knew exactly what they were doing.

He turned around and studied the rear of the Command Center. If he stayed he would die. That's why he joined, right? To die in defense of his country. But was he defending his country, or just an oil field? And those "enemies," weren't they fellow countrymen who only wanted a few gallons of gas for their cars?

Two Humvees sped toward the rear gate, one of them the UAH he'd left. As it roared past him, he made up his mind to save himself. He would have a family to support. He jumped to his feet and sprinted, hoping to hurl himself in the side door.

The distance between him and UAH lengthened as the vehicle turned up speed to crash through the locked gate. But as quickly as it accelerated, it stopped, almost crashing into the lead Humvee that jerked to a mud-flying stop in front of the gate. A soldier jumped out of the first Humvee and went to unlock the gate.

You must be kidding me! What an idiot! The Humvee could break that gate wide open. But thanks anyhow.

He sprinted to the passenger's side of the UAH just as the gate-opener returned to the lead Humvee. He yanked open the door. Sergeant Rector stared at him.

Jeff froze. Why would a battle-hardened veteran flee? Jeff wondered if he should run the other way.

The vehicle jerked forward. Jeff bulled his way into the UAH onto the lap of Rector and the door flapped against his boots.

Rector shoved him through to the laps of the men in the rear seat and slammed the door shut. "Bout time, Corporal. What the hell kept you?"

CHAPTER 49

The private who had almost left Rector once, repeated his excellent open field driving: a Pac Man of the field, Andretti of the swamps. They bounced and jangled for fifteen long minutes. The men seated in back snugged their seatbelts and pushed one hand against the roof protecting their skulls. Two men, Jeff and another, flew like flotsam in a wind storm, weightless in freefall half the time, the other, like dice in a cup right before hitting the betting table. Where they landed nobody knew.

The explosions receded behind them, and the driver eased off the accelerator. Jeff didn't know his name, but he thought Private Cole Trickle Ricky Bobby Pac Man summed it up. The UAH veered behind a clump of mesquites and stopped. Rector opened his door and popped his head up with binoculars.

"Holy mother of God," he mumbled and crawled back in his seat. "Private, get us the fuck outta here." They shot ahead.

Jeff and the other floating man grabbed seatbelts and seats. The engine whined; men grunted; equipment rattled. But words? None. Jeff wondered if they were all thinking what he was: *I just deserted my post. The Army is going to track me down and what? Court martial and prison. Or maybe they'll just shoot me on the spot.*

The open roof turret invited him to climb up, jump out, and walk back. He might be taken prisoner, but at least he'd accompany the guys who fought and didn't run.

He glanced at Rector, their leader, a hero of war—running away.

Nausea squeezed his stomach. What would he tell Dad? Dad had worked all over the world trying to preserve democracy, protecting Jeff and their family and the rest of the U.S.A. from all enemies, both foreign and domestic. Isn't that the same oath Jeff had sworn to uphold not two weeks ago?

Damn!

He held his head in his hands and wondered if they played basketball in Army prisons. They did in the movies. Played it outside too. But maybe deserters never got to see the light of day.

"I know what all of you are thinking." Rector's firm voice cut through the rattling and thudding of the UAH as it scurried south—a prairie dog's frantic sprint for a hole. "You're thinking you want to go back and help your buddies—that you'd rather fight than go on this mission." He paused, letting the last two words sink in.

Jeff raised his head. *This mission? What mission?*

"That's right. We're on a mission: orders from Captain Hoag to head south and report our situation to the Colonel at Southern Command Center. Since our oil well command lost all COM, we're tasked with filling them in."

He eyed Jeff. "Get your minds straight and your shit in one bag. We got about six hours of this peaceful smooth ride before we get there. Who knows what we'll run into before that?"

"Sergeant?" Jeff said. "Can I assume my post?" He needed fresh air to clear his head and the gagging smell of sweat and fear.

"Thought you'd never ask. Be more room in here if you were up there anyhow, Corporal."

Jeff twisted and climbed up into the turret. As he moved by, Rector's throaty whisper advised him, "Careful, Jeff. We need you."

"Thanks, Sarge."

So this is war. Hog shit to hero in one minute.

CHAPTER 50

In the wee hours of the next morning, Bernadette eased the trailer door open and crept inside. Dan had figured out how to fold down the table and make a bed out of the kitchenette area. He'd scrounged blankets, and though warm and comfortable, far from cozy, and even farther from sleep.

Bernadette reeked of cigar smoke and whiskey. *Must have been a good night for her.*

Where was Lisette? That nagging question hit him again for the—thirteenth—yes, thirteenth time. Had she really gone looking for Sam? Probably not. She paced somewhere out there, sulking.

Distant thunder rumbled closer. Drops of rain pattered on the trailer roof, and the dusty wet smell filtered in. A breeze sung through the screen and feathered his face.

A flash of lightning lit up the entire trailer. After a three-count, a shattering crack rattled the trailer.

That's it.

He closed the window and dressed. *This is ridiculous. Lisette is out there getting drenched.*

"Bernadette, are you still awake?"

A low, gravelly slur muffled against the sheets. "Don't worry Daniel. The trailer has been through many a Louisiana thunderstorm. Go back to sleep. Sorry I woke you, sweetie."

"It's not that. I was awake. I had an argument with Lisette, and she went for a walk trying to find you or Sam. Do you have a raincoat or two? Maybe I could try to find her." He rummaged around in a closet next to the door. Unsuccessful, he peered into the darkness.

Bernadette's sheet-covered form gradually sat up like a ghoul rising from the grave. The lightning flashes lent a strobe light effect to her movements, making her movements even more zombie-like. He half expected that in the next lighted view she would come at him, teeth gnashing.

"Don't worry about her, Daniel. She's been out in worse weather than this. She was raised in this country. If she does not want to be bothered, neither you nor the U.S. Marines will find her."

He closed and leaned on the closet door and drummed his fingers. He tapped out dit-dit-dit, dah-dah-dah, dit-dit-dit.

"Daniel. I know Morse code. I told you not to worry."

The pitter of rain quickly changed to a deafening roar. The trailer shook with the wind. *A tornado?*

Bernadette's voice snuffled against the sheets. "Count prime numbers. Erect Heinz rectangles. Whatever. Get some sleep. She'll be back when she's good and ready."

He sat down on the kitchenette bed and peered outside at the blowing trees and sheets of rain. The violent shaking of the trailer diminished to a gentle rocking with the gusty wind, lightning and thunder more distant. How could he concentrate on adding prime numbers to form a Heinz rectangle?

Where was Jeff? Was he okay?

Sonorous sighing came from Bernadette's bed.

He undressed and crawled back into bed, pulled the sheets over his head, and did what he hadn't done in years. *Please, God, let Jeff be okay. I know it's been awhile and it always seems like you hear from me when I'm in trouble. But please, make Jeff, Marci, and Katie safe. And don't forget Lisette. Bring her back here safe, too. Thanks.*

Oh, yeah. I'd like to survive this mess, get back to my family, and convince Lisette she'd be better off without me. That'd be great. Thanks.

The wind buffeted the trailer with rain, Bernadette snorted once and turned over to a more peaceful sighing, and Dan's eyes finally closed, ushering in a hazy land of shadows and hopes.

Prime numbers coalesced in greens and blues and violets to form Heinz rectangles:

$$5+7+11=23$$
$$7+11+13=31$$
$$11+13+17=41$$

He dreamed of kissing soft lips and Jeff crying out his name in a ghostly swamp.

He awoke with a start to a sun-backed silhouette standing over him. He blinked and squinted, shading his eyes with his hand.

The shadow spoke. "Have a good sleep, Danny Boy?"

Sam.

"Not really. Kind of a pissy night."

"Be glad you weren't getting the full stream all night like we did."

Dan sat up quickly and grabbed Sam's arm, his voice strained with concern, "Did you see Lisette?"

"Right over here, Dan."

He frowned at Lisette's mocking tone. She stood next to Bernadette, a cheerful face sipping on steaming coffee, wet coils of hair clinging to her neck. *God, what a neck.*

"Welcome back to the world of the living, Daniel," said Bernadette.

Dan closed his eyes, blew out a sigh of relief, and stretched, raising his head to the heavens. *Thank you.* "How 'bout a cup of that coffee?"

Sam slapped him on the back. "That a boy. Get those brain cells percolating."

Lisette handed him a cup of coffee, and he inspected their clothes.

"So if you were out all night in that rain, how come you're so dry now?"

"We changed while you were doing your Rip Van Winkle imitation." He waved Lisette and Bernadette off. "You two need to go help Ron and the others outside while I fill in Danny Boy."

The two women walked away, silent.

"Others?"

"Reinforcements. Remmy St. James's relatives want to get him back as much as we do. We scoped out Xoflex and poked around all night, but no luck. It seems the U.S. Army has a keen interest in Mr. St. James and has detained him at the Xoflex plant."

"Can't imagine why," Dan slurped coffee.

"Yeah. No shit. Speaking of connections, Bernadette tells me you might have something."

Dan frowned, then wanted to jump up and down. "Yeah, it's cool." After last night's turn of events with Lisette he had forgotten about the video file he'd copied.

While he waited for the machine to boot up, he peered at Sam. "Did you talk with Lisette at all about last night?"

"Not much."

"What do you think I should—"

"I like Lisette and she likes me. She likes Ron, too. I don't get involved in her private life. Whatever's going on between you and Lisette is your business. Capiche?"

"Right." *This guy is no Fred.*

The computer beeped and Dan clicked on the file *UAEAEH_cleanup. vid.* The video software logo preceded the clip about a Greenpeace splinter group and their efforts in cleaning up oil spills in the North Atlantic. A spokeswoman asked Remmy St. James if Xoflex could speed the clean-up process. It cut off before Remmy could respond.

"Play it again." After the third time Sam said, "Okay, that's enough. Did you recognize anyone?"

"El-Hamain behind the woman?"

Sam raised his eyebrows and flipped his palms out, as if to say, Is that all?

"Okay, there's El-Hamain, probably responsible for the OPEC Vienna disaster and subsequent failing OPEC oil wells, meeting with Remmy St. James, Xoflex's chief oil production guy. It's no great stretch to believe the two of them are responsible for the worldwide oil disaster. Which is probably why the Army has Remmy, since no one's been able to locate El-Hamain."

"That's what I thought. But his aunt and uncle say Remmy had nothing to do with it and he's been working hard to find a way to fix things."

"Of course he would tell *them* that. I sure wouldn't want my aunt and uncle thinking I just destroyed the world."

"Yeah, that too. But he told his aunt that he knew how to reverse things, and had to get back to Xoflex to prove it. If he was in cahoots with El-Hamain, why go back in knowing the Army had the place surrounded?"

"He would more likely be on a private plane to Dubai."

"Bingo." Sam, nodded, and kept nodding. Waiting. Waiting.

The *Jeopardy* tune played in Dan's head. "You're going into Xoflex to get Remmy? Are you nuts? I mean come on. That's the United States Army. And, in a way, we work for them. Use the radio and tell them you have vital information about Remmy."

"I tell you what. You get me into Xoflex and I'll tell you the rest of the story. But in case something happens to us and you get busted, it's better you don't know some things."

Dan felt the pang once again of being left out—the old "support staff" and "the need to know" bullshit.

"Okay. Whatever. Just give me Bernadette. I can't do this by myself. Their security software almost had us last night. We may not have much more than a couple of passes at the security system before we are shut out completely."

Sam patted Dan's shoulder. "Thanks Dan. I'll do more than just Bernadette. There's a guy named Bear, friend of Remmy's, who'll be roaming outside keeping you safe. And believe me; it'll take a platoon of Army guys to get by Bear."

Sam strode out the door. Dan thought about the wave of Humvees that had passed them several days ago on their way to Xoflex. That was a hell of a lot more than a platoon.

CHAPTER 51

Remmy disappeared from the lab and fell into black water. He pushed off the bottom and put a defiant fist in the air as he swam to the side of the Big Black Toilet. The Flusher had worked perfectly. No one except the guy who built it and maybe two other members of the lab staff knew about it, a contingency procedure for contaminations in the lab. He had stepped through an apparent closet door, hit the button, and whoosh: gone. The door closed behind him and no one the wiser. He splashed into a large tank of water loaded with black, ionized charcoal that absorbed most nanoparticles.

He climbed out of the tank, peeled off his wet clothes, and grabbed a towel, blotting off some of the black powder. He entered the Magneto room. Xoflex had engineered their nanobots to be magnetically attractive. He hit the pulse button—one millisecond of magnetic pulse. A slight pang in a lower molar reminded him of the old, cheap filling. He toweled off, let the towel drop and exited. He opened the locker outside the room. Inside hung running clothes he'd used during the summer. The shorts and tee-shirt wouldn't keep him very warm, but if he kept moving he should reach his destination soon.

This exit emptied out on the far side of the Xoflex property, and they usually kept it double locked. Phipps probably didn't know about it, and he hoped Sinclair's mercenaries relied more on the lock and security cameras than a real guard. He disabled the alarm and quietly unlocked and cracked the door. No guard. The security video camera outside rotated to point away from the door. He bolted, hidden in the nearby woods before the camera caught anything but leaves flying in his wake.

He ran for about ten minutes, trying to put as much distance between him and Xoflex. When he stopped, he felt like he'd been on at least *two* all-night Mardi Gras benders. His hands shook, he could hardly get his breath, and ... up came the coffee and donut. He heaved twice more, the last only bile and spit. Wiping his mouth, he wished for two quarts of cold water, maybe even a gallon. He glanced over his shoulder, then tried to spit one more time, but his mouth felt like fly paper sprinkled with sand. *Should have left that IV in a bit longer.*

He trotted in the direction of the nearest road, hoping for a ride and water.

After another two minutes of trudge-trotting, his vision grayed, he felt faint and stumbled to a walk, putting his hand out to steady himself on a nearby tree. He missed the tree and fell, landing on his back.

Everything spun out of focus. He felt like heaving again.

What the hell is this? Did they put a drug in the IV?

He concentrated and focused on a distant patch of sky through the canopy of trees and vines. Puffs of white clouds in the blue. You didn't see blue sky like that the rest of the year. Only in the winter. Too much humidity and heat. At least he wasn't hot. And the plants and earth smelled so fresh.

The scrub bushes and palmettos waved in his vision. The cool grass and mud cradled his arms.

Got to get up. Move.

But he couldn't. At least the nauseating vertigo finally stopped.

Stay still and it will be okay. Sleep. Yeah. Get up later and conquer the world.

Maybe Tony will help. Tony with curly golden locks, twinkling brown eyes, perfect eyebrows hovering over an Indian nose with high, flushed cheeks, and a red, sensitive mouth—like his prize roses.

They knew about us, Tony. That's okay though. I don't care. After all, it's New Orleans.

He closed his eyes. *Think of Tony. Smell his roses. That will help.*

Then he felt strong hands on his arms, and he opened his eyes.

Must be dreaming. Uncle Joe? Auntie?

"Remmy? Dat you? How you get here?" Joe said as he cradled Remmy's head.

"Uncle Joe. I don't feel so good. Drugged me." Then he grinned and said, "Outfoxed 'em." His eyes glazed over. He shivered and mumbled, "Thirsty. Need water."

His eyes closed.

"Remmy. Remmy!" But Joe's screams got no response.

The sniffers hounded them this time from the get go, so Bernadette and Dan got nowhere fast. Dan needed an excuse to escape Bernadette's prying eyes. "I'll be right back." He said. "I have a program on my laptop in the van that might help."Once in the van, he closed the door and concentrated on getting in and finding his program, the one he should have never written, the one he had to destroy.

While Dan was in the van, oblivious, Joe, Sam and Bear hauled Remmy into the house and put him on Bernadette's queen bed. Lola bent over him. "I don't like this at all," she said, dabbing Remmy's face with a cool damp cloth.

Lisette took his pulse, pulled his mouth open and inspected the shrunken tongue.

"He's dehydrated. Smells like he vomited, too. Do you think he can drink?"

Lola grabbed the glass of water from Sam, cradled Remmy's head with her hand, and tried to pour water into his mouth. It ran down the side of his cheeks.

She started to cry. "Dammit, Joe. Can't you get him awake? He gotta drink sometin' or he gonna die. Do sometin'!"

Joe cocked his elbow and slapped Remmy on the cheek, nearly knocking his head out of Lola's hand.

"What the hell?" Remmy's eyes fluttered and he tried to sit. He rubbed his cheek.

"Remmy!" Lola said. "Praise the Lord. Now here, you drink dis water." She eased the glass over to his lips. He grabbed it and slurped down the water, asking for more and more until after four glasses he sat up on his own and looked around.

"I thought I was a dead man. Thought they drugged me."

He licked his lips and asked for more water. After four more glasses, he stopped and thumped his stomach. "Think I'm ripe now."

He squeezed his eyes shut a few times, then gazed at each one of them and croaked, "So, where am I and who are all these people?"

After brief introductions, Sam said, "We were coming in to get you when your uncle nearly tripped over your body in the woods. You saved us from having to figure out a way to overcome the U.S. Army. How'd you get out anyhow?"

"It's a long story, but the short version is I had a secret passageway that they hadn't figured out."

Remmy frowned at Sam. "If you're with the CIA, how come you would have to overcome the Army? Aren't you guys on the same side?"

"Normally, yes. But—"

The door to the trailer sprung open. Lisette popped her head in. "Hope he's ready to move. We got company."

CHAPTER 52

A day earlier, Abdullah observed from the turret of his own Humvee, pondering as René rode the war machine forward and shattered the enemy. The enemy. Other human beings, mostly young boys volunteering to be heroes, but in reality only needing their college tuition paid. It was not their fault. They were not there when the birds had suffocated from oil spills. They did not spill the oil that made ashes of Asiyah, or cut the melody out of Tamara's hand.

His thoughts became a whirlwind, twisting into the next one without waiting. *Always wanted to save life—now I'm taking it—had to be done—teach them a lesson—bring back the good earth—destroy the oil tyrants—end the age of the automobile.*

He shook his head trying to make sense of things. But the thoughts spun on. *Not right—killing all these men and women who were just their tools, their blind and innocent tools. If you destroy the hammer you don't even faze the carpenter; he only gets another hammer. But take away all the wood, and ... no need for a carpenter. And we did that already. So why? Why kill so many?*

He keyed the microphone, "René stop. No more. We have to stop!"

But it was too late. Fires poured out of tanks behind the now breached barbed wire. Only a handful of shells had fired from their powerful tanks before the black diesel smoke stopped, the fuel gone. With René's onslaught, soldiers fell like petals from a dead rose.

Abdullah screamed into the microphone, "René! René! Stop firing. Stop killing! I can't do this anymore. Can't you see? Stop! Pleeeease!"

His words ended in a cracked wheeze. It was useless. He buried his face in his arm, unable to watch anymore.

René's voice crackled over the radio, "Cease fire! Cease fire!"

The firing stopped. René's calm baritone soothed Abdullah over the earphones, "It is over sir. We will not massacre them. Do not worry. It is over."

Abdullah unfolded his head from the crook in his arm, tentative but hopeful.

He'd seen this before, only with different weapons and over different causes. Wrecked machines smoldered and coughed fire through ragged holes. Dead or writhing men and women littered the green and brown field, moans and mumbles intermittently punctuated with tormented screams, a barked order, a name called several times without answer. Burnt gunpowder mixed with diesel oil, blood, wet earth, and burning flesh—all smells familiar to war-seasoned veterans. One unfamiliar odor floated in: the burnt popcorn smell of biodiesel-fueled machines, the only vehicles still moving through the maze of human and metal detritus.

A tattered, white handkerchief waved in the wind behind the barbed wire.

Abdullah vomited over the side of the Humvee. He retched over and over, his body draped over the edge of the turret like a rag doll. He sobbed between spasms, an upheaval trying to exorcise the evil he had become.

He realized his political agenda had accomplished what all politicians thirsted for—more power. And he'd used the best tool a politician had when faced with a powerful enemy: violent overwhelming force—war. He hated what he'd done, what he'd caused, but at the same time he knew it would have come eventually, just from someone else, someone evil. After all, he wasn't evil. No, he was not.

He retched again, sour bile burning his throat. His hands flailed at his head and yanked out patches of hair. He enjoyed the pain. He ripped his jacket and shirt off and started tearing at his skin with his nails.

If only I can reach the real Abdullah inside, then I can show them.

Ethan, who had occupied the Humvee behind him, saw the beginning of Abdullah's break and quickly jumped in beside him, pinning his arms to his side with a big bear hug. "Tamara needs you, Abby. It's okay. It is almost over. You must calm yourself. *We* need you. The *world* needs you. *Please,* sir."

Ethan had to hold on with all his might to the wriggling, cursing, spitting animal that Abdullah had become.

A final heave and the animal quieted, sobbing and moaning, "What have I done. It wasn't supposed to turn out like this. Allah, I am so sorry. God, please forgive me."

Abdullah coughed and stood straight and still, as if a switch flipped. "Thank you, Ethan. I am fine now. I know what I must do." His was as calm as the eye of a hurricane. He pulled his shirt and jacket back on.

René, who had returned in his vehicle, peered over at Ethan and Abdullah. "Everything all right?"

Abdullah motioned forward with his hand, "Let us get inside and set up. We still have work to do. Only ..." a momentary crack in his voice returned, "No more killing."

"Yes, sir. We can manage that."

Abdullah's driver followed René and they moved through the nightmarish battle scenes. Abdullah stared straight ahead, batting at flies that flocked for the feast.

Deep inside the barbed wire enclosure, oil derricks intermingled with scattered oil pumps in the field. He gradually walked his gaze around him. It reminded him of the Iraq-Kuwait war.

What had they called it? Operation Desert Storm. Good name.

Only it turned out like a typhoon—the initial storm surge proved horrible, a thing of awe, but the aftermath clawed and haunted and persisted, eventually overcoming any memory of the beginning of the storm.

That feeling began sneaking into the back of his mind. He saw the smoking debris on one side of the barbed wire, and relative calm on the other side. Only it was all turned around. In Kuwait, the wells had belched fire and soot high into the air. Here, the oil wells did not smoke. But the rest appeared identical—dead bodies on a landscape that had once appeared beautiful, now scorched and pock-marked with craters, leveled but for burning machines and scattered charred trees.

This is only the beginning.

A light of hope lingered. If he could change the course an iota, maybe, just maybe, the rest would play out as he had foreseen. Not this ugly thing that strangled his mind.

He jumped from the Humvee and waved for René to get things started.

Finish one part. Begin the next.

CHAPTER 53

Jeff zipped his soft shell cold weather jacket all the way up. The bright sun seemed to bounce off the freezing air that penetrated his bones. The UAH jogged to the left and right as it had done for the last few hours. They'd made good time traveling within sight of the highway, but never on it, fearing IEDs.

Rector's voice crackled in the headset, "Come on down, Corporal. We have a good view. Besides, it's getting cold. You need to get warm."

"I'm okay." He said it with a conviction he didn't feel. His teeth ached and his ears had gone from burning to numb.

"That's an order, Corporal."

Jeff scrunched down into the warm cab of the Humvee and shut the turret door. He took off his helmet.

Two men in the back seats slept; Rector sat in the right front; the private drove. Jeff occupied the middle: the central dot on a number five dice. He sat cross-legged, Indian style on the flat metal that he usually stood on to see out the turret. His helmet lay in his lap. The driver's eyes popped so wide a margin of white completely encircled light blue irises that twitched back and forth like blue marbles in a pin ball machine, noting every rabbit, every bug that moved.

Rector, on the other hand, slumped with his back halfway on the door, his helmet pitched low almost covering his eyes. Eye slits gleamed like a cobra, focused directly on Jeff. Rector switched off the intercom and leaned forward. Something he wanted only Jeff to hear.

The Humvee's engine, a low-pitched purr, growled louder uphill and quieted when they coasted. The sleeping men in back jostled in unison at turns and bounces, occasionally groaning or changing positions, but never waking. Jeff and Rector seemed alone together. The driver existed in his own world.

"So, Jeff, is this about what you expected?"

Jeff stiffened. Rector never called him Jeff. Maybe once. But not like this—casual, like a friend.

"Not exactly." Yet it jibed with what he'd read about war—unpredictable, terrifying, but somehow rewarding.

Rector cocked his helmet back and studied him. Jeff could see his eyes better, hooded, but not sinister. He stared at Jeff, expectant. Jeff wanted to give him an answer but had nothing. He was empty, and afraid he might say the wrong thing.

Rector pulled out a can of Copenhagen from his coat pocket, twisted off the top, and held it out to Jeff.

"No thanks." The sharp smell of tobacco nauseated Jeff. He shifted on the platform with each bump.

Rector shrugged, took a pinch and shoved it into the corner of his mouth. He stowed the Copenhagen and grabbed an empty Coke can from behind him and spit into the top, then moved his cheek and jaw back and forth and spit into the can again. He leaned his head back against the side of the Humvee and scratched the side of his neck.

"You're from Denver, right?"

"Yeah." Jeff put his hands on his face, his elbows on his knees, mimicking a yoga master preparing for a long meditation. He'd slept like this before, but only in fits. Rector should leave him alone if he slept. He put a hand over his nose to block the faint odor of piss.

"Don't guess Denver will ever be quite the same after this shit."

Jeff eyed Rector and sat up. "What do you mean?"

Rector slurped after spitting into the can. He wiped his lower lip with his sleeve. "What do you think happened back there?"

Jeff cleared his throat. "We got the shit kicked out of us." He hung his head and lowered his voice, "And we deserted our buddies." He felt humiliated.

"Now, the first part is true, most definitely. And I ain't use to that, for sure. But we didn't desert anybody. I was ordered to report to

Southern Command Center. The COM lines were down and Lieutenant Robison said, and I quote: 'Sergeant, get the hell out of here. Take any men you need and one other Humvee squad. But move!' So that's what I did. I stopped and was goin' to look around for you and you jumped in. Saved me the effort. Now maybe you think we were desertin', and you jumped in to save your ass. We did save your ass. But you ended up on a legal mission. If you'd rather go back, I'll stop and let you out. If you want me to report you as a deserter, I could do that, but it would be hard to support as the only evidence is in *your* sad mind. And everyone knows that in combat your mind plays tricks. So what's it gonna be?"

Jeff glanced at everything but Rector.

Rector continued, "Okay, now that we got that settled, let's try again. What do you think happened back there? Besides getting the shit kicked out of us."

Jeff scratched his chin. "We ran out of fuel?"

Rector waited, raised his eyebrows and gave Jeff the Charades hand sign for more.

The Humvee dove into a big ditch, bottomed out, then flew up the other side: a sensation of weightlessness followed by an instant three G's. Jeff gripped Rector's seat back and pushed his other hand up to protect his head. Guns and helmets rattled. Two men in back snorted and mumbled. The ride smoothed. Easy breathing resumed.

Rector cocked his head at Jeff, like a curious dog after a strange sound.

Jeff relaxed and shifted his gaze back and forth, searching for something right there, at the edge. It *was* strange. *Why had the U.S. Army run out of fuel?*

"Shit! We were set up." Jeff blurted it, a touch of anger in his words.

Rector nodded and smiled. "I think LT figured it out real quick, and that's why he sent me out of there. Someone has to find out what the hell is going on."

"Why would they set us up?"

"I don't know for sure if that's what happened. I'm just following orders. But I think we need to be damn careful what we say when we get to where we're goin'. We all gotta be on the same page. You get me, Corporal?"

Jeff got it. There were two messages: once they got to the Command Center, let the Sergeant do the talking; the second was the oldest code of the soldier—watch your back, and your buddy's.

"Yeah, Sarge. I got it."

That brought a thought that had smoldered hazy all night and finally crystallized.

"Sarge, do you ever get the feeling that . . . like we're not doing the right thing out here, I mean killing all these people and everything. Do you always do exactly what they tell you to do?"

"It's like this, Corporal: I'm a soldier in the U.S. Army and I do what the U.S. Army orders me to, no questions asked. They decide what to do, tell me, and I do it. Simple."

Jeff needed more. It was maybe the reason he was here and not still back there, blown to bits.

"What if they made the wrong decision? You know, politicians have been known to make the wrong decision every now and then. And they pass it down to the military and wham! We're the bad guys. And, what if they don't know if we're killing civilians and shit? I mean . . ."

"This is the way I see it." Rector spoke with a calm assuredness, as if he was explaining how to field strip an M16. "Those guys that are in power, they're supposed to know everything that goes on, and they're supposed to be responsible for it. If they *don't* know, then they're fucked. Cause they're still responsible. That's their pledge. Without that pledge every one of us would have to be rethinking everything we did. We would lose the edge. Our slow-motion decisions would lose any battle, any war we entered. The way I figure it, if they don't want to be responsible for us, then they shouldn't be leaders. The best ones know. The other ones ... They become bad politicians, or find a grenade in their tent."

Rector looked at Jeff square-on, no flinches, no doubts—and something else—a seriousness Jeff wouldn't want to cross. Not ever.

Rector's eyes softened. He spit in the can and backhanded his mouth. "That's why I entered the U.S. Army: to be a soldier, not a politician. Now, get ready to hop out, Jeff."

Jeff frowned and his heart flip-flopped. Was Rector letting him go?

Rector smiled, "We need to use one of the spare fuel cans before we get too low. Can you handle that?"

"Oh." He let out a breath. "Sure. Fuel cans. Got it."

Rector tapped the driver on the shoulder and pointed, "Hey, Cole Trickle. Stop in that grove of trees. We need gas. You know, you should be telling *me* that. Don't you watch the fuel gauge?"

The wild-eyed private stopped the vehicle and glanced back. "I don't know much about these things. I just drive 'em, Sarge."

Jeff jumped out and emptied one of the spare fuel cans into the Humvee. They traveled until dark in relative silence, then pulled over for the night. Rector nodded off to sleep, and Jeff slid into a semiconscious state, afraid of going to sleep but finally giving in. He would need his rest for tomorrow.

CHAPTER 54

Dan sat in the front passenger seat of the van, concentrating on finding his program in Xoflex's files. Now that Bernadette wasn't hovering over his shoulder, he might have time. He found the right area, opened the file and—

The side door burst open. Sam and Ron crowded in with some other guy while Lisette jumped into the driver's seat. Sam handed Dan a jacket, his Beretta and a full clip. "Sorry to interrupt, but we gotta split. Stow your gear and get ready for a fast ride."

Dan closed the laptop, hoping he didn't appear guilty. He stowed the laptop inside the satchel at his feet, put the gun and clip in the outside pocket, and zipped everything closed.

"Dan," Sam said, "this is Remmy St. James. Remmy, Dan Trotter. Lisette, get us out of here. Follow that truck."

"What about Bernadette?"

"She's in the truck." Sam pointed. Little Pee Pee materialized in front. A huge mongrel of a man sat in the bed of the truck holding on with hands that Dan felt sure could take a piece out of the metal if he gripped hard enough.

"Who the hell is that?" Dan pointed.

From behind him, Remmy answered, "That's Bear. He's with me."

Looks like he got the right name, Dan thought.

"Sam, is that the same Bear you said helped me while you searched for Remmy?"

"The same."

Lisette swerved the van out of the trailer park and followed Little Pee Pee at breakneck speed. Dan held on. The mutant man in the bed of Little Pee Pee appeared relaxed: just an easy ride through the park, barely moved from side to side.

Dan felt he would be thrown into Lisette's lap any moment. *Lisette's lap? That would be kinda—*

WHAT is your deal? Get a grip!

Must be the stress. Gotta get a less stressful job.

The side view mirror gave glimpses of the other truck, Blue Titty, about twenty yards behind, splattered with mud from the van. Dan had never seen the driver and gaped at him. *Jesus! He's just a blonde-headed freckle faced kid, barely able to see over the steering wheel.* The head and chest of a very tall guy loomed above the cab. The guy held onto the truck's roll bar.

Dan blinked hard, squinted at the front truck and back in the mirror. The guy riding Blue Titty like a bull rider at the rodeo was a mirror image of Bear. Maybe taller and thinner, but the face—only a mother could love that.

Dan squinted in the mirror and spotted a lady in the passenger's seat of that truck. One thing for sure, the big guy holding onto the roll bar was not a progeny of that lady. She had classic beauty, worn down a bit, but still—

The van jerked to the right, went over a very large ditch and bucked like a wild mustang. Dan's hand slipped off the door handle and he instinctively clutched the laptop with both arms, unable to keep his head from connecting with the metal roof. *Shit! That's gonna leave a mark.*

He rubbed his head and cinched his seat belt. He started to put on his jacket, but froze when the truck in front slowed and they closed in. Bear smiled, obviously enjoying the carnival ride.

The two muddy ruts they slogged through entered a narrow corridor. Tree limbs and palmetto branches lashed the windshield.

POP!

He ducked instinctively, hugged the satchel between his chest and knees, and stopped breathing as his heart tried to run out of his chest. Had someone shot at them?

Wonder if the Company psychiatrist can help that?

He blew out his breath and sat up to see his fate. A spider web of cracks radiated from a central spot on the windshield where a plum-sized pine cone lodged.

Less stressful job. Soon.

The truck in front splashed through a large pool in the middle of the ruts. The muddy water splattered their windshield, blinding them. Lisette hit the wipers, but it only smeared a brown finger painting over the windshield. Dan rolled down the window and peered ahead.

"Stop!" he screamed.

Lisette slammed on the brakes and the van slid, canting Dan's side forward. The right corner of the hood tapped the already stopped rear end of Little Pee Pee with enough force to twist the van all the way sideways. The wheels clipped something and tipped the van over onto the right side.

Dan smacked the side of his head on the door jamb. A palmetto leaf crammed through his open window, almost tearing the computer satchel from his arms. He held on, but screamed in pain as the saw-toothed branch sliced into his right forearm.

"Son of a bitch!" His yell seemed distant, blunted by a feeling of unreality, mixed with a cacophony of curses and grunts from the back seats. The smell of composted earth and grass filled his nose. The seat belt cinched too tight and cut into his hip bone.

Lisette, hanging from the seatbelt, peered at him. "You okay, Dan?"

She winced when she moved her left hand. The thumb jutted at an odd angle.

But yet her first concern had been me.

"Yeah. Cut my arm. What about you. Looks like your thumb is dislocated." He thought he was speaking normally, but his voice sounded distant.

"Probably," she said it like an afterthought and glanced in the back seat. "Sam, you guys okay?"

"Fine. Peachy. Never better."

Ron chuckled. Remmy groaned.

Lisette's door was wrenched open by the mutant Bear. Dan

expected him to rip Lisette out of the van, but he handled her as gentle as a kitten.

His deep voice rumbled, "Ya'll gots to get outta here. Dem Army guys is right on our tails."

Dan reached down with his left hand and struggled to unbuckled the seatbelt as Remmy and the other two started clambering over the seats to get out through Lisette's door.

Another compact man leaned into the window and said, "Remmy you awright, you?"

Remmy pulled himself over the side of the driver's seat and grinned wanly. Blood dribbled from the side of his mouth.

"Sure, Uncle Joe. Just got into a tussle with the window."

Dan finally scrambled out of Lisette's door and slopped through the muddy water toward two boats sitting in a canal. Everything tilted and moved like a carnival fun house.

His right forearm oozed dark blood from the palmetto gash. It was probably a shallow cut, though, because he could still grip the computer. In front of him, Lisette walked and nonchalantly pulled on her left thumb, grunted, and shook her left hand like it had gone to sleep. She waded out to the first boat and pulled herself over the side, turned around, and put her hand out to help Dan get in.

He handed her the computer satchel first. "Make sure this doesn't get wet."

Uncle Joe scrounged two white plastic trash bags and stuffed the satchel into one, then the other. He wrapped it between life vests, saying, "Never wear the damn tings. Might as well git some use."

Dan pulled himself up onto the gunnel of the boat, but got hung up halfway. Lisette hauled on the back of his belt and flipped him over into the floor of the boat. He flopped around for an embarrassing eternity until Lisette helped him up and guided him onto a seat at the back of the boat. Drops of his blood freckled one of her cheeks. She sat beside him and tore two thin strips off the lower half of her tee shirt, folded one and placed it on top of the wound, then cinched the other around his arm, giving pressure to the wound.

He couldn't help but glance down at the exposed alabaster silky skin of her waist.

You are hopeless.

He wet his left index finger and wiped at the flecks of red on her cheek. Her nose really wasn't too bad, and her lips were fine. Water lapped at the hull. They're eyes locked for an instant, an eternity of instants. She blinked once, a close-up caress of those beautiful blue eyes, and stared deep inside him.

That he would remember. Forever.

CHAPTER 55

After that, for Dan everything blurred into a dream of emotions, water, and sound. He had a hard time focusing, all his thoughts scrambled. He touched the goose egg on his aching right temple, and cradled his throbbing arm. He licked brackish water off his lips.

Lisette sat in front of him. Her ebony locks trailed behind like the moss that hung from cypress trees. The trees floated by, their delicate Christmas tree tops widening down to their trunk, olive stanchions disappearing into chocolate-milk water.

A constant bumping and thumping crowded his brain. He imagined the cypress knobs unfurling long fingers that reached out under the water and tapped the hull of the boat, trying to grasp it.

He shook his head to clear his mind. *Crap! That hurt.* And it didn't clear anything.

In the back of the boat, something else thumped. A vaguely familiar person flopped from side to side, huge elbows and hands, heavy, knocking at every turn.

Knocking. Trying to get in? Out? He should be trying to get out. Why would he want to stay here? Of course! He liked this swamp—raised here, ate shrimp, gators. Hell, he could probably wrestle one and tear its head off. *Look at the size of those mitts.* Dan held out his own hand. *Tiny. I'm a midget compared to that guy.* That guy was probably a mutation of Southern intermarriage. So there was really no comparison. Like comparing a marmot to a gorilla. Same species, only a different subspecies. Was a marmot the same species as a gorilla?

Didn't matter. The guy's mother didn't care. On the other hand, maybe she did. She'd ridden in the other truck and now sat beside Dan: light red hair, carroty, mixed with white streaks, tangled and flowing back from strands stuck to her cheeks and temples, wet with tears. Anguish scrunched her beautiful face. Couldn't be the guy's mother. How could she give birth to such a—Dan glanced back at the huge man—hulking mutant? Did they even do C-sections back here in the woods? A guy that big would have been huge as a baby. Probably killed her coming out. Jesus.

He glanced at the woman again. Crying, so she must love him. Maybe he was knocking trying to get back to her.

The boat swerved hard, brackish muddy spray hit Dan's face. *Didn't even flinch. Nerves of steel.* Instinctively he started to wipe his face. *Shit! Not that hand.* More like nerves and brains of snot. *Can't even remember not to use that throbbing appendage. Stupid shit.*

That big guy was trying to use his whole body to crawl out the side. The last curve must have spooked him. *Maybe big, but shit, this is nothing. Try running through a Venezuelan jungle carrying a suitcase with a helicopter on your tail.*

The guy was definitely trying to get out, now face down, arms outstretched above his head trying to claw out the side of the boat, his left leg half covered with the tan swamp liquid. So heavy the whole boat tilted. Was the boat leaking? If the guy wanted out that bad Dan would happily help him. Keep them from sinking.

The boat swerved again, slapping one side against a tree, flopping the man onto his back. His shoulders were nearly as wide as the boat. Not as big as cousin Bear, though. Maybe it was *brother* Bear. Wasn't that a cartoon movie?

But the man's face was not a 'toon. *Jesus. Not alive either. Can't be with that.*

Lisette eyed the big man with the mangled face. Her wild hair twisted in the breeze like Medusa's snakes. Her eyes dazzled like two perfect blue diamonds, reflecting every bit of light at that huge man. Dan felt the hope in that fiery gaze. Hope that she could bring the hulk back to life. Hope, but also sorrow and love. She had a lot of love. Man, if she loved him the guy was definitely knocking trying to get back in.

He winced at the face. *He's dead, you idiot.*

The boat slowed; the big outboard stopped its incessant grind. Lisette stood.

Time to get out and swim? Out of gas?

She stepped around the big man and adjusted another puny motor with a long axle ending in blades she angled into the water. A high pitched hum accompanied the big outboard motor tilting out of the water.

She reached under a gunnel and pulled out a torn white towel. She wrapped it around the big man's head and face. Tears streamed down her face.

The puny motor spluttered to a start, a put-put, and they eased forward.

She glanced at Dan, and wiped her cheeks.

Is she sad about me?

"That's Dad," she said. "We had to take him with us. I love him dearly."

She put a hand on Dan's shoulder for balance getting back to her seat. *Warm, strong hand. It would be okay.*

Dad? Doesn't look like her dad. No beard and way too big

This was the South and the age of divorce. Maybe one was her step-dad?

He pondered that and stared at the white towel on the huge guy's face. Everything glazed over. He lost track of time.

The boat stopped. He snapped his head up.

No more *put-put* sounds, no more knocks, only dull, gentle thuds of the boat against the dock, footsteps on the dock, talking, flapping and quacking of ducks.

Shadows floated over the white towel across the man's face.

A firm hand took his left forearm. The sun dodged in and out behind trees, and he squinted through it at a person's head.

"Dan, are you alright?"

He blinked at the voice and the winking sun. The hand pulled him. He pushed up from the seat with his right arm. The pain in his forearm shot straight through to the dull ache behind his eyes causing him to squeeze his eyes shut and resist any further movement. Another hand held him steady.

The pain eased. He blinked again and saw who held him.

Sam.

"Hi Sam. Where have you been? Had a boat ride. Dead guy in the back. Big guy."

"Yeah, that's Dad. Are you okay, Dan?"

Sam touched Dan's temple. "You must have hit your head. Got a bruise. Probably a concussion."

"Yeah. Had one before. Feels like that. Arm hurts, too. I didn't know you were related to Lisette. That guy was your dad, too? Hey, where's my computer?"

Sam patted Dan's shoulder. "No, he's not mine or Lisette's dad. Worried about the silicon brain, huh? That's a good sign."

Dan nodded. *Silicon was better. Didn't think. Didn't hurt.*

Sam helped him out of the boat onto the swaying dock. He wobbled and stumbled once to his left. Had to get his dancing feet back.

The compact man—*What was his name? Jake or Jeb, something like that*—handed a bundle to Sam, who carried it from the boat and grabbed Dan's left arm again.

Now that his right arm wasn't supported he let it hang and it throbbed with the building ache in his head. The knocking sounds now pounded inside his head.

Great.

"Does anyone have some aspirin, or Tylenol? Motrin maybe?" He asked as politely as he could while he tried to follow Sam on the swaying dock, one step here and two stumbles there. Maybe he had a hangover. Did he drink too much last night?

Last night. Something important happened last night.

He searched for Lisette, but instead saw Bernadette. Mud spackled her cheeks, and a big glob matted her hair to her left ear. Lipstick smeared her upper lip into a snarl, and mascara smudged her eyes like black butterflies.

She will know. She was there. Wasn't she?

Her smile improved the snarl. But she shook her head and walked into the cabin.

"Maybe some coffee? I read once that coffee helps migraines. And I'm getting a whopdoozer of a headache. But aspirin would be my first choice. Stomach's not quite right either. Coffee might—" He shook his head slowly at the mere thought of vomiting.

Sam guided him into a chair. "I'll see what they got, buddy. You just sit here and I'll get Lisette to tend to your arm."

Sam went away, then came back and handed Dan a big white and orange parcel. "Here. Unwrap this and make sure it's okay."

The orange parcel sat in Dan's lap. He blinked several times, then picked and pulled at the duct tape, winced at the pain in his left arm, but found an edge to the tape and wound the gray turban off the orange life vest until he smiled at the black satchel. He eased the laptop out and put his cheek on the cool, soothing metal. He cradled it on his knees, opened it and powered up. The Windows musical theme started him swaying and smiling, and he tapped his foot to the chugging sound of the hard drive as it loaded the necessary programs.

Those sounds and the crisp recoil of the keys on his fingers along with the weight of the laptop on his knees finally brought him back to reality. He rolled his head around and loosened the muscles in his neck. His headache felt better already. 313,353,373,383 all floated in pulsing fluorescent green across his indigo mind screen. He loved threes. The cloth wrapped around his right forearm seemed a part of him now, the pain distant.

The chugging sound got louder. His stomach sank. The hard drive motor must have been damaged in the boat.

The usual messages and numbers scrolled on the screen. The chugging sound got even louder and changed into a *whop-whop-whop.*

It was not coming from the computer, but from outside the cabin.

CHAPTER 56

Yesterday, Abdullah's forces conquered the Army command center in the middle of the East-Texas oil fields. Ethan had sequestered Abdullah into a corner behind tall dividers, previously the Army commander's desk. Last night and early this morning, Abdullah reworked his speech, changing it first one way, then the other, then yet another. He stared into space. Everything had been so clear when he started this quest so many years ago.

He took a break and walked around the new center. Though early, people bustled about, setting up computers, routing wires, positioning furniture, blackboards and whiteboards, some shouting orders, others laughing or hammering on the floor.

Abdullah hid behind dividers, observing. A young man and woman picked up bright ornaments from the floor and carefully hung them on a three-foot Christmas tree sitting on a desk. The woman switched an ornament out for another three times. The man plugged in the lights. A collective approving hum and patter of clapping hands spread around the room.

After the clamor subsided, Abdullah walked toward the exit to get a breath of fresh air and heard another sound.

Outside, a young blond-haired man sat on a bench and sobbed with his head in his hands. A woman with auburn hair bent over him, held his shoulders and murmured into his ear.

Abdullah walked over and touched the woman's shoulder. "What is wrong?"

She jumped at his touch and gazed at him with hollow, bloodshot eyes. Tears tracked down her cheeks. "It's his sister, sir."

The young man lifted his head. Close-cropped amber hair high-lighted red cheeks glistening with tears, and his turquoise eyes had a sadness that pricked a distant memory in Abdullah.

"I'm sorry, sir. I can't help it. I know what we are doing is right, but ...When I saw her staring at me from the mud, I couldn't believe it. She only joined the Army Reserve to help pay for school. She was always good at hunting, so I guess they thought she should be in the infantry. But to see that beautiful face smeared with blood and her dead eyes staring up at me. Maybe I shot her. Killed her. Shit!" He shook his head and squeezed his eyes shut, pushing his hands against his eyes as if he could push out the memory with the tears that rolled down his cheeks.

"It is hard," said Abdullah with a gentle tone. "To do great good there is always a price. The greatest good extracts the highest price. We have always respected those who gave of themselves for the greater good: doctors, ministers, or even greater people like Ghandi, or Jesus. We give them high praise for their shining example of how humans can endure hardship and torture and still do the right thing. Maybe even save all of humanity."

He cradled the man's chin in his hand and raised his head. Red rimmed his blue eyes. "And how will you respond to this trial?"

Not waiting for an answer, Abdullah released his hold, turned around and walked briskly away. After walking behind one of the huge tanks to shield him from view, he broke. His entire body trembled. He fell to one knee, holding onto the side of the tank with one hand, the other bracing his body as he retched once more.

It's too much. I am not Jesus. I cannot go forty days and forty nights. Not another day of it.

His eyes traced the rocks, the mud, the bent stubs of worn grass, and ended on the hard metal of the tank tread. A machine of war. His war. Without his impetus, none of this would ever have occurred: brother killing sister, father killing son, a nation imploding because he had not predicted how far they would go to keep their throne, their paradise.

Their power.

A twisted twig in his mind snapped. The end of the twig contained a fruit that had become too heavy for the branch. The old tree was too weak. His previous constitution couldn't bear the stress any longer.

His inner tree trunk quickly evolved to a different bark: harder, pulsed a different blood: colder, and fed a different fruit: unremitting violence.

He traced the symmetric lines of the tank's wheel as his inner eye followed the broken twig. The last of the old fruit of compassion and love fell into an inky pool and caught fire. Now the other branches poured nourishment to the new fruit: vengeance, violence, and war. His new tree began to rotate, swinging the branches loaded with shiny sharp knives like a tornado of razor blades.

Cut them all. Make them bleed. Fillet their souls. He felt new, dangerous, and more sure of himself than ever. He would prevail.

He stood, wiped his mouth and marched back toward the command center.

The young blond man stood tall, recovered from his sadness. On seeing Abdullah striding towards him, he reached out his hand in thanks.

Abdullah locked eyes with the man for an instant, then strode away.

The tow-headed young man stepped back, as if struck in the face. He cocked his head. What he saw before had reached into his being and pulled him into the light of hope, an angel of mercy. What he saw now? Steely hard emptiness. The soul had departed, leaving only a ruthless well of emptiness, a black hole that would suck life into nothingness.

The young man pressed his hands to his heart, making sure it stayed put.

CHAPTER 57

The *whop-whop* sound filtered into Dan's concussed brain. A helicopter.

Lisette leaned over the kitchen counter and stretched to peer out the window. It reminded him of a day not so long ago: her in a helicopter pulling him out of the Venezuelan jungle, her black hair pulled back in a ponytail, flipped over her shoulder as she had stretched to haul him into the chopper. Now, her hair coiled on her shoulders, loose and damp from the boat ride. He ached to snuggle against her neck, the smell of her skin and wet hair close.

The helicopter moved off. Lisette walked out onto the veranda. Dan placed the open laptop on the coffee table in front of him and gently closed it, not taking his eyes of Lisette.

Sam returned with a couple of Tylenol and a glass of water.

"Thanks, Sam. I'll be with you in a minute. I need to . . ." He gazed at Lisette.

"Take your time. I think we'll be safe here for a while. We need you with a clear head."

Sam left. Dan swallowed the pills and stood. His head and arm throbbed in syncopation, but he gritted his teeth, placed the glass on the counter, and walked out the door.

The beating helicopter faded quickly. The marsh quieted.

No breeze. Calm.

Spanish moss hung from the cypress and live oaks, wet from last night's rain, sparkling in the sun like tinsel on a Christmas tree. Ducks nuzzled their tail feathers, chortled and milled around in a cove on the far side. A great blue heron stalked with slow-motion, snake-like movements that suddenly stopped, head retracted. The heron's head struck into the shallows, a wriggling fish speared in its needle beak. It deftly flipped the fish high in the air and caught it in its open gullet.

Not far from the heron, a gator sunned its prehistoric plated body on the mud, apparently sated, though its eyes followed the heron, then switched to a nutria that scampered out of the water within easy striking distance.

"Beautiful, isn't it?" Dan eased out the words—a gentle start to an anticipated tough journey. The mere sight of her eased his pains.

Lisette jerked her head slightly toward his sound, then relaxed and sighed deeply.

"Oh Dan. It's just so . . . so different."

He waited, not sure what was coming, but knowing it was time.

"You know, before the Big K, life was so different, but yet in many ways it's better now, even after the oil spill. Thank God the marsh way up here didn't get much oil. After Katrina the marsh was washed cleaner, more animals, the water sweeter, and the trees greener. But Jesus. I never want to go through that again."

She sighed again, shook her head and gazed into the trees.

"What do you mean?"

She blinked and turned her head back to him, warm blue irises telling the story before her voice continued.

"I was doing something . . . really stupid."

"I don't think so."

She smiled, her thin lips crooked. "You are such a kind man, Dan. I'm so sorry I put a wrench in your life."

"Lisette, every man my age should have such a wrench thrown in his life's bicycle tires so he can figure out what's important and what's not."

She gazed at the marsh.

One of the ducks chuckled louder, flapped its wings and paddled back and forth across the water. The gator slunk back into the water.

She sighed and punctuated it with a grunt. "Yeah, it was stupid, me coming back here right before the hurricane. You see, Daddy—He had a few things here that I didn't want him to lose: a picture of him and momma before she died, his father's old hunting knives, and other important things. Maybe more for me than for him. Guess I also came back for the guy I told you about—the one you remind me of. Your names are similar. His was Stan. Anyway, I came down here, I thought in plenty of time. But things happened faster and . . . not like I thought."

"Stan, huh?" Dan thought she liked him for himself, not because of some guy.

She chuckled and looked deep in his eyes. "Yeah."

She glanced away. "Anyway, I got to lookin' at the family pictures and saw one of my baby sister, Clarisse, right next to a pressed rose from Daddy's beautiful garden. She was so young when we lost her in a storm years ago. Daddy gave all of us one special rose for each birthday. She only got one."

She turned her back to Dan and lifted the hair off her neck. "That's why I got this."

Dan sucked in a breath.

Below her hairline, a tattoo of a single red rose stared at him.

She shook her hair back in place and studied her shoes. "Clarisse was special. I got sad. Found a jug of moonshine. Had a problem with alcohol back then. Started thinking and drinking and . . .

"Next thing I know, God dammit, the front door slammed open. When the wind blew, that door always flopped back and forth. There was no floppin'. The door stayed open and didn't move, like something or someone was holding it. It was dark as hell's night and the wind howled like a banshee. I jumped up and grabbed Daddy's knife.

"A wave of knee-deep cold water hit me and in another two minutes it was chest high pushing me around the room. You see, the old house wasn't like this one. The back door was way on the side. So the water came in and the house filled like an aquarium."

In the swamp, the gator's eyes and nostrils on the surface of the water eased closer to the ducks.

"Oh, Jesus," she continued, "I was scared. Knew that I was dead. I swam, trying to get out. Couldn't get out the front door; the water was coming in too fast. The back door must have busted open cause I got sucked towards it, like a big whirlpool. If I got out into the flooded swamp I would be worse off than dead—too many gators and moccasins. So I grabbed the door jamb and held on."

She slapped the railing of the veranda with an open palm. The ducks startled and flapped to the other side of the cove.

"Lucky for me my great, great gram was part Viking. Got more upper body strength than most girls."

"So that's where you got that, huh?"

"Yep. You should have seen pictures of her. She could out-canoe any guy." A quick smile faded. "Damn, I wish I could have saved just one of those pictures.

"Anyway, I hung on until the water flow lessened. Then I got my toes onto the hinges and clawed my way onto the roof. Let me tell you, that was worse than any damn obstacle course the Marines ever invented. Had to lay flat 'cause that wind would have flicked me off that old tin roof like a potato chip if I sat. Lucky I was on the leeward side; the other side was peeled up like a sardine can."

The gator's nostrils and eyes swung around and eased toward the nutria that sat on the edge of the mud, scratching its ear with a hind leg. Dan wondered if maybe he was wrong: Maybe people did have eight interesting layers.

She gazed at the trees. "After an eternity it started to get light and the water moved the other way, back-washing the dregs of New Orleans into the Gulf. Only, half of it got caught in the trees. The wind had blown so hard the trees had no leaves, like a Yankee winter. Their witch's fingers reached out and caught clumps of people's lives: dresses, pants, toy trucks, stuffed animals. Only these were people I would never know. Except one. Stan floated by. I wanted to swim out and grab him, but he was dead." She put her face in her hands and cried.

A breeze fluttered the leaves in the trees like rain on water.

Dan didn't know what to do. He felt alone, something he enjoyed in the past. But now he wanted to hug her. He stood with his hands at his sides.

After a moment, she wiped her face and smiled at him. "Weird things happened in the hurricane. I can see it like it happened today, a couch floating by with a stuffed teddy bear sitting upright, the morning sun catching its orange eyes, watching me. Watching me. Kinda like it was puzzled but having a great ride.

"But the stench." She wrinkled her nose. "Like a big toilet had been flushed with fluttering toilet paper and shit caught in every branch and bush."

"I wondered what that was in the trees," he said. "Thought it was moss, or maybe torn paper from fallen kites."

"Yeah, we tried to pick most of it out 'cause it was so damn ugly. But you couldn't get all of it."

She picked at a fingernail. "Anyway, I must have passed out on the roof for most of the morning. Woke up hot and thirsty. All the water I'd brought lay in the back of the Jeep. It lay on the other side of the bayou, tires up. I looked around for a boat or canoe, 'cause there was no way I was gonna swim to that Jeep. Gators and cotton mouths swam everywhere. Plus my left leg was all swelled up. Must have got bit by a moccasin."

She stopped and closed her eyes.

Dan waited.

Tears trickled down her cheeks onto pursed and trembling lips. Jerks and spasms accompanied each breath.

"What's wrong, Lisette?"

She held out her index finger, and he waited again.

Finally, she shook her head and whispered, "It was Dad."

"Your father?"

"No. No. You know . . . with Bear. Dad's short for Crawdad. He was good at getting mud bugs."

"Oh."

"Anyway, Dad saved me. He came through, paddling a big canoe. Don't know where he found that sucker. Guess somebody told him I'd gone to the house and he decided to come get me. I was delirious, probably dehydrated and sick from the moccasin bite. I remember those big strong arms lifting me and the next thing you know I was in the bottom of the canoe watching the sky and the passing trees. I felt like a kid, back when Daddy and Momma took me out in the boat to go fishing. I'd lie down and watch the trees go by with the fluffy white clouds and the blue sky."

Dan glanced over at the boat. The gray tarp covered the big man. "I'm so sorry."

She faced him and wiped her cheeks. "So you see, that night made me realize how fleeting life can be. I guess when I pulled you out of that jungle and saw how hurt you were and how happy I made you, I thought, you know . . . might as well. Never can tell what the hell's gonna happen tomorrow, or for that matter, in a couple hours."

She had peeled off the last layer and flung it at him. He closed his eyes and tensed his abdomen, forcing tears to stay away. All she wanted to do was help him.

He opened his eyes to splashing in the bayou. The nutria scampered away from the gator's lunge. A deer bounded into the trees, a free spirit throwing its rear hoofs at the gator.

CHAPTER 58

Jeff slept. He dreamed of riding in a truck, searching for a Christmas tree in the Rockies. His dad joked about prime numbers, then hummed a tune. The crisp, spruce air wafted in the open window. It all felt like home. He jolted with a bump. Home disappeared, but the humming continued. He opened his eyes to the gray light before dawn. The Humvee bounced and sped around a low patch of tall grass.

The private drove and hummed a high tenor melody, soft but distinct: *God Rest Ye Merry Gentlemen.* Jeff hummed along in a lower octave, remembering it must be close to Christmas.

The private stopped humming. Jeff said, "I'm sorry, but I don't even know your name."

"It's Joshua. But most people call me Josh."

"Okay, Josh. Sorry to interrupt, but it seems like you might have a better handle on this than I do. Is it Christmas?"

Josh pulled the steering wheel to the left, avoiding a large clump of mesquite bushes. "Christmas Eve or Christmas, not sure."

"Big fuckin' deal." Rector's voice growled.

Jeff jerked his head toward the voice. Two ebony crystals sparked under the rim of Rector's helmet.

Rector edged closer, pushed his helmet back so Jeff could get the full advantage of his glare.

"You think those assholes that killed our buddies back there gave a rat's ass if it's Christmas Eve? They sure didn't give a fuck about it in Iraq or Afghanistan. No, I take that back. They knew exactly what day it was, and they loved it. Just like Nam. The biggest offensive attacks came on Christmas. 'Cause that's when the sentimental Americans let their guard down. We got wise to that, and instead, let our guard down on *their* holiday. Be a nice guy. Let them have their holiday. That's when the Tet Offensive killed a thousand U.S. troops in Nam. Tet was a celebration of *their* lunar new year."

He pointed at Jeff, extending his whole arm like a straight arrow. "There are no holidays in war, theirs or ours. You are a soldier. You're not a civilian going to the mall buying last minute gifts for your mom. You're job is to protect those people from harm."

He turned his head toward the private. "And if you want to hum anymore, the only tune I want to here is the theme from *Rocky*. Keep that sentimental crap to yourself."

The other two men in the Humvee had awakened to the Sergeant's tirade and traded glances with each other between unbelievable stares at Rector.

Rector met their stares and they looked away. "That goes for each and every one of you. Forget about Christmas. You must be stronger than the enemy. Celebrate victory! Pray for *that*. Envision *that*. Dream about *that*. Once we have victory you can put *that* on your calendars every year and you will know a real celebration."

The Humvee bounced and everyone hunched down. It lurched to the left and jerked to a stop, the men in the back thrown into each other.

"What the f—?" started Rector.

"We got company," the driver said.

Through the windshield, Jeff could see only a clump of mesquite and a grassy knoll.

"Lock and load!" Rector said. "Corporal, get up there and give us a report."

Jeff donned his helmet and weaseled up into the turret and stood on tiptoe for a peek.

The Private had done a good job of stopping behind that knoll, and in the nick of time. On the other side, five camouflaged Humvees cruised abreast of each other in a wheeling search pattern through a grove of trees and marshland. The outermost vehicle in the spoke of that wheel had already reached the other side of the knoll and was moving away.

Jeff reported what he saw to Rector.

"Okay, we'll stay hunkered down here awhile. You keep an eye out, Corporal."

He climbed up and knelt on the outside rim of the turret intermittently craning his neck, his head only high enough to see over the knoll. The sun shown from behind him, allowing a great view for him, but only glare if they looked towards him.

After a half hour of playing bob and peek, he felt chilled to the bone. Finally, Rector ordered him inside.

Entering the closed quarters of the Humvee, it took him awhile to adjust to the low light. He took a drink of water from his canteen and hugged himself to get warm. He never thought the south could get this cold. Rector had a map flattened out on his knees and traced lines with his index finger.

"What's goin' on, Sarge?" he asked.

"I think those guys might be part of the Southern Command Center. We're close to their coordinates. Did you see anything that might point against it?"

"Nope. Like I said, they have U.S. ARMY clear as day plastered on the side of each vehicle."

Rector shook his head. "They aren't answering the preset frequency."

He folded the map. "Private, turn us around. We need to backtrack about five miles. I'll try the frequency again once we're on higher ground."

After only minutes, the closed quarters, their nervous energy, and days without showers, the Humvee reeked like sweaty socks that had seen one too many basketball game. That and the jostling ride squeezed Jeff's puke muscles. Rector glanced at Jeff and cracked the turret top to let fresh air circulate.

The UAH coasted to a halt. Rector spoke into the radio, listened, mumbled some more, then keyed off. "Listen up. We're going in, getting some grub, re-supplying and heading out again. Southern Command needs us to help with a search for a guy who escaped from their command center at a place called Xoflex."

CHAPTER 59

They arrived at the Xoflex building, and a lieutenant colonel with a chest full of medals waved them over. Rector opened his window and saluted. The colonel directed them to the back of the building for food, water, and ammunition. A large green sign above the back entrance read, "U.S. Army Post Number 234." Something about that seemed odd to Jeff. But odd didn't cover the extremely tall hawkish man in a lavender business suit who ambled back and forth. Now and then he stopped and peered into the woods with binoculars.

When the UAH stopped, Rector caught Jeff's gaze and muttered under his breath, "Watch yourself."

They all piled out and collectively sighed. It felt good to be on solid ground and out of the Humvee. Rector led them into the building. The other men glanced back and echoed Jeff's thoughts, murmuring about a "purple suit," and "What the fuck?" Jeff had other priorities now. He needed to take a dump in a real sit-down toilet, and get some chow.

In front of them a white-walled hallway with linoleum floors held three card tables surrounded by several metal folding chairs. On the tables sat paper plates, plastic silverware, two five-gallon Gatorade thermoses full of iced tea and lemonade, and food. Not MRE's but real food: fried chicken, shrimp, ham, hamburgers, French fries, mashed potatoes, gravy, pecan pies, peaches. Everything a growing boy could want. Jeff became even more suspicious. The Army never gave them real food in the field. His stomach growled and the odors overcame all worries.

The others took off helmets, leaned rifles on the wall, set up chairs, and helped themselves. Jeff found a toilet and returned. He rubbed his hands and filled his plate.

They sat, munching, and in general feeling good to be alive, when the lieutenant colonel walked in with "the suit." The man in the lavender suit was so tall he ducked coming in the door. He was all bones with sharp angles tenting the suit's shoulders like a scarecrow. His sharp-edged face highlighted predatory eyes. As thin as he was, Jeff knew that gliding walk and the gaze. He'd seen similar men on the basketball court who could travel full court in ten lopes, and would drive an elbow through your eye just to get a rebound, smiling at your pain as they ran by.

The lieutenant colonel spoke, "Gentlemen, we are glad to have you with us. Our resources have been stretched very thin and you are a welcome sight. Excuse us for interrupting. I know you must be tired from your long journey, but we have a priority mission. Continue eating while we explain."

He paused as he set eyes on Rector first, then each of the men in turn, like he was trying to be a dad, smiling and making sure each felt like he was on their side. Jeff thought that strange for an LC.

"This is Mr. Sinclair. The Army is working with him closely trying to figure out how this whole loss of oil thing came to be. I'll let him take over now."

"The suit" towered over the lieutenant colonel, and clasped his long fingers in front of his chest, as if praying. Probably not the Lord's Prayer, Jeff thought.

"Good afternoon, men. I will get right to it. This building houses the cause of our woes, and the man who started it also knows how to end it. He escaped earlier today into that … that swamp out there. We need you to find him and bring him back. We have others searching for him, but they are not as … shall we say, well-trained, as you are. We have heard great things about you from your lieutenant. He says you're his best. That's what we need. This man's name is Remmy St. James. He is very smart and is being helped by a terrorist, Abdullah El-Hamain. They want to control the entire world's oil and destroy the United

States. When you find Mr. St. James, and I know you will, bring him back to us. This is probably the most important mission you will ever have. We need you. The U.S. Army needs you. The United States of America needs you. You have seen how ugly this civil war has become. If we do not find this man, it will get worse and last for decades. Without oil, our country is powerless to defend itself against our enemies. You are our best hope, and perhaps our last."

He finished by studying each man's eyes with a sincere gaze before he turned and strode back down the hallway. Jeff wanted to throw food at the man and his false bravado.

The lieutenant colonel stood. "Gentlemen, you have your orders. I will give Sergeant Rector your search area and photos of St. James. If you can bring him back before midnight tonight, I will see to it that each and every one of you gets a silver star. As Mr. Sinclair said, this mission eclipses anything anyone has ever done in the history of the U.S. Army. Make us proud."

He summoned Rector to his side. Rector glanced at the squad. "You heard the colonel, get moving. We ain't got all night."

As the colonel explained the search map to Rector, the men shoveled in several mouthfuls, gulped down lemonade, grabbed their equipment, and headed back out the way they'd come.

Alongside the UAH, three camouflaged-dressed PFC's jumped out of a jeep that pulled an open trailer full of ammunition. The other men went straight for the ammo, but Jeff turned around and peered at the U.S. Army sign below the roofline.

He stood transfixed.

Rector exited and motioned with his head and eyes to get moving. The alarm and warning in his eyes hurried Jeff back to the vehicle, though he glanced back once at the sign.

They all packed in the now cold seats of the UAH, and PFC Josh, alias Cole Trickle, wasted no time in getting them back into the jungle of southern Louisiana. The acrid odor of sweat returned.

After bumping along in silence, Jeff noticed Rector staring straight through the windshield, his jaw clenched and his right hand clutching the map with white knuckles.

"Sarge," Jeff said, "You wanna tell me what happened back there."

Rector flinched, jerking a long distance gaze right through Jeff, but said nothing.

Jeff waved a hand in front of Rector's eyes.

Rector grabbed his wrist in a vice grip, leaned in and said in a guttural whisper, "You tell me, Corporal."

"Sorry, Sarge. You looked . . . kinda . . . kinda like I've never seen you before, and I thought . . . It just scared me, that's all."

Rector focused in on Jeff and the intensity went out of his eyes, voice, and grip all at once. He whispered so only Jeff could hear him, "Fear, Corporal. That's what you saw. I was scared shitless."

"Yeah," Jeff murmured. "That was it. Glad I took a dump back there."

Rector smiled and breathed so close Jeff could smell the fried chicken on his breath. Not as good as it had smelled twenty minutes ago.

Rector leaned in, touching his helmet to Jeff's. "So, what were you staring at back there?" He still spoke in a low voice, apparently not wanting the others to hear.

Instinctively Jeff did the same. "The sign. But that's not all. There were a lot of things." Then Jeff had a flashback to a comedy routine where the next scene they would scream at each other, then break out laughing.

"Like what?"

"Like the scarecrow purple suit with laser eyes. What the hell was he doing giving us orders? And the LC. He had on all those ribbons. That's not right. What the hell did he tell you that got you so jumpy?"

Rector folded his arms and sat back, eyeing Jeff. "He was real broken up about us losing our friends. He said he was sorry about the massacre back at our base camp, but they were going to take care of El-Hamain real soon."

CHAPTER 60

Abdullah was past being ready for his speech. Way past. Over the last two hours he'd paced back and forth like a caged tiger in his cubicle, intermittently stalking out and glaring at René or the men setting up the computers.

His glare shifted to the Christmas tree he had thrown onto the floor after he came back inside. The shattered ornaments twinkled in the light.

Do they think a pretty tree with sparkling ornaments and multicolored lights will make everything okay?

No one but René would meet his eye. Others glanced up when he ventured out of his divider cubicle, but immediately looked back to their work.

Wish it didn't have to be this way. But that is the way it is. The world has changed. We have changed it and it is for the better. They must understand. They will understand.

Two hours earlier, after he'd stormed back in, René had tried to calm him.

"Sir, what is wrong?"

Icy words laced with sorrow followed. "Everyone dies. Suffering is life. I suffered and some of them will suffer. It will happen. But the end is justified. Now is the time. You get me on the air and I will tell them."

"Sir—"

But he would not let René speak, pointing back into the room. "Get me on the air! That is all I need."

René's puzzled and hurt look still faded in and out of Abdullah's mind.

He's strong. He'll see once I tell them. He'll see.

And so he had paced and glared and thought. And thought. About his two loves and *their* love. And about life.

Asiyah: She had always taken care of the weak. He'd seen her first taking care of a young abandoned camel after the Soviets had decimated a village in Afghanistan. He couldn't believe anyone could care so much for a filthy animal like a camel. But she had bottle fed the gangly thing until it could fend for itself.

In the next year she'd risked her life on one of the boats blocking Japanese whalers. So brave. Luckily for him a harpoon sliced open his leg. She'd tended his wound, nursing him back to health and winning his heart.

Why had God taken her from me? And in such an ugly and painful manner?

Later there was Tamara. Ruthless Tamara. Her violin solos in Vienna had wooed him. But her strength and wanton sexuality had won him. Though he knew she would not play the violin quite as beautifully as she had before, she would not give up. He smiled. She would have slapped his face when he had vomited over the dead. She would have said, "Get a grip. We cannot afford to be weak. We have a war to win."

Absolutely correct. It was war. Politics and negotiations were over. They had refused to relinquish their thrones of money and oil. Time to pay the piper. And the tune would be a dirge.

If only the oil barons had tried a bit harder. After all, they made billions of dollars in profits. Not in a year, but in months. And only spent a token million here or million there for fuel efficient cars, or spill resistant tankers, or cleaner burning engines.

What *he* felt, *they* would feel. Even more. In his life he had taken for granted so many things. As an adolescent in a wealthy family he always got what he wanted: the best schools, the latest computers, the flashiest cars. As he aged he realized that losing those things, those material things, caused less pain. Losing friends and loved ones, those he had taken for granted, he remembered. Those wounds crusted over but recurrently split open and sometimes bled worse than the initial wound.

Losing their power and money would hurt. But losing their own? That would change their tune forever. This time those lost would not be unknown sons of poor Hispanic or African Americans that had "volunteered" for their wars of the past twenty years. The dead would include neighbors, friends, brothers, sisters. It would cut deep. They would understand what the Bible had said about "wailing and gnashing of teeth."

How do you win a war? Overwhelming force. They thought their big military an overwhelming force. Yet they would be conquered by a life force smaller than most could even imagine. The force he had used was not the beat-you-over-the-head type, but as in jujitsu, the enemy's own force would defeat them.

In a way he embraced the delay. The longer it took the harder the other side would fight to keep hope. The harder they fought, using their oil guzzling machines, the quicker his success. His microbes would halt their machines. He would win.

They probably thought they could bring back all the East-Texas oil. Merely obtain the right antidote and everything would resolve. Perhaps they thought Mr. Remmy St. James could correct the problem with the right cocktail, and presto: Oil's back. Everything's okay.

He froze.

Lurking in the back of his mind, a tiny prickle grew to a thorn.

Could Remmy do that?

Unlikely.

No, impossible. After the bacteria ate the oil it could not be recaptured. He'd gone over that a hundred times. More like a thousand.

What about the Professor in Vienna?

He was dead. Dead. No one could get anything out of him. And he was wrong anyhow.

Those spiders were his idea, and a good one. Everyone hates spiders. The OPEC members predictably smashed the spiders with their shoes, grinding the microbes into every crease and stitch of their soles. In hours the microbes multiplied, populating the creases of their clothes, their hair, and their very skin. A good idea that worked. No traces could be left of the mastermind, though. The Professor was too weak. He would have spouted valuable information with any torture. He had to die.

But Remmy was still alive. He was smart. Greedy and smart. *Perhaps we should go after him.*

Right after the message.

Abdullah sensed a presence and jerked his head up to see René.

"Sir, we are ready."

Abdullah stood abruptly. "Finally."

He followed René to the one-room studio they had constructed. A blue screen for computer generated images would show oil spills, smog over Beijing, melting glaciers in Greenland, the devastation of Katrina, the burning oil fields in Kuwait, the mansions and yachts owned by oil tycoons and CEO's of GM, Ford, Chrysler, and more.

He plugged into the microphone and Ethan said, "You are on in five-four-three." He finished by putting out two fingers, then one.

CHAPTER 61

An hour after Rector left, one of the soldiers at Xoflex interrupted Sinclair in his meeting with the officers, "Sir, you need to see this."

"Surely it can wait." Sinclair glared at the man. "We are planning an attack here."

"Sir, it's him, El-Hamain."

Sinclair's hooded eyes went from anger to puzzlement.

"What do you mean?"

"He's on the TV. On every channel."

Sinclair and the lieutenant colonel traded glances as they both stood to follow the soldier.

In the next room a group of soldiers stood staring at the TV. On the screen, Abdullah El-Hamain pointed to photos of industrial accidents and smog laden cities, and said, "As you can see, the big oil companies have been working to destroy the earth for a long time."

Sinclair muttered to the lieutenant colonel who quickly seized control of the remote and changed channels.

El-Hamain's rendition continued.

Sinclair glared at the screen and chopped his flat hand at his throat. *End it.*

The screen went blank and the lieutenant colonel said, "Man your battle stations." Then he snatched the wall phone and barked more orders. Twenty seconds later the floor vibrated and dull roar emanated from outside.

"You see, Colonel, that did not require much planning. You push a button and," Sinclair smiled wanly, "boom."

Abdullah warmed to his live presentation. He had reviewed the ugly past, he would present the dirty present, and in another ten minutes he would show them two possible futures: big oil's barren and bleak earth or his green and grand utopia. He smiled at René who visibly relaxed. Yes, Abdullah thought, it *has* been a long time since your boss has smiled in true happiness.

Next, Abdullah started the slides about how powerful the oil barons had become. Someone pulled open the outside door and yelled, "Missiles incoming!"

Before anyone inside could take more than one long step, their world erupted in blinding light and a deafening crash.

The lieutenant colonel glanced at Sinclair. "Yes, but I thought you wanted to save the wells. It is going to be quite difficult now."

"No shit, *Colonel*! But we can't have a terrorist taking over control of our media and spouting out all that propaganda, now can we, *Colonel*."

The colonel glared at the blank TV screen, then at Sinclair. "Now what?"

"What do you mean, now what? And don't you look at me like that. You're getting a pile of money out of this. Take your men and make sure the job is done. Remember, no survivors and no prisoners. If you have to burn it to the ground, do it. The extra oil tanks I told you about will survive. But make sure El-Hamain is finished."

"We are going to leave you unprotected here. What if—"

"Leave a handful of men for the machine guns and one Humvee. El-Hamain is the main force we must destroy. That damn tree hugger has done enough damage. I want him dead. Now go!"

The Colonel walked away, muttering to himself, "Fucking suits."

Sinclair watched the colonel leave. He threw his pen at the door and screamed, "Morons!" If they would have acted on his recommendations four hours ago, none of this would have been necessary. They could have had the force in place for a surgical strike, avoiding the collateral damage to the oil wells.

He stared out the window at the cadre of Humvees and tanks moving north. Their gray-white exhaust seemed puny vertical strings against a distant bank of charcoal clouds. Lightning flared and the blackness shifted toward them, filling the sky with a pregnant under-surface of roiling pods, as if aliens would sprout forth any moment. He shuddered and turned away to the eastern tree line with their hidden swamps.

Thoughts of Remmy St. James returned. Now that El-Hamain was out of the way, Sinclair could concentrate on finding Remmy. *Why had Remmy left?* Didn't he understand that the entire United States needed him? That Octex-Penta would pay him handsomely for his help in res-cuing the oil from those terrorists?

Perhaps those imbeciles and their rough treatment . . . Remmy seemed tougher than that.

Surely my apology and . . . empathic acknowledgement of what we shared would . . .

He sighed.

Remmy, Remmy, Remmy. We will find you. Then it will be all the more difficult. I won't be able to hold back the imbeciles and their . . . treatment of you this time.

He glanced out the window again and noticed movement at the base of a tree. What appeared to be a huge, tailless rat skulked around the tree. The nutria stopped and its hollow eyes seemed to stare right at him. Its nose and whiskers twitched and it disappeared into the forest.

He shuddered again.

Rats! And everyone wants to get back to nature for what. Bigger rats? Probably have cockroaches the size of squirrels, too.

A soldier opened the door. "Mr. Sinclair, the Colonel advised that we all go into a fortified room away from windows until he can return."

"Fine, soldier. I must get a bottle of wine and I'll be right there."

Nothing better than a winter afternoon and a good bottle of Cabernet. Never travel without it.

CHAPTER 62

Dan stared after the deer, wondering what to do.

"Dan . . . Dan!" Sam shook his shoulder.

"Alright already. What is it?" The throb in his arm and head returned.

"I hate to bother you two, but we need to get moving. Don't you have questions for Remmy?"

"Sure." He stood and glanced at Lisette, who smiled and shooed him away.

He walked into the cabin with Sam, still thinking about what Lisette had said. All this time she thought she was helping him out.

Remmy sat in the chair that Dan had vacated, the laptop wide open.

Dan rushed in. "What the hell do you think you're doing? That's U.S. Government property. And besides, it's *mine*."

"Sorry. Sam said you had some files that—"

Dan reached over the table, grabbed the laptop and pulled it to him, wincing at the pain in his arm. He wanted to hold it close to his chest, but he spun it around to see what the stupid guy had done.

Prime numbers inside colored balloons floated across the screen. Remmy had not gotten past the screen saver. Dan breathed a sigh of relief.

He glared at Remmy. "You don't just grab a guy's computer and start using it. Especially someone who works for the CIA. Who do you think you are anyhow?"

"I was just trying to—"

Sam pushed his palm out like a stop sign. "Dan's right. I should have told you to wait." He looked at Dan. "It's my fault, Dan. I'm in a hurry and thought he could get started."

Dan pursed his lips and frowned. He did not want Remmy wandering around his computer. It might remind him Dan had written that program last year for Xoflex.

Remmy tilted his head down and peered up at Sam, as if over reading glasses.

"Come on, Dan," Sam said. "We need to work together on this. What were the files?"

Dan closed his eyes and shot out a breath through his nose like a bull getting ready for battle. He would have to work with this guy who might expose Dan's secret, show everyone that Dan had started this whole thing. He glanced outside, his insides gnawing and ripping. He had to get Jeff back, get back to Marci. Out here things were too crazy.

He studied the computer screen. His fingers ran over the keys so fast it was hard to tell if he actually touched them.

"Okay. There. You wanted it so bad. What does 'S_Am1 , US1 , N3, and *UAEAEH_cleanup.vid*' have to do with all this?"

Remmy gawked at Dan, eyes wide.

Dan smiled. "Thought you erased it all, huh?"

Sam patted Dan on the back. "Didn't expect a computer genius like old Danny Boy here, did you?"

Remmy sat back in the chair, closed his eyes, sighed, and ran his fingers through his hair. He sat forward and gave Dan a half smile. "I'm sorry about . . . Anyway, I guess if you could find this you'll probably find more." He stood and started pacing. "I thought they needed my help. And they paid well. So, what the hell. Right?"

Lisette had entered the room, and said over Sam's shoulder, "So, you *were* in cahoots with El-Hamain, like the TV said." Not a question, but a statement of fact.

Dan wanted to stand up and cheer for Lisette. *Hit him again.*

"No." Remmy said. "Hell no. I never wanted to help him at all. It was Octex-Penta."

Sam cocked his head back, like a bird preparing to peck. He scowled and blinked several times. "Scuse me? Octex-Penta wanted you to help *them* with El-Hamain?"

"That's right."

Dan frowned and started to shake his head, then winced. Everything tilted again, but it wasn't from his head. "I don't follow you. Why would Octex-Penta want you to help El-Hamain? He wanted to destroy all the oil. Right?"

"True."

Sam, Dan, and Lisette traded glances.

"So," Sam said, "Octex-Penta wanted El-Hamain to destroy all the oil?"

"Except." Remmy held his hands out like the answer was obvious.

"Except . . . except . . ." Dan struggled to find the answer.

"Not in the U.S.A." Lisette finished and whistled: a good whistle through skinny lips.

"That's right." Remmy held his index finger up. "Have you ever studied a map that enumerates the location of terrorist attacks?"

Sam shook his head quickly, a confused shudder. "Come again?"

Dan wondered if Remmy made this up as he went or had the story all thought out beforehand.

Remmy smiled. "Where on the globe do most of the terrorist attacks occur?"

"Well," Dan said, "The Twin Towers killed the most people."

"True, but most of the terrorist attacks occur in the Middle East, Africa, Europe, Asia, Venezuela, and Indonesia. In other words: where most of the oil outside the U.S. is located."

"So you think that Octex-Penta wanted to eliminate all the rest of the world's oil to do away with terrorism?" Dan shook his head. "Sh-yeah, right."

Lisette nodded. "Without the oil, many of those countries have no money. Without money how will the terrorists, who mostly come from those countries, get funded?"

Dan bent one eyebrow down at her. *Don't agree with this numskull.*

"So, eliminate the source of income and do away with terrorists?" Sam said. "I don't buy it. Big oil companies don't give a shit about terrorism in any country except the U.S."

"Right!" Remmy slapped his hands on his thighs and sat back down with authority. "But they tried to convince me that the President was pushing this plan to get rid of terrorism. That's why I didn't go along with them, even when they said the President was hoping our company would help the country out on this one. The President does hate terrorism, and he is not the brightest bulb, but come on."

This guy *is* making sense, Dan thought. "I bet they didn't like that." he said.

"Actually, they were extremely nice about it. That should have been my first clue. They thanked me for my time, made me sign a non-disclosure statement threatening jail, etcetera, and said they would contact me in another week to see if I had changed my mind. In the mean time they said they had other avenues they were going to explore."

Bernadette stepped into the room. "Y'all want some tea or lemonade or something cool to drink?"

"That'd be great," Dan said. He felt parched. Maybe if he got more hydrated he would think better. This was so confusing.

"I could use something more fortified," Sam said.

Lola's voice carried from behind Bernadette, "We got that, too. I'll get Joe."

Sam smiled at Bernadette, who smiled back and left.

He nodded at Remmy. "Go on."

"Okay. A few weeks after I turned them down, I got the order for Makers for the Maracaibo well. I went down the next week and implanted our nano-bacteria, I call them Makers. No sooner had I returned home than the Venezuelans called me back saying something was wrong. I was in the middle of figuring out why their production had taken a huge nosedive when you're man arrived."

He squinted at Dan. "I had nothing to do with killing him. It was those hot-blooded, trigger happy spi—I mean Venezuelans. They're worse than the damn Arabs. I swear they'd all kill their own brothers over nothing. That's why they do so well as terrorists.

"Anyway, when I found out he was in disguise and then his cell phone self-destructed in my hand, I figured that the CIA, or maybe Octex-Penta, had a contract on me to shut my trap, get rid of any loose

ends. So, I skedaddled back here to try and buy time. That's when I figured it all out."

In the other room Bernadette and Joe laughed so loud Remmy
stopped and strained to listen, as if he needed to hear something funny
now. But the laughter quieted.

He nodded at Dan. "Those files you found were files that enumerated my research on all the U.S. oil wells and how much we could boost
their production. I showed Octex-Penta that with our product they
could increase production in the U.S. back to their figures for the 1970s.
I believe they decided to keep this a secret, all the while appearing as if
they were the nice guys, trying to lower the price of gas. Of course, they
would not lower the price much, but enough so that America would
continue to drive their favorite gas guzzlers. They would rake in the
profits for another twenty years before the bottom dropped out.

"Needless to say, they were ecstatic, even showed me a good time
deep-sea fishing in the Gulf with four of the top GM execs. Then they
said they wanted a video with me helping El-Hamain to prove to the
world that we got along with OPEC. The next week we had the discussion about getting rid of the terrorists and their oil."

He dropped his head. "Funny how money makes you stupid. I
wasn't thinking too well or I'd have figured they only made the video
to prove I was in bed with El-Hamain and that he and I were the bad
guys."

"So what do you think is actually going on here?" asked Sam.

"It took me awhile to put it all together. But I believe Octex-Penta
waited until I had implanted the producers in all the U.S. wells and
then they sabotaged the producer vat with bacteria that destroyed oil,
I call them Takers. They got their video and, behind my back, allowed
El-Hamain to get a load of Takers. They wanted to blame El-Hamain
and me for trying to take away all the world oil, when in reality they
had engineered it so that the only oil left would be U.S. oil. No com-
petition, no terrorists. They would retain all the power and ability to
regulate the price of oil without worrying about OPEC. The President
loved them. He would get reelected by a jubilant America—no more
terrorism, no more OPEC, and they could drive their SUV's and muscle

cars for less money. The rest of the world would be in chaos, but would have no way to fight us. No oil, no military—not to mention crippling their economies and squelching all travel. We could finally become that island across the big pond like we were before WWI."

Sam murmured in disbelief, "The only game in town."

The door from the kitchen swung open and Bernadette, Lola, and Joe came in carrying the drinks.

Lola scrutinized their faces and called out, "Joe, I think we might need more lightnin'. They done seen da boogie man out here."

CHAPTER 63

Sam grabbed the first glass of moonshine and took a large gulp. He bugged his eyes and squeaked out, "Jesus!"

"Yep," Joe said. "You might want to sip it. Have the same effect, just not burn yo insides so much."

Remmy sipped the clear liquid and continued. "Only problem is I think their plan went haywire. I believe they underestimated El-Hamain. I'll bet they were going to kill him after the OPEC thing, but he got away, and made it to Texas."

"What makes you think that?" Lisette said.

"Well, when I was at Xoflex yesterday, this guy Sinclair acted like I was responsible for screwing up the Texas wells."

"Texas wells?" Sam said. "Last I heard those wells were being attacked by good old boys trying to get to the oil, like the wells were still producing."

"Yeah, that's what I thought, too. But I had a little torture session that made me change my mind. Sinclair, that bastard, believes I am partnering with El-Hamain and that we did something to their Texas oil to stop production. I pretended to break under the torture and told Sinclair I had the solution to save their Texas wells. That's when I escaped."

"Can you? I mean, bring back the oil?" Sam said.

"I'm not sure about the OPEC wells. It may have been too long since the Takers hit them. But Texas? Possibly. I have a good idea how

El-Hamain did it, but it would be nice to question him personally to see how much time we have. Also, we still need the antidote, the Regulators, and they're back at Xoflex, and I am *not* going back there."

Sam sipped more of the moonshine, then stopped and seemed to think about the rest of the glass. He poured a glass of lemonade and eyed Dan. He then inspected Remmy from head to foot. "You may not have to. Who's manning the video shack, you know, the camera at the front gate? Is it the Army dudes or one of yours?"

"Last time I was there, it was one of the Xoflex guards. I think the military had their hands full."

"Dan," Sam said, "can you make me up to look like Remmy, not perfect, but pretty close? And fast, like in the next half hour?"

Dan peered at Sam, and back at Remmy. They were about the same height and had about the same roundness to their faces. If he changed Sam's nose contour and perhaps a bit more cheek bone that might cover it. Eyes were about the same, maybe a little liner to give Sam the lateral up-tilt of Remmy's. The only thing left was the hair, and a ball cap would do most of that.

"Sure, and I can do it in twenty minutes, give or take."

"Make it a take. I'll be at the video camera at the front gate and that's not high resolution. Am I right?"

Remmy nodded.

"Since they want Remmy so bad, I'll lure some of them to me; we take them out and get in and gone before they know it."

Remmy shook his head. "You don't have a chicken's chance on a gator farm. There's soldiers crawling all over that place."

"Dat's fo sho," Joe said. "Dat's fo damn sho. Though we *do* owe dem shitholes for killin' Dad."

Sam held up his hand. "Let me figure that out. If I'm not back in a couple of hours, you'll know. Remmy, you help Dan figure a way past all the other security into that, uh Regulator's office."

He motioned to Lisette and Ron. "Get your gear." He nodded at Joe, "We'll need help navigating back to Xoflex."

"I'll git Bear to hep you wit dat." Joe left.

Dan fixed Sam's eyes first, while Remmy sat still and modeled. Not perfect, but damn close. He glued on a latex nose and cheekbone combo that thankfully fit Sam with minimal modifications. Doing the makeup made him think of Fred, and Dan closed his eyes and stopped working. He opened his eyes and Sam stared into them, pulled him close and whispered, "Remmy's a good guy. Work with him. Okay?"

He nodded, though he couldn't help a sideways glance at Remmy. Remmy was there when Fred died. Remmy could expose Dan. Remmy would be hard to trust.

He finished and Sam started off, then came back. "Let me see that arm." Sam took off Dan's arm dressing, placed a bead of superglue on the now dry cut, and rewrapped it with fresh gauze and tape. He handed Dan a radio. "That should do for now, even water proof it. I'll call you on the radio when I get in place."

Dan gave Sam's face one last inspection, pressed on one modified cheek to get it right, and Sam left.

"Come to the back bedroom," Remmy said. "I'll use *my* computer. I doubt the Army changed the basic security system, since they have all those guns and guards. We should be able to get in quickly."

Lola regarded Bernadette, "You want to hep them or hep me wit da gumbo and crawdads?"

"Only two computers. Left mine at the trailer. And I can always use another good recipe for gumbo." She tussled Dan's hair. "You gonna be alright without me watching your back?"

"I think so. Remmy probably knows a lot of back doors into the security system where the sniffers won't find me."

Remmy smiled. "Oh yeah. They'll never know what hit em."

"Okay then. You boys have fun." She walked to the kitchen.

Dan wasn't so sure about things, despite what he'd said to Bernadette. First, he didn't like Lisette going back into the lion's den, even with Sam. He studied the door she'd walked out, then turned his attention to Remmy. *He* was another story. It seemed like he was on their side and his speech about Venezuela and Octex-Penta came across as sincere. But Dan kept replaying Fred's last words, "It's the Nano guys." Remmy stood and walked to the bedroom.

Dan folded the laptop and placed it in the black satchel. He shouldered it and unzipped the side pocket where the Berretta lay. He followed Remmy, studying every move. He flexed his bandaged arm. It felt good.

Any quick movements and—

"Shit!" Remmy ran forward toward his desk.

Dan pulled the shoulder strap over his head, slid the radio inside, and touched the Beretta.

Remmy stopped suddenly and blew out in relief. "Whew! Thought somebody took it. But then I remembered, I put it under the desk when I left."

Dan gripped the gun as Remmy reached under the desk.

When he pulled out a laptop computer, Dan relaxed, but kept his hand in the pocket. Then he realized: the gun was not loaded.

Remmy sat down to put the laptop on the desk and glanced at Dan's hand. "Trusting soul, aren't we?"

Dan smiled with his mouth only. "Not really." He wanted to shove in the clip.

Remmy returned his eyes to the screen, his hands on the keyboard, his posture relaxed.

"Nature of the business, I guess. You never know about someone you just met, especially if you found out they were present when your *best friend* was murdered. Mind telling me who *did* kill Fred?"

Remmy faced Dan, leaned back in the chair, and lifted his hands like he was under arrest.

"Dan, I see your point. I'm not too fond of strangers right now, either. But to answer your question, I don't know who killed your friend. I arrived post mortem, so to speak. It was probably one or all of the board members—a loose term, really—they were Venezuelan Mafioso. He had a bunch of holes in him by the time I arrived. Why did they kill him? I don't know. Maybe he didn't act quite right. Who knows? They're a trigger happy bunch. Been watching too many old western movies and listening to too much rap. And since they have most of the money and politicians in their back pocket, they can just about kill whoever, whenever."

Dan nodded, only an outward conciliation. "How did you know we were staying in that little vacation casa?"

Remmy scratched his head and frowned.

Dan's eyes narrowed. *Was it an act?*

"Sorry, Dan. Vacation casa?"

"Never mind. I guess the proof will be in the pudding. Show me what you got. I'll watch."

Remmy put his hands down, shrugged, and started typing.

Dan took his hand out, sidled behind Remmy and peered at the screen. Remmy entered Xoflex's security system. In seconds they shot through firewalls that had taken Dan and Bernadette hours to crack. Up popped a totally new area, then another, and another. The different layers of security that unfolded mesmerized and impressed Dan.

The cool cylinder of a gun barrel under his chin impressed him even more.

CHAPTER 64

Jeff could not shake Rector's steady gaze, despite the rocking of the UAH as they sped away from the Xoflex plan. The initial acceleration soon became the herky-jerky Pac Man ride of yesterday, though Jeff agreed with escaping as fast as possible.

They slowed and Jeff asked, "How does the LC know where El-Hamain is?"

"He knew about El-Hamain because they are supposed to know. Intell, spooks, informants, whatever." The answer was full of unknowns, raising more questions.

Jeff blurted, "Let's say they had an informant. That means they knew about what El-Hamain was doing all along. You'd think they would have stopped him."

"Not really. And you know why, too. Don't you, homeboy?"

The UAH danced over a hill and around a swampy area, shifting Jeff so close to the sergeant that Rector's lips almost touched Jeff's ear when he whispered, "They ain't us."

That was it! Jeff sat back and stared out the windshield, remembering a time long ago . . .

He's a teenager, back at the Fort Carson Army base in Colorado Springs. He and his dad are waving miniature U.S. flags in a large crowd welcoming back soldiers from Iraq at the base airport.

"Dad," he says, "it seems funny that the guys in battle fatigues have no medals. I mean, they fought at the front. Shouldn't they have something to show for it?"

"The combat uniform should be drab, no flash. In the old days the flash of officer insignia would be a target for the enemy. After learning the hard way, officers no longer wear flashy insignia when at the war front. Instead, they are sewn on in cloth and drab colors. No one in combat wears ribbons. Besides, when you're thinking about eating a bullet in combat, no one cares how many ribbons you've got. If you get captured, they will go after the ones with ribbons preferentially because they have the respect of the men. Once they are broken, it will be easier to break the others."

It was a good rule that anyone in the U.S. Army obeyed. Another thing that anyone in the *real* Army knew: the only location you advertised with a sign was the medical area, and that with a big red cross. You didn't go around advertising that you were the U.S. Army base in enemy territory with a huge sign like at the Xoflex building, "U.S. Army Post 234."

The Xoflex Army is all bogus.

Jeff focused on Rector's face and his flat grin. No amusement there. More like a bland welcome to his world, a world where everything he had previously believed in, honored, even cherished, did not exist. Not here.

If it wasn't the U.S. Army out there, who was it?

"Sarge, who do you think—?"

The UAH stopped so fast a helmet from the rear flew forward and hit Jeff's back.

Rector snatched the helmet and tossed it back to its owner, saying gruffly, "Strap it on, Private, or the next thing rolling around this Humvee will be your head."

"Yes, Sergeant."

Rector turned to the driver. "Hey, Cole Trickle, why the sudden stop?"

"Ran out of solid ground." The driver pointed. The marsh ended abruptly at a bayou.

Outside, the wind had picked up enough to sway the hanging moss in an undulating ballet, causing a ripple of shadows on the Humvee's dusty windshield. A flock of grebes flapped away, the racket of their take-off a percussive crescendo to the idle of the diesel. The wind whistled through the doors.

"Check it out." Rector raised his head toward the turret.

Jeff snugged his helmet, stood up into the turret, and surveyed the area. High clouds of an hour ago had given way to gathering cumulus with smudged bellies. A splash in the water riveted his eyes to that area, but he saw nothing except a fluttering wake from a spooked animal. He methodically searched for a way around the bayou. Something caught his eyes and he stared.

"Sarge, I think you need to get out and look at this before we leave."

"What is it?"

"Not sure. But I think someone's been here recently."

Rector got out and walked to hood of the Humvee. He squinted at Jeff, who pointed at what he'd seen.

Rector's boots sucked in the mud with each step. His stance got increasingly wider, the water deeper. Abruptly, he sloshed up to a dry peninsula. He stopped and peered at a smooth indentation at the land-end of the bayou and tracked it to higher ground and a clump of bushes.

He returned. "A boat's been landing there. Several times. Could be our dude. Keep an eye out. He might be coming back."

Jeff's heart rate jumped. He twitched his head, scanning everywhere. Rector gave orders to the driver to back up and hide. They would wait awhile. They backed up twenty-five yards behind cypress trees, live oaks, and tucked the Humvee into a stand of palmettos.

Once they stopped, Rector ordered everyone else to get out for a good stretch and to relieve themselves before what could be a long wait. Jeff returned first and walked to Rector. "What are we doing here, Sarge? We know those orders are not from the real Army. Not legally binding."

Rector craned to see over Jeff's head and said in a low voice, "We are trying to find out the answer to your last question, Corporal: Who the fuck are those guys if they're not Gung Ho Mo Fo's like us? Maybe if we find out who they're after and why, then we'll have a better idea of who they are."

He strode off toward the bushes. "I need to take a piss. Stay here and watch for company. I'll think better when my bladder's not pinching my brain."

Jeff inspected the bayou: quiet, no movement. Muffled voices and steps from the others came closer. Jeff turned to greet them. The clouds over the northwest sky now bulged black and indigo. Rumbles of thunder followed flashes of lightning; he judged about fifteen miles away. He hoped the Sergeant would let them stay in the Humvee through this storm. He didn't relish another wet night.

A distant whine of an outboard motor turned his attention back to the bayou.

CHAPTER 65

Bear drove the boat. Lisette sat in front. Sam wore Remmy's clothes and to a casual observer looked exactly like him. The others sported duck-hunting camouflage clothes borrowed from Lola and Uncle Joe, a close match to the camouflage on the aluminum boat that carried them to the tail of the bayou. Bear timed the landing perfectly, shutting off and lifting the outboard so that the boat skimmed onto a groove in the swamp grass worn down from prior excursions. As soon as the boat stopped, they all jumped out. Bear secured the boat with a rope around the willows and palmettos, then led the way. Winding through a vague path in the thick bushes and cypress trees, they reached the edge of the clearing that sloped gently up to the Xoflex building.

"Bear," Sam said, "you stay with the boat and be ready for an immediate departure. If we're not there in thirty minutes, get out of here."

"Don't tink so. Dat motor starts just fine and dandy. First pull. No need to keep it warmed up. I'll just stick around here, in case you need some hep."

"Come on, Bear."

"You look like Remmy, so I's stickin' wit you."

Sam shook his Remmy head. "Okay, let's do it."

He called Dan on the radio who instructed him about the quickest route in, once they overpowered the security guards.

They made their approach.

CHAPTER 66

The hunting boat landed and the occupants evaporated into the woods. Jeff wondered why Rector did nothing. "You want me to check out the boat, Sarge?"

Rector stood on the running board and peered over the top of the Humvee with binoculars. "Nope."

"What?"

"You heard me. Sit tight."

"Okay, Sarge. But we haven't got any idea who they are. Maybe the boat has clues."

Rector let the binocular dangle from the strap around his neck and looked at Jeff. "Come on, Corporal. Tell me what you saw."

Jeff thought for a moment. "Three civilians in camouflage, one in civies came in on a hunting boat and headed toward the Xoflex plant."

"Think they were civilians?"

"The big guy, and the other one for sure. No way could he get into the Army. Too damn big."

"And the others?"

"They were different. Didn't move like he did. Seemed like they followed him, like he was a scout. The others aren't Army, but I don't think they're locals either. Those baseball caps didn't quite fit in with the camouflage."

Rector smiled, "Good. You got your first lesson. I've seen that kind before. They fit in much better as the war wears on. They grow beards;

lose their ball caps, and begin to take on the appearance of locals. Those are spooks, Corporal. Either CIA or another clandestine special ops."

Rector peered through the binoculars. "And the real question is: Why are spooks going to the place that advertises itself as U.S. Army, but ain't?"

Jeff let his binoculars hang and studied Rector. "If they are *with* Xoflex, why would they be sneaking back there? They must not be with them. Maybe they're trying to figure out who the hell is at the Xoflex plant, like we are."

Rector eased his field glasses down and eyed Jeff. "If that's the case, who are the good guys and who are the bad guys?"

Jeff snorted. "No way in hell that scarecrow in a suit is a good guy."

"You haven't seen the majors I've seen. Sinclair's a bit weird, but maybe he really is on our side. I mean, he is going to kill this guy El-Hamain. And that's the guy who started it all, right?"

In the last two minutes Rector's voice had gone from "sure as shit" to "what the fuck is going on" with a splash of "let's bolt!"

Jeff shifted his stance, unsure what just happened. "Maybe El-Hamain did start it all. That weirdo suit back there is no major, though. I can't see trusting him. I got the feeling he would just as soon feed us to gators as pin a medal on us."

Rector's eyes had changed—a crazy look, like a part of his brain had cracked. His voice trembled with a weird vibration. "Yeah, but at least he was surrounded by Army uniforms. Those spooks . . . they're . . . Had me an experience with spooks in the hills. Can't trust spooks. They'll—"

Then Rector's eyes got wider and seemed to stare right through Jeff. Maybe the rumor that Rector was on some psych meds was true. Maybe he forgot to take them.

They both glassed the Xoflex building in silence. Several minutes passed, and Jeff leaned as far away from Rector as he could get, feeling like the man had just blown a gasket. Rector dropped his binocs down a few times and squinted at Jeff like Jeff was some kind of alien insect.

Then Rector jerked his binoculars to his face and hoarsely whispered, "Jesus!"

The four who'd come in the boat ran down the grassy slope,

dodging right and left as chunks of dirt and mud spewed around them. The face of the guy in civies seemed to be peeling off in pieces. Flashes preceded the barks of rifle fire from two soldiers who had run out of the Xoflex building. But they were too far away, and too late. The four fugitives were already into the boat.

Rector raised his rifle.

They disappeared into the bayou.

"You were going to shoot them?" Jeff said.

Rector pulled the rifle from his shoulder. "Only one. Interrogate him. Find out what the fuck. You know. Do our job. Right?" Rectors eyes seemed glazed with a dangerous detachment.

Jeff added another file for war: *Smart men got stupid and stupid men got smart.* Or was it scared shitless? All he knew was that Rector was not quite what he'd been yesterday. Shit, nothing like he'd been an hour ago.

Rector's gaze shifted—as creepy as the words that crawled from his mouth. "We gotta find a boat. Go after them."

"Come on, Sarge. Where the hell are we going to find a boat?"

The other men in the Humvee mumbled and stared at Rector.

Their peering eyes must have twisted an inner switch. Rector faced them and ordered, "Okay, everyone out of the Humvee except Corporal Trotter. Rifles ready and get that RPG out too. They come back, hit 'em with everything we got."

He placed each of the men where he wanted them, snatched off one of their dog tags, and strode back to the Humvee, motioning for Jeff to get down into the cab.

"What's going on, Sarge?" Jeff asked quietly, trying to steady his voice.

Rector clambered into the driving seat, his rank mood and crazy eyes pricking at Jeff's get-the-hell-outta-here reflex.

"We're going back for reinforcements and to get rid of a traitor."

Jeff relaxed and took off his helmet. "So you agree with me about that suit, Sinclair?"

Rector said nothing and drove, bouncing in the seat and easing the steering wheel from side to side to avoid stumps. The further they went, the more hunched over he became, like he was protecting the wheel from a thief.

Halfway up the rise Rector slammed on the brakes, and Jeff put both hands on the dash grab bar, bracing himself. Something hit him in the temple and his world turned off.

CHAPTER 67

Dan thought, Impressive? Yes. Not because he couldn't imagine how Remmy had manipulated the keyboard and somehow retrieved the gun that, with a trigger pull, would put a hole up through Dan's tongue, pallet, and tear out his frontal lobes. Though, that was impressive enough for now. Besides, Dan couldn't think of anything else except the top of his head blowing off.

He felt the warm puffs of Remmy's words on his ear.

"Trust is a key issue here, wouldn't you say, Dan?"

Dan spoke through clenched teeth, not wanting the movement of his jaw to jostle Remmy's trigger finger.

"Sorry. Won't happen again . . . Really."

The pressure of the gun barrel disappeared, and Remmy backed off, twirling the .38 revolver like Wyatt Earp, but stopping with the gun still aimed at Dan.

"Okay, I've shown you mine. Now where's yours?"

Dan reached into the outer pocket of the carrying case.

Remmy cocked the hammer of his .38 revolver. "Slowly there, Mr. G-man."

Dan pulled the Beretta out and laid it on the table.

Remmy smiled, eased the hammer—a sound Dan heard distinctly—twirled the gun around once more and ended with a flourish of putting the .38 beside the Beretta.

Dan let out a breath that had been sitting in his lungs so long it must have been pure carbon dioxide. The grainy edge of his vision began to clear as he gulped breaths.

"Jesus. I might have to change my shorts."

Remmy went back to typing and said calmly, "Want me to wait?"

Dan wanted to say, Yeah, why don't you wait here while I go outside, find a boat and get the hell out of here. But he had no idea where to go. So he sighed and said, "No, I'm good."

A breeze from the bayou fluttered the curtains at the window and cooled the sweat on Dan's forehead.

Remmy kept typing. After a few moments of unsuccessful attempts at keeping Remmy's computer screen and both guns in focus, Dan took his laptop to the other side of the table, and pushed the guns between them so he could use his own computer. He booted up. "You know, mine isn't even loaded."

"No kidding?" Remmy pointed his revolver at Dan and clicked around each cylinder with a clear view of all six bullets. "Mine is."

"Okay. You made your point. Can we get to work here? Sam is trying to help you."

Over the next half hour they worked together and actually laughed at a few wan jokes, though Remmy's laugh sounded creepy to Dan, hoarse and high pitched. Dan had to admit, someone who knew all the security tricks made it easy. They traded stories about Colorado, New Orleans and to Dan's surprise, roses.

Remmy came to a file that Dan recognized, even had the name he'd used when he sold it to Xoflex: *Nanohiway*. "What's that program do?" Dan asked, trying to slow down his heart.

"That's probably one of the key components to our patent. It allows the nanobots to communicate with the bacteria. Without that, we might not be here."

"Did you write it?"

"No, that one we contracted out."

"Why not just change it so the nanobots can no longer communicate with the bacteria. You could send it like a virus into Xoflex's main frame, or give it to DoD and stop this war. You wouldn't need the Regulators."

"I tried already. It's too complicated and whoever wrote it made it too secure."

"What about contacting whoever wrote it?"

Remmy sighed. "Look, I've been doing the best I can. I tried contacting him, but he didn't answer my e-mail. We need this now, not next week. Are you going to help, or not?"

Dan smiled. "Sorry, I've been too busy to even look at my e-mails."

Remmy's mouth opened and he stared at Dan. "You wrote that program. Son of a bitch! The CIA has known all along."

"No. They don't know, and I don't want them to know now. I did it for some extra money to help pay for my kid's college. It was strictly off the record. They'd probably fire me if they find out."

"What do you care if they fire you? You could make millions being a private programmer."

"No, I have issues—don't work well with people."

"You seem to do okay to me."

Dan realized that he had changed in the last several days. Maybe Lisette had been good for him.

A mouth-watering aroma filled the room, reminding Dan of crab feasts and beer in Maryland.

Bernadette strode in. "You boys about done? We got good food out here."

"Give us a sec," Dan said.

She squinted at Dan, the guns on the table, then Remmy and turned back around. "It's better hot." The door closed behind her.

"What do you want to do?" asked Remmy.

"Maybe I can work on this program and—"

The radio in Dan's briefcase crackled with Sam's voice. "Dan, you there? Over."

Dan lifted the radio out and pressed the talk button. "Yeah, Sam. Over."

Sam's voice chattered fast, firm, though somewhat garbled, so Dan frowned in concentration. "Okay, over and out."

"What?" Remmy said.

"He said we're leaving in ten minutes. Didn't sound too interested in other opinions either."

Remmy grabbed his gun and folded the laptop down. "Guess I'll chug some gumbo and suck some heads. I'm going after the Regulators. I *know* they will work."

Bernadette stuck her head back in. "Did I hear that radio?"

"It was Sam," Dan said. "He's coming back and wants to leave right away once he gets here. Something about the security being down at Xoflex."

Remmy slid past Bernadette, who eyed the Beretta by Dan's computer.

Dan grabbed the Beretta and shouldered past her. "Funny story. Tell you about it soon."

The kitchen table had a pot of gumbo and reddish-pink crawdads in two separate pots. The aroma touched off hunger that Dan had ignored for hours. *Fasting is supposed to be good for you every now and then. Right?*

Joe walked out the door when Dan sat down.

"Where's he going?" Dan asked as he filled a plate with steaming crawdads and ladled gumbo into a large bowl. He briefly closed his eyes and breathed in the steam, remembering the back of a Cajun seasoning can: salt, red and black pepper, onions, ginger, paprika, celery, bay leaves, cloves, cinnamon—he could go on, but he stuffed his mouth. The aroma sat him down in a chair ten years ago outside *The Gumbo Shop* in New Orleans. What he would give to take his time and *dine* instead of wolf down this great food. He also needed about an hour to change that program.

"He gone to gas up da plane," Lola said.

"Are you leaving us?" Dan said.

"No," Remmy interjected between bites, "but I thought it might be a good idea to be ready for anything." He strapped on a shoulder holster and eyed Lola. "Do you still have that dynamite?"

"Sho, Remmy. We got a whole box." Lola's smile showed nearly perfect teeth.

Dan swirled the spicy gumbo in his mouth like a fine wine. It had been a long time.

Suddenly he sat up, eyes wide. "Dynamite?"

Remmy gave a snort. "What'd you think? We had missiles on that plane?

Lola patted Dan on the back. "Don't worry child. We been droppin' doze sticks on revenuers 'fore you was ever even thinking 'bout being a G-man."

Dan decided that was good advice. It was like worrying about crawdads being tainted for a hundred years after the big oil spill. He cracked crawdads and slurped a spoonful of gumbo, the taste so good he dismissed those worries and his mind turned to another concern that had been nibbling at him for the last hour.

Was she okay? Surely Sam would have said something, though his voice sounded distressed, hurried. True, but what could you tell from two quick sentences? *He did say, "We." Yes he did.*

A distant burring sound made him stop chewing. An outboard motor. He wiped his face and stood.

"Finish up, Dan." Bernadette said. "You might not get anything else for a while." She eyed his frowning worry and shooed him off with her hand. "That's okay. Go on. I understand."

He scooted the chair back, mumbled a quick "Excuse me" out of habit, and stood at the door after three steps.

The afternoon sun squeezed his eyes to a squint. But it didn't stop him from searching.

He heaved a big sigh; the ebony pony tail bounced in the breeze.

What the hell are you doing? You've been through this. Made a decision. Haven't you?

Apparently not.

The boat's keel cut through the calm tan water; the wake danced in the sun. *Mesmerizing.*

Whatever. He could not move. Good excuse.

His gaze tracked higher. She stared right at him, cheeks flushed.

Whatever, squared.

CHAPTER 68

Abdullah was lucky. Though the missile did not make a direct hit, the impact tossed him like a rag doll over a desk and into a stand of electronic equipment. He tried to stand, but pushing with his left hand turned a dull ache into a grating, searing pain in his elbow that made him queasy. The lights had all been extinguished so he could only gingerly feel with his right hand the jagged splinter protruding from where his left elbow should have been. He sat still and breathed deeply, waiting for his heartbeat and nausea to decrease.

He turned over on his one good hand and knees and slowly stood, clutching his left arm against his body with his right hand.

Through the dim light and sparks, beams of flashlights added to the appearance of a nocturnal magic show, only the huge spotlight with the magician in the center never materialized. Instead, low moans accompanied the searching beams. A silhouetted figure reminded Abdullah of a medieval knight with a long jousting spear ready for battle. Closer inspection revealed the pain-frozen face of René with a death grip on a tent pole. It protruded through his chest. Abdullah gently closed his friend's sightless eyes.

He picked his way through the rubble to the door, leaned against what remained of the frame and surveyed the smoke-hazed jumble of off-kilter desks, computers, and boxes, interspersed with a foot here, an arm there, sticking out at odd angles. Uniformed figures roamed over and between the isles helping survivors. He stumbled outside into big raindrops. A flash of lightning made him flinch.

It is over.

He had tried to tell them the truth and to get them to see his way. He trudged further away from the complex and it struck him: It didn't matter. Whether they agreed with him or not, they would have to change.

He concentrated on placing each step until he could not go further. He stood, staring at puddles. A man lay under a huge fallen tree, his skull crushed. He felt faint and his whole body shivered uncontrollably. He lifted his head. A black tent seemed the only undamaged structure, so he stumbled over to get out of the freezing rain. He fumbled with the tent flaps and finally stepped inside. Twenty pairs of eyes stared. Soldiers stood or sat on cots or the floor. He gave them a weak grin and two or three smiled back.

They must not recognize him soaking wet and disheveled, because none of them said a word.

His eyes adjusted to the dim light and he noticed their odd stance: they stood or sat as if at parade rest with their arms behind them.

Then it hit him. The prisoner's tent. These soldiers were prisoners and their hands were tied or cuffed behind their backs or around tent poles.

"I'm sorry." His voice rattled the silence. "Let me see if I can help you. I'll be right back."

He remembered the man under the tree and stumbled outside. Perhaps he'd been the guard. He leaned over the dead man and felt in his pockets for a knife or a key. He found both and returned to the tent.

After cutting several ropes and plastic cuffs, his arm screamed and he stumbled to one knee. He gave the handcuff keys and knife to one of the released soldiers and crawled onto a cot. Feet shuffled, voices murmured. Then nothing.

He's in a similar tent, but much colder and it smells of burnt flesh. Sad, unbearably sad waves of sorrow pass through him like a convulsion. His lower legs are wrapped in gauze; the pain is dulled by morphine. Turning to his side he sees her charred remains on the cot beside his. Did it move?

Asiyah. Are you alive?

She is wrapped in plastic but the odor makes him gag.

But there, he sees it again. The blackened mass moves inside the plastic.

Oh, Allah! Oh, God! Oh, Jesus! Is she still alive?

A hand breaks through the plastic and Asiyah's upper body slithers out, half covered in her burned parka, the other half not burned at all. The parka hood slides off and she smiles at him, one half charred and paralyzed, the other half the smooth skin and sparkling eyes of his love. She reaches out to him with her good arm. He reaches toward her delicate hand. Like a miracle the charred skin flakes off from her other side.

But her face is different and her hand is now bloody.

She winces at his grasping her hand and she is...Tamara.

The empty eyes no longer smile but are accusing and hateful.

"It's all your fault." Her voice is like a snake's his. "You did this."

She holds up her hand. Blood spurts from the ragged finger socket.

"I know it! It is! You're right! I'm sorry!" He startled awake, realizing he'd been dreaming.

A gray-eyed young man peered down at him. His face was calm, dirt-streaked, and he wore a tattered camouflaged baseball hat cocked back on his head. Abdullah quickly glanced at the cot beside him.

Nothing.

"It's okay sir. You had a bad dream. That happens every now and then when you get morphine."

Abdullah frowned, puzzled.

"I thought it would help, what with that broken bone sticking out. It's okay. I'm a medic."

Abdullah tilted his head down to see his arm. It was wrapped in white gauze and swathed close to his body. A burgundy spot stained the area over his elbow. A dull ache throbbed, but bearable.

He glanced back at the cot beside him. *Tamara. I'll be there soon, my dear. Don't worry. It will be as we planned. A rose garden. We'll raise goats. You'll play Brahms again.*

"We have a good doc back at the aid station. I've seen him with bones and he could probably set that elbow perfect. Are you okay? Do you need water?"

The young man—hardly more than a boy, Abdullah thought—spoke in a soft Southern accent amidst compassion—compassion that Abdullah knew he did not deserve. After all, he might have, probably would have killed this . . . this child only hours earlier.

"Thank you. Water would be good." His own voice sounded distant, a scratchy record playing behind his head. The air smelled of burnt plastic and gunpowder with a hint of alcohol antiseptic.

The medic was so gentle, hardly moving as he retrieved a bottle of water while lightly cradling Abdullah's head to drink.

After several swallows, Abdullah lifted his chin, and the man took the bottle away.

"She said it's my fault," Abdullah said. "But it's not." This time his voice was closer and smoother, resembling his real self.

The young man's eyes searched. "How could it be your fault?"

"I guess she thinks I started it but didn't finish it."

A twinkle came into the man's eye. "Yeah, my girlfriend said the same thing. That's why I married her before I left."

Abdullah shifted his weight. Wind popped the tent. Outside, the shouts and running feet came closer. *Tamara was gone. Yes.*

"Where are you from, young man?"

"Town not too far from here. Ennis, Texas."

Abdullah huffed and wheezed a slight chuckle, even as he winced at the pain of moving his elbow. "How small is the world. I was there a few days . . . perhaps weeks ago. A pornographic motel in the middle of the Bible belt. Your country is full of dichotomies."

The man's smile broadened, bending the dirt streaks. "Oh, you mean Terrell. Folks round there have been trying to get rid of that place for ages. Granny said you can't get rid of the other side of man. You just have to realize it's there, avoid it, and do the right thing. Then, no matter what happens, God will see you have a clean heart. That's why I became a medic."

The shouting got louder outside and the tent flapped more incessantly. Plopping sounds on top added to the flapping. The twilight of their tent world flickered with intermittent brightness. Thunder rumbled.

"I lost my clean heart a long time ago," murmured Abdullah to this . . . this boy angel at his side. That's what he had to be. And this was a final confession. He was tired of all the lies, all the killings. Perhaps this angel could forgive him.

"Oh heck. I'm not sayin' I got a perfectly clean heart. I keep trying, though."

It felt like the gray eyes searched Abdullah's soul. Wherever they touched, a wound healed. He felt lighter. Peaceful.

"I figured that the Army would be the perfect place. I could help our guys who got hurt tryin' to keep us free. And, I could help out the other side too, if they wanted it."

Abdullah nodded.

The perfect place. That is all I ever wanted.

It had taken the lieutenant colonel some time on the road from Xoflex. Now, at almost noon, he saw their objective: the smoldering camp of that terrorist El-Hamain. Through high-powered binoculars it appeared that the first missile he'd launched from Xoflex had been well off center. At first it puzzled him, until he remembered the lightning. That was war, he thought. Unpredictable fuck-ups. The storm had passed. The next shots would not miss. He spoke into the microphone, "Fire!"

The salvo from the tanks was deafening.

CHAPTER 69

The Humvee's door slammed shut and Jeff awoke, disoriented. He remembered Rector driving them up a hill. Now, they stood still, Humvee idling.

"So much for reinforcements." Rector's voice sounded frustrated, but oddly cheerful. He now wore a camo ball cap and smiled at Jeff.

Jeff's head throbbed over the left temple. Handcuffs tethered him to the dash grab bar so he couldn't sit back in the seat. He pulled at the cuffs and winced.

Rector's smile broadened and he shook his fist at Jeff, jangling dog tags. "You awake now, homeboy?"

"What the hell did you do, Sarge?"

Rector put the Humvee in reverse and backed up. He pointed at the Xoflex building through the windshield. "I wanted to see if they had any reinforcements to help us out with those spooks."

Jeff rattled the cuff chains and leaned over to feel his chest. No tags. He narrowed his eyes to slits and flexed his jaw muscles so hard it hurt.

"Oh, you mean the cuffs and tags?" Rector seemed way too cheerful.

Jeff nodded stiffly, wondering how long he had to live.

Rector drove back down the hill, away from Xoflex. "That was a precaution. The way you've been talking about authority figures, I needed to think things through while you cooled off. I took one of the other guy's tags, too. He's weak. He won't live. I have to write to your mommas. It's always been that way. I live. You die."

Jeff concentrated on the floor while trying to ignore the ache in his left temple. It felt like a thumb pushing into his brain. The sun had barely changed in the sky; not much time had passed. What could he say to save his life?

After a minute of jostling back and forth in the seat, his wrists chafed so hard on one bump that he decided. "Sarge, I guess I was a little stressed out. Do you think I'm a traitor?"

Rector nodded his head so many times and with such force that Jeff thought he might hit his head on the steering wheel.

Knock yourself out.

But Rector didn't hit his head. He stopped nodding and peered at Jeff. "That's my homeboy, Jeff. You're no traitor. Neither is that guy, Sinclair. We're all on the same team. I know that, now."

Rector's voice made a wave of prickly flesh run up Jeff's back, even before he saw Rector's eyes.

Just get the key.

Jeff glanced away from the white-rimmed irises and eased a breath out. "That's good, Sarge. I was afraid you might be mad at me. I was scared. I'm not used to this stuff. Not like you."

The head bobbed again.

Jesus!

Before Rector could answer, Jeff added, "So, Sarge. I want to help as much as I can. Maybe you could let me out of these cuffs?"

Without hesitation, Rector plucked the key out of his shirt pocket and pressed it into Jeff's hands.

He winked at Jeff and clicked his tongue like he was making a horse get up and go.

"No prob, bro."

First a traitor, now his brother. Going well I'd say.

In the last few minutes all hell broke loose at Remmy's cabin. As soon as the boat touched the dock, Sam started issuing orders, loud and fast. He explained that the Xoflex plant was extremely undermanned. They had to get in fast, take them by surprise and Remmy could get all the information he wanted.

He pointed at Ron, Bear and Lisette. "Get all the guns and ammo we have. We'll need two boats."

He nodded toward Joe, who was fueling the plane. "Good idea. We also have grenade launchers for an air assault."

"Never you mind," said Lola, coming out the door. "We got dynamite, young feller. We done this a hunerd times before. Why don't you git some chow and keep those grenade launchers for yourself. You might need 'em."

Sam chuckled. "Okay. Maybe I'll take a bag lunch for later."

Bernadette came out behind Lola juggling a large thermos bottle while stuffing a parcel of tinfoil-wrapped mudbugs into a rucksack. The front door slammed shut only to have Remmy pop it open, cradling his plastic wrapped computer.

Dan stood on the dock. She got out of the boat and walked inside. He tried to break the spell—rubbed his forehead, coughed, stretched— but his feet stayed planted.

Is this it? What will happen to us? To her?

"Dan!"

He jerked his head toward the voice. *Sam.*

"You're disguise worked like a charm, but now we need you to go with us." Sam was already halfway changed into his field gear.

"Right," Dan said. "Wait. I need to talk to you."

"What?"

"I may have found a way to stop all this without getting the Regulators for Remmy."

"How long will it take?"

"Maybe an hour. I don't know. Could be longer."

"Are you sure this will work?"

"Probably. Well, no I'm not sure. Maybe I could stay here and work on it while you got with Remmy." Computers he could do. He didn't really feel like getting shot at again.

Sam put a hand on Dan's shoulder. "Remmy's Regulators are a sure thing, and I can have them in twenty minutes if we hurry. I need every man I can get to help me at Xoflex. Can I count on you coming with me?"

"Sure." Sam was right. The program had already done its damage. If he couldn't save the world, he could at least do his part to let Remmy and Sam save it. Besides, he still had a chance to prove himself as a field agent.

He turned and tripped and nearly fell off the dock, moving before his feet were ready.

You geeky moron. Get your ass moving. He hated looking clumsy, expecially with Lisette around.

He plowed into her going through the front door.

"Dammit!"

She gawked. "Sorry, Dan."

He glanced back at the others bustling about outside, then took her by the arm and eased her into the house, shutting the door behind them.

She frowned at him. "Dan, we've got to leave."

"Wait. Wait one minute. Please. I need to say something."

A crescent lock of ebony hair fell across one of her puzzled eyes.

He released her arm and sighed, "I'm sorry, Lisette. From day one you have tried to help me and I've been . . . Well, anyway, I think . . ."

He sighed again and gazed directly into those deep pools of quiet.

"I think I love you. I wish . . . maybe in another life—

She slapped him.

The force teetered him against the door. He stared at her with open mouth.

"Get your shit together, Dan. We have work to do. Nothing happened that night except some sex. Got it! You were drunk. I was, too. We had fun and fell asleep. End of story. I never said I loved you. We're friends. Get your computer. We are going to need you!"

She pushed him aside and left, the door crashing closed behind her.

The sun shone through the kitchen window, the only bright spot in the room.

The light finally dawned on him. She was right. He *had* been drunk, not only that night, but drunk over her for the last week. Now he realized she had been tearful because Dan reminded her of Stan. She was just emotional. They were friends that had great sex. He started to feel less guilty.

Guilt returned. She was trying to protect him, to alleviate his pain.

He put a hand to his slapped cheek. It was hot and wet. Why the hell was he crying?

He wiped his eyes and charged back to the bedroom for his computer.

CHAPTER 70

After Sam and his crew escaped, Sinclair had radioed the colonel, but got no answer. Then a few minutes later that sergeant, the real Army sergeant, what was his name, Rector, returned and told him they would capture Remmy St. James very soon. But then Rector left without warning. He had abandoned them, the son of a bitch.

Sinclair tried twice more and reached the colonel. "We need your men back here on the double. We just had a visit by three . . . people. I think they were from the CIA or perhaps another Special Ops."

"Yeah, what makes you think that?" The colonel's voice dripped sarcasm.

"They got past all the security, overcame two of your men, and stole something from Remmy St. James's office. They may be back. Send your men, now."

A long pause and static filled Sinclair's ear.

"Colonel, are you there?"

"Yeah, and I'll be here for a long time. It seems there's no fuel where you said it would be."

Sinclair frowned at the radio. "Did you use the key I gave you?"

"I opened the big tank and all that came out was a cloud of black gnats. The tank is empty. Nothing. Nada. Get it? We are stuck right here. Period!"

"Nothing? That can't be. I need you here."

No voice or static answered. It seemed the colonel was done with Sinclair.

Sinclair felt the eyes of the soldier behind him and finished speaking to the dead radio in a voice as calm as he could muster. "I see, Colonel. We will expect you then, tonight. Have a good trip."

He clicked the radio off. "Corporal, please get your comrades and watch the east entrance. The colonel will be here as soon as he can."

The corporal left and Sinclair eyed the half empty bottle of cabernet. More would feel good, but he already felt a warm buzz, and would need all his faculties very soon. He crossed the room, uncorked the bottle, and took a long pull. Red wine always did it for him.

Rector drove away from Xoflex with crazy-eyed glances and robotic speech, rational thought a shattered glass needle, shards scattered in a huge haystack. Jeff must escape from him. After the last two days he ached to go home. It wasn't about his dad being right about finishing high school, nor about getting out of this war, though that was definitely a high priority. It was about a responsibility he had run away from. Being a hero was highly overrated, underpaid, and . . . not his bag. So he had to be very, very convincing to this nutcase sergeant, or he might end up with a bullet instead of a rap to the temple.

Rector white-knuckled the steering wheel of the Humvee, dodging trees. The bayou loomed and Jeff spotted the other three concealed comrades, their rifles and RPG up and ready.

It's now or never.

"Sarge, I'm ready to help in any way I can. What's your plan?"

Rector's head ratcheted around to stare at him with those wild eyes. "Are you?" Eerie was too casual for the sound of his voice.

Are you what? As crazy as me? Ready to help me or just pretending? Willing to go all the way?

I'm dead!

Be calm. Make him believe.

"Sure, Sarge. I'm ready. Tell me what you want."

Rector's head ratcheted, machine-like, back to looking straight ahead. "I want to kill all those spooks. When they come back I want to split their hearts and tear out their livers." His now monotone voice grated like fingernails on a chalkboard.

Jeff turned his head so Rector could not see his eyes and the expression on his face that would surely give away his sense of doom.

As calmly as he could muster, he said, "So, what can I do, Sarge?"

No answer.

The Humvee came to a gentle stop. Rector took it out of gear, but kept the motor running while he stood on the brake. His head turned on a slow-motion motor until the trance-like stare rested on Jeff, his voice loud with authority. "It's you and me, Jeff. You get up there and fire that 240 bravo at everything that moves in those boats that are coming. I stay down here, making sure you heat 'em up. Simple. You up there. Me down here. Got it?"

"Sure, Sarge. I'm on it."

Jeff grabbed his helmet and rocketed up into the turret. He gulped in the fresh air, ignoring the cold. *Anything to avoid those eyes.* Relief died at the next thought: Would Rector shoot out his legs? Probably, if Jeff didn't shoot the shit out of anything that entered the bayou.

The roar of two separate outboard motors approaching triggered his combat mode. He cocked the 240, made sure the bullets fed in properly, tightened his helmet straps, and took aim into the bayou, only too high. He would *not* kill anyone for Rector or anybody else.

Though the initial sound of the outboards seemed very close, Jeff soon realized the quiet of the marsh had magnified the sound. They must be further away than he thought.

The Humvee's powerful engine vibrated Jeff's perch and the sights of the big machine gun. The gentle rocking and diesel fumes reminded him of a high school skiing trip to Winter Park last year. He remembered the back of the bus with his Krista, cozy and warm, sated after a good meal, content after a long day on the slopes, hoping for a score on the ride back with her. Her blond hair, flushed cheeks and green eyes had attracted him the first time he saw her.

He could still see that face, streaked with tears, pleading with him not to leave as the bus pulled away for Army boot camp.

Soon, Krista. Soon I'll be back.

One of the men in front of him took off his helmet to adjust the straps and exposed his pale, shaved pate. It reminded him of his father:

shooting hoops with him in the back yard, seeing his cheering face in the crowd at games, talking with him about life and future plans.

Why didn't I listen? Sorry I didn't quite get it, Dad. I do now.

He felt a tug on his pant leg and his heart raced.

"Are you there, Corporal?"

"Yeah, Sarge. They're coming."

"Okay. Make me proud, homeboy."

The dissonant whining of the two outboards interfered with thought, pushed out the pleasant past. His nostrils flared, chest thumped, and he focused to slow his breathing. He wondered what a bullet felt like in the back of the knee.

The bows of the two boats gently swayed back and forth, following the channel. The first boat was nearer to him and aluminum. The big man guided the outboard in the stern, Dread Locks sat in the middle, and Miss Pony Tail hunched at the bow. The second boat was a wooden boat, poorly balanced, the bow riding too high to see inside.

Jeff aimed at the first boat and tightened his finger on the trigger, bracing himself for the buck of the gun. The other soldiers opened fire. He pulled the trigger, only shot a bit too high to hit anything. Bullets from the others hit the aluminum boat and ran from bow to stern. The big man slumped forward. The second boat careened off behind an island, splinters flying.

Rector punched him in the leg and he involuntarily jerked the bullet line down. His bullets hit the outboard of the aluminum boat. The stern exploded into flames and black smoke.

Jeff swore under his breath, hoping no one was injured by the explosion.

He heard the other boat, but the island and scrub trees hid it from sight.

One of the soldiers stood and fired the grenade launcher toward the sound.

Jeff jerked on the trigger, fearing a shot instead of a punch from Rector. Aiming high again he peppered the area, tearing off the tops of trees and bushes.

Another burring crescendo assaulted his ears when he stopped shooting.

Maybe a third boat?

He recognized the sound as a plane, just as it popped over the low trees, already on top of them.

A gleeful woman hanging from the plane door threw something down at them.

Her laughter reached him at the same moment he realized she'd just thrown a fizzing stick of dynamite. Too late. The explosion lifted the Humvee off the ground.

CHAPTER 71

Dan held onto his satchel with the computer and Beretta, and his thoughts piled up on the boat ride to Xoflex. *I have to talk to Lisette, tell her it's okay. I must find a computer at Xoflex and change my program, send out a virus. I have to find Jeff—*

Gunshots pinged off the boat. Sam gunned the outboard and ran the boat high into the swamp grass, killing the engine. Out of the corner of his eye, Dan registered that Lisette's boat had been machine-gunned. Sam jumped out and yelled over the gunfire, "Come on, Dan! We need to get out of here before they—"

But Dan didn't hear the end. He was already out and running the wrong way, toward the gunfire, toward Lisette, high stepping and slogging through the water toward the now topped scrub trees, raggedly trimmed six inches shorter by the machine gun. *I have to get to her.*

"Dan!" Sam's scream registered, but was like a dream voice, a dream Dan could ignore if he kept his mind focused. *Faster. Through these bushes and—*

An explosion ahead jerked his gaze up. Smoke rose over the trees. *Jesus, God, no!*

Pushing his legs to move faster through the shin-deep, cold water he ignored the splashing behind him. Someone jerked him backwards by his jacket collar.

He swung his arm around and tried to wrench himself free. "Let me go! Maybe I can save her!"

He swung without direction, wild, like one of his grade school fights when he didn't know how to punch. Just try to smash their face.

A strong hand gripped his wrist and pinned his arm behind him.

Sam's face filled his view. "Dan, come on, buddy. I need you here. I'll go. I'll get Bear and Ron, and Lisette. I need them all to help get us into the Xoflex building."

Another explosion set both of them scrutinizing beyond the trees. Sooty smoke rose even further away and the swamp plane flew toward them with Lola and Bernadette waving out the open back door. Lola pointed back at the explosion and gave them the thumbs up sign.

"What can I do here?" Dan yelled, perturbed with Sam.

"Go back there with Remmy. I think he's been hit."

Dan twisted his head. Splintered gashes traced the side of their boat. Remmy smiled and waved, but sat hunched over like an old man.

"Okay, but if you're not back—"

Sam trounced through the scrub trees, moving away quickly.

Dan sloshed back, unhurried. He occasionally glanced at Remmy and muttered, "She's okay. A Marine. Survivor. Lived through a hurricane. Strong. Smart."

He stopped, turned, and craned his neck, wishing he had x-ray vision to see through the bushes.

Ten seconds passed.

Twenty.

"Dan, I'm sure Lisette will be fine." Remmy's soft voice ended in a weak, wet cough.

Dan glanced back at Remmy. Standing knee deep in water, Dan's view was too low to see anything but Remmy's shoulders and head. Shiners under both Remmy's eyes accentuated his haggard look and he teetered from his slouch, struggling to keep from falling.

Dan sloshed faster. "Remmy, I'm sorry. I'll be right there."

He made it to the boat and peered over the gunnel. Remmy clutched a blood-stained side.

"Shit, Remmy. You *have* been hit. Why didn't you say something?"

"You really think you would have heard me? Sam screamed his head off and you ignored *him*."

Dan clambered into the boat just as Remmy's teetering struggle failed. Dan caught him before he hit the deck and laid him down, placing a nearby towel under his head. Dark blood soaked Remmy's left flank.

"Let me look at this," Dan gently lifted the coat and shirt. A deep gash beneath Remmy's left ribs leaked scarlet.

"Turn over easy. This might hurt. I need to see how deep this is." He helped Remmy roll onto his right side, and tore a strip of his shirttail and dabbed at the wound. He saw his computer satchel lying in a pool of water and almost dropped Remmy. He'd never forgotten about his computer before.

He rolled him back and Remmy coughed hard, groaning and clutching at the wound. "Hurts like a bitch."

"Yeah, the bullet tore through your stomach muscles, but not into the abdomen. Lot of blood from the muscles, but not lethal. Hold pressure there. Maybe once we get back to Xoflex we can find a proper dressing."

Dan eyed his computer then stood and squinted where Sam had disappeared.

"Dan, if I die, you've got to do what you said, change your program and get it out."

"You're not going to die. Lot of blood, but nothing vital."

Remmy gripped Dan's arm. "Promise me you'll do it."

"Okay, already. Geez. You'll be fine." Dan finished while gazing back at Lisette's boat.

"Go ahead, Dan. I'll wait right here."

Dan jumped out and ran through the water, shouting over his shoulder, "Thanks, Remmy. Back in a jiff."

He gained footing on harder ground and moved quicker, but the branches of the low trees slapped at his cheeks. Something tripped him and he fell forward and dodged a broken branch sticking out from a fallen stump. The branch grazed his eyelid and gouged his cheek. He grunted, righted himself, untangled his foot from a vine, and crashed forward.

Breaking through the other side, he saw Sam picking through the remains of the other boat: shredded aluminum and gray metal from the outboard housing. Dan passed the propeller, only it wasn't attached to the outboard motor. The foot of the outboard had broken off and was impaled in a stump. The propeller, still attached, spun in the breeze like a pinwheel.

"Sam, Remmy's okay. Only a flesh wound. What can I do? Have you seen—?"

Sam held up his hand. "Stop right there!"

The sound of a revving diesel engine on the other side of the bayou made Dan duck. A Humvee eased away from them on the grassy rise. A soldier in the top of the Humvee rotated his gun around.

Dan dove to the side. "Sam, take cover!"

Sam flipped over the side of the boat as bullets pelted the water where he'd been.

The shots ended and Dan ventured a peek. The Humvee bucked twice and stopped.

Dan ran towards Sam.

Sam's head appeared over the side of the boat and he held up a hand. "Dan, please. Don't."

Dan no longer heard Sam. He'd thought the initial warning to stop was about the Humvee. But now he suspected otherwise. He thrashed through the water, stumbled once, then picked his way to what remained of the bow of the boat. He sank into deeper water and pulled on the gunnel and craned to see over the side. Sam's face sagged, his eyes baggy, the corners of his mouth deep creases. He looked ten years older. When he noticed Dan watching he lifted the sides of his mouth, and pulled a jacket over Ron's head, a head missing a cheek and ear. Then Sam hung his head and placed a hand on Ron's chest.

Dan's foot found a solid ledge of sand and he pushed high enough to see inside the boat.

Her black pony tail was there.

Sightless eyes burned into him.

CHAPTER 72

"I told you. Didn't I? Fucking spooks! They did it again. Killed the whole squad. Just like in Afghanistan!" Rector screamed as he drove. "You didn't believe me? Never trust a spook. Always go with the Army."

Their Humvee had survived the dynamite explosion, and Rector had forced Jeff to fire again at the other side. Mercifully, the 240 bravo jammed. They still had two M-16s, Jeff's Beretta and Sarge's .45. Jeff feared Rector would make them stay and fight.

But Rector had become frantic when the machine gun jammed.

"It's a jinx," he'd said. "Need reinforcements."

He'd tugged on Jeff's pants and belt until Jeff had come down from the turret. "Gotta go. Be safe. Help me navigate inside."

The corners of Rector's mouth snarled and frothed, eyes so wide the eyelids must have sucked into his brain. Jeff wanted to open a door and run. But Rector still pointed that .45 at him.

He hated to look at Rector, but he had to watch him. No sucker punches this time.

He thought of Rector getting together with that Sinclair guy: Hitler meets Jason. *Oh yeah.*

Rector holstered the .45 and put the Humvee in gear and floored the accelerator. The Humvee started bucking and stalled not thirty yards up the slope towards Xoflex.

Rector frantically turned the key and screamed, "Shit!"

The engine coughed once, twice, and caught again.

He put it in gear and pressed the accelerator.

They chugged forward once and stopped.

Rector hit the steering wheel. "Fuck!" He twisted the key. This time only the starter whined and groaned.

He punched and slapped the steering wheel and dashboard while stomping the floorboard.

He jerked his head at Jeff.

"Get your ass up there and see if they're coming."

Jeff stared at him.

Rector wrenched out his .45 and pointed it at Jeff. "Now!"

"I'm going, Sarge. Jeez. Put the gun away, okay?"

Jeff's back crawled sweaty fear as he poked his head up through the turret.

He could either watch Rector face to face, or jump out. But Rector pointing a gun at his legs was not good.

Not even close.

He swiveled the 240 sideways, peered over the turret shield, and surveyed the swamp.

The blond-headed driver, Josh, ran towards them.

Distant movement caught Jeff's eye. He squinted through the smoke to see and then screamed and waved frantically at Josh to go back.

When Dan saw her, he smashed his palms to his temples and squeezed his eyes shut.

No. Not her. Not now.

He opened his eyes. Blue doll's eyes stared back. But she wasn't a doll. She was a human being. She couldn't blink because she'd been caught by surprise and now she couldn't sleep. Couldn't rest. God knows she needed a rest. Why won't God let her rest?

Close them and she'll rest. Be okay.

He moved around the bow of the boat to get close to her. He stared at her eyes.

Don't look at anything else. Just close her eyes. Let her rest. She'll wake up in a minute and slap me again. Hell, I needed it. Numberless idiot. If I had gotten ready a little faster, it would be me in that boat, not her.

His feet no longer sucked in the muddy bottom as he stepped higher onto swamp grass, close enough to touch her. A breeze cooled his face, flipped a lock of her hair over one open eye. He tenderly lifted it off and, fingers barely caressing her lids, he closed her eyes, extinguishing the thousand-yard stare.

Her alabaster neck pinched crooked against the camouflaged coat collar. He cradled her head in his hand and lifted it like an egg. He straightened out her neck and eased her head down.

There. No more kinks. Much more comfortable. Rest a few minutes. That's all you need, Lisette. He traced a finger over her nose and lips—too big and too thin, but her.

A firm hand gripped his shoulder. A voice spoke in a hollow box behind him.

The hand shook him.

"Dan! Let's go. We need to get outta here." Sam tugged on Dan's arm, but he didn't budge.

Like he moved through Jell-O, Dan faced Sam and ripped his arm away. "It was the right thing." He nodded his head methodically, a vertical metronome ticking up, down, up, down.

"Okay, so you fell for Lisette. Hey, we all loved her. In her own way, she loved all of us, too. I'm sure it was more difficult for you, being married. But to say that Lisette dying is the *right* thing?" His voice went flat. "It might make things easier for you, but I don't think I'd go that far."

Dan frowned. "But it was. Even though it was the last ... the *very* last thing she did. When she slapped me it was the right thing to do." His voice sounded weird to him, like a machine inside a box on the moon.

Sam glanced at the Humvee, and Dan followed his gaze. The machine gun pointed sideways. Dan smiled at Sam. He tried to make it a satisfied, relaxed smile.

Sam's eyes grew big. "Are you okay, man? I'm sorry, I thought you were referring to her ... you know ... being killed."

Dan squinted and glared at Sam. *She's dead. No more looks. No more laughs. Dead!*

Sam shuddered and backed off. "Hey, I didn't do it, Danny Boy. Remember *them?* Machine guns? Rat-tat-tat?" Sam glanced across the swamp.

Dan tracked to the Humvee and back to Sam, repeatedly. Each time he frowned deeper, glared harder, and breathed deeper and deeper, until finally he snorted like a bull ready to charge.

He moved so fast Sam jumped. Dan grabbed one of the rifles from the boat and sloshed quickly around the edge of the bayou.

"Dan, come on, man."

Dan flung the gun into the water. "You're right. Something bigger. They fired a grenade launcher, right?"

He ran, splashing water like a retriever after a downed duck.

Lola had blown them to pieces, but surely not the grenade launcher.

"Come on, Dan. We need to get back to Remmy and get going."

Dan sloshed faster, his thoughts spinning. When she had slapped him it had been the right thing because she wanted him to forget her—to get back to his world, his wife, his kids, his job of disguising reality. It *had* been the right thing.

But it must have hurt her to slap him. It would keep her from resting in her grave. All he wanted to do was tell her it was all right. She did the best thing.

Now he couldn't tell her.

That fucker with the machine gun is gonna pay.

He reached the other side. The water lapped onto the upper torso of a young soldier, his shaved hatless head face down in the mud. His ragged entrails waved in the water, leaking black cherry Kool-Aid. For a moment Dan stared at the broad powerful shoulders under the camouflage, expecting them to push up, shake the mud and water off his face, and drag his shredded belly off into the grass.

He shuddered. *Not going to happen. Dead. D-E-A-D! Just like Lisette.*

He glimpsed Sam by the boat, waving his arms wildly, shouting.

Sorry, Sammy Boy. Can't come right now. Have to finish it.

He scanned the shore above the lifeless torso and spotted what he needed, just like the one in ordinance class: a long brown cylinder with a trigger and a sight. Beside it, a box of grenades littered the grass, like a child spilled tinker toys. A picture of Jeff and scattered tinker toys in their back yard flashed in his mind. He wondered where Jeff was and stumbled, momentarily disoriented.

Then he remembered his mission and slogged through the black cherry mud, reached through the reeds and vines and yanked at the grenade launcher. Something held it fast.

A vision of a dead soldier's hand still gripping the trigger flashed through his mind.

He closed his eyes, sighed through his nose, and pulled hard. It gave way and he stumbled, sloshing backward, holding the grenade launcher high in the air. No hand! A gnarly piece of vine dangled from the trigger guard.

He clicked a cone-shaped grenade into the business end and hoisted the launcher to his shoulder. He sighted in on the Humvee. A soldier in the top turret waved his hands frantically. Another ran from the water towards the Humvee.

Trying to run away, huh? You SHOULD be scared. Bet you thought you got us all. Guess what? Time for you to taste the other side of war. You gave, now you get.

He took a deeper than normal breath and let it out . . . slow . . . calm . . . steady.

"This is for Lisette."

He pulled the trigger. Something blew in his eye and blurred his vision.

Jeff saw the tube on the man's shoulder. The screaming and thrashing of yesterday's burning soldier blazed in his mind. Pain. The worst kind. Not dead until the nerve endings seared to a crisp.

Smoke puffed out the back of the tube. The RPG headed straight towards him.

He yelled, "Incoming!" and jumped.

CHAPTER 73

The cold front that had spawned the thunderstorms and prevented the direct hit on Abdullah's camp pushed its arctic head further south, meeting a moisture-laden low spinning up from the Gulf. Something that Louisiana rarely saw started falling from the sky—snow.

A single snowflake stung Dan's eye when he pulled the trigger. Flash, smoke, boom. The Humvee lifted into the air. The boom lingered. Thunder rumbled. A burned-firecracker odor lingered in the air. A curtain of snow blew across the swamp. Lightning flashed.

He ducked at the flash, then cheered. "Yeah!"

He threw the grenade launcher to the side and danced around with his fists in the air. "Got you, motherfucker!" The elation at finally shooting someone that mattered, avenging Lisette's death, and proving to everyone he could do it, overcame him.

He loved the snow, especially when it came down this hard. He'd seen thunder snow before, but it still felt eerie. The muffled sound of the thunder enveloped him, and the dispersed lightning made each individual snowflake glow like a flock of Tinker Bells. Already, large flakes blew across the swamp so fast that he could barely make out the smoking Humvee. Had the blizzard come one minute earlier he would have never been able to see well enough to make the shot.

He lifted his chin up and gazed into the white, extended his arms, and twirled around slowly.

"Thank you, God!"

He stopped and put his tongue out to catch the cold flakes. It reminded him of the first time he'd been to a Bronco's game with Jeff. The snow had started half way through the first quarter. Six-year-old Jeff had put his tongue out and held his cherub face to the sky, laughing and saying, "It's God's cotton candy, Dad." That's what he'd always told the kids: God wrapped the earth in cotton candy just for us to play in. It was his winter present to help us get through until spring. It was wonderful to romp in, and if you put your tongue out, it tasted cold and sweet. Dan had snapped a photo of Jeff and the snow. It hung in his cubicle.

He jumped at a gripping of his arm.

"Okay, Wyatt Earp. Now that you've finished off the Okay Corral would you please help me with Remmy?" Snow coated Sam's hair and eyebrows, and he shielded his eyes as he peered at Dan.

"Good shot, huh?" Dan beamed. *Might be a field agent yet.*

"Yeah. Great. Now, about Remmy?"

"Okay. I'm coming. What do you make of this snow?" Dan followed as Sam slogged around the head of the bayou.

"Weird, but I guess it's as it should be."

"Why's that? Doesn't seem like anything like this should be happening today. It's the Deep South. Since when is snow to be expected?"

Sam turned around and Dan bumped him in the chest. "Don't you know what day it is?"

"Yeah, it's Monday."

"True. And it happens to be a federal holiday."

Dan frowned. "Jesus."

"Yep."

"Christmas?"

"You got it, Danny boy. Now, how about we go join Remmy and make those assholes at Xoflex give us a great big present. After all, Remmy said he could save the world if he got inside there. Maybe we should help him."

"Sounds good to me." They slogged further and he mumbled, "Christmas. I'll be damned."

Joe had landed the plane in the bayou and was standing by Remmy at the boat by the time Sam and Dan struggled back. Bernadette waved and smiled at them through the cockpit of the Albatross that barely fit into the upper reaches of the bayou.

"How ya'll doin'. We blew them to smithereens, didn't we?"

"You sure did, Berny." Sam beckoned her to join him. "We might need your help with these Xoflex computers. Come on over here."

She shook her head and her smile faded. "No, I think I'll just wait here."

"Come on, Berny. There's no snakes out. It's too cold."

She shook her head and eased back into the cockpit, her voice floating out. "I'll wait and travel by plane, thank you very much."

"Forget it, Sam!" Joe shouted. "She no use. Already tried. Hep me wit Remmy, you."

With a dejected Joe under one arm and a weeping Lola the other, Remmy stood. Sam and Dan helped ease him out of the boat. He was pale and stumbled with weak legs. The wet snow clung to his hair, making him appear an old man. He sat down on a log, held his hand on his flank, and attempted a weak grin. "Whole lotta noise over there. What happened?"

Dan stood and turned his head in the direction of Lisette, then peered into the sky and the snow.

Sam looked off to the side, then at the teary Lola being held by Joe. "They got Ron and Bear, and ..." he gazed at Dan, "Lisette." He clapped Dan on the back. "Danny Boy here blew up the Humvee that killed Lisette. First shot, with a grenade launcher no less. On target. Needs to join the Marines."

Remmy sighed. "Oh . . . Ron and Bear and Lisette." He gazed at Joe and Lola and held out his arms. They all hugged and cried.

Remmy wiped his face and peered up at Dan. "I'm real sorry, Dan." He winced and squeezed his side.

"Thanks. I guess she went out like she wanted to. Blaze of glory and all that." He peered at the hill, trying to see the Humvee through the blizzard. "Fuckers."

"Hell," Sam said, "they were only doing their job—Army guys trying to protect Xoflex."

Remmy coughed. "Shit!" He grimaced and groaned holding his side with both hands, and grunted out, "Not Army."

"We gotta git Remmy medical hep. Let's git goin'." Joe started to duck under Remmy's arm to help him to the plane.

Sam put a hand on Joe, holding him back. "What do you mean, not Army?"

Remmy sniffed once and straightened his back. "I don't think those guys are real Army. They had on the wrong shoes and wore medals. Probably mercs hired by the oil companies."

"Mercs?" Sam shook his head. "Just like Iraq. Can't get the military to do your dirty work? Hire a contract mercenary. Some people will do anything for money."

"True. So what's the plan?"

"Right now they only have a few people. What part of the building do you need to enter?"

"The north end on the first floor."

Sam pulled out a sketch of the plant from his inner jacket pocket. He shielded it from the snow and traced his finger along a path. "Okay. I think if we drop a stick or two of dynamite, and maybe some grenades into the east entrance, that should get rid of what's left of the soldiers— I mean mercs."

Dan shivered and brushed the snow off his coat. "Whatever you do, do it soon or I'm going to be an icicle."

The wind picked up and big drops of rain plopped into the bayou. The last of the snowflakes disappeared into the muddy water.

"Okay, Dan, you help them get Remmy back into the plane. I'm going back for that grenade launcher. We'll need all the firepower we can get."

Sam sloshed off across the bayou while Dan and Joe helped Remmy over to the plane, Lola leading the way.

The snow, freezing rain, and the smell of aircraft fuel reminded Dan of a March day at Washington National Airport eighteen years ago. He'd flown back from Afghanistan, a nation embroiled in a Russian war and a CIA covert mission. He was trying to get out of D.C. to see Marci at Presbyterian Hospital in Denver. She was in labor and he feared he would miss the birth of his second child, too. Just like Jeff.

How many other things had he missed in Jeff's life? Then again, he *had* been there to play rugby with him, teach him how to hit a baseball, and show him a thing or two in *Resident Evil 4*.

He glanced back in the direction of Lisette. He missed her. Not as a lover, but as a friend. He didn't really remember the sex, but he did remember her honesty and love of life. He ached for her smile, her soulful eyes. Just one more time. He sighed. At least he had last week.

"We need to come back, you know," he said.

Joe didn't turn around. "Don't you worry, you. We be back to get dem. No swamp gon take our Bear, and yo Lisette. Make showa dat."

Once they got to the seaplane, Remmy seemed to regain most of his former vigor, and got into the cockpit without much struggle.

Dan sat on the pontoon. The cold seeped into him as he stared out into the dead gray swamp. He blinked back the rain. The downside of the RPG adrenaline rush sucked at his energy and something deeper. Inside the plane, Joe and Lola fussed over Remmy, their voices small and distant.

He closed his eyes, but it didn't help. Lisette's dead orbs stared at him. He wondered if he would ever enjoy Christmas again.

He started to climb into the plane when Sam sloshed over. "Wait a minute. I'm gonna need you and Joe with me to storm the place after they drop the dynamite from the plane."

Joe craned his head out and frowned. Dan shivered and stuttered with cold. "S-s-storm the place? With th-three men? You've got to be kidding."

"We'll have surprise on our side. Plus, they'll think we're with them. Here, put this coat on. I got it off a soldier." Sam tossed the camouflage coat to Dan who shrugged it on but shivered harder. He thought of the hand-walking torso now without his coat.

"Joe, you think Lola can handle the plane?"

"Shit! You kiddin' me? She fly dat thing better'n me any day."

"Okay, I got the grenade launcher with ammo, and three M-4s. You guys wait on shore. I'll brief Lola, Remmy, and Bernadette."

Dan and Joe sloshed to shore. The coat felt good up top, but as soon as Dan walked out of the warm water the cold chilled his legs to the bone. The long walk up the hill to Xoflex should warm him.

The snow mixed with sleet and huge dollops of rain. Dan wondered how Lola could take off in this; much less navigate well enough to drop anything accurately on the Xoflex building. The plane revved and wind from the props blew across the water as the amphib turned around. Diesel fumes whiffed by.

Sam sloshed up and the three men trudged through the remaining brush at the edge of the clearing that rose to the Xoflex building.

The plane's increasing rpm's reverberated in the swamp. Then it was gone, leaving only their steps, rustling clothes, breaking twigs, and the patter of rain. Drizzle replaced the sleet and made it tough to see through the gloom. Dan squinted at the outline of what must be the hulk of the Humvee that he'd exploded. Mist rose from the thin layer of cold sleet on the warm ground. Blue-black smoke hung in a cloud around the Humvee, and the air smelled of burnt plastic and flesh. It reminded him of a horror film—or maybe this was hell.

A metallic click like a rifle cocking flopped all three men onto their chests—a loud slap on the soaked earth.

Was someone alive in the Humvee?

CHAPTER 74

*H*ow could that be?

Dan was sure he'd demolished the Humvee. Then again . . . He wrestled with the memory. The explosion. The vehicle lifted into the air. Fire. Smoke. The celebration. He'd been so happy he actually scored a direct hit that he'd thrown down the launcher and danced a Super Bowl end-zone victory jig. It didn't feel so good, now. In fact, thinking about that soldier being blown up, Dan's vision blurred.

He tried to concentrate. Had he actually seen the Humvee explode?

What about the instant before the explosion? Did that soldier, the one who surely murdered Lisette, did he jump out of the top and escape?

Could that be his gun cocking?

The metallic click, again.

Is it a gun cocking or metal cooling?

He whispered to Sam, "What was that?"

Lightning lit the sky and flashed a clear view of the Humvee. The Humvee sat upright, intact, on all four wheels.

The drizzle filtered back into snow and blew across the field as if the electricity had shocked the storm back to its original state. Thunder clapped so hard that Dan thought his skittering heart might bounce out and race down the hill to safety.

"I dunno," Sam whispered. "But if it's that 240 bravo we're in a world of shit." He nudged Dan with his elbow and pointed. "See that clump of bushes?"

He saw a shadow that could be a bush, a bear, a Volkswagen beetle, or three men huddled together with machine guns. "How do you know that's bushes?"

"Saw it in the lightning. Trust me. We need to get over there for cover. Let's move."

Sam and Joe crawled up the incline toward the shadow, their backs slithering, snow-covered wrinkles. After a minute they blended into the shrubs. Dan felt paralyzed.

Move!

He was on their heels in a flash. In crawl overdrive, he passed them and tumbled into the shallow depression surrounded by scrub brush. His gun and canteen clattered. He twisted and jerked like a wind-up toy on its back, and finally sat up and scooted to one side of the hollow to make room for the other two men. They quietly crawled in behind him.

"Nice, Dan. Veeerry sneaky move. You want to pop orange smoke now to give them a visual?" Sam's voice seeped sarcasm.

"Sorry. Got a little nervous. Guess I'm not the best field agent."

Sam patted him on the back. "Forget it. You did good back there with the grenade launcher. Right?"

Dan hung his head. "Maybe not. The Humvee's still functional and somebody is—"

"I know you fucking spooks are over there." A yell interrupted from the Humvee. "We're gonna blow your ass to pieces. You didn't even faze us with that grenade. Shit, I been through worse in boot camp."

A loud click sounded, a cocking sound, a metallic tick.

The loud click, again, followed by the tick.

A muffled "Shit," two loud pops, and the unmistakable sound of footsteps running away from them through the sloppy grass.

Dan crawled on hands and knees and peered over the mound, through the bushes. A dark ghost ran up the hill, away from the Humvee.

"*Pop, pop, pop!*" Sam's M-4 fired in single action mode, right next to Dan's ear. Dan jumped back and landed on his butt, his hands splayed behind him, catching his fall. His ears rang.

Sam fired twice more and squinted into the blizzard, nodded a grunt of approval, and turned back to Dan.

He saw a wide-eyed, open-mouthed statue, eyebrows white with snow—an old man waiting for the grim reaper.

"He won't be bothering us again," Sam said, calm and nonchalant, but dulled by the ringing, as if wrapped in a musical blanket. He held out a hand to Dan. "Let's go. I think he was alone."

"H-how do you know that? He said 'we.'" Dan rose to a low crouch. He shook his head, trying to get rid of the ringing.

Joe swatted him on the back. " 'Cause dey ain't no more jawin', an nobody else shootin' at us. Lets git goin' or we be late for de party. I hears Lola gittin' close."

The whining buzz of the plane *did* sound closer, though another sound worried Dan—a distinct miss in the previously smooth engine noise. Sam and Joe led the way, but this time Dan didn't wait. He followed in their footsteps, though he tripped twice peering at the charred Humvee instead of watching the path. The blackened area extended up one side, but all doors appeared solid, the vehicle probably operational.

About twenty yards away lay two soldiers, one on top of the other, like a cross.

The one Sam killed must have fallen on top of one killed by Dan's RPG, the machine gunner.

Seeing them this close, flopped on top of one another, face down, dead, unmoving, Dan dropped his head and felt drained. The high whine in his ears had subsided, though he wished it would get louder and blot out everything.

The plane flew over and he raised his head. Black smoke trailed behind and the engine missed, then caught again.

Sam motioned for them to flatten against the wall of the Xoflex building. The security cameras followed their every move. Sam fired up into the air, single shots like he was after the plane, his line of fire gradually creeping in on the camera. Pop! Son of a gun. Hit the camera by mistake. He swore for the benefit of the other camera, then, son of a gun, hit it, too.

"Okay, wait for the—"

The explosion on the east end of the building blew rubble all over them.

"That's our cue." He ran around the building, gun ready. But he didn't fire one shot.

Dan rounded the corner of the building, and the sight nauseated him. Five soldiers sprawled in various states of dead, most with pieces missing or holes bleeding. Snow and dust from the explosion filtered down like moths onto the rubble and bodies. Through the room's new sky-view, lightning flares revealed frozen death masks. No matter how many times he blinked, the freeze-frame agony on the soldier's faces would not disappear.

During his career he'd never been as close to the real action as during the last month. The adrenaline rushes had been cool, but this scene stuck on rerun convinced him he'd made the right career choice many years ago. He could never be a field agent. He had sluggish reflexes, wasn't the best shot—he'd obviously missed a huge Humvee with a cannon for Christ's sake—and now he realized he really did *not* have that killer instinct or the ability to shrug it off.

The snow vanished and the rain pounded in earnest. Mud-blood rivulets trickled between Dan's shoes, the blood not quite mixing with the thicker mud, streaks of red in the brown. He pulled his hood on and followed Sam over the bodies and rubble, barely keeping the bile in the back of his throat from joining the mud.

They filed under a jagged piece of roof into a long hallway. The oddest thing yet confronted them: down the hall a table was piled high with food and drink. Lightning flashed, and plain as day, weird as shit, on one end of the table sat a cake with one piece missing and a cake knife beside it.

"Guess they knew we were coming," Sam said.

Thunder cracked loud, almost hiding another low rumble that tailed off as Sam slung his rifle, cut a piece of cake, and crammed it in his mouth. "Carrot cake. My favorite. Dee-lish-ous," he mumbled around the mouthful. He pointed at the table, beckoning for them to join him.

"I ain't too hungry right now," Joe said.

"Me neither." Dan nearly vomited in Sam's face.

"Whatever. I didn't get to eat much at the cabin." Sam gnawed on a fried chicken leg, then slurped on the pitcher of lemonade, the fluid gushing over the sides onto his cheeks. He wiped his mouth, cut another piece of cake, smiled after each bite and drank the rest of the lemonade. Finally, he leaned his back against the wall and sighed. "Oh, yeah. I needed that."

Dan wavered on unsteady legs and leaned on his rifle. Sam glanced at him, licking his fingers. He fit the bill. Field agent. Soldier.

Not for me. Never again.

Sam eyed him. "What?"

"How can you eat after Ron and Lisette and seeing that back there? Those men and . . ."

"That? That was nothing. You should have been at Bosnia. Now that—"

A hole popped into the wall inches from his head, followed by the crack of a gun down the hallway.

CHAPTER 75

All three men flinched and ran in a crouch behind the food table. Pieces of food flew as bullets pocked the wall and table.

As suddenly as it began, it ended.

A familiar voice echoed from the end of the hallway, "Sam, come on out. I got the bastard." Remmy's voice sounded stronger than when they'd left him, or maybe it was anger.

Sam's face had flecks of cake and icing on one cheek. Red splotched one ear.

"You've been hit," Dan said.

Sam frowned, felt at his ear with a finger and licked it.

He smiled. "Nope. Cocktail sauce."

He grabbed a shrimp, dipped it in the sauce on the table and bit it off at the tail. "Good, too." He ate another and started walking down the hallway, saying over his shoulder, "Come on, you two. Sounds like Remmy's feeling better."

"Hard to git dat Remmy down, no." Joe had more bounce in his step at the sound of Remmy's voice.

Dan moved a pace behind the other two, but miles behind in his head.

How had Remmy gotten up there? Who did he have? How the hell could Sam eat at a time like this?

He glanced back at the table of food, the bullet holes in the wall, the rubble, and one soldier's arm sticking out at an odd angle. Rain drummed on the roof. Their steps echoed in the hallway. Fried chicken mixed with the smell of wet mud and acrid sulfur—a rainy Fourth of July.

He didn't feel like celebrating.

He pinched his cheek hard. *I'm here. This is real. When will it end?*

Concentrating on the back of Sam's head, he put one foot in front of the other, though he felt like his feet belonged to someone else.

By the time they walked the length of the hallway, his mind caught up with reality, and he became reattached to his body, just in time for another jolt.

Remmy sat on a chair with his foot planted in the back of a prone, extremely tall man wearing—*Is that a purple suit?*

Dan squeezed his eyes shut and opened them again. *Yep, purple.*

The man's hands were tied behind his back. Lola stood with one foot mashing his head against the floor, a handgun pointed at his back. The struggling man's inky orbs sparked at Dan around a knife-like nose and an angry sneer. Though the man seemed completely restrained, Dan felt like any moment he would rise up and . . . smite them.

Smite? Dan shook his head, blinked hard, and studied the scene. *Not really biblical. Get a grip.*

"Hi, guys." Remmy's voice was cheerful. "The plane caught bullets in the wrong places, so Lola had to make a slightly less than watery landing that took us right to the back door. Sam, meet John Sinclair, formerly Texas University basketball's star center, one of Daddy Sinclair's favorite sons, now just another big, oily asshole wanting to take over the world."

Remmy dug his heel into Sinclair's back. "He thought since I was gay like him that we could get along like old buddies. But it didn't quite work." He put all his weight on his heel and ground it into Sinclair's back. "Did it, Johnny Boy?" He hopped off and kicked Sinclair in the flank.

Sinclair started to grunt an answer, but Lola ground her heel into his cheek. "Shut it, you."

Remmy sat back down, grabbed at the dark wetness on his flank, gritted his teeth and breathed hard. He finished with a voice smooth as honey, laced with sarcasm. "Of course, it was a bit hard for me to concentrate while gargling a fire hose." He lifted his rifle high and, putting all of his weight into it, jabbed the butt of it into the back of Sinclair's leg, right behind the knee.

The tall man vomited a gush of reddish fluid onto the floor. Lola didn't flinch.

Dan knew that spot Remmy had hit. Lots of nerves there. It was one they had told him in the torture training camp he'd gone to years ago—one he'd never seen used. *Definitely a good spot.*

Sinclair coughed and the smell of sour vomit and sweet wine filled the room from the claret fluid pooled on the floor.

Remmy chuckled, then laughed. Dan had heard that laugh in movies and once in a prison. Not crazy, not maniacal, only haunting, piercing and . . . *Can I leave the building? Now?* Another soul had been lost in this war, but the body was still alive, and his vocal cords worked well.

Remmy's laughter abruptly stopped, and he screamed at Sinclair, "Wine? You were drinking wine, enjoying the afternoon of death and mayhem?"

He raised the rifle butt again.

Joe moved in and grabbed his arms. "Remmy don' do dat, son. You betta than him."

Remmy strained against Joe, eyes fierce. Joe's small stature contained wiry strength that stifled any movement of the rifle. Gradually, Remmy let go of the rifle and slumped his head forward, muttering, "Sorry, Unc Joe."

Sam looked crestfallen when Joe eased Remmy back into his chair. He shook his head and helped Joe prop Sinclair to sit with his back against the wall.

Lola only moved enough to hold the point of the pistol against Sinclair's bruised cheek. Claret-colored saliva strung down from one edge of his mouth. But his eyes didn't care. They seemed to smile at Remmy, a smile without happiness, a smile of a predator about to pounce. "Did that satisfy you, Remmy St. James? Make you feel more of a man?" His voice was a hiss straight from hell. Dan unconsciously took a step back.

Lola gouged the pistol deep into the man's cheek and said, "Shut it, you, less you want yo' brains mixed wit dat fancy wine."

That was interesting, Dan thought. After a rifle that nearly took

Sinclair's leg off he had the gall to be sassy. But a woman screwing a gun into his cheek resulted in, Dan was sure of it, a flicker of fear. *Wonder what your momma was like? Freud would have loved this triangle. The joke would start: Two gay guys and a Cajun grandmother walked into a bar . . .*

"It's okay, Lola. Back off a bit, but keep him covered."

Sinclair peered at Sam as though deciding on his next live meal.

"And who are you, little man? Mr. Save the Gay?" A dirge of sarcasm.

"Nope," Sam's voice was cheerful and bright as a boy with a new toy. "I'm the one guy in this crowd who could write a book about torture. For instance, I would not have used the rifle butt. I would have used *this*." He punctuated *this* by flipping out a four inch razor sharp knife blade. "Push it into the right nerve, slice the right tendon, stick it into the right bone, and Mr. Sinclair, you will lose more than your wine."

Definitely more than a flicker of fear, now. Dan stepped forward to see better. Sinclair's mouth twitched and the entire smile faded from his eyes.

Sam traced the knife around Sinclair's eyes. "If you want to see the best chapter of my book on torture, keep up your 'Fuck you' attitude. I don't have time for a piece of shit like you. I need information. NOW!"

At the NOW! Sam suddenly leaned into the man's face and placed the knife blade against the entire length of Sinclair's nose. He spoke quietly, but as sharp and serious as the blade. "Why are you here?"

A simple question, but one Dan thought might have numerous complex answers. Was it to find Remmy? To get his secret for why the oil was disappearing? To partner with Xoflex so they could use their nanotechnology to improve U.S. production? Though why would they need to have the Army, or mercenaries that dressed like Army soldiers here as well? Had they paid Special Forces to do all of the above so—?

"To save our oil interests." Sinclair croaked.

Sam moved the tip of the blade to point at the pupil of Sinclair's eye; an eye that contained a widening rim of white and followed the tip with unfaltering interest.

"That *sounds* right." Sam's words sprayed fine spittle on Sinclair's cheek. Yet neither man moved or blinked.

Remmy stood again and commented over Sam's shoulder, "*Your* interests. Yes, I believe that. Forget about what others need. Just keep the money rolling in. Did you count on this fucking civil war when you decided to rid the rest of the world of oil? Or is that why you needed the Army, or mercenaries, or whoever they are: To quell any uprising?"

Sinclair licked his lips, but still didn't blink; the knife was so close it would cut his lids.

Sam pulled back the blade and stood. "Guess that's it, then. The rich want to stay rich. I'd always wondered how long you guys would go on allowing those mid-eastern 'turban heads,' as you call them, to control your oil. I mean, you *do* think it's all *your* oil, right?"

Sinclair wriggled to a straighter sitting position. "We helped discover it, market it, and refine it, not to mention protect it with U.S. soldiers. I'd say we have stake in that oil. The Army was too busy this time so we improvised."

"But why get rid of the entire world's oil? If you had a beef with the mid-east, why not just destroy their wells? Or better yet, why not flood the market with electric cars and then no one would want their oil. Oh . . . I forgot . . . They wouldn't want *your* oil either. Guess that wouldn't work." Remmy said each word with effort and sat down hard, the anger now gone, fatigue overcoming his prior passion.

Sinclair glared at Remmy. "You think *we* planned all this. It was you and that damned A-rab. You made the bugs, he spread them. We're only trying to clean up his mess. And we need your help, Remmy. That's why we captured you to begin with."

Dan thought he had everything figured out. Bad guy—Sinclair. Good guy—Remmy. But things kept getting dim, gray, hazy. All he wanted was a computer program: 0=off 1=on. Simple.

Something simple happened because Sinclair had long legs and they were not tied down. Sinclair kicked the gun from Lola's hand. Then he kicked Sam, hard, right in his knife hand. The knife stabbed Sam's thigh.

Sinclair ran. He could run, too. Even though he had a slight limp in the knee Remmy had smashed, he had long legs. And once he had actually played pro basketball.

CHAPTER 76

Remmy had no love for Sinclair. So when Remmy smiled and shot Sinclair in the back, Dan was not surprised. But when he strode forward, jammed his foot in the man's back and blew off the back of his head . . . Dan squeezed his eyes shut. All the colors clashed, indigo and orange, black and yellow. No prime numbers came to him. The colors swirled into a whirlpool of bile green. His eyes snapped open.

Sam uttered a miniscule grunt of a scream when he pulled the knife out of his thigh. He quickly unbuckled and pulled his belt off and cinched it around the top of his thigh. Those thigh wounds could bleed like a mother. Good thing Sam was so quick and level-headed.

A belt. Never have thought to do that. Possibly after a minute or so. Seen it on TV. But Sam simply whipped it out and—

"Dan!" Sam's voice penetrated his haze.

"Oh yeah. Sam. Nice job with the belt."

"Forget the belt. Would you go help Remmy get what he needs. We need to get out of here."

Remmy was walking back, his eyes glaring with hate. *Maybe I'll wait a sec.*

Pop! Pop!

Dan ducked.

He peered up and Remmy tilted, then crashed to the ground. A jagged, bloody hole replaced one side of his face.

Dan was jerked backwards and down by his coat collar. A loud bang sounded right by his ear and he fell backwards.

Sam must have fired at something. After that, everything moved in slow motion, accompanied by muffled, distant sounds laced with a high pitch ringing.

He felt a writhing movement under his back, a rifle jammed in his hands, and heard Sam's muffled scream, "You've got to shoot him, Dan. He's coming right at us."

Dan sat up. A figure ran at them through the haze of the gunfire. Dan pulled the trigger. It felt like an eternity, watching the figure and pulling the trigger again, and again. Just like the video games, though, the figure fell down. Simple. But that kind of simple was not . . . not really . . . no, it wasn't.

A ringing, white noise stuffed his head with cotton, cotton with little bitty nano tuning forks that only emitted middle 'C.' *Little bitty nano tuning forks?*

Bernadette walked towards him. Her lips moved with intermittent words. "Dan, can . . . off of Sam?"

He searched side to side. Sam? Where? He was right here a second ago.

A wriggling movement played under his butt.

Sam. I'm sitting on top of Sam.

Bernadette helped Dan stand. "Are you okay, Daniel? You look a bit frazzled."

"Shit yeah. Can't hear. Just shot a guy. Lost Lisette. Great day. Couldn't be better. Sorry, Sam. Didn't know I was sitting on you."

He flung the rifle to the ground and walked away.

"Danny boy! Daniel! I could use your help here." Bernadette's words had an authority that Dan could relate to. Orders. That's what he needed. Simple direction.

"Right."

He wheeled around to help Bernadette and noticed the man Dan shot lying on the floor. Water dripped from the hole in the roof, splattering the neat, black hole in his forehead, and filtering through what was left of his brain, falling to the floor where it plinked in pink. A gust of wind puffed at the man's hair. Sheets of rain dappled the rivulets of red, splaying like fingers from his head.

Sorry, buddy.

Dan shut his eyes and shook his head. The tiny tuning forks

continued a shrill accompaniment to the film clip of gore. Where was twenty three, or eleven, or even two. He needed a prime.

After a minute the ringing improved. It smelled like someone lit a match in a restroom filled with moldy, dead leaves. He opened his eyes. Lola stood over Remmy and shook with grief.

He trudged to Sam, pulled him up to stand on one leg. Sam put his arm around Dan's neck and they limped toward Lola.

Dan spoke softly in Sam's ear. "What now, Sammy boy? Don't think Remmy will be saving the world. What do we do now?"

Joe had his arms wrapped around Lola and was murmuring soothing sounds.

Sam let go of Dan and slid his back down the wall until he sat on the floor. Bernadette sat beside him. Dan stared at Lola and Joe. *What do we do now? What the HELL do we do now?*

Sam peered at Dan. "I guess we're done here, Danny Boy."

"Do you think? Everybody's dead. We've got . . . let's see, nobody who knows anything about the nano shit to get the oil back. I have no idea where my computer is. We're blown to hell. What else is there?"

"Since there are no more big things to worry about, why don't we start with something simple? Find a first aid kit. I don't think that knife hit an artery, but I could use bandages, tape, and antiseptic, so I don't have to go around pulling on this belt all day."

"Okay. That's good. I can do that." Dan said it like a kid. He simply needed direction.

Bernadette produced a first aid kit she'd brought from the plane. Dan patched up Sam. Lola and Joe stumbled on a pile of body bags and put Remmy in one. Dan stared at the body bags and wondered why there were so many. Then he remembered all the dead men and grabbed his head with both hands and tried to shut it all out.

They all sat with their backs against the wall. Joe and Lola huddled together, Bernadette and Dan flanked Sam. Lola sobbed, Joe murmured in her ear, but no one spoke.

The wind howled across the jagged hole in the roof. Rain splattered and cleaned the corpses. The red ooze of life faded. Lightning flashes seemed brighter, but the thunder receded. The skylight darkened. Night was falling.

Dan thought of Marci, of her yelling at him and crying at the door before she left. He shook his head and pushed that out and remembered another night when she held his hand and led him to the bedroom after a bad mission. She always knew what to do in the early days when he thought more like a child, when his social faux pas needed maturing. Maybe that's why she'd been angry and cried. She didn't want him to grow up.

He surveyed his surroundings and suddenly longed to feel the chipped surface of his pressed-wood desk, to hear the hum of computers and clatter of the office, smell coffee and the secretary's perfume. He shut his eyes and tried to envision Marci. He wanted to thank her for trying to keep him safe. A red haze obscured her face.

He hoped she would forgive him. She did it before, like when he'd missed Jeff's birth. She'd slapped him when he missed their anniversary one year, drunk with the guys. But she still forgave him.

She had slapped him, hard, like Lisette.

Exactly like Lisette.

"We have to get Lisette and Ron and Bear and bury them you know." His voice sounded distant and weak.

Sam rested his temple against the wall and faced Dan. "We will, Danny Boy. We will. Kinda wet and cold out there right now and soon it'll be pitch black. Besides, I'm pretty tired. Let's see if we can find a warm place to sleep before it gets too dark to see anything."

They climbed one flight of stairs and found Remmy's office. Had his name right on the door: Remmy St. James. There was a pull-out couch, blankets in a closet, and a nice thick carpet. Must have been an important guy.

Sam gave Bernadette and Lola the comfort of the bed. The guys huddled together under one large blanket on the carpet. The carpet smelled like it had been recently cleaned.

Joe said in a fading sleepy voice, "Lola said the plane is crashed. No good. We cain't take no bodies wit us. We need to bury Remmy and Bear too, y'know."

"Sure, I know," Sam murmured. "We should probably bury those soldiers too."

"To hell with that," Dan said.

"We should look for their dog tags, too," Sam continued. "Some of them might be real Army."

Lightning flashed through the floor-length windows. Wind blew the trees and sheets of rain. Dan envisioned the rain pelting the charred Humvee, the wrecked boat, and the bodies left in the open, mixing oil and blood into the Louisiana mud.

CHAPTER 77

Morning brought gray skies and unfamiliar aches in parts Dan hadn't thought of in years.

He remembered pieces of the night: sleeping like a dead dog for several hours, waking intermittently, rearranging, trying to find a comfortable place on what hours before had seemed like a plush, thickly padded carpet. He'd covered his nose once at Joe's acrid scent, and covered his ears to Bernadette's low soothing voice punctuating Lola's weeping. In the early hours he'd finally dozed and dreamed of saving Lisette from a murderous cackling demon who strafed the swamp with a powerful machine gun. After realizing he'd saved a corpse whose hollow eyes crawled with worms, he couldn't go back to sleep, and didn't care if he ever slept again.

The wind crackled scant rain against the window.

What now? Go back to work?

Work didn't seem so important anymore, though if he could get to a computer that actually worked he could yet modify that program. There were no lights, so probably no power.

He needed to see Marci, Katie, and Jeff. And even Watson, that happy little Scotty. He unconsciously smiled. Soon, he would be taking him for morning walks with Marci through the snow. They all loved the snow.

Maybe when he got back, Jeff would come home on leave, and they'd all celebrate Christmas. Late, but right. With family. Put all this shit out of his mind.

Sam sat up and groaned. "Gonna need something for pain. This leg feels like I got a bad tooth down deep that needs pulling."

Dan stretched and sat up. "I think there's pain meds in that first aid kit. I'll go see." He walked by Sam. "After we do all this burying, I want to go home. I'm not like you. Not cut out for this stuff. Need to see my wife and kids."

"Let me see if any of the phones work. Maybe we could drop Remmy's nano-briefcase and laptop on the way and I could help you get back. Besides, I have a feeling the burials are going to be quick and—" Sam stopped and glanced at Lola. "Just find me Percocet or Morphine. Hell, I'd even take Motrin or aspirin. Then get back here. We do have a few things to decide."

Dan left and immediately hunted for a computer that worked. He searched the entire floor before he found a blinking monitor. He stopped and did a three-sixty. No one was watching. He hacked into the Xoflex mainframe, found his program, entered the code, a beautiful prime: 1201021—a palindrome with computer codes: 0 and 1, all the numbers added to a prime: 7. Then he radically modified the program. What he thought would take an hour, took him twenty minutes. But now the nanobots had no program to communicate with the bacteria. He e-mailed it to DoD, CIA, and as an afterthought, to a hackers website he knew. He signed it, "Remmy St. James," then turned off the computer. He found a bottle of Motrin and headed back.

When Dan returned, everyone was sitting on the couch. At his approach, they all caught his eye briefly, then found something interesting elsewhere.

"What?" he said. Had someone seen him?

Sam said, too quickly, "Nothing, Dan. Did you find the—?"

Dan tossed him the bottle of Motrin. "Sorry, no morphine or anything more powerful."

Everyone except Sam stood and walked to the window or studied the paintings on the walls.

"All right, what the hell is going on? I leave for five minutes and now no one wants to look at me. Did I do something?"

Bernadette moved over and put an arm around his shoulder. "No,

Dan, it's not you. Or rather anything you did. It's that we don't want to upset you any more about . . . about Lisette."

Dan shrugged her arm off his shoulder. "How could you upset me any more? She's dead. She died in battle. A Marine. Should be happy. Besides, I'm done with all this. Let's get on with the burials."

"We can't bury her," Sam said. "No one is coming to help us, nor do they really care. They have their hands full elsewhere. Any moment now the mercs might come back. We don't have much time, and besides ..."

Dan paced the room. "Why not? She's not with them. We can leave those asshole soldiers. But we have to bury her. And Ron and Bear and Remmy. That's what you said last night. We'll grab the soldier's dog tags and bury our three and hit the road."

"Dan, let me finish. Sit down." Sam tried the firm approach, but Dan glared at him and kept pacing.

Sam persisted. "Please. I need to tell you something."

Dan stopped pacing and frowned at Sam, trying to appear angry, though he felt worried.

"Not only do we not have much time, but the ground is too wet and too close to sea level. If we bury them they'll float up and the animals—"

Dan raised a hand, interrupting that thought before it formed. "Okay, I get the message. So, what do you propose, we carry them with us?"

Sam's eyes darted to Bernadette and Joe. "No. We have to . . . burn them."

"What?"

"Cremation. Bernadette thinks Lisette would love nothing more than to have her ashes floating in her beloved swamps. Lola and Joe feel the same about Remmy, and Bear. And, Ron? He was a free spirit and I think the idea of his ashes floating off into the atmosphere and into the Gulf of Mexico would appeal to him. We have to think of it like the Norse did, send them to Valhalla the right way."

Dan crinkled his nose and squinted, his voice in an unbelieving crescendo. "Valhalla?"

"Yeah, you know, Norse heaven, great place to go, home to all the heroes slain gloriously in battle. Hell, they get to drink all they want and have battles and ..."

"Whatever. Let's just do it and get out of here." Dan rolled his eyes and sighed.

Sam gazed out the window and pursed his lips. "That's not all."

"Please, no more about Norse heaven." Dan shook his head. *Sam's gone over the edge.*

"No. Not that. It's . . ." He paused and peered into Dan's eyes. "They are not the only warriors who died yesterday."

Dan raised both hands. "Of course! You still want to send all those . . . soldiers to Valhalla too. I thought going to Valhalla was only for honorable warriors. What's so honorable about ambushing and killing a woman?"

He was through talking. He walked away from Sam toward the door that would take him anywhere but here.

"Dan, did you forget that Lisette was in this as a soldier, too. She fought with the knowledge she could die in battle, a combatant, not a civilian. There is no difference between female or male. War is unisex now."

Halfway through Sam's discussion, Dan slowed. At the end he opened the door, but he stopped and turned around. All the fire was out of his soft reply. "You think that matters to me?"

"I know you had feelings for Lisette. Hell, we all know that. But let me put it this way. Those soldiers only followed orders. They did a good job, too. Hey, they managed to find us, didn't they? They waited until the right time, and they almost got us. To me, they did their job remarkably well. They died fighting for a cause they believed in. And, for all we know, it could have been the right cause. Maybe Remmy did get this whole thing started. Maybe those soldiers truly were trying to save the good old U.S. of A. by defending the last hope of saving our oil supply."

Dan shook his head, one foot against the open door. "And all this time, I thought we were the good guys."

He glanced at Joe, Lola, and Bernadette, all huddled together against the wall. They'd been watching Sam, then Dan, then Sam, like a tennis match. Who would win this round? "What about you three? Don't you think we are the good guys? Can you believe we are even in the same league as that asshole Sinclair? Jesus, he tortured Remmy, he tried to kill us. All he cared about was the goddamn money."

They stared at him.

"You know what?" Sam said. "I thought you would have already figured this out. But I guess not. You think good and bad are synonymous with right and wrong. Sorry. Not true. Sometimes doing the right thing can make you feel bad, and doing the wrong thing can make you feel good. Or, let me put it this way, there have been many times in the last twenty years that I thought I was a good guy, but ended up the bad guy. So I learned that no matter what side I was on, I still had to do the right thing. Otherwise I couldn't sleep and wouldn't have this bright cheery disposition." He smiled.

Dan huffed through his nose. "I don't care how you cut it, Mr. Cheerful, those assholes that followed Sinclair can rot in the mud as far as I'm concerned."

Lola cleared her throat. "What if one of those soldiers out there was your son. Wouldn't you want him to get a proper burial, or cremation, or whatever? Even Sinclair had a mother. Don't you think she deserves to know her son was taken care of at his death?"

Dan's voice quieted. "First of all, my son wouldn't be working for that guy. And second of all, if he was, he would see right through him and get the hell out of here."

He stepped back into the room and eased the door closed. "But I guess I see your point. Let's quit talking and get on with it. I'll tell you this, though. You're not going to burn Lisette in the same pile as those stinking soldiers. That's my final offer."

CHAPTER 78

After all the talking, Dan had to admit, Sam was right. Giving those men, and even Sinclair, a proper funeral pyre would set much better on his conscience than later dreams about worms coming out of eye holes. When he walked out, the bright sun warmed him, birds chirped, the morning air smelled fresh, and the night's bleakness ebbed away.

They all had their assignments: Bernadette and Lola would gather twigs and branches in two separate piles, and siphon JP5 from the plane to ignite the wet wood. Joe, Sam, and Dan would place the soldiers and their—Dan groaned at the thought—pieces onto one pile and Lisette, Ron, Remmy, and Bear on the other. It was warming up fast, so they all took some bottled water they found in Remmy's office.

Before they left the building, the men began the gruesome task of filling body bags with bits pulled out of the rubble. They dragged those down to the Humvee. On the way down, Sam's limp became more noticeable, and he stopped and sat on the bumper of the Humvee. "I need to rest this leg. Then I'll try to start this vehicle. We'll need it if the plane doesn't start."

Dan and Joe filled body bags as they worked their way down to open ground beside the swamp. The trick was not looking at the cold stiff corpses of Lisette, Ron, and Bear when they tugged the body bags over their heads and wriggled them down to the feet. Dan gagged twice and propped his hands on his knees, breathing hard. Distant grinding sounds of Sam's repeated attempts to start the Humvee accompanied their grunts and shoves. After a minute of silence from the starter, Dan peered up the hill.

Sam waved his hands over his head and yelled, "Won't start. You'll have to carry them up here a ways. "I'll get this guy and bring him down."

Dan nodded slow and obvious, and yelled, "Okay. If you need help, holler."

After getting their three comrades pulled off to the side, Dan and Joe went further into the swamp for the soldiers. Dan was surprised when he retrieved a U.S. Army dog tag from the first torso's neck. Shooing away the flies that buzzed around the melee, he searched for more, and found two.

By the time they finished the sun was high in the sky, melting away most of the clouds. Tree frogs peeped and flies buzzed. A scant breeze rustled the trees. Dan and Joe sat on a downed cypress log, wiped sweat from their face, and sipped bottled water. Dan tried to ignore the rotten-meat and excrement smell from the bags, but soon moved upwind.

"Why don't we go see if Sam needs help?"

But Sam was almost on them, accompanied by Lola. They dragged two body bags behind them. Bernadette lugged the last load of wood.

Sam stared at Dan, then glanced away.

"You okay, Sam?" Dan said.

"Yeah. Leg throbs, though."

Joe stood and scowled. "Gawd Ahmighty dis stinks. Dis de woist day o my life. Don't tink I'll ever sleep right agin."

Bernadette threw the wood down. "I thought you were right in doing this Sam, but Jesus, I agree with Joe, I'll be having nightmares."

Dan felt more upbeat than he'd been in two days. "I disagree and want to thank Sam for making us do this. I know I'll sleep better having said good bye to our fallen comrades, and to these soldiers. By the way, I got some dog tags here." He reached into his coat pocket and dangled them in front of Sam.

Sam quickly took them from him. "Who was it?"

"Don't know. Let me look."

Sam pocketed them. "You know, it might be better if we don't know who they are. I'll send these tags to the Army when we get wherever we're going."

Sam barked out orders. "Okay, let's get the wood soaked first, then get the bodies on top and soak them. Sooner we get going, the sooner it's over. Let's go people."

Within a half hour, the smell of burning JP5 blotted out all odors, and seemed to chase away the critters. Joe held an arm around Lola, Sam leaned on Bernadette, and Dan stood off to the side, closest to Lisette's bag. No one moved.

Dan felt trapped in a black and white silent picture show: black body bags atop white wood; black swamp, white sky; black mood, empty white mind. Sweat trickled down his neck, and he could barely hold his eyes open.

Sam bowed his head. "We commend these bodies and souls to you, God. They were warriors."

He lit the pyres. Soon the heat forced them to step back. The smell of burning flesh initially reminded Dan of a barbeque. Then the thought of singing hair and melting eyes gagged him and he covered his nose with his sleeve. The acrid smell of the burning plastic in the bags filtered in and actually helped. He walked to the swamp.

Sam limped over to Dan and touched him on the shoulder. "You ready?"

"For what?"

"To go home."

Black smoke snaked into the white sky. "Yeah, sure."

CHAPTER 79

Dan remembered mini-bites of the next two days. Sam got the Humvee started. They crammed in and bumped along until they boarded a plane, a special CIA plane, Sam said. But only Sam and Dan. The others—he couldn't remember. They were gone.

Out the plane window, long stretches of I-70 appeared without one car, then downtown Denver, roads littered with cars. Abandoned. No gas.

Sam clammed up. Almost like something inside him died in that funeral fire.

When they landed at Buckley Field, the fresh air slapped Dan awake. His mind cleared. It must have done the same to Sam because after they deplaned he hugged Dan long and hard and whispered in his ear, "I'm sorry, Dan. I'm . . . so . . . sorry."

"Yeah, I know. Thanks, Sam. I'm sorry, too. You knew her longer than I did. And Ron? I guess you had two losses. Right?"

While in the terminal they heard the news: the oil in Alaska had been saved. The DoD said a new program helped to rid the wells of the destroying nano-bacteria. They mentioned Remmy St. James as the savior, but that he died getting the program off.

Dan wanted to leap for joy, tell someone, anyone that he had been the one, he had been the hero. But he could never tell. Not a soul.

Sam grabbed him and hugged him again, his voice a whisper. "Go back to your wife, Dan."

Marci was waiting for him when he returned to that same great house in the same great neighborhood with happy Watson bounding through the snow, yapping and licking. Her wonderful blue eyes, though not the deep blue of Lisette's, felt warm, and when he kissed her full lips and touched her pixie nose, he dropped into a rabbit hole of bliss.

It snowed all day and they worried Katie might not make it home. But that night, Katie rode a friend's borrowed horse in from the foothills. No gas for cars. The useless cars had been pushed into the streets to make room in the garage for animals.

After she put the horse in the garage and gave him hay, she stomped into the house, wiped her feet, and hung up her coat. Wet horse smell hung in the air around her. She smiled at Dan and hugged him. "Love you, Dad."

He held onto the hug. "How was the ride?"

"It was so beautiful," she said, "no plowed roads, only smooth hills. The moonlight on the snow glittered like a fairytale or the Christmas poem about Santa Claus."

Katie, he, and Marci enjoyed a grand supper of Raman Noodles and spaghetti sauce. He didn't care what they ate. They were together. He actually felt great. He had saved at least some of the U.S. oil, and that might be enough to keep the U.S. of A. from going down the tubes.

Dan kept hoping Jeff would walk in on special Christmas leave. But that was unlikely. After all, they were at war.

After supper Dan hung his coat in the closet and noticed a rattle of metal in one of the pockets. He pulled out a white envelope with *Danny Boy* scrawled on the front. He opened it to find a pair of dog tags and a letter:

I struggled with telling you this the whole way back. Thought you'd been through enough. I found these on one of the soldiers by the Humvee and the name hit me right away. I believe I killed him, not you. I don't know what else to say but I'm sorry.

Sam

CHAPTER 80

"Danny Boy, that's me. Been gone awhile. They said I was depressed. Lost, more like it. Everything gray and black. No colors. No primes. Back with the program, now. Kinda. Most of the time. Guess I missed the event when Krista had you. Jeff and Krista hid her pregnancy well. War baby. And here you are a year old. Little blond-headed Adam. Think you'll be left-handed? Who knows? It'll be a surprise! Lots of them—surprises, and babies—with war. Don't forget that. You won't. Will you? Some do, you know. Eventually. That's why it comes back. Repetition forgot to teach them about it. War. Hell. Maybe if they lost a son they'd find a different way."

Dan sat outside in his rose garden. Bright sun warmed the cool morning, the air fresh with the sweet odor of early June roses—pink ones, orange ones, and his favorite: American Beauties. The tow-headed toddler in his lap smiled at him, with eyes that made him clench his jaw and blink hard. But he must continue this . . . confession.

He gazed into liquid eyes. "First, you can never tell anyone about this. It's between me and you and Sam. And even Sam can't know about the program. Okay?"

He nodded at the toddler who nodded back, then wriggled to get down. Dan helped him down and felt a twinge in his right forearm, rubbed the scar and remembered that night when he'd found Sam's note. He had held it together long enough to do three things: destroy the original note in the fire, retype it but omit the sentence about Sam killing Jeff, and feign a rediscovery of the note and tags, this time showing Marci. Then he had fallen apart.

Throughout the fog of the past eighteen months, those tags had never been far away. He dangled them by their beaded chain between him and Adam. They twisted and rattled.

"You know, I loved your father. It was good of Sam to take the blame. But I killed him. And now you will never have a father."

He squeezed his eyes shut and gripped the dog tags so tight the edges cut into his palm. Prime numbers floated by in green and orange and blue—2,3,5,7,11,13,17,19—Jeff never made it to 19. He relaxed his grip and opened his eyes. No blood on his palm. In the end, people mattered. Numbers existed. He slipped the tags into his pocket. He'd been through this a thousand times in his mind this last year. This would be the last.

"What is a father's love for a son? I've had some time to think about this. You toddle around and I'll tell you the whole story.

"You might say it is, at first blush, the love of a name—my name, carried past death; a celebration of his birth realizing the continuance of a line, a pedigree. How stupid is that, right? It's only a name."

Adam tripped and fell, and Dan leaned over to help, but halted. The boy did not cry, but pushed up quickly and ran a few steps, stopped and twisted around with a satisfied gleam in his eyes.

Dan grinned. "Yep, the boy-things I loved next. We were both guys, so we did rough and tumble things, testosterone-enhanced, like football, rugby, baseball—pitting strength, one against another."

He traipsed behind Adam, who occasionally jutted his head to smell a rose.

"The next part is a bit complicated, but bear with me."

Adam gazed happily at him, and his open-mouthed smile revealed dimples.

"I hoped he would be better—in the areas I failed, he would excel. So I pushed to make sure that my failures did not become his, that his life abounded in new opportunities. Then it happened, he grew into *himself.* I had to accept him as his own person: a *different* contribution, not only to the daily human conundrum and the DNA of life, but to the future. Whether I liked it or not, he traveled in his own direction; he was the future, and he would do it *his* way."

The toddler reached for a rose and pricked his finger. This time he cried and ran to Dan, who lifted him to his hip, sucked the coppery tasting blood from his finger, and wiped his tears. He hugged him until he wriggled, then held him tight for a moment more before kissing his finger and letting him down.

Dan wiped his own eyes and sighed. If he did not keep talking, hell would twist and burn his mind back to oblivion.

Adam reached out for a rose again, but before grabbing the branch he stopped and looked at his finger, then backed away.

"You're as smart as he was. After I accepted him as Jeff, not Dan's son, it was cool to see him puzzle a scenario in *Resident Evil*, show Katie how to solve an algebra problem, and feel his strong arms hug me. I didn't always like hugs, you know. Or him caring enough to show affection in public.

"Now he's gone. Hope, identity, joy: Lost. How is that possible?"

The tears streamed down his cheeks, he sniffled, and backhanded his cheeks, all the while watching Adam who frowned at him.

He blew out a breath. He would not go back to that place where a dirty lance pierced his heart with tetanus and made the muscle freeze; that place with no colors, no stars, no rising sun, and a moon that frowned; where all he wished to see was four white walls, all he hungered for was choking dust; a place with muffled and hollow sounds, dull and putrid smells; a place where bitter bile coated his tongue.

Adam raised his eyebrows and Dan had to smile. "She did it, buddy. Your grandma. She raised the sun, made the stars twinkle, the moon smile, took care of you and everything around here while I was . . . away. Like always. There's my Katie, too. So you've got your grandma, your aunt and me. Sorry about your mom. She's with your dad, now. There's always a little good."

He held up his thumb and finger a millimeter apart. Adam giggled. The pincher sign usually meant "tickle time."

Dan lowered his hand. "It'll be a different world out there, but we'll do okay together. Guess last year was pretty bad, huh? Should be glad I missed it. They tell me I got my war, in spades. D.C., L.A., Israel, Jerusalem, Iran, Iraq, Egypt, The Vatican. All gone. No more oil or holy places to fight over. Except Alaska. The last great wilderness. No one but the U.S.A. will see that oil. I did that." He smiled. He had done something good: saved at least part of the U.S.

White smoke curled from the chimney at the house next door. Though early summer, the days remained cool. Some said the ash from burning cities dropped the temperature. El-Hamain's followers said he did it. The new Mohammed of green got rid of global warming. Local climatologists from CU and CSU argued for the natural earth's cycle, nothing to do with humans at all. Dan was simply glad there were so many beetle-killed trees—made great firewood. Maybe things did happen for a reason.

Their milk cow craned her head out of the garage. George the horse grazed in the back yard. Adam toddled over to Dan's legs and pulled on his pants, wanting up. The neighbor, Harvey, waved as he herded his goats around his back yard. Dan waved back and picked up Adam, held him high and jiggled him. Adam laughed and that made Dan want to live.

"I love you, little man. I wish Jeff could be here to see you. And Lisette." He clenched his jaw. "She would teach you about history stuff. She would love you. She could probably help us with this back-to-nature stuff, too. Though your Grandma has done damn good. Look how she took care of this rose garden. I planted them when your dad was born. Dark red roses. American Beauties. Don't they smell sweet? And so velvety. I'm going to smell them every morning with you, Adam. Smell them every morning."

Jeff woke to another day in the bowels of Dallas and lifted the cardboard shelter. He winced at the odor of the sour rabble that surrounded him in this asphalt city. He pulled his camouflage coat closer. With no car and no ID it had taken months to get this far. His thigh ached, but the shrapnel wound had healed.

Stay under the radar. No trial for desertion.

Now that it was warmer, he could start out again. A long trip, but he had to do it. Why Denver? He'd only remembered his name yesterday. The headache kept him muddled. A deep urge pushed him. Maybe he would remember more when he got there.

The End

ABOUT THE AUTHOR

Milt Mays is a graduate of The Naval Academy, a retired U.S. Navy Captain, and a Cheyenne Veterans hospital physician, having learned the value and seen the results of war. His novel, *Dan's War*, was a finalist at the Pikes Peak Writers Contest in 2009.

Visit the author's website at http://www.miltmays.com

www.ingramcontent.com/pod-product-compliance
Lightning Source LLC
Chambersburg PA
CBHW050916250626
47155CB00001B/256